Black Arts

"[A] perfect balance of action, relationships, magic, and healing, fans will love it, and new readers will get sucked in."
—All Things Urban Fantasy

"An action packed thriller.... Betrayal, deception, and heartbreak all lead the way in this roller-coaster ride of infinite proportions that will keep readers twisting and turning until the very last page."
—Smexy Books

"Hunter's mastery for writing suspense-filled chapters that keep the reader on pins and needles turning pages shines through. She manages to juggle multiple story lines, letting them touch just enough to give hints of what's to follow until the story reaches its breathtaking conclusion."
—SF Site

Blood Trade

"Faith Hunter's Jane Yellowrock series is a high-octane urban fantasy that follows its own rules and keeps you guessing until the very end."
—Smexy Books

"There is nothing as satisfying as the first time reading a Jane Yellowrock novel."
—Fresh Fiction

"With a new twist on vampires and action-packed suspense, *Blood Trade* takes readers on an exciting ride!"
—RT Book Reviews

Death's Rival

"Hunter has done it again, delivering a thrilling combination of mystery and romance that will delight her fans."
—SF Site

"A thrilling mystery with epic action scenes and a kick-ass heroine with claws and fangs."
—All Things Urban Fantasy

continued ...

"Holy moly, this was an amazing read! Jane is the best urban fantasy heroine around. *Death's Rival* catapulted this series to the top of my must-buy list." —Night Owl Reviews

"A wild, danger-filled adventure. The world building includes a perfect blend of seductive romance, nail-biting action, intriguing characters, and betrayal from all sides."

—*RT Book Reviews*

Raven Cursed

"A lot of series seek to emulate Hunter's work, but few come close to capturing the essence of urban fantasy: the perfect blend of intriguing heroine, suspense, [and] fantasy with just enough romance." —SF Site

"Hunter doesn't disappoint.... I say you can't get enough of one of my favorite kick-ass heroines, so if you are new to the series, give yourself the gift of books one through three. You won't regret it." —Fresh Fiction

Mercy Blade

"Has all the complexity, twists, and surprises readers have come to expect ... a thrill ride from start to finish.... Hunter has an amazing talent for capturing mood." —SF Site

"There was something about the Jane Yellowrock series that drew me in from the very beginning.... *Mercy Blade* is top-notch, a five-star book!" —Night Owl Reviews

"Faith Hunter has created one of my favorite characters, ever. Jane Yellowrock is full of contradictions ... highly recommended." —Fresh Fiction

Blood Cross

"Readers eager for the next book in Patricia Briggs's Mercy Thompson series may want to give Faith Hunter a try."

—Library Journal

"In a genre flooded with strong, sexy females, Jane Yellowrock is unique.... Her bold first-person narrative shows that she's one tough cookie but with a likable vulnerability ... a pulse-pounding, page-turning adventure." —*RT Book Reviews*

Skinwalker

"Seriously. Best urban fantasy I've read in years, possibly ever." —C. E. Murphy, author of *Truthseeker*

"A fantastic start to the Jane Yellowrock series. Mixing fantasy with a strong mystery story line and a touch of romance, it ticks all the right urban fantasy boxes." —LoveVampires

"Stunning.... Plot and descriptions so vivid, they might as well be pictures or videos. Hunter captures the reader's attention from the first page and doesn't let go." —SF Site

"A fabulous tale with a heroine who clearly has the strength to stand on her own...a wonderfully detailed and fast-moving adventure that fills the pages with murder, mystery, and fascinating characters." —Darque Reviews

More Praise for the Novels of Faith Hunter

"With fast-paced action and the possibility of more romance, this is an enjoyable read with an alluring magical touch." —Darque Reviews

"The world [Hunter] has created is unique and bleak ... [an] exciting science-fiction thriller." —*Midwest Book Review*

"Entertaining ... outstanding supporting characters.... The strong cliff-hanger of an ending bodes well for future adventures." —*Publishers Weekly*

"Hunter's distinctive future vision offers a fresh though dark glimpse into a newly made postapocalyptic world. Bold and imaginative in approach, with appealing characters and a suspense-filled story, this belongs in most fantasy collections." —*Library Journal*

"It's a pleasure to read this engaging tale about characters connected by strong bonds of friendship and family. Mixes romance, high fantasy, apocalyptic and postapocalyptic adventure to good effect." —*Kirkus Reviews*

"Hunter's very professionally executed, tasty blend of dark fantasy, mystery, and romance should please fans of all three genres." —*Booklist*

BROKEN SOUL

A Jane Yellowrock Novel

Faith Hunter

A ROC BOOK

ROC
Published by the Penguin Group
Penguin Group (USA) LLC, 375 Hudson Street,
New York, New York 10014, USA

USA | Canada | UK | Ireland | Australia | New Zealand | India | South Africa | China
penguin.com
A Penguin Random House Company

First published by Roc, an imprint of New American Library,
a division of Penguin Group (USA) LLC

First Printing, October 2014

 REGISTERED TRADEMARK—MARCA REGISTRADA

ISBN 978-0-451-46595-5

Printed in the United States of America
10 9 8 7 6 5 4 3 2 1

To the Hubs, my Renaissance Man,
for everything you do and are, that makes my life a joy.

ACKNOWLEDGMENTS

Mindy Mymudes for beta reading. For being a font of knowledge. For being a great friend.

Lee Williams Watts for being the best travel companion and assistant a girl can have!

Beast Claws! Street Team extraordinaire!

Jason Gilbert for introducing me to Michael Edgecomb with Summerwood Fencing Academy of Rock Hill, South Carolina.

Michael Edgecomb for the fencing lesson and introduction to the garb of fencing. (Which I changed some . . . But, hey, it's for vamps.)

Mike Prater for all the little questions you answered.

My mom, Joyce H. Wright, and Lynn Hornsby for being my own personal fan club.

Let's Talk Promotions at www.ltpromos.com, for getting me where I am today.

Lucienne Diver of the Knight Agency. There are not words enough to say in thanks for guiding my career, being an ear when I need advice, and working your fingers to the bone. Thank you so much for everything!

Isabel Farhi of Ace/Roc for keeping me on time through the copy edits.

Valle Hansen for wonderful help (and polite queries) on the CE of *Broken Soul*.

Cliff Nielsen for all the work and talent that goes into the covers. I have to say—this is the BEST one yet.

Jessica Wade of Penguin/Roc. The best editor I could have. You make me into a much better writer than I ever would have been alone. I don't know how you keep the high quality up, book after book, especially now, with the Kicker kicking things around. Thank you.

CHAPTER 1

Half-Dressed Vamp Gave a Come-Hither, Toothy Smile

Visiting the Master of the City of New Orleans was always challenging, but it was worse when he was in a mood. Leo Pellissier's Clan Home and personal residence had burned to the ground not so very long ago, and the rebuilding was taking longer than he thought he should have to wait. Combined with the accidental media release of the upcoming arrival of a delegation of the European Mithrans—fangheads of state to the rest of us—and making the arrangements to house and feed his unwanted guests according to their usual kingly standards, his patience was wearing thin. Any equanimity he might have feigned to was long gone.

His Regal Grumpiness had demanded my presence. Yeah. I had called him that—from a safe distance, on my official, military-grade, bullet-resistant cell phone. I'm brave and all, but I'm not stupid.

I parked the SUV I had been driving lately—one of the MOC's, a heavily armored gas guzzler fitted with laminated polycarbonate glass, the stuff often called bulletproof glass—in front of the Mithran Council Chambers and ascended the stairs, checking over the changes in the building's security arrangements. The razor wire on the brick fence around the property in the French Quarter had caused quite a stir, various injunctions, and political posturing, but New Orleans' Vieux Carré Commission had caved when it was pointed out to them that Leo was currently, technically, something like a head of state or maybe a Mithran ambassador, and the property was, therefore, currently, technically, not quite U.S. territory. The political relationships between the Secret Service, the Treasury Department, the United States legal system, and the vamps were murky. Congress was still debating fanghead status and whether to declare them citizens or something else. I was betting on *something else* as the most likely outcome. It would be cheaper than rewriting the laws to include penalties for human blood-drinking; nearly immortal vampires, who were deathly allergic to sunlight, were strong enough to tear out iron bars, fast enough to be difficult to spot on standard security cameras, and had the ability to use their stalking compulsion and their blood to enslave humans and make them want to do stuff. Like let them walk free one night from any high-security prison. It was cheaper to consider them some form of noncitizen and therefore not subject to all U.S. laws.

I was in the middle of upgrading the security of the council house from an embassy-security precaution level to White House–security precaution level to provide super-duper protection during the EVs' upcoming shindig. Hence the razor wire; the increased number of dynamic cameras all over, with low-light and infrared capability; the new, top-of-the-line automatic backup generators in case of power failure; the new automatic muted lighting that was being installed along all the hallways inside; the replacement of the decorative iron-barred gate in the brick fence with an ugly, layered-iron gate that weighed a ton and could resist a dump truck filled with explosives. Just for starters. The measures I had instituted were not Draconian but they were more stringent than the historical society liked on the outside and that the vamps themselves liked on the inside. All this for the visitation that no one wanted but no one could refuse. Not even the American vamps themselves.

A lot of ordinary humans in the U.S. were unhappy about the planned—but as yet unscheduled—visit by European vampires too, and there had been death threats made against the undead, mostly by extreme right-wing religious hate groups, neo-Nazis, fascist groups, one ultraliberal group, and several homegrown jihadist groups. No one was surprised at the reactions, but security preps had to include explosive, bacterial, and chemical attacks—as in weapons of mass destruction—and electronic attack. Even the State Department was getting in on it all.

But maybe odder than anything was the question that my team at Yellowrock Securities were all asking. Why did the European vamps want to come here anyway?

As the head of YS and one of Leo's current part-time Enforcers, it was my job to see that the Mithran Council Chambers—aka vamp HQ, aka vamp central—was secure. Go, me. His Enforcer-in-training, Derek Lee, was helping and learning the ropes, even as he was trying to adjust to being an occasional dinner for Leo. Submitting didn't come easy to any former active-duty marine, but several things had persuaded Derek: money; he'd get to kill vamps; he'd get to play with all the toys Uncle Sam and Sam's R & D department came up with; his men would have constant employment. But there was something bigger too. Derek's mother had been diagnosed with an aggressive form of breast cancer, and Leo had agreed to feed her his blood to help her heal. Family was more important than pride to Derek. More important than anything else.

It was an uneasy alliance just yet, made worse when Derek's men had razzed him about the new job as Enforcer requiring him to provide blood-meals for Leo. But the men were settling in as semipermanent security, and most of them had found a vamp to feed. Vamps were hard to resist when they turned on the charm and the compulsion, and even marines had their limits when a gorgeous, half-dressed vamp gave a come-hither, toothy smile.

I went through the security precautions at the council house door, relinquished my weapons, and was led through the building by Wrassler to Leo, who was clearly not in his office, since we went down the elevator, not up the stairs. I'd known Wrassler long enough to expect an honest answer when I asked, "How's Leo?"

Wrassler—nicknamed so because he would make a professional wrestler look puny—rubbed a hand over his pate. It needed a shave, and his palm made a rasping sound on the bristles. "He broke a lamp after you hung up on him." I laughed and Wrassler added, his tone mild, "An original Tiffany worth over thirty thousand dollars."

I stopped laughing. "Ouch."

"Mmmm. His Mercy Blade was out of touch for an hour, and Leo needed to blow off some steam without killing any-

body, so I invited Brian and Brandon to spar with him. Thanks
to them, you'll get to sit this one out and watch, rather than
fight him when he's annoyed." Wrassler looked down at me
from his several inches of additional height and said, "It ain't
pretty."

And it wasn't. The hot smell of sweat and blood hit me when
I entered the small gymnasium with its fighting rings, and my
Beast perked up at the scent, interested. Brian and Brandon
were Onorios, two of three in the entire U.S. They were faster
than humans, had better healing abilities than humans, and
probably had other mad skills and abilities that I didn't know
about yet. The rarity meant that few people knew what they
were truly capable of or what their full abilities were. But it sure
wasn't besting a ticked-off master vamp in full-on kill mode.

Leo was barefooted, wearing black gi pants of a style I'd
seen him fight in before, his upper body bare and smeared with
blood that hid most of his white scars, his black hair plaited flat
to his head except for loose strands flying as he moved. He was
vamped out, his three-inch-long fangs clicked down and his
pupils black in scarlet sclera. Despite the vampy-ness, he
looked in control. Barely. Drawing on my skinwalker abilities,
I took a sniff to determine the pheromone level of his anger
and aggression.

One of the twins was out, lying off the fighting mat, his chest
rising and falling, so still alive. The other twin was in play, but
his face looked like it'd been used as a punching bag. Which it
had been. There was blood all over his white gi, the cloth hiding bruises and torn flesh between the fang rents. The sounds
of thuds and slaps and grunts resounded on the air, echoing
brightly through the open space. The standing twin spun away
and hit the wall. I felt the impact through the floor and my
Lucchese boot soles. He slid down the wall, leaving a bloody
smear on the painted cement block.

"This isn't good," Wrassler murmured to me. "The two of
them should have been able to hold their own against him."

"Hmmm. Who else did you call?" I asked softly, as Leo
screamed his triumph into the room, fists raised to the ceiling.
My Beast peeked out and purred, and I shoved her down. *This
is not the time,* I thought at her.

"Grégoire. He's on the way." Wrassler checked his cell.
"And Gee DiMercy should be here any minute."

At his words, Gee DiMercy, Clan Pellissier's Mercy Blade,

walked through the door on the far side of the room. "Halle-lujah, holy Moses," Wrassler murmured beneath his breath. It was a Southern Bible Belt phrase uttered by people in a cer-tain age group, and though Wrassler looked too young to use it, he drank vamp blood, so he didn't look his age, whatever it was.

"Your gramma say that?" I asked, as I watched Girrard Di-Mercy from a safe distance. The Mercy Blade was dressed in tight black pants and a billowing royal blue shirt, and he car-ried twin flat blades, both long swords with hand-and-a-half hilts for one- or two-hand fighting. His hair was back in a queue, tied with a narrow black band. The first time I'd seen him fight, he'd been saving my butt, and I hadn't had time to admire his technique. Leo was focused on the approaching man, arms out, hands and talons ready, shoulders tensed, mo-tionless as a crouching predator. Unbreathing, in that statue-still way of the vamps. *Funnn*, Beast murmured.

"Used to," Wrassler murmured. "My mama. My daddy." He added, his tone mesmerized, "Me."

When he was twelve feet away, the Mercy Blade tossed Leo a blade, the overhead lights glittering on the steel edge. The vamp leaped high and whipped it out of the air, but the small swordsman was already moving. His blade left a long cut on Leo's side. The Master of the City landed on the balls of his feet and slid away before the blade could bite deep, but his blood flowed fast from the slice.

Beside me, Wrassler tapped the mouthpiece of his headset and called for blood-servants to join him in the gym, his voice soft but demanding. Yeah. No matter what was going on, Leo was gonna be hungry; it would be wise to have donors on hand.

On the mat, the men danced with the swords, their bodies moving with deadly grace. Scarlet droplets flew on the air, the clang of steel so bright and sharp it hurt my eardrums. It was probably stupid, but I walked closer to get a better view.

The stench of pheromones increased and I rubbed a wrist on my nose to keep from sneezing. It was potent and heady, with the reek of violence and an underlying hint of wet feath-ers from the Mercy Blade and of raw power from Leo. But I'd smelled Leo fighting both ways: out of control and using his anger to power his vamp gifts. The difference was negligible, but it was there. Out-of-control Leo stank, an acrid taint on the air, tart as a rotten lemon. This was the other fighting scent. A show, controlled and planned, no matter how out of control and bloody it looked, no matter how bloody it *was*.

The fighters pirouetted away and back, the swords so fast they were a blur of light on steel and the clash of menace. Inside, Beast chuffed with delight. *Down, girl,* I thought at her. *We're not here to get sliced and diced.* She huffed and turned her head away from me—a pointed insult.

The men on the mat locked blades and Gee grabbed Leo's wrist, sticking out a leg and shoving his master across it. Leo landed with a thump. The point of Gee's blade nicked Leo's throat. The others in the room went silent, not even the sound of breathing echoing off the bare, white walls.

I lifted my hands and clapped, the sound slow enough to pass for bored. "Onorios heal fast. So do Mercy Blades. But it was a pretty show, boys."

Leo kipped to his feet, actually breathing now from the exertion. Off the mat, the twins rolled over, groaning, gasping, and smelling of pain. One of them cursed under his breath about the need for realism being "effing painful." Gee DiMercy chuckled softly. "Indeed, you are a bruised mess, dear boy." To me he asked, "And how did you know this was all a play, little goddess?"

Studying Leo, I tapped my nose and then tucked my fingers in my jeans pockets. "You smell different."

Leo blew off his irritation and looked up at a blast of air from the door. He said something in French, and Grégoire, standing there, said something back. There was a time when I'd wanted to learn Chinese. Now I'd give a bundle to be able to speak French, even though I was betting Leo and his best boy-pal, sparring partner, combat comrade, and probably lover, were rattling off in some archaic form of the language that no human alive today could understand. Leo and Grégoire had both learned the language centuries ago, and languages evolve faster than most people think.

The two vamps helped each of the twins rise, and gave them sips of their own blood to drink to speed the healing. It was a little too much PDA for me, all the lips and teeth and tongues and bare skin, but then, I'm a prude by most standards, even by the cultural criterion of the Cherokee of the eighteen hundreds. I know that for certain because I was alive back then. Cherokee skinwalkers live a long time. And then we go insane and eat people. Go figure. I guess everything has a price.

"Will others discern that we do not fight in a rage?" Grégoire asked.

"I did warn you she would not be easy to dupe," Gee Di-Mercy said. He was cleaning his blade as he walked, head down, a soft cloth that looked like silk on one side and chamois on the other stroking the blade in a hypnotic rhythm.

Answering Grégoire, I said, "Probably." And then asked, "What others?" as I followed the vamps to the door where I had entered.

"The European Mithrans," Brandon said. He balled up the hem of his torn gi top and wiped his chest. Grégoire's eyes followed the action with a look that spoke of hunger, and not just blood-hunger. I was pretty sure Grégoire was polysexual. Or maybe pansexual. I wasn't sure whether they were different and didn't really want to know. That whole *prude* thing again.

"And you want them to think you're fighting mad for what reason?" I asked as we pushed into the hallway.

"For *les* demonstrations," Grégoire said. "So as to lull them into thinking they can defeat us, of course." Which made no sense until he added, "They will challenge us to *les Duels Sang*, no?" His tone was excessively patient, the way an adult sounds explaining something to a three-year-old who's been asking "Why?" all day long.

Duels Sang. Sang meant "blood" in French. They were training for Blood Challenges, the totally legal duels that established place and importance and right to rule. And were sometimes fights to the death. "Oh," I said. Then I realized that likely meant me too. "*Oh.* Well, dang."

Grégoire laughed again, the sound not unkind. "You will fight wonderfully, little cat. I have seen you."

"Take Jane to my office," Leo said to Wrassler. "See that a small repast is prepared and brought up *maintenant*. We will see to our *toilette* and join you."

"Twa-let?" I asked when the males had entered the locker room set aside for bigwigs, and we were alone, heading to the elevator. "Like a French potty? One of those bidets?"

"He meant hot showers," Wrassler said, "changing clothes. *Healing wounds*," he finished, with a particular emphasis.

I nodded, pursing my lips. *Hanky-panky. Gotcha.* Well, at least they'd let me have food while I waited. Though I had to wonder how long the *healing wounds* would take. I only had all night, and *mant'non* could mean anything.

The elevator doors closed behind Wrassler and me. In the past, to reach most of the lower floors, a passenger had to swipe a security card. Now Wrassler rested his palm flat on an open plastic boxlike thing for his handprint to be read. I had implemented the security upgrades, but I'd wanted either retinal-scan devices or units that required a body-temp handprint, displaying adequate blood flow for life, to prevent anyone from cutting off the hand of an employee and using it to get around. Unfortunately, vamps didn't have remotely human retinas, nor did they show signs of life as measured by a biometric screen, so I'd had to take the chance that no one would try an amputation. The system I had settled for recognized and stored all human employee and vamp handprints and gave the passenger the rights to access only specific floors. There were restrictions for most humans, and—because Leo couldn't bind me like he wanted—that included me.

I had right of entry via the usual button control panel to all the normal floors, but none of my measures had gotten me onto any of the mystery floors. Until now. The elevator started going down. "Uh, Wrassler? I thought we were supposed to be going up to Leo's office. Why are we going down?"

A small explosion of breath escaped Wrassler and he looked up at the display in shock, his face going paper white. "I don't know, Janie. Something ain't right."

"How many subbasements are there?" I asked.

"I don't know," he said again, which was a surprise. "I think five. But I've never been down all the way before." His face looked pale in the bluish light, and his sweat suddenly smelled of worry, which was odd. Wrassler topped my six feet and probably weighed in at 350, all of it hard muscle. He could take being rammed by a rhino and not even look ruffled. Something about his stance and expression made me pull my weapons. A silver stake from my bun and a small throwing knife from my boot. They weren't much, but they were all I'd been able to conceal past the new security guys. The last crew woulda caught me in an instant, but the new rotation was not quite up to their level of awareness. Yet.

Beside me, Wrassler also pulled a weapon. It was a handgun—or a small canon; take your pick—the five-round Taurus Judge model .45/.410. It was capable of chambering both Colt .45 ammo and .410, two-and-a-half-inch shotshell ammo. The ammo would punch a hole through a pine tree. Wrassler's gun had been fitted with a fiber-optic sight, and he held it steady as the doors opened to a storage room. His shoulders relaxed and he holstered his weapon as he repalmed his print and hit the floor button. The doors closed.

I put away my weapons, analyzing the floor I'd seen. The room had been full of cardboard boxes and old metal-covered, hump-backed steamer chests, the kind that actually went on steamships, full of rich people's clothes. Or maybe on sailing ships, long before steam. It also contained lots of old books on shelves. And paintings. One or two had been in Leo's home before it burned to the ground. Or maybe in Grégoire's clan home. I couldn't remember, but they were familiar. In one painting, I recognized the spotted fur on the lapel of a man wearing tights and poufy drawers and buckled shoes. Sitting at his feet were three beautiful vamps. One was Grégoire; the other boy and girl were unfamiliar, though all three wore period clothing like the vamp who stood over them. They also wore jewelry, Grégoire a red-stoned ring, the girl a delicate bracelet, and the dark-haired boy a necklace of a bird in flight, set with blue stones.

In another painting was Leo and another vamp, Leo's predecessor, his uncle Amaury Pellissier. And then there had been the painting of Adrianna and a female vamp in clothing from the eighteen hundreds. Adrianna had tried to kill me on several occasions. Next time I saw her, her head was mine.

"Wrassler? Why'd we draw our weapons on a storeroom?"

Wrassler didn't look at me when he answered. "Elevator's been acting up all week. Taking us to the wrong floors. And there've been stories. Tales. For years. About a dark floor. Boo stuff." Which I translated as stuff that went *boo* and made you jump in fear.

"Okaaay." The elevator was rising again, and his scent now smelled of relief and the breakdown products of adrenaline. "So we're good?"

Wrassler nodded, still not meeting my eyes.

"You know . . . Really. I need to see all the lower levels and all the access stairwells to determine the security needs. And I need admittance to them in advance of the EuroVamps' visit."

Wrassler pursed his lips as if holding in a comment. We'd discussed this before, and Wrassler had orders from Leo to keep me on the upper floors and the gym level. Leo was being stubborn, which meant that Leo had things to hide. I shook my head and looked from the conflicted blood-servant to the doors with proper elevator etiquette.

"This is essential, Wrassler. You know it is."

When the elevator stopped again, it opened to the correct floor and we stepped out. I flipped open my fancy cell phone in its upmarket, Kevlar-topped carrying case and hit the number for home. The Kid answered, "YS," pronouncing it *Wise Ass*, which he could do without a head slap because of the distance between us.

"Funny. Can you dial in to the elevator system at vamp HQ?"

"It's not on the communal system, but Eli wired it during the upgrades. Why?"

No one had mentioned wiring the elevator to me, but we could deal with that later. In private. "The main elevator's been taking people to the wrong floor. Get in and take a look-see, digitally and any other way you can figure out. If you can't find anything, we need to get the Otis people in here, pronto."

"Otis?"

"The elevator repair company."

"Will do."

I closed the cell. If Eli's unauthorized wiring had caused these problems, I might be in a world of hurt. Literally. But until I had proof that YS had caused the problems, I'd keep my worries to myself.

The small repast in Leo's office was not small. By the time the waiters—wearing new liveries of black tuxedoes and white gloves—were done delivering food, setting it up to look pretty, and telling us what everything was, I was starving. There was a ten-pound bison roast on the center of the tea table, a copper tray of roasted, stuffed quail, a tray of cheeses, and one of fruit. There were also several bottles of wine—the dusty kind, with dry, curling labels that practically screamed *expensive*. Things were changing at vamp central and—with the exception of the varieties of meat—I wasn't sure I liked all the hoity-toity alterations. Something about it set my dander up, as one of my housemothers used to say. "Why all the new duds?"

Wrassler explained while I loaded up a plate. "Leo will be moving into his new clan home, and with the Europeans coming, he wants the serving staff trained to present food and drink in the Continental manner, both here and there, for as long as the Mithran guests stay. Everything is to be perfect."

He sounded worried and I had a feeling that the last line was a direct quote from Leo. Thinking, I plopped down in an upholstered chair and put my Lucchese-booted feet up on the coffee table. The boots, a gift from Leo, had been damaged the first time I wore them, and Leo had handled the repairs or replacement. I never asked which. They were gorgeous, and having them on the table was perfect for what I wanted to say. "Leo never read *The Taming of the Shrew*, did he?" I propped my plate on my flat belly and took a long slurp of wine. It tasted like, well, like wine. I grimaced and set the elegant crystal goblet aside. "Got any beer? That stuff is vile. It dries out my mouth."

Wrassler pressed a button on the oversized desk. "Ask Quesnel for an assortment of beer, please," he said. When he stood straight, he studied my posture. "*Taming of the Shrew*? You read Shakespeare?"

I lifted a leg, holding up a boot—black leather with green leaves and gold mountain lions embossed on the shafts. They were hand-constructed, hand-tooled, hand-stitched, hand-everything Lucchese Classics that sold for around three thousand bucks a pair. But they did not belong on a table. I crossed my ankles and set them back on the table.

"Past tense." I chewed a bite of quail that simply exploded in my mouth with spicy, bacony, wild-bird flavor. "Holy crap," I said around the mouthful of quail and bacon and some tiny little grain. "This is good." It was also greasy and bony. I pulled a small bone from my mouth and dropped it on the plate with a piercing, crystal tinkle before licking my fingers. "In high school. For a while I thought I might like to go to college. Turned out there wasn't money in the children's home's budget for a kid whose grades were only a little above average. Anyway, before I figured that out, I took some courses. The story's based on the concept that if you try to please someone, they'll only turn on you and look down on you. But if you act like a barbarian—"

"Like the one licking her fingers right now?"

"—then the fancy schmancy folk won't know how to act and you'll win by default of not doing the expected thing."

"I don't think Leo will go for that, Janie."

Behind him, the door opened and one of the penguins entered, carrying a tray of cool bottles. Not cold the way we serve them here in the U.S., but cool, the way they serve beer in Europe, the temp of a root cellar. *Ick*. But I popped the top and drank half of an Einbecker Ur-Bock. "He'll never impress the EuroVamps. He'll have to kill them all or prove he's something different—more modern and newer than they are. Whatever. But not better at being what they are. Won't happen no matter how hard he tries."

Wrassler said a low "Hmmm" as I finished off the quail and started on the bison, picking the meat up with my fingers. I had noted the number of chairs in the small but opulent office, and figured that if I didn't get my fill now, I might not get anything. It looked like a much bigger meeting than usual, and I had to wonder why we weren't in the security conference room.

By the time my plate was empty, the men entered, smelling of various colognes and scented soaps and aftershaves. And endorphins. Yeah, they'd gotten happy.

They stopped in the foyer of the office proper, clustered in a fanghead/blood-meal group, and stared at me in what smelled like shock. I grinned up at them and licked my fingers again.

"Little Janie has suggested that we act the Petruchio to the Europeans' Kate Minola," Wrassler said, his voice toneless but his eyes dancing as he took in their reactions to my lazy sprawl. "American barbarians."

Leo tilted his head, studying me, and he did that single-eyebrow-quirk thing that was so classy and that I totally could not do. I'd tried. In that moment he looked completely human, if a bit like he'd stepped out of the pages of a historical novel. He was wearing a shirt with draping sleeves and a round collar that tied at the throat, the ties hanging open. High-heeled leather boots went to his knees, with a pair of nubby silky pants tucked into them. Except for the boots, I'd seen him wear this outfit before. Either he had a dozen of them or he was wearing this one out. I saluted the group with my beer and slurped, watching them.

Leo chuckled, his eyes crinkling up at the corners. When he laughed, he looked so normal, so human. It was uncanny and kinda scary that one of the most dangerous nonhumans I knew could appear so ordinary. He crossed the office proper and took up my deserted glass of wine. He drank deeply, his eyes still on me over the rim. "Barbarians, eh?"

"And tech experts. Modern people. Just a suggestion," I said, and sucked the rest of the beer out of the bottle with one long, low-class glug. "So. Wha's up, dudes?"

CHAPTER 2

It Is Ðone . . . *Factum Est. Consummatum.*

"We have a minimum of three months to prepare for our . . . visitors," Leo said, the last word sounding forced, as if he'd rather have said *invaders* or *attackers* or *enemies*. Leo leaned over the desk, resting his weight on his fingertips, and studied us from his standing height. Leo wasn't tall, but his posture gave him a commanding presence I had used myself.

Dominance posture, Beast murmured at me.

There were a bunch of us in the office, as I'd guessed: Adelaide (Del) who was Leo's new primo; Bruiser, who was Onorio and Leo's old primo; Grégoire and the bruised-up Onorio twins; the Mercy Blade, Gee DiMercy; and Derek Lee, Leo's potential new full-time Enforcer. It was an eclectic group, not what I had been expecting in terms of attendees. Everyone was dressed in what I'd call Victorian Age Chic except for Derek, Adelaide, and me.

Derek was wearing casual slacks and a tailored shirt. Unlike me and my slump, the former marine was sitting upright in his wingback chair, taking notes on an electronic tablet, looking every inch the up-and-coming businessman that he was developing into. Well, except for the shadows in his eyes every time his gaze moved to Leo. He was having trouble adapting to the position of Enforcer, and the requirements that went with the job.

He said, "*Six* months *might* be long enough to get your people ready. Assuming that we have the same team here straight through. Rotating out teams means constant retraining. My men need to work with whatever security will be here then, to integrate a real team, people who can almost read each other's minds in hazardous situations."

Leo looked at Del, who was wearing a little black sheath dress and low heels, and she checked her own tablet. "Clan teams end their two-month rotations in two weeks. We'll get a new batch then."

I interrupted. "Why do you rotate out that way? Why every two months? Why not have a full-time crew here all the time?"

"It is the way things are done," Grégoire said with a sniff.

It might have been a disdainful sniff, which made me smother a grin. "You mean, the way they did things back in feudal Mithran times?" I asked. "The way the EuroVamps do things? The way that will let them know exactly what we are going to do and when?"

"Predictability is a liability," Derek said, agreeing.

I expected Leo to differ, as he usually did when I suggested a change of plans or methodology. Old vamps get set in their ways, the school of thought that went, "If it ain't broke, don't fix it." For centuries, sometimes. Instead he asked, "What alternatives do you suggest, my Enforcers?"

Coulda knocked me over with a Mercy Blade feather. If they ever showed their feathers to the world instead of the layered glamours they wrapped themselves in so they'd appear human. "Uhhh," I said, not prepared for him being agreeable. "A permanent crew here would be good."

"I got some of Grégoire's new people in the swamps, training," Derek said. I looked up at that. I knew he intended to integrate the two security forces—Grégoire's Atlanta team and Leo's New Orleans team—at some point, but not that it had already started. "Most of 'em washed out and got sent back to Atlanta. We still got a few sticking with it."

"You training them like SEALs?" I asked, meaning was he wearing them down to skin and bones and guts, the way Uncle Sam trained his best fighters.

He grinned at me and said, "I'm trying not to kill any."

"We could bring Grégoire's crew in as permanent security," I said to Leo. "We could also make the rotating clan home security teams' cycles longer," I suggested.

"Six months at a stretch," Derek agreed. "And stagger them

so that the council house doesn't get a complete batch of new recruits all at once."

His voice silky, Leo said, "My Enforcers have been plotting."

"Nope," I said. "Just great minds thinking alike." To Derek, I said, "I've suggested that to him about ten times now. He's kinda stuck in a European rut, doing things the old-country way."

Leo and Derek both frowned, but Leo said to Del, "Adelaide, compose a letter addressed to the masters of the other clans, detailing the changes and asking if their own security or comfort will be negatively affected by such a modification to protocol."

Derek frowned at me and I shrugged, even less prepared for Leo to capitulate. Maybe Leo had needed to hear it from a guy? Or maybe he was worried and finally listening to his paid troops? I was betting on the guy thing.

"George," Leo said. "You will send my card to each of the other clan homes announcing an official visit. You and Adelaide will then deliver the letter requesting the protocol changes, by hand, and introduce my new primo."

Del looked down at her lap, avoiding Bruiser's eyes. Bruiser looked at me and smiled as he answered, "Yes, *dominantem civitati*—Master of this City and Hunting Territories. It shall be as you say."

I don't know what I was expecting, but it wasn't that, spoken in Latin and archaic-sounding English words, words that seemed to have a power of some kind over the others in the room, because their scents changed, smelling bitter, of shock, and maybe a little of horror.

Yes ... Master of this City ... It shall be as you say ...? And then it hit me. Bruiser didn't call Leo *my master*. The phrase he used showed respect to the master of a city, but no more respect or loyalty than anyone might use, anyone unassociated with a master's household. And the phrase had been all formal, in Latin. *Crap.* Bruiser had just announced publicly that he was no longer Leo's ... employee? Dinner? Sex partner, if he had ever been that? I hadn't been comfortable enough to ask. Still wasn't. But the phrase said that he was certainly no longer Leo's blood-servant. Bruiser's eyes were warm on me, a little smile on his lips.

My cheeks heated and I couldn't control the speed of my

Faith Hunter

heart rate. I sure as heck couldn't control the scent of my pheromones, which were suddenly all over the place. The vamps in the room looked from Bruiser to Leo and then to me, picking up cues from each of us that we might rather have wished kept private. What did this public announcement mean to and for Bruiser? In the odd silence of the room, he let his smile drop and turned to Leo, who was still leaning over the desk, maybe frozen there in shock.

Leo held Bruiser's gaze for a long moment before turning that predatory stare to me, his nostrils widening as he scented the air. I could feel the ice of Leo's gaze as he spoke, but I kept my eyes on Bruiser. "Are you certain, *primo quondam meus*?"

"I am certain, *dominantem civitati, magister quondam meus*."

"You give up much," Leo said, his tone slightly hoarse. As if the words were pulled from him, as if they hurt as they left his mouth. I didn't know what was going on, but it sounded important. Life-or-death important. And everyone in the room seemed to think so too. There were a lot of wide eyes and very little breathing, even from the humans.

Del, her face white with shock, mouthed a translation. *Master of this City. My former master.*

Holy crap. Bruiser was really . . . quitting?

Bruiser smiled and looked at me, his eyes heated. It was as though some closed, dark place inside me opened, revealing a painful, raw wound in an oddly empty space. "I gain much more, *dominantem civitati*," he said. And the lesion in the dark, empty place within me seemed less painful somehow.

"It is done," Leo said. *"Factum est. Consummatum."*

Which sounded like a death sentence. Or the end of the world. Or something equally awful. But Bruiser's smile widened, and it didn't droop when Leo leaned forward and added carefully, "All of my regulations and proscriptions shall stand. And you will remove the last of your belongings from the council home tonight, before the sun seeks to rise."

Bruiser hesitated only an instant, as if measuring what the words meant before saying, "Yes, Master of this City. I shall abide by all regulations and proscriptions that pertain to me."

Leo looked like that was less capitulation than he wanted, but he went on. "I require that Jane Yellowrock remain in the position of Enforcer, along with Derek Lee, for the duration of the Europeans' visit. Derek and I have reached a settlement on remuneration for his services. Do you agree, Jane?"

I looked back and forth between Derek and Leo and held out my hand to Del. "You got a pen? A piece of paper?"

Without speaking, Del leaned forward and took both from a small drawer in the front of Leo's desk, passing them to me. I half folded the paper so no one could see what I was writing and penned a number on the paper. *$1,000,000.00.* I folded it and passed it to Leo. He opened the paper and burst out laughing, the laughter again making him seem so human and so dang gorgeous. Monsters are supposed to be ugly; Leo simply wasn't. His eyes glistened with amusement. The black hair he usually tied in a little queue came forward and brushed his pale olive cheeks. Still laughing, he passed the note to Grégoire, whose blond eyebrows went up in surprise that quickly translated into amusement. *"Vous avez été correct, mon seigneur,"* Grégoire said, his tone formal.

I didn't know what that meant, but did catch the *correct* part, and when Grégoire pulled a ring from his finger and passed it to Leo, I realized that they had bet on my reply, and Leo had won. I narrowed my eyes at them, as Leo slid the ring onto his pinkie. The ring was gold, the band smooth and worn, centered by a ruby cabochon. It looked old and valuable, and a lot like the ring the much younger Grégoire had worn in the painting downstairs. I sat back in my chair, irritated for reasons I didn't understand.

"Half that," Leo said. "No more. However, I will also pay expenses for you and salary for your crew. Take or leave it, *mon petit chat.*"

I thought about it, remembering the room full of books and papers in the basement, and decided to up the ante. "Leave it," I said. Leo looked up from admiring his winnings, surprise on his face. Yeah, he hadn't expected me to refuse. I adored surprising a vamp. It happened so seldom with the old ones and their expressions were priceless. "This is a negotiation, so you don't get to demand. Half, plus expenses, Younger's salary, and also access to everything in every vamp database, library, and storage available to you, no matter the language, about the history of witches and Mithrans, and the existence of other magical beings. I want access to anything and everything that you and any of your people have."

Leo murmured, "Witches again. Are your loyalties divided, my Enforcer?"

I thought about what he might be asking me to claim and I

said, very carefully, "My loyalties are perfectly aligned according to who I am, what I am, and according to my word and to my contracts."

Leo watched me, sniffing slowly, smelling for a lie. "This bargain is acceptable to me."

"Done," I said.

Leo nodded. Still watching me, he said, "We have an infiltrator."

I dragged my gaze from Leo's to Bruiser's. "Reach?" I'd shared my suspicions about the mysterious researcher and electronic security genius with Bruiser previously, and had since proven them. Reach wasn't quite a traitor, more an entrepreneur, gathering and selling information to the highest bidder, instead of keeping proprietary info secret. I still hadn't decided what to do about him. For that matter, I didn't know what we *could* do about him. He'd made no secret of working for the customer who offered him the most money; he had no blood-bond with Leo to keep him loyal; and Reach had ways of finding out things that bordered on the mystical. Once he had his electronic claws into a system, it was nearly impossible to remove them. I more than halfway believed that he had his claws in my own system and in Leo's, and there was absolutely nothing I could do about it.

"No, *we* have not been infiltrated." Leo waved a lazy hand as if wiping away the thought of Reach. "I have a well-placed and well-paid infiltrator on the European Council of Mithrans."

Every eye in the place settled on Leo, and he gave a languid smile, enjoying the astounded stares and olfactory responses. "You have a spy in Europe?" I half asked, half stated. "Dang."

Leo's smile widened and he did that eyebrow-lift thing. "Yes. This person has been in place for many years."

I noticed that he didn't say *Mithran* or *blood-servant* or give a gender. Cagey, Leo.

"This person has informed me that this visit by members of the European Council will be used to discover weaknesses in our organization. This information is nothing new. However, this person has confirmed that the preliminary delegation will be followed by a larger mission whose purpose is to destroy us. They wish to acquire our territory and bring it under the control of the Europeans, and not simply because we have grown too powerful."

Grégoire sat up slowly, horror on his face. *"Pas François!"*

Leo said, "Not your sire, my friend."

"Who?" I asked.

Bruiser leaned toward me, his mouth at my ear. "Grégoire's sire was François Le Bâtard, an illegitimate son of François d'Angoulême."

I had heard Grégoire's titles once, and they were as sparse as they were royal, as I recalled. It helped that I had a file on him. I pulled up the file on my official cell, which was mated to my laptop at home, and discovered that there was nothing in his titles about a François d'Angoulême or a Le Bâtard. He was simply "Grégoire, blood-master of Clan Arceneau, of the court of Charles the Wise, fifth of his line, in the Valois Dynasty." So I looked up the royal Charlie the Wise.

As I searched, Leo added, more gently, "But your brother and your sister Batildis have begun to rally their supporters to this end." I remembered the painting of the man wearing tights and poufy drawers and buckled shoes, spotted fur on his lapel. Grégoire close by. The boy and girl vamps with him had been unknowns, but maybe not for much longer. They had worn jewelry, Grégoire with a ruby ring. The girl's face had been terrified. "And yes," Leo said, "that might eventually garner the interest of Le Bâtard, though he is not scheduled to travel to these shores with the European Council."

Grégoire snarled. He actually snarled, like a ticked-off big-cat. A perpetually blond, fifteen-year-old vampire big-cat. I looked up from under my brows to see his face, vamped out and furious, his hand on the hilt of a dagger. Leo placed his own hand over Grégoire's and a tingle of power swept through the room, smelling spiky, of pepper, papyrus, and plant-based ink. I looked back to my research as Leo soothed his bestie in French, the syllables soft and fluid, like liquid lovemaking. I *so* wanted to learn French.

According to my notes, François d'Angoulême was born on September 12, 1494, in Cognac, France, and died on March 31, 1547, in a place I couldn't pronounce—Rambouillet. François Le Bâtard meant Francis the Bastard, and he was the illegitimate son of d'Angoulême. Of the Bastard, there was no birth date and no death date, which was a good indicator of . . . not much. Had he been human, he could have perished at sea, languished in a jail, or been sent to a penal colony. He could have chosen to disappear, or been involuntarily disappeared in dozens of ways and never heard from again. But in his case, Le

Bâtard had been turned, making him not true-dead, but undead. Charming. A bastard had made Grégoire. After what I'd
guessed and heard about his maker, the title was appropriate
on other levels too, because Grégoire's maker had been evil
personified. He had liked little boys in the "You want some
candy, little boy?" kinda way. He was the sort of vamp I liked
to hunt, stake, and decapitate. Call me a lover of slasher porn,
but some dudes just deserved to lose their heads. Both of them.

"What has been happening *en le court*?" Grégoire asked,
sounding more controlled, and even more Frenchy. When Grégoire and Leo spent time together, they tended to talk more in
French, and it was totally seductive. Not that I'd tell them so.

"There have been many changes," Leo said, "and some of
our number tonight know nothing about the Europeans' history. Adelaide, enlighten them, if you please."

She raised her tablet and said, "A brief history. The European Council's highest-ranking members were originally Se-
mitic in origin, arising from the first three, the father of
Mithrans, Judas Iscariot, and his sons—the Sons of Darkness.
They were located primarily in and around Jerusalem and
comprised largely of members who carried the witch gene.
During these years, there was relative peace between the vampires and the witches, and many artifacts of power were created. That changed during the Roman siege of Jerusalem. The
atrocities committed by the vampires to stay alive in a starving
city were unimaginable. Following the diaspora in the year 72,
they were under persecution from their own people due to
those atrocities, and were hounded by the Roman conquerors.
Many vampires resettled in countries along the northern coast
of Africa, the southern coast of the Mediterranean, and later
in Rome, under the noses of their enemies in the Holy Roman
Church. They followed the Roman Empire to Constantinople,
and when it fell, the vampires—then known as the Mithran
Council—moved to France."

I had heard parts of this, and had put other parts together,
but the summary answered other questions, like why so many
of the older vamps I'd seen were olive skinned. They shared a
common origin with the early Christians—the cross of
Golgotha—though for very different reasons. The earliest
vamps moved with the Hebrew people to nearby territories
during the diaspora, including to Africa, so the second generation of vamps had often been people of color.

"According to what we've learned," Del said, "from sources inside the council itself, the Mithrans in many parts of the world are facing new and deadly troubles."

I looked up at that. Leo was being awfully free with the info that he had a plant in European vamp headquarters. Leo did nothing without a reason. Maybe nothing more than slapping them in the face with a glove, but there was a reason. Or several reasons. Vamps tended to layer on reasons and meanings and old emotions like a lasagna.

Del continued. "In the nineteenth and twentieth centuries, in a number of key governments, in countries ruled by despots or a military elite, the Mithrans were able to place blood-servants or powerful Mithrans in high levels of the military, intelligence, and banking."

She added, "Today, these Mithrans and blood-servants are being hunted by anti-Mithran fanatics, many using methods that are . . . barbaric." Her mouth twisted down. I assumed she had been reading reports, and none of them were good reports about bunnies and butterflies.

"Led by the growing popular support, some governments are enacting stringent laws against the Mithrans in their midst, and have judged them as dangerous as witches. Perhaps more so. We are seeing an increase in witch hunts and Mithran hunts across the Middle East and in Eastern Europe and Russia," Del said. "The Mithrans are fighting back. However, a number have been staked in recent days and the ensuing power shifts have been dramatic."

I thought about the power plays and unrest in the Middle East. Many religions had proscriptions against drinking blood and therefore hated blood-drinkers. So, yeah, she had a point, but I'd never connected that to fanghead control or vamp deaths. So that meant that minor—but growing—political groups have seen the influence of vamps and staked them, which has resulted in world political power shifts. Interesting.

"The violence is moving into Europe and the council is becoming desperate to find both safe haven and the artifacts of power that they lost during the diaspora. According to our source on the council, they believe that with the icons in their hands, they will find security in this modern world, a world which is changing with such speed and creating such threat to them.

"There have been murmurs in the European Council," she

said, "about moving their headquarters to the New World. Our source believes that they would do so only if they could move into a well-established territory and hunting grounds—which means the extensive territory of New Orleans or New York, as the largest and most well-established hunting grounds in the Americas."

"New York has been making overtures to the EC for decades," Leo said, his face cold and hard as a block of white marble, "paying what amounts to a tithe to them. My predecessor never paid such a tithe in either monies or blood-servants, and neither have I. In return for New York's tithe, I believe that they would leave him in peace and attempt to take this land."

"And if they come here?" I asked him.

"If they come, they will challenge me for the territory, cattle, and magical artifacts. To protect themselves, they may well capture or kill every Mithran, witch, and other supernatural creature alive in the entire United States. Certainly in my territory."

That meant my friends, my employer, his servants, and me. As if he heard my thoughts, Leo turned his black eyes to me. "They are wise to suspect me and my motives. I have dallied reporting to them about many things to secure my power base, to keep the status quo long enough to build my strengths. That includes the ongoing attempt to reach *rapprochement* with the witches of the United States and the attempt to locate and secure *les objets de la puissance*, *les objets de magie*. And that long before you came to my lands, *mon cour*."

Toneless, Del translated, "Objects of power. Magical devices." Leo's statement implied that Leo had successfully found some magical items, but that was a conversation for another time.

"The original vampires *were* witches," I said. "I've never understood why they would want to kill them off."

Not breathing except to speak, his body as still as white marble, Leo said carefully, "The European witches and Mithrans were in a state of political neutrality until the time of the Spanish Inquisition. The persecution by the Church, and by Tomás de Torquemada, their instrument of torture, created a rift between the races, and both came here, to the New World, in great numbers. But not together. They were, by then, separate in all things. Torquemada and his desire to obtain *les ob-*

jets de la puissance is the cause of the chasm that divides the Mithrans and witches."

To me Adelaide asked, "Have you heard of the Inquisition?"

I was raised in a Christian children's home. Of course I knew a little about the history of the Church. I nodded and waffled a hand back and forth. "Nothing about how it affected Mithrans and witches."

"Torquemada lived from 1420 to 1498," Del said, "and he used the offices of the Church and European royal politics to take the lands and possessions of those deemed heretics by the Church. He tortured and killed uncounted numbers of people, and a great many of those who died were Jews, Muslims, witches, and vampires. From the beginning, he hated them all as being children of Satan, but after a time, his interests changed, and he began to drink blood from captive Mithrans. He began to search, not only for the heretics themselves, but for their objects of power. He played the witches and the vampires against one another, and, in a matter of years, the schism between the races grew wider, turning into outright enmity."

"If the Europeans come here," Leo said, his black eyes piercing me, "they will not be under my control. I will be under theirs. The media footage of my Enforcer fighting and defeating a demon, and killing a witch using a magical implement, reached them some time ago."

I froze in my chair, putting it all together, how my life intersected with the history, the danger, and the future that was headed our way. I had killed a rogue witch who had summoned a demon with the blood diamond. Directed by the witch, who had long ago lost her mind in contact with the dark spirit, the demon had been killing humans in a bid to get to Leo Pellissier, whom the witch believed responsible for the death of her daughter. Even with the power of the magical artifact at her command, I had killed her and called an angel to defeat the demon. All caught on TV. Go, me. And now I had the blood diamond in a safe place. But the Europeans probably thought I had given the evil thing to Leo.

Leo gave me a regal nod as he watched me putting two and two together in my mind. "My enemies, and yours, know that many of the objects they have long sought are here, in my domain. They believe that the artifacts are in my hands, or, less likely but still possible, in yours."

"Holy crap on a cracker," I muttered. I had a number of magical trinkets, and Leo knew I had some of them. For reasons I didn't understand, he hadn't pressured me for them. Much. But maybe a battle was about to begin for them. I had some blood-iron discs made from pieces of the iron spike of Golgotha, vamp blood, and skinwalker blood, and I'd managed to keep the making of the magical discs secret. I had some pocket watches powered by the discs, and a black-magic focal stone called the blood diamond, as well as some other trinkets in my possession. Most of them were in safe-deposit boxes, which was even better—harder to get to, harder to break into, harder to steal. Vamps and vampire witches had done some pretty terrible things with the objects over the centuries, some of those horrible things since I'd been around. No way was I giving the witchy things up to the fangheads, but I kept that off my face. I hoped.

"The Europeans' greatest desire," Leo went on, reading my every twitch and heartbeat, "is for the remaining iron from the spike of Golgotha."

"I don't have it," I said. "I never saw it." I knew he would smell the truth on me. The spike could still be in Natchez. Or in Baton Rouge. Or in any of a hundred small towns or cities that had been settled by the white man for hundreds of years. It was too dangerous to leave in the wrong hands, and I'd had my own tech guy running searches for it. And then it hit me. "But they don't know that, do they? The EuroVamps think I have the spike."

I was sure that the EVs had paid good money for research on me, which made it likely that they had used the services of Reach. Which meant that they had *everything*. I closed my eyes.

On some level, I had—once upon a time—stupidly thought that Reach was a friend of sorts. Even knowing that he'd sell his mother to make a buck. It was a stupidity that might cost me.

Leo let his fangs click down on the little hinges in the roof of his mouth and spoke around them. "Soon, little kitten, you will have to find the spike. Or there will be nothing I can do to protect you. Nothing at all."

I remembered the ferocity of the fight I'd witnessed in the gym, and my mouth went dry—my shoulders wanted to tense. Beast wanted to slash Leo across his perfect, beautiful face. But none of this was actually Leo's fault. I had drawn the attention of the most powerful fangheads to me by my own actions, and by not finding a way to cut Reach out of my life and out of Leo's. And mostly by killing a demon-calling witch on national TV. Go, me.

She had been using the blood diamond, one of the most powerful black arts devices in the witchy world. But the spike . . . it had been made by vamps, the very earliest vamps, smelted of the spikes from Golgotha, the spikes melted, welded, or forged into one single spike, covered with the blood of a murderer, a thief, and a holy man who rose from the dead. And according to the snatches of stories I had heard, it had been turned to evil from its first use.

I didn't know whether the spike still existed or what it did, exactly, except it was believed to allow the handler to control vamps. So far as I knew, the spike had been carved up or melted down. Whatever form it now had, it was rumored to be here, in the States somewhere. Discs made from it had been used in black-magic ceremonies that slowly stole the life from witches who had been forced to fuel a huge working circle in Natchez. It had been ugly. Yeah. The vamps would hold me down and drink me dry if they had even a hint that I knew where the spike was.

Leo nodded once as he saw that I understood. "If you bring all the *objets de magie* to me, I will try to shield you and the witches you seek to protect."

Yeah. I just bet you would, I thought.

Leo went on. "Before the Europeans arrive, there are several things that must be accomplished." He inclined his head, as if to make a point. "Things that pertain directly to you, my Enforcer.

"In the following months, you will continue the work on this New Orleans Mithran Council building, bringing it to the highest level of security that can be achieved. You and Derek Lee will continue to oversee the security arrangements of the Pellissier Clan Home, as construction nears the end. And you will discover the location of the iron spike that you claim you do not have. You may also be called upon to assist in *rapprochement* with the witches in the Americas, but we shall discuss that another time."

CHAPTER 3

Boo Stuff

I left Leo's office a half mil richer but filled with a gnawing worry. Following Wrassler, Derek behind me, I called the house—*my* house, which was so cool—on my cell, dialing the new business line, one that rotated over to a business cell when we were out. Working for the fangheads had been good for my bank account—not so good for my conscience, but good for my bank account.

"Yellowrock Securities. Alex Younger speaking."

I grinned, because the Kid could see who was calling. Like the "Wise Ass" greeting of earlier, he was yanking my chain, but, this time, I could hear the enthusiasm in his voice, which meant he had something for me. I pressed the cell to my ear so we could talk without the humans hearing. "Elevator?"

"Is still malfunctioning. The floor buttons being pushed by passengers aren't being correctly routed, and instead are sending out incorrect pulses and taking the car to the wrong floors. By the way, I can't tell if the errors are all electrical, digital, or mechanical. The elevator company is doing an online diagnostic before they send out a repairman. They'll call me with an update on the time, but I'd like to test it once more, with someone on board I can talk to. Can you use the elevator while I watch what happens digitally?"

"Ummm." I was trying to figure out how to get the Kid to remember that I had no way to test the elevator, because *he* wasn't supposed to have a way to test the elevator. And then I remembered my bargain with Leo. "I'm hoping to get some written material from the basement of vamp HQ. So I'll be a while getting back."

"Huh? Oh. Yeah. Whatever. I'll watch."

He ended the call and I turned to Wrassler. "So can I see the storage basement again?"

Wrassler shrugged his massive shoulders, ushered Derek and me into the elevator, placed his palm on the openmouthed display, and punched a button. We started down. And kept on going.

After a too-long descent, that odd smell of panic came again from Wrassler and he pulled his big-ass weapon. Derek pulled a gun too, a snub-nosed .32. I had an image of Mini Me from some old movie. Smothering a totally inappropriate titter-giggle, and only an instant behind them, I pulled my stake and the tiny knife. Micro Mini Me.

The lights flickered in the enclosed space. My breath caught, laughter mutating into something darker.

The elevator car came to a stop. The doors opened. And everything went black. Derek whispered a curse, soft, fierce, and emphatic.

The space around us and before us was blacker than the mouth to hell. Wrassler clicked on a small penlight, holding it to the side of the laser sight, which did nothing to penetrate the darkness of the room/hallway/cellar/dungeon/whatever-the-heck-it-was in front of us. The narrow bands of light were swallowed.

The stench that hit my nose nearly buckled my knees. It was a combination of old blood, rotten herbs, vinegar, sour urine, and sickly sweat. And then I heard breathing, a slow inhale. Slower exhale. Above us, the lights came back on, blinding after the dark. The space beyond remained black even as the elevator closed with a soft *whoosh* of sound.

"Palm," Derek murmured to Wrassler. "Fast."

Wrassler transferred the heavy gun to a one-handed stance, slapped his hand on the laser-reader box, and hit the button for the main floor. *Yes. That. Do not attempt to stop on the storage floor. Just take me outta here.* The elevator began to rise, and I realized I had spoken aloud, not just in my head. I hissed softly, inhaling through my teeth.

Derek had started to curse, a single word, over and over, under his breath. In the moments we had faced the blackness, he had sweated through his shirt. So had Wrassler. So had I.

"Someone want to tell me what the hell that was?" Derek demanded, when he could say something more coherent.

Wrassler, a faint tremor in his hands, holstered his weapon and said, "Don't know. Tall tales. Stuff to scare children. Stories the regulars used to tell the newbies, about a dark room, where things are kept, things that used to be human. Maybe. Or maybe never were."

"Boo stuff," I quoted, hiding my weapons again.

"Boo stuff," Wrassler agreed. "Tall tales. Till now. And we gotta get you better weapons," he said to us.

"Yeah," we both said.

The doors opened and we stepped off onto the main floor, full of lights and milling people, and the bloody smell of vamp digs—herbs, funeral flowers, blood, humans, sex, alcohol, food cooking. Somewhere someone laughed. So normal. Only now did a shiver tremble along my spine, as my adrenal system did a quiver and shake. My mouth suddenly tasted bitter.

I pulled my keys and headed for the door, dodging Bethany, one of the outclan priestesses. She was dressed in a vibrant crimson skirt and shawl, with a purple shirt and bell-shaped earrings that tinkled. As always, she was barefoot, and her toenails were painted the same shade of red as her skirt. Either that or she had been dancing in blood. I turned around in midstride and got another look. Yeah. Polish. With Bethany, one never knew.

On her heels was Sabina, the other priestess, dressed in her starched, nun-habit-like whites. It was good to see them in the same room, though I wasn't sure what that might mean. They didn't always get along. Sabina's whites weren't splashed with blood, so at least they weren't killing anyone together. Today. Yet. I grabbed my weapons from the security guy at the front door checkpoint, without speaking, without glad-handing, without good-byes, and blew out of HQ into the night.

It had rained while I was inside, ensconced in windowless offices, on middle floors—and lower floors—and now the night smelled fresh, of water-water-everywhere, the air still so full of rain moisture and ozone from lightning that it soothed and energized both. To the south, lightning still flickered between clouds, brightening the horizon in white-gray flashes. Thunder rumbled far off, a long, low echo. It was probably a great show over the Gulf of Mexico.

I strapped into the SUV and took a deep breath, seeing my

hands on the steering wheel. They looked calm, steady, competent, not terrified, shaky, or useless. I turned the key and managed not to put the pedal to the metal and fly around the circular drive. The new iron gate rolled back along its tracks as I approached. I timed it so that the sedate pace allowed the gate to be fully open as my SUV—one not driven by a heavy-footed speed demon or a panicked evacuee—reached the entrance.

And then I was gone, the gate pulling closed behind me. My panic started to ease. I gulped air, hyperventilating, trying to analyze what I had heard and smelled and tasted on my tongue while standing in the dark. It had felt cloying and heavy, the taste oily and vinegary, like really bad salad dressing and raw meat, rather than anything dangerous. My hindbrain, however, said otherwise. That subconscious, reptile brain had informed me that the lightless room contained a horrible, deadly . . . something.

Beast pulled on the power that lay between us, the gray place of the change, and our energies danced along my skin with a faint tingle, like holiday sparklers. She rumbled deep inside, a snarl of anger. *Dead things. Hungry things. Do not go back to den of dead hungry things.*

The laughter that had remained hidden inside me tittered out, sounding as panicked as a twelve-year-old kid at a Halloween slumber party—not that I had ever been to one. Whatever had been there, in the dark, waiting, something about it had hit me and the men with me, and even Beast, on a primal level, something so primitive that I couldn't even name it except by nightmare titles—the bogeyman. Yeah. That was what had activated my Spidey sense. Something dark and malevolent. The bogeyman. And it was hiding in Leo's basement. Not good. Just freaking not good.

I rolled on through the French Quarter streets, the mutter of the engine and the tires splashing through rain the only sound, shaking off the fear-sweats as Beast let go of our magics. I was still getting used to the time it took to get anywhere in a car in New Orleans. Like forever. The Harley had been so much faster, what with being able to take back alleys, go the wrong way up one-way streets—as long as a cop wasn't around—and slip between cars stuck in traffic. The city seemed a lot bigger and a lot more crowded in the SUV. I didn't particularly like it. Not at all. Everything took too long to get to.

One block out from my house and business, something hit my SUV door. Rammed it hard, knocking the vehicle into the oncoming lane. I yanked back on the wheel, righting myself and the vehicle. It hit again, harder, denting the door, rocking the SUV on its tires. A squealing sound pierced my ears, maybe fury, maybe pain. Maybe both, with a frenzied edge to the scream, like a buzz saw sliding along metal.

Before I could find it, the thing busted against the side window, creating a round impression of circular cracks with straight-line cracks radiating out from the center, like the spokes of a broken wheel. It looked like damage from a shotgun, fired point-blank into the laminated polycarbonate glass. I whipped the heavy vehicle back into my lane and gunned the engine. From the corner of my eye, in the rearview mirror, I caught a glimpse of rainbow-hued light and an impression of glittering wings. And then it was gone, leaving behind only the sound of its screaming.

I was gripping the steering wheel so hard the leather squeaked. I slowed and came to a stop on Canal Street, not sure how I'd gotten there. I was shaking, breathing all wonky. Eyes darting around, searching for an enemy. Seeing nothing. The street was empty at this hour. No attacker, no witnesses. As my eyes darted around, I spotted a security camera. And then realized that I had stopped after an attack, instead of clearing the scene at all speeds. Too much adrenaline in my system in too short a time had made me fuzzy-brained. "Not smart. Outta here." I pressed the accelerator and drove on. I wasn't attacked again.

But I did notice a black SUV, paralleling my progress one street over. Black SUVs were a dime a dozen, but this one . . . Had I seen it from the corner of my eye while the light thing attacked me? It looked familiar. I slowed, and the black vehicle continued on. Paranoid me.

When I got back to my place, I stepped from the SUV and inspected the damage. It looked like the kind that could be caused by a two-hundred-fifty-pound deer in a full run ramming an ordinary vehicle. But unlike a deer accident, there were no short brown hairs or blood in the indentations. No indication or evidence of what had hit the vehicle, though the rain may have washed some away. I had seen the sort of thing that hit me before, several times, in fact. The first time was when it wrecked Bitsa, my Harley, and most recently in Chauvin, Louisiana. It had been all teeth with vaguely humanoid features. Had the creature I had seen down south been the same species as the thing that hit my SUV? Maybe the same creature? And did this mean the creature was hunting me? Not a happy thought.

Feeling the damp in my bones, I shook off my misery, entered my house, acknowledged the guys sitting in the main room with a wave and a promise of info, and went to my bedroom, closing my door. I stripped and climbed into a shower, letting the steam and the water pressure pound the stress out of me.

The thing that had attacked my vehicle was similar to the being that was my ex-boyfriend's partner in the department called PsyLED under the umbrella of Homeland Security. Her name was Soul and she was brilliant and curvy and gorgeous and deadly. And not human. When lives were at stake, she moved like the thing I'd seen, the thing that had now attacked me in the streets several times. The thing I had seen splashing in the water of the canals, like a dolphin playing, below Chauvin, Louisiana. A thing others didn't seem to see at all, except for Bruiser, with his Onorio magics. Whatever she was, Soul changed form in a swoosh of light, just like the things, the lightbeings, though she didn't smell like one. Thinking of Soul and Chauvin made me think of Ricky Bo. Which just ticked me off.

Before I went back into the main room, I dressed and texted Soul, not that she had come here, or done anything substantive, when I saw the previous things. But informing her seemed the right thing to do. *Another thing like you attacked my SUV. Dented it.* I listed the time and sent the text. And stared at the screen, hoping Soul would call or text me back, but she didn't. I knew how hard it was to step up and deal with the "I am not human" problem, but I had hoped Soul would come through sooner rather than later.

Back in the main room, I curled up on the couch and said, "Update."

"Not trying to be rude or anything, Janie, but you look like crap," the Kid said.

"It's been an interesting night."

To my side, Eli appeared, carrying a huge mug of tea, smelling of spices, with a dollop of Cool Whip on top. He put it in my hands and wrapped my fingers around the warm stoneware. His hands held mine on the heated mug, his flesh warm over mine. It was an odd, kind, unexpected thing, that touch. Tears burned under my lids. "Thanks," I whispered, not trusting my voice for more than that.

"Alex is right," Eli said aloud. He dropped into the chair across from the couch, watching me. "Debrief. Take it slow."

As I sipped, I filled them in, step by step, while the Kid typed up a report. We had discovered that it helped to have a running record of the weird stuff in our lives and business.

When I got to the part about the thing in the basement, Eli asked, "What did it smell like? Did you recognize it?"

"No. It was . . ." My nose crinkled, remembering the oppressive dark and the stench.

"You didn't have a record of the scent in your skinwalker memory?"

"The closest I can come to it is to say that it smelled like a village full of sick and dead humans, mixed with the strong odor of lightning, and the scent of vamps when they had the plague. And vinegar. Sick and dead and dying and electrified salad dressing all at once." I shook my head as if shaking away the memory. "Anyway, we went back up the elevator and I got the heck outta Dodge."

The Kid said, "Otis Online Repair did a diagnostic and told us nothing we didn't already know. The palm scanner and the button control panel are functioning according to specs, just as our own diagnostic showed. They speculate that the problem with the elevator may be an electrical pulse in the HQ wiring, maybe something not digitally traceable in the control panel. I pulled up an electrical schematic of vamp central." He whirled the laptop to display a floor plan with varicolored lines on each floor, including five layers of basement, which was really unusual, what with New Orleans' high water table. "The basements should be permanently flooded from water seeping in from the ground, but they aren't," I said, "which means that magic went into the construction. Some kind of spell that keeps water outside the basement walls." Which meant witch assistance in the building process several hundred years ago. But what was most interesting were the different-colored lines threaded through the building, floor to floor.

"The colored lines," he said, "are the electrical systems according to date of installation. The red lines are the original installation in—get this—1890. Most of the original wiring has been updated, some parts repeatedly, for decades," Alex said. "Some were torn out—that's the yellow—and replaced, especially after insulated copper wires first came on the market to replace the original uninsulated ones. The major updates were done in 1893, 1906, 1947, 1969, 1998, and again in 2005, after Hurricane Katrina. In fact, all the rewiring dates followed major hurricanes, and twice in that time, all of the aboveground floors were totally rewired due to a storm surge that supposedly flooded the basements from above."

"So the spell that keeps water from seeping in through the walls won't stop it from entering from above."

"That's what I'm getting," Alex agreed. "But according to what I can find online and in the databases of vamp HQ, the lines in the two lower basements have never been upgraded, and are still in use."

"And the two lower basements would have suffered the most from aboveground flooding, so that excuse to rewire was bogus. If our problem isn't the control panel of the elevator—which is the most likely suspect—then maybe something about the wiring—"

"In that case, most likely, water is seeping through the walls," the Kid interrupted, "and is collecting on or dripping on the wires. That would cause the stuff you're seeing, brownouts and blackouts and loads of glitches. The electrical is tied into everything from food storage to the computers to the security systems."

"Ducky." The word sounded as tired as I felt. "Just freaking ducky." Because our jobs had just gotten harder and we all knew it.

"I'm waiting for a final arrival time for the Otis repair people. I'm aiming for after six a.m. on whatever day they can come. You'll want to have security personnel with each member of the repair team." We both looked at Eli.

"Okay by me. I'm always up for a rappel down an elevator shaft. I'll make coffee," Eli said, sounding psyched. He disappeared into the kitchen. The Kid and I blinked and shook our heads in unison. Eli had weird ideas about what was fun.

When he came back, bringing with him the smell of espresso and a mug, I said, "Now we get to talk about my SUV. I got attacked again, just like that time that thing, whatever it was, attacked me on my bike." I looked at Eli. "The SUV is damaged."

Eli dropped back into a chair across from me, his eyes crinkled up in delight. "Really? Leo will be so ticked off at you for damaging his loaner. Can I watch you tell him?"

"Thanks for the heartwarming concern. Leo won't care. *Raisin*, now, *she'll* care," I grumbled. "She'll probably take the repairs out of my pay." Raisin was the name I had given to Ernestine, the in-house CPA, the woman who ran all things of vamp financial natures, and kept the vamp social calendar. She was, like, three hundred years old, and got decades older every time I saw her, dry and wrinkled and *old*, like an unwrapped mummy, and she wrote my checks—yeah, old-fashioned checks written with a pen dipped into ink—and paid the vamp taxes and kept the bills and paid the food service vendors and clothing expenses and collected tax money and tribute money from the subservient clans and worked with financial advisors to make money with the money she collected. And she took care of paying for cars. And paid repair people. And she didn't like me because I cost money. Raisin terrified me, maybe because she had authority and wasn't above slapping the back of my hand with a ruler to punish a transgression.

"Being boss has to suck." Eli looked positively happy about my having to face Raisin.

"Yeah. Back to the thing that attacked me? It was probably caught on a security camera in front of the Cigar Factory on Decatur."

"On it," the Kid said.

"The last time I was attacked in the streets, I was on Bitsa and was hurt pretty bad. This time, it didn't get near me, but I was surrounded by steel and glass, so maybe it can't tolerate either. Bruiser injured it that time with a steel blade." It had happened in the gray place of the change, which I hadn't gotten around to telling the guys about. The weird thing was that I'd never seen a nonmagical being in the gray place until Bruiser strode into it. Somehow. And Bruiser and I had, so far, managed to not talk about that. In fact, I had managed for us to not talk about much at all, except for work. Nothing personal. Nothing about . . . us. Whatever we were. But from the looks I'd gotten this evening, that wasn't gonna last. Whatever space Bruiser had been giving me in the wake of Ricky Bo's betrayal was used up. He was gonna do . . . something. Whatever. And soon. That left a hollow feeling in my middle, and I drank deep from the tea, licking the melting Cool Whip off my lips.

"So, steel," Eli said. "Possible to hurt it, then, as long as we're faster than it is."

"Good luck with that," I said.

The Kid was still typing, his fingers clacking on the keys. He might like touch screens and the newest model of tablets, but when it came to reports, Alex was old-school, using an ergonomic keyboard and Microsoft Word. All important files were encrypted and triple backed up, unimportant files were just backed up and e-mailed to himself. For his birthday, as a surprise, I had opened accounts for him online at three different electronics stores. Of course, I had put a limit on all of them—I wasn't *that* stupid.

"This light creature. Was it the same one that attacked you last time?" Alex asked. "I mean the exact same creature or just one like it?" Which was the question I'd asked myself.

"I don't know. Maybe. Why? How's the research coming on them?" I scooted across the couch, closer to the small table he used as a desk.

"Not good." He shoved his hair behind one ear, the curls getting kinky as his hair grew out. I didn't know the Younger brothers' ethnic backgrounds, but African figured prominently in there somewhere. "And if there's one, there's usually more."

Not always, I thought. A pang went through me, shrill as a cracked brass bell. I'd seen only one other of my own kind since I walked out of the mountains at age twelve. And he'd been insane.

Unaware of my reaction, Alex went on. "Maybe all of them hate you," he added with glee. "The closest I can find for it is the lillilend, a mythical creature adopted by gamers as a lillend."

"Wait a minute. My dragon made of light is a role-playing-game creature? Seriously?"

Without looking up from his tablets, Alex gave me a lopsided grin. "Gamers adopt a lot of mythical creatures and then crossbreed them to get new creatures. The lillilend is a shapechanger." He glanced up at me from under his too-long hair to see how I'd respond to the presence of another shape-changing creature in the world, besides weres and skinwalkers.

I sipped again, which he took as "No comment," and went on. "It has a female human or elf-like form, one with legs and arms, but also has hybrid forms, sometimes winged, with a twenty-foot wingspan. When it's in the hybrid shape, it's been reported to have a humanoid upper half, or humanoid head, and a snakelike lower half, with coils that can reach twenty feet. And wings. When it's in one of its hybrid forms, it can acquire a pure energy structure. Like a creature made of light, as seen through a prism."

Light forms. Like what I saw in the gray place of the change? I thought back to the creatures I'd seen. I didn't remember a twenty-foot wingspan, but if the wings had been made of light, or had been pulled in tight, then maybe I'd just overlooked them. And if they'd been half-furled, maybe they had looked like a frill. And maybe the one I'd seen wasn't fully grown. A lot of maybes.

Alex went on. "All sorts of legends mention the lillilend, perhaps even the Adam and Eve story of the snake in the Garden of Eden, and even the apocryphal Lillith story. Similar creatures in mythology are the Fu xi, the Lamia, the Nuwa, the Ketu—which is an Asura, but none of them have wings."

I had no idea what kind of creatures he was talking about but I nodded. I'd discovered that agreeing meant less time listening to explanations that I didn't care a whit about. Listening to descriptions of things that weren't what I was looking for seemed like a waste of time, and the Kid could run on for hours about gaming and mythological stuff.

"I've been compiling artistic renderings of all the mythical creatures, but—"

"But since they're mythical, no one really knows what they look like," I said.

"Right. Here." He spun two of his three tablets and I pulled them closer, skimming through the paintings, the graphics, the friezes of snakelike creatures carved in stone from long-lost civilizations, the comic-book renderings of big-busted beauties.

"Nope. None of these match what I saw. In fact, if I had to describe it and didn't mind the funny looks I'd get, I'd call it a dragon made of light or a spirit dragon." I pushed the tablets back. "So, on to other things." I filled them in on the minutiae of the vamp meeting, and finished with a question. "Where do we stand on the spike of the crosses? The Europeans want it. Leo wants it. And no, they're not getting it. We need to find it first and toss it in the Mariana Trench or a volcano somewhere."

"Poseidon, Pele, and Vulcan might think they're being dissed." Alex was grinning, teasing.

Too bad I couldn't appreciate that. "Whatever. It needs to be destroyed." Every magical implement used in black arts needed to be destroyed. The old saying about absolute power was totally true when it came to vamps. And witches. And humans. And probably skinwalkers, come to think of it.

"And what did you do with the other weapons of power?" Eli asked softly.

I turned to the former Ranger sitting across the rug from me, his legs stretched out, his fingers laced across his stomach. He looked deceptively relaxed, but I knew better. He could strike across the room almost as fast as a cobra, and he was always armed. Always. "Uncle Sam can't have them," I said flatly, my tone soft.

"So you're the only person who has the right to them?"

It was an old argument, one we had been having for weeks, and we were stuck. "I'm the only person who won't use them."

"And if using one would save Angie Baby's life?"

Angie Baby, Molly's daughter, my godchild. I knew what he was doing. He was telling me that I would, eventually, find a need for the blood-magic. "Uncle Sam can't have them," I repeated. "Not now, not ever. We need to destroy them."

"Stop it," Alex said, his voice low.

Eli and I looked at him, but he was staring at his screens, his head down and his eyes hidden behind slitted lids. His lips curled up on one side, a smile so like one of his brother's understated gestures that it shocked me. And then the half smile stretched into his own wry grin. "I don't like it when Mommy and Daddy fight."

I threw a line drive at his head. It would have been deadly had I used something other than a couch cushion. As it was, he did a good imitation of a bobblehead doll before he scooped the pillow off the floor and threw it back at me. And missed. Eli was grinning at our antics—actually showed a hint of his pearly whites. "Bro," he said to his brother. "You throw like a girl. And, Jane, so do you."

We both grinned back, Alex flipped him off, and on that happy family-time moment, I stood, stretched until something popped in my back, and said, "'Night."

"What's left of it," the Kid griped.

I woke at eleven a.m. when a knock sounded on the front door, and I threw on a robe. When the guys moved in, I'd discovered that I needed a better robe, so I bought three, all matching, blocky-shaped, black terry-cloth robes, and gave them out at a Sunday breakfast. The guys had rolled their eyes, but they wore them when they came downstairs in the mornings. Most of the time. I tossed my hair over my shoulder and peeked out the window in the door, then looked back over my shoulder at Eli, poised on the top landing, a handgun in each hand. His robe hung unbelted, revealing the sculpted body of a warrior, and the pale scars that had nearly killed him. He had new scars on his throat and chest caused by a vamp eating on him. He didn't remember much about the event but I did. He said it didn't bother him, but it bothered me. A lot. I'd nearly gotten my partner killed.

Keeping the remembered horror of that night out of my voice, I said, "It's Bruiser."

Eli safetied both weapons, lifted one in acknowledgment, and trudged back to bed. Keeping vamp hours was hard on us all. I remembered the expression in Bruiser's eyes from the night before and my shoulders drew up. Feeling stupid, or maybe uncertain, which was stupid come to think of it, I pulled my robe together, tightened the belt, and tossed my hip-length black braid out of the way before opening the door.

A peculiar mix of scents met my nose: cooked grease, sugar, tea, green things, citrusy something, and gun oil. Less intense was the smell of New Orleans: water, exhaust, food, coffee, old liquor, spices, and urine. I blinked at the combo, trying to take it all in. Bruiser was dressed in dark brown khakis and a light brown shirt, the sleeves rolled up, his muscled arms showing beneath the cuffs. He was holding the handle of a basket in one hand and flowers in the other. Flowers. Stems wrapped in lavender paper. Like . . . *flowers*. Like from a fancy florist. White calla lilies framing three bright red calla lilies with yellow stamens, all nonaromatic. And a wide frill of catnip in bloom, tiny white flowers with a scent so delectable Beast rolled over on her back and purred.

I just stared at the flowers. Feeling weird.

Bruiser had brought me flowers.

CHAPTER 4

An Offer to Dish

"Jane?"

I started, realizing I had been standing, without greeting him, my eyes on the flowers. "Ummm." Moving woodenly, I opened the door and stood aside to let him in.

Wearing a faint, quizzical smile that would have done my Ranger partner proud, he said, "You act like no one ever brought you flowers before."

"Yeah. Once." *Rick*. Rick had brought me daisies and sunflowers. But I didn't say that. "What do I do with them?"

Bruiser's face changed, and I had no idea what the new expression meant. I didn't take my eyes from the flowers to get a better look. His voice soft, he said, "They go in a vase. On the nightstand by your bed. Or on the kitchen table. Or on the coffee table in the living room. They go where you can see them most often, and, seeing them, remember that you deserve flowers." When I still just stood there, he said, "I'll get a vase from the kitchen. I'm sure Katie left some here. Why don't you get dressed. And then we can have breakfast. I brought beignets from Café du Monde, and tea."

"Yeah. I'll go get dressed." I could tell my voice sounded weird, but I turned and went to my room, shutting myself in. I stood there, my back to the paneled door, staring stupidly. *Flowers?* I pulled on jeans and a T-shirt and braided my hair, debating on makeup. I finally put a touch of lipstick on my bottom lip and smeared my lips together to mush the color around until there was just a tint left. And found myself staring at my reflection in the mirror, my amber eyes catching the light. Rick had brought me flowers. Rick had deserted me. Now Bruiser had brought me flowers.

Flowers. With catnip.

My Beast was silent but excited, alert, and curious, ears flicking, eyes intent.

I walked back into the living room and followed the smells of beignets and flowers to the kitchen. Bruiser was facing the window, drying his hands, backlit by the window light, so I could see only a profile, his brown hair darkened by glare, his nose a tad too strong for classical beauty, yet well formed. It was a totally sexy nose. He was tall, strong-looking, capable. His stance said he could handle anything, protect anyone, or die trying. Something tightened in my middle.

Behind him, on the table, was a cut crystal vase that had been in the butler's pantry, the bouquet inside it, the blooms fluffed. Short snips of stems lay in a small pile, where he'd trimmed them. I vaguely remembered that the stems of cut flowers had to be trimmed every few days.

Beignets were on china plates from the top cabinet. Tea had been poured into matching china cups. They were sitting on saucers, with tiny little napkins beside each. There was real cream in a tiny pitcher I had seen somewhere on a shelf and a matching sugar-holder thingy. And polished silver spoons. And the flowers. In a vase.

Beast was peering out through my eyes, staring at my bouquet. She sniffed and filled our/my head with the scent. *Catnip?* she asked. *For Beast?*

Yeah. Catnip. The fancy flowers were bad enough. The catnip was something much worse. The aroma expanded as if trying to fill the house.

Bruiser had moved in here not that long ago, a temporary arrangement, he'd called it. Then he had moved back out, and back into vamp HQ, to help with the transition of the old primo—him—to the new primo—Adelaide. Now he wasn't even a full-time blood-servant, or at least, that was the way I had interpreted the meeting earlier. I didn't know what he was to Leo. And I didn't know what he was to me. We had danced. We had killed rogue vamps together in Natchez. We had shared a few intense physical moments brought on by mutual attraction and once by magic. But I had no idea what any of it meant or where I wanted us to go.

Bruiser seemed to sense me behind him and turned. I stuck my hands in my pockets and frowned. His face emotionless, he moved around the table and pulled out a chair. I knew how to do this. I'd been taught proper Southern manners in the children's home. But I hadn't practiced in more than a decade. Shoulders hunched, I took my seat and lifted my weight in the ungainly half crouch that allowed him to push my chair in the requisite few inches.

Bruiser handed me a napkin, which I placed over a thigh. He moved my teacup and the sugar and creamer closer. I added both to my tea as he took his seat at the corner, ninety degrees, and only inches, away from me. The house was mostly silent, one of the boys upstairs snoring softly. My palms were slightly moist and my heart was beating fast. The air conditioner came on. It was May, and already hot in the Deep South.

I expected Bruiser to put food on my plate and make me eat it with a silver fork. But he didn't pass the beignets. Instead he lifted a box from the basket and set it in front of me, to the side of my dainty cup.

The box was maybe twelve inches by fourteen, wrapped in shiny gold paper with a darker gold bow, the ties all long and curly. From the way he handled it, the box was too heavy for jewelry, which was my first panicked thought. Just from looking at the box, I could tell that whatever it held was expensive. Even the paper looked like it cost a small fortune. I stared at it. I was doing a lot of staring. I was pretty sure I wasn't breathing.

I dragged in a breath, scrubbed my sweaty hands dry on my jeans, and reached for the bow, pulling the ties until the ribbon fell away, My fingers were stiff and clumsy, but I got the paper open without tearing it. It seemed a crime to tear that paper. I set the stiff wrapping to the side and opened the plain white box. Inside was a second box, this one of carved wood, put together with wooden pegs. The wood felt old when I touched it, but well-oiled. I lifted the lid. Nesting within, on a swath of red velvet, was a knife, secured in a scabbard.

My mouth went parched, my hands icy and dry. A faint tremor ran along my fingers and vibrated through my core. I felt a small smile tug at my mouth, and I shook my head, feeling like there wasn't enough air.

Bruiser said, "It's a Mughal Empire, watered-steel dagger from India." When I didn't say anything or lift my eyes from the wondrous scabbard, he went on. "The knife was made in the seventeen hundreds, and has a slightly curved blade with a central ridge and double grooves. It has a gold-overlaid palmette and cartouche at forte, with a gem-set, jade-hilted handle."

Still smiling slightly, breathing deeply to catch up on lost air, I lifted the scabbarded dagger and pulled the blade free, holding it to the side so the window light fell on it. The steel was beautiful, with a blued sheen that spoke of careful work with forge and hammer. There were nicks in the blade, but Bruiser hadn't honed them out, and I was glad. They had history, each nick and scratch.

Bruiser, his voice the caressing lilt of a weapons lover, said, "The jade hilt has hand-carved scroll quillons centered with a carved stylized lotus leaf, and the pommel is in the form of an African lion's head with gold inlay and set with golden topaz for the eyes."

He didn't have to add that the stones were the same shade as my own human eyes. I ducked my head, feeling the weight of the knife and its history in my hands.

"The scabbard," he said, "is velvet-covered wood, jade-mounted, nineteenth century, with a carved jade chape and lock. A certain wily salesman suggested that the blade is charged with a spell of life force, to give the wielder the ability to block any opponent's death cut. Pure balderdash, but it makes a nice tale."

Silence fell between us, and I sheathed the blade, sliding it into the scabbard that had been shaped and carved just for it. The chape of the scabbard and the quillons met, the carved lotus flowers snapping together perfectly, with a small tap of jade on jade. "Why?" I asked, gesturing to the table with the dagger and scabbard, and then to the knife with my free hand. "Why this combination of . . . stuff?" *Why flowers and catnip?* But I didn't ask that part.

Bruiser reached forward and took the blade, placing it in the nest of scarlet velvet. He took my hand. His palm was heated, the skin callused, and his fingers closed over mine. Deep inside me, something that was raw and ugly and bleeding stopped aching. Just . . . stopped.

"I thought for a long time about how to approach you. I thought about jewelry, or a Harley. I have a beautiful, fully restored Indian I thought you might like. I thought about a piece of Cherokee pottery I have somewhere, packed away. But each of those things touches on only a part of you."

I tilted my head, watching our hands, not his face. His hands were well formed, fingers slender and strong.

Not reacting to my silence, Bruiser went on. "I chose these things because they seemed to speak to the heart of you. To the deep darkness that is part of you. That still, lightless, solemn place where, I think, no one has ever gone."

My hand tightened, ever so slightly, when he described me, the hidden me, the soul home where all that I was, and all that I am, and all that I might someday become, lived. My soul home, in the tribal fashion, was a cave, an empty cave, with water-smoothed rock walls, and a fire pit in the center.

"You have honor," Bruiser said. "That is a rare quality in this world." He lifted my hand and pressed my knuckles to his mouth. His lips were hot and firm on my icy flesh.

I was now breathing too fast and shallow and I felt the cold prickles of hyperventilation.

"Men don't think to give you flowers," he murmured, his lips moving on my skin before he let our hands drop, still clasped, "because you have the heart of a warrior. The soul of a priestess. The heat of a long-burning fire. But we should give you flowers, all of us, if for nothing but to share their wonderful fragrance and beauty." He smiled slightly, his lips moving in my peripheral vision. His thumb stroked the skin on the back of my hand, once, twice, slowly. "That is why the flowers. The catnip, that quiet, delightful scent, is for your beast, the cat I saw you become, one night."

I pulled in a slow, nearly painful breath. Smelling the catnip. Inside, Beast rolled over, paws in the air, and purred.

"The dagger? Because you are a weapon, from the soul out. And because I have been such a weapon, and shall be one again, if you agree. The china and crystal, the linen napkin and silver spoons," Bruiser said, "are more for me than for you. Because I have been all those things, once, long ago, and I would share that world with you, if you will let me. If you will let me stay with you."

I pulled in another breath, feeling light-headed again. The scents of catnip, tea, and steel filled me like a mist fills the night.

"For a reason or a season," he said. "For a year or a lifetime. For a poem or a song. For a victorious battle or a bloody death. For honor. I would stand by you for as long as I might live."

Questions filled my head, bouncing like balls in a box. I looked up from our clasped hands, into his brown eyes, afraid of what he might be asking me. His eyes had golden flecks. Had I noticed that before? And his nose. I found his nose so captivating. It was bony and commanding all at once. His hair, the color sable in this light, fell over half of his forehead and down into one eye, tangling with his lashes. Through the falling strands of hair, I could see, barely, his widow's peak and the tiny mole that rarely showed at his hairline.

As if he knew my questions before I thought them, he said, "If we survive this coming war, you and I, we may live three or four human lifetimes, far longer than any human has lived since the flood, since Methuselah walked the Earth. Jane Yellowrock, I want you to be part of that life, in whatever form or capacity you may choose. I won't push; I won't demand. But I wish to be with you, if you will allow me to do so."

"And if Rick comes back?" I hadn't expected to say the words. Had no idea where they had come from.

"You deserve someone who will honor you first and last. And if you choose a man who dishonors you, then you are not the woman I believe you to be."

I smiled at that, because that was how I felt, but hadn't had the words to frame the thought. "Touché. And if Leo objects?"

"I was quite careful of the legality of my wording this morning," he said. "Leo may not like that I court you, but he will have no choice."

Court? I pulled my hand from his, unsettled. "I don't know how to talk about relationship stuff. You need to know that. I have no idea."

"I, however, have decades of practice," he said, with an amused, almost lofty tone. "Later, when you've had time to think, we'll talk. Now we need to eat," he said. "And drink this lovely tea. It's a special, finest, tippy, golden, flowery orange pekoe from Ceylon, a first flush tea that I brought with me from the council house."

"You stole Something Far Too Good for Ordinary People?" I asked.

Bruiser grinned at the old tea lover's joke and indicated that I should taste the tea. I did. And it was indeed SFTGFOP, and by far the best tea I had ever tasted. I sighed and closed my eyes as the flavors moved along my throat. When I opened my eyes, Bruiser had placed a beignet on a plate and put it by my tea saucer. He could have used the silver tongs I hadn't noticed until now, but he didn't. He set the beignet on the china plate with his bare fingers, white powdered sugar on them. He lifted his hand . . . and licked his fingers.

He licked his fingers . . . The sight went through me like the antique weapon might through silk gauze. This man, this Onorio . . . He was way more than silver and fancy manners. He was Bruiser. I smiled and picked up the pastry. Bit into the cooling beignet. I set the beignet on the plate and sipped the tea. In silence, we ate the picnic breakfast, me coming to understand that Bruiser wanted me. *Me.* When he could have any sexy blood-servant or vamp he wanted. And . . .

I wanted him too. I always had.

But there were so many things that lay between us: I'd taken a mate recently and it hadn't worked out so well. Bruiser had helped to hold me down so that Leo could force a feeding and attempt to bind me. That he'd had no control over his own body at the time didn't help a lot, not on an emotional level. Also, Bruiser didn't know about Beast. I wasn't sure I was ready to take a man to my bed without telling him about Beast. Without telling him everything about me. And then there was Bruiser's Onorio status and what that might mean about him and his life and his future. More secrets. There were chasms of the unknown between us right now. Deep and dark chasms, full of shadows and wraiths and the gloom of darkness.

After the meal, Bruiser washed the dishes and poured us both something more familiar—me a big mug of my own tea, with Cool Whip and sugar, just the way I liked it, and himself a mug of coffee, from the espresso machine in the butler's pantry. Holding the mugs, he gestured to the living room. "Shall we talk?"

I wasn't sure I could, exactly, or not right now. But I also couldn't find a good reason to refuse, so I led the way and sat on the sofa, curling my legs under me, and accepted the mug, sipping, waiting.

"Leo received a new communiqué from the Mithrans in Paris," Bruiser said, his voice easing into a more businesslike tone. "Because of the contents of the letter, he intends to train his people in European Mithran tactics and fighting methods, lessons to begin at nine thirty tonight. Eli and you and I are to attend. A meeting and discussion about the European Mithrans will follow."

"I thought he threw you out today."

"He did." Bruiser's gaze met mine above the rim of his cup, his eyes filled with amusement. "Unlike Grégoire, who chose to keep his Onorios with him, and they chose to stay, I am no longer part of Leo's personal servants. He will not have a live-in whom he cannot bind."

"Leo has trust issues?"

"He's stayed alive for five hundred years because of those trust issues. So, yes. However, I know more about the ins and outs of Leo's personal household and the council's day-to-day activities than anyone alive. For that knowledge, I am still a valuable employee to the New Orleans council and to Clan Pellissier, and I was sworn to that service from an early age." He sipped, thinking, and shrugged. "As Onorio, I have other, less specific uses and great value. So, after you left, Leo and I struck a bargain, one I found exceedingly beneficial financially. I will continue to be employed by the clan, under one-year contracts, for a period of three years, at which time we may renegotiate the terms of my employment or I may choose to leave the clan entirely."

"Fancy words for he offered you a lot of money and you took it."

"Essentially, yes."

"Sooo, you go to work there every day but you sleep somewhere else?"

"I have a small apartment on St. Philip Street, just around the corner."

"The Saint Philip Apartments?" I was getting to know the Quarter and the businesses and people who comprised it.

"Unit eleven," he said, sounding wry. "I rented it the last time Leo threw me out. I moved the last of my everyday things into it this morning." He shrugged. "It's only nine hundred square feet, but it's one of the few units to be completely renovated. It isn't quite the exquisite accommodations of a lair of the Master of the City of New Orleans, but for the moment it's mine, and comfortable enough."

"Ah." There seemed to be not much of anything to say to that.

He seemed to notice the uncomfortable silence that followed, and said, "And on that pithy note, I'll take my leave. I'll see myself out. Until tonight." Bruiser left his mug on the small table beside the couch and strode toward the door. He left me sitting sleepily on the sofa, a cooling mug in my hands, and a glorious memory of his backside clenching in the lightweight cotton pants as he left. Bruiser had a really great butt. "I'll pick you up at six for an early dinner. Wear a dress."

As the door closed, I murmured into my mug, "You could move back in here. We have an empty room upstairs." And felt how the words tasted, how they felt on my tongue, the texture of the invitation, and the faint thrill that ran along my skin. "Or maybe not. Maybe I'm not ready for a man in my life again." And then I heard his parting words. *Dinner? In a dress?*

My cell vibrated and I looked at the screen to see a text from Soul. *Must rearrange current case. Will be in NOLA soonest.* Which told me little, but did at least indicate that she was taking me seriously.

A moment later, I smelled Eli on the stairway. He moved like a cat on his bare feet, and he'd lived here long enough to avoid the squeaky spots on the old stairs, but there was nothing he could do about the air currents, and with the AC on, his scent preceded him. "Hey," I said.

He leaned around the corner. "Is it safe to come in?" I nodded, and Eli went straight to the espresso maker. He was wearing jeans and layered T-shirts, and managed to look deadly even without shoes. Moments later, he sat across from me in the chair he favored, his hands holding his own mug. "You want to talk about it?"

I don't know what I'd expected, but an offer to dish wasn't it. My eyes widened in reaction and Eli flashed me a quick glimpse of teeth. "I overheard part of that. The floors are un-insulated, you know. And that was a proposal if I ever heard one. Which is interesting since I believe you two will be having your first official date tonight."

"No, it wasn't." The words said themselves before I could think them through. "It's not a date. I mean, no ring, no lovey-dovey words, no—"

"Flowers. Catnip. Food. Tea. And a knife that might be worth thousands. Dinner and a dress. Proposal and a date night."

My eyes stayed wide and I hunched my shoulders. "No," I breathed. "He didn't propose. He didn't. I don't want him to propose. I don't want him to love me. I'm not ready to be shackled into a relationship."

Eli's grin widened, taking on a teasing twist. "A proposal tailored just for you. Thoughtful, reasoned, romantic. As much as food, flowers, and knives can be." When I said nothing, Eli added, "Maybe it wasn't a *marriage* proposal. But it was a *something* proposal. I think you just have to decide what that something is." He stood and moved silently to the stairs.

"You are an evil, evil man," I said. Eli just laughed.

A nap was out. No way could I sleep when I had a date . . . a *date* . . . with Bruiser and martial arts practice afterward at fanghead HQ. Was I supposed to wear a dress and bring sparring clothes to change into? And clothes suitable for a vamp meeting afterward? What kind of dress was I supposed to wear? Something I'd put on for a security gig for the vamps? I wandered into my bedroom and opened the closet. It was . . . full. Or nearly so.

When I moved here, I'd arrived with the clothes on my back and a change of undies, my few other clothes and boots sent on by the postal system in a big brown cardboard box. Back then I'd had more weapons than clothes. I'd lived in jeans and tees and leather. Now. *Crap.* Now I had a girl's closet. Full of clothes. Girl's clothes. Long dresses suitable for vamp ultra-formality. Shorter skirts for the more casual occasions. Pants for the same. Dancing skirts. A fuzzy purple T-shirt with a dragon on it, the shirt charged with healing by a witch friend. It wasn't a pretty dragon, either, but one of the toothy, village-terrorizing dragons, its body striped like a coral snake, wings spread wide, covered with striped red skin and feathers. So ugly the dragon was beautiful. I had jackets, and a turtleneck sweater made of silk knit. I had shirts. Lots of shirts, some made of cotton that had to be starched, and some of silk, and some that could be tossed in a washer and dryer and looked perfect immediately. I had boots and boots and more boots, and two sets of fighting leathers and three pairs of dancing shoes. Of course I still had guns and knives and the small box of vamp-killing charms that Molly had made for me before I came to New Orleans. I reached onto the top shelf and my fingers found what my eyes didn't want to see, the box hidden by an obfuscation charm. The box was smooth and beautiful, once my eyes could finally focus on it. I clutched it to me and looked back into the closet.

I had . . . stuff. My heart was beating wildly. The tea I had just drank rose in an acidic swirl. Choking. Burning. I pulled the box tighter against my chest, the wood corners pushing painfully into my flesh, but not grounding me. Not giving me ease.

I had a dry cleaner. A grocery store that delivered. I *owned a house.*

Holy crap. I had put down roots.

I dropped onto the bed, clutching the box of charms to me, and stared at my closet. A closet full of dresses.

Somehow I had become a . . . a *girl.*

CHAPTER 5

I Needed That Head Slap

I banged out of the house, needing to be gone. Badly. Or maybe I just needed to get away from the person I had become. Once upon a time, and not that long ago, that would have meant a ride on Bitsa, fast roads, weaving in and out of slow traffic, wind in my hair. Well, under my helmet, but it was the same feeling of freedom. Unfortunately, Bitsa was still in repair, and that meant the SUV.

Which was better than nothing. At first. Then I got stuck in New Orleans' horrible traffic. Worse, I was pretty sure I was being followed by a black SUV. When I made turns, weaving through the one-way streets to avoid fender benders and snarls, it always showed up again. Or one like it. Fingers banging on the steering wheel in frustration, I pulled out and headed for the river. If the vehicle showed up again, I'd know it.

I meandered a bit to get on the bridge access and crossed the Mississippi, looking down on the churning water and the barges and personal craft. It made me want to get a boat. Like I had time to go play. I reined my stupid brain back in line and checked behind me; the black SUV didn't show again. But since I was headed in that general direction, I figured I could check in on the clan home property, which was one of Leo's directives from the meeting the night before.

As I pulled down the tree-shaded drive, the branches arching over the roadway like something from Tara in *Gone with the Wind*, I wove between workers' trucks, trailers, and a few beat-up, rusted cars. The SUV Derek drove was also here, so I pulled in behind it, parked, and got out, stretching in the over-heated afternoon light before approaching the house. A heat wave was on the way, the temps in the high eighties and the humidity already close to dripping. Living in the Deep South was a sultry experience and not always in a good way. Mosquitoes were buzzing around me and honey bees were invading the blossoms on the azaleas beneath the trees. Birds were calling. It was as peaceful as it ever got around a vamp's home.

Inside the construction site, the walls rose three stories, the top story under the beams of the mansard roof. Two basement levels were belowground, an uncommon occurrence for a place with a high water table. I still hadn't asked how Leo was keeping the basements from flooding, but from the tingle of magic on the air, the construction boss had a water witch on payroll.

The workers smelled of cigarettes and old beer and exhaust and unwashed bodies and perfume. A generator had left clouds of exhaust on the air and electric tools had left their own stink. The port-a-potty nearby contained a reek of worse things. But it was all overridden by the smells of fresh wood, chalk, spackling, and turned earth. Faintly, there was brick and mortar, concrete and cement curing—alkaline, earthy scents.

The new house looked nothing like the old one, being brick and stone with a French country feel. It reminded me of the footprint of vamp HQ. I'd been told it was based on the Château de Dampierre, but on a smaller scale. The château must be huge, because this place was oversized enough to make security both a nightmare and easier than normal: a nightmare to wire and put cameras on all the doors and windows and make sure they all triggered an alarm when needed. Easier to position cameras to cover the grounds and easier because I could position safe rooms anywhere I wanted. There were several, one on each level, each with escape tunnels leading out to different areas of the grounds or garage or another exit. During the planning stage, I'd had a ball adding in all the security details and watching the eyes of the architect and the engineers as I moved things around—ignoring things like load-bearing walls and pipes and stuff. They tended to freak. But everything was in place now and everyone seemed satisfied, if not happy.

Today there were probably twenty men and women from all areas of construction represented, electricians and plumbers and carpenters, three guys who were wearing stilts on their boots so they could mud wallboard on the twelve-foot ceilings. It looked like a Larry, Curly, and Moe moment waiting to happen. They were all working hard, no loitering on this job site. I had to admit that when it came to getting things done, Leo's money and favors talked. Unlimited funds and the ability to help heal a sick loved one meant that he got fast and competent service with a smile.

I confiscated a yellow hard hat and plopped it on, my braid dangling behind me. Walking through the place, I looked up through the unfinished stairs and out through the windows in the mansard roof high overhead. This place took the word *mansion* to new levels.

Inside the kitchen was a guy with a hard hat and a set of plans under his arm, talking to a woman in jeans and a tailored jacket, and Derek. It looked like a high-level meeting while the plumbers adjusted PVC piping and electricians and heating-and-air guys tested the floor-warming system that would soon be covered by tile. It was noisy and energetic, but the activity looked good-natured and easygoing, unlike the frenetic way office workers often looked. These people were having fun; they liked their jobs.

I tucked my hands in my back pockets and moseyed toward the bosses. Derek was talking security. Separated by a wall made only of studs and nails, I stood behind him listening as he discussed the sprinkler system. It had to disperse enough water to put out a major fire, which meant taking water from the Mississippi not so far away. Leo's previous house had used Mississippi water, grandfathered in under a law that hadn't been written when the first house's kitchen was retrofitted with a sprinkler system. Now the MOC wanted the whole house sprinklered, and had discovered that he needed permits from people like the EPA and the Army Corps of Engineers. From Derek's tone I could tell that Leo wanted fast action but the initial-agencies were balking. Big surprise.

Like all post-active-duty military men, Derek seemed to have a sixth sense when he was being watched. Or he was just paranoid all the time. He turned to scan the surroundings, eyes probably picking out likely spots for snipers, and saw me. His eyes narrowed, and he frowned. I grinned and gave him a little wave. "The Enforcer is here," he said. "Maybe she can help with the kitchen issue."

Kitchen issue? Not likely. But I walked over, willing to pretend. Sometimes a cold look and a little Beast in my eyes was all it took to get things done. "Sup, y'all?"

The woman got this *look*. This "You are not in my league" look. And she was right. She looked chic even in a hard hat, though I'd never have worn three-inch heels to a construction site. I set my hard hat on a counter and slouched against a stud to listen to the problem. The woman was a decorator and her paint colors weren't matching the tile colors and she wanted something more au courant than beige, white, cream, and snow in the room. She wanted bronzes and coppers and earth tones. Like I cared. But I let her talk and listened with half an ear as I worked out how many cameras we would need to cover the five-car garage. The woman also wanted the two sets of double ovens to be moved across the kitchen from the place where they were in the plans, so she could put a window in the exterior wall. Yada yada.

I glanced at Derek while she chattered and had to swallow down a laugh at the frustration on his face. It wasn't easy being boss. All bucks stopped with him—and better him than me. When the decorator wound down, Derek said, "If moving the ovens didn't cause problems elsewhere"—he thumbed at a wall that hid a safe room, and suddenly I understood the problem—"I'd let you have your way on the ovens. But it's no deal." He looked at me when she started to speak again, and said, "Jane? What do you say?"

Great. So much for bucks stopping with Derek. To the decorator, I said, "As I understand it, you have two requests—color scheme and light in the kitchen. Right?"

She nodded and I went on. "But you also have a job to do. Your *job* is to make Leo happy. Derek's *job* is to keep Leo safe. And that's my job too. You can't move the ovens, because that makes it harder for us to do *our* job. Putting the ovens there"—I pointed where Derek had thumbed—"isn't going to happen."

"But—"

I held up a hand to stop her. "Let me finish. Request number one is color. Leo likes whites and beiges and he's outlived au courant several centuries ago." I studied the space and realized that I had the attention of the entire crew. Lucky me. "You can't change Leo's white-toned color scheme but you could make the faucets and knobs bronze and put in some aged copper panels in the ceiling if you want. Drop some bronzy lights over the island." I'd seen that at Katie's and it looked really good. "Hang some big copper pots over the island or along the wall next to the cook top." I pointed. "And . . ." I turned in a circle, trying to see the room as it would be soon. "Maybe put in a copper or bronze exhaust hood. Instead of the white quartz or granite cabinet tops like on the rest of the counters, put copper sheeting on the island. You could even get the oven and refrigerator doors done in copper or bronze, all without changing the color scheme." When the decorator's mouth fell open, I said, "What?"

"That's . . . perfect, actually," she said. Then jumped in quickly with, "But this room needs more light."

"Yeah. Vamps don't care about light. They care about security. Why don't you knock out that wall there"—I pointed to the back of the house—"and put in some French doors and tall windows if you need light in the daytime. Just be sure to get the engineer to work with you on the sizes and necessary measurements of the bullet-resistant glass and the support I beams for the stories above."

Her red-lipsticked mouth made a moue of surprise. "You'd let me do that?"

I looked at Derek and the construction boss and the architect, who had wandered over to listen. They all nodded. "Sure. So we're good on not moving the ovens?"

"We're fine." She looked down at her notebook and wrote *Copper Cladding* in big letters.

Derek walked away, shaking his head. I followed, not understanding his reaction. I didn't usually bother with multisyllabic words like *consternation*, but that was how Derek looked—consternated. Derek and I had had some issues over the months when I'd been under contract to Leo, and while some matters had worked themselves out, some hadn't. I wasn't sure they ever would. As soon as we were out of earshot I said, "What's with the head shaking?"

"You solved everything. That woman was driving me nuts. She had been driving everyone nuts for over an hour."

Crap. I really was turning into a girl. When the heck had that happened? I kicked a chunk of two-by-ten out of the way. Maybe a little too hard, in my frustration with my life, as it hit a freshly hung piece of wallboard and bounced back at me. I jumped out of the way, but the wall now had a huge dent in it. *Dang it.*

But I owed Derek an answer. I said, "You were trying to answer her questions without trying to solve her problems. I solved her problems. It'll cost Leo another small fortune, but with what he's spending on this house, what's a few thou more?"

He looked confused and mimicked me by kicking a cut piece of two-by-four out of his way. His didn't cause any damage. "So . . . I need to solve problems, not answer questions?" He stopped at a cooler and passed me a can of Coke. He took a Mountain Dew for himself. We popped the tops and sipped as he considered my answer.

Derek led the way out the front door and partway down the steps, which had been salvaged and re-mortared from the burned original house "because they are part of history," according to the expensive architect. We sat on a step, looking out over the property and the massed vehicles. I listened to the myriad conversations on the work space, watched a helicopter on the horizon, and saw a black SUV drive slowly past the entrance to Leo's place. Seeing it cleared my head. "Make sure security is here all night," I said to Derek. "Someone's been tailing me, and might have been tailing others."

Derek was instantly alert, and any anxiety over his lack of personnel problem-solving skills slid away. "I can put a shooter there." He pointed across the property to the barn. "There's a nice spotter location on top. Flat, protected from wind. We could put another guy inside the house. Talkies and we're good to go."

"Yeah. Do that. Now, you want to tell me what else is up? Because you're—" I stopped dead. *Spilling pissed-off pheromones. Nope. Can't say that.* "Upset." Yeah. That would do. "More upset than just dealing with a construction site and a decorator."

Derek frowned and studied the barn where he could put a shooter. He didn't look at me at all when he said, "It's this Enforcer stuff."

"Uh-huh," I said, drinking from my can, waiting for him to get to the point.

"How'd you deal with the blood-drinking part? And the sex part?"

I pulled in a breath that was part Coke and coughed. And coughed. Which wasn't planned but was really handy for thinking of an answer to the sex part of the questions—which I totally had not expected. After about ten seconds' worth of coughing, during which Derek's face told me all sorts of things, I realized that he and Leo weren't having sex, but that Leo had come on to him, with that whole vamp-blood-makes-it-feel good thing. This was delicate territory. And despite my win with the decorator, I wasn't so good at delicate territory.

I rolled my Coke between my palms, deciding that the bare truth was my best choice. "Long story short: When I got here, I wouldn't let Leo drink from me. Not ever." I sipped my Coke and it burned going down, making me cough more. When I spoke again my voice was hoarse and rough. "I was afraid that if he tasted my blood, it would have given away my skinwalker heritage. But I got mauled when I first got to New Orleans and I couldn't figure out how to tell him no when he offered to heal me. He healed my arm, got a taste, and he didn't know what I was. So I was safe. Then I stupidly used a nonexistent Enforcer status to get something done."

"I remember. You claimed to be his Enforcer without knowing what it meant." Derek was darkly amused. "That was in Asheville, right?" I nodded. "Not the brightest thing, there, Legs."

"Yeah. Stupid, I know, especially by Mithran law. When he needed me to be his Enforcer for real—" I stopped. This was way more confessional than I wanted to get with Derek. I didn't want him this close. I didn't want to share. I bent my head to my knees and wrapped my arms around them, hugging myself. Thinking. Rocking slightly back and forth on the front stairs.

If I was honest, I didn't want to say the words aloud to anyone who didn't already know. And I didn't want to look at my reasons for not looking at the event again. Meaning I was a coward who needed talk therapy. "Crap," I muttered.

I forced myself to go on, gripped my knees so tight it hurt, talking so fast it was a garbled strand of words. "When he needed me to be his Enforcer for real, Leo was within his Mithran legal rights to make it happen. Bruiser had been injured and his mind wasn't working. His ability to do or think anything of his own will was gone. Mentally he was"—my free hand made flapping motions before re-gripping my knees—"basically a puddle of goo." Bitterness laced through my words when I continued. "Leo used compulsion to force Bruiser to hold me down. Then the Master of the City forced a blood feeding and binding on me."

My breath ached on the words, way deeper than I'd expected.

Derek cursed softly. I smelled his shock and his protective instincts as they kicked in. It was an odd scent from a man who didn't trust supernats, and who surely didn't trust me. I didn't look at him, watching the helicopter as it moved away on the horizon. Seconds ticked by, neither of us talking, not looking at each other, staring out over the cars and trucks. High over the front drive, a hawk circled, riding the air currents. Gliding. Hunting. *Free.*

"It's taken me some time to get over it," I admitted long after the silence had become uncomfortable. "Okay, I'm still getting over it. I got some revenge, which helped, but not as much as I thought it would, to be honest. Mostly . . . I've just had to work through it. I'm a skinwalker. I understand the animalistic need to dominate another creature. In lots of animal life, especially mating rituals and pack dominance fights, one animal dominates another. Animals accept it or die fighting it. But I'm not an animal." *Liar, liar, pants on fire.* I smiled cynically at my own thoughts but Derek wasn't looking at me. I went on. "Resistance is normal for me. I resisted. He partially bound me. I found a way free. Now he's apologized to me for taking by force what was his by legal right—according to his point of view—and might have been his by a more, mmm"—I searched for the words—"more socially acceptable means, had he tried to go that route." I glanced at Derek, gauging his reaction.

Derek frowned harder. He had a fresh marine haircut, which was a pretty dreadful lack of style but he made it work, especially with that frown. It pulled his face down hard and made crevices beside his nose and down along his mouth. His dark skin had a slight sheen in the day's heat. "I don't understand," he said finally.

I frowned back at him. "To be the permanent Enforcer, you have to be bound at least a little, but humans have a choice," I said. "Being a blood-meal doesn't have to be painful or degrading or sexual. It can be simple. A few drops so he can read you, and know you're not compromised by another vamp. So he can know and feel your loyalty to him."

"Like drinking a few sips from my wrist. Nooo." He flapped a hand. "No other stuff. No sex stuff."

If Derek had been white, the blush would have been scarlet. As it was, his skin went darker and his flesh smelled of a mix-

ture of anger/shame/worry. "Yeah. Like that," I said. "It de-
pends on what you want. What you need. What you can
handle." *How much of your soul you are willing to give up for
the price Leo is offering.* But I didn't say that. Derek was already there.

He held his head in both hands, scratching it. Maybe using
his upraised arms to hide his face from me. "I need my mama
alive."

"Ah." I felt weird being in the position of comforting him,
of being all Florence Nightingale or Mother Teresa or one of
those loving, caring women that I had no idea how to be.
But . . . maybe I didn't have to be any of those.

I said, almost harshly, "Let me get this right. If Leo's drinking your blood felt painful, then it'd be okay when he drank
from you? But it feels good, and you're all macho, and so the
drinking gets mixed up with the feel-good part of your brain.
Then your little brain starts to think sex and your big ol' macho
self goes all homo-terrified on you, right? And that petrifies
you because . . . I don't know. You're a marine, and your head
gets all wonky?"

Derek's mouth opened as he started to deny it, so I went all
guy on him. I slapped the back of his head. Hard. "What am I?
Your shrink? Life sucks and then you get sucked on. And
sometimes it feels good. I'm not saying to like your body's reaction if you don't swing that way. But get over it. Do the job.
Get your mama well. Or quit and hope for modern medicine
to heal her."

Derek's eyes filled with tears, quickly gone. If he'd been a
big-cat, the look he gave me would have been a snarl, all teeth.
His muscles bunched; his balance shifted, ready to attack me
as my words penetrated his thick skull.

"You made a deal with the Devil," I said, "and now it's time
to pay. As to *feelings*," I snorted, "talk to a priest or a counselor
about the gay part. Or talk to Leo. Lack of pain and having
Leo's mouth on your wrist isn't the same thing as getting laid
or turned into a sex toy. Drinking from you is the way Leo
protects himself. And he knows you don't like it."

Derek looked at me in surprise, his anger melting away.
"Say what?"

"You had to know that. He's reading everything you feel as
he drinks. Dude. He's playing with you the way a cat plays with
its dinner. It's his nature. So you can accept that it feels good

and decide that it doesn't have to lead to sex, or you can tell him it bothers you. Honesty might make him quit the predator games. Leo will accept it either way. And like I said, he can make it hurt if that makes you feel better."

"Jesus, Mary, and Joseph," Derek cursed, bending his head back down. More embarrassed.

Out front, a black SUV drove in front of the driveway, going the other direction from the last one. To Derek I said, "I think that's the same SUV that went by earlier. How fast can you get someone out to the road for the next pass and get a look at the plate?"

"I don't have any of my guys here. I— Wait." Derek, for all that he was having a crisis of manhood, stood and shouted a name. "Mannie. You still got the feet?"

"My brother, I got the feet and the hands. *They* wasn't hurt when I got sacked in my last game." He tapped his head. "Only the old brain box."

"There's a black SUV cruising past out front. Get out there and get a look at the license plate next time it comes by. Make sure they don't see you."

"I'll take a pic with my phone, bro." Mannie dashed down the drive to the street.

"Mannie Dubose? From LSU? Injured in his second season with the Saints?" I didn't live with a sports nut for nothing. Eli loved the Saints.

"The same. Nearly lost his eyesight when he had bleeding behind his eyes. Quit with his signing bonus, two years pay, and a well-crafted injury bonus. Now he and his dad own the construction company that his ole man used to work for. They mighta lost a football career, but they used the money right and parleyed it into a family business. He's good people.

"Legs," he added, without looking at me. "Thanks. I needed the head slap."

"Not the tough talk?"

He pursed his lips to keep from grinning. "Eh. I mighta needed that too."

"Talk to Leo. Or I'll slap your head again."

"You need me to hurt Leo for what he did to you?"

This time I smiled, feeling all mushy inside. Derek might not be family—yet—but in his own way, he was a friend and that was good enough for now. "Nah. He gave me a big honking boon when he asked for forgiveness."

Derek's eyebrows did that soldier-micro-twitch thing that Eli's did when he was surprised. "He asked your forgiveness? For real? *Leo?*"

I shrugged with my eyebrows. Turnabout was fair play.

"A big honking one, huh? Not bad, Legs. Not bad."

We sat in the sun for a while until Derek's phone rang. "It's parked down the street, bro," Mannie said on speakerphone. "I zoomed in and got the plate. Sending it to you now. Also a shot of the driver, but it's not too good through the glass."

"I'll send it to the Kid," Derek said to me. "I gotta get back to work."

"Later," I said.

We bumped fists. I pulled out of the driveway, passing and waving to Mannie, and then passing the empty SUV. No driver. Or rather, a driver lying down in the seat. That. Because an SUV appeared behind me a mile or so later. I lost him by taking a back road, one that was sinking below the water table in this alluvial landscape. Two turns later, I was free to go where I wanted. People were so stupid sometimes.

CHAPTER 6

Carrying a Vamp Head

Hours later, I looked at myself in the mirror on the closet door. I was wearing one of the first outfits I had bought when I got to New Orleans, clothes purchased because it was too hot for my mountain wear, and because they were colorful and beautiful. Now I knew enough about clothing to recognize that they were made of inexpensive fabric, with inferior workmanship. I knew that the seams were sewn cheaply, the drape wasn't quite right, and the skirt would likely last only a few washings before it lost its shape entirely. Dumb, stupid stuff to know, of no value in a world where my most important bit of knowledge should be how sharp the blade, how well it was balanced, and how true the sights on the gun. But I'd bought the clothes with my own money and with my own taste. I'd worn the outfit on the first night I'd gone dancing in New Orleans, my first week here.

The silk, calf-length, asymmetrical skirt was patchwork, a dainty, flared, delicate confection of tiny, two-by-four-inch patches of teal and purple, a skirt for an impoverished princess. The hem flipped when I danced and the elastic waist rode low on my hips if I wanted it to, or higher, on my waist. I'd put on a few pounds of muscle since I bought it, but most of that was in my shoulders and thighs and the skirt still looked good on me. Rad, as the salesgirl had said.

I wore the skirt low on my hips, paired with a peasant top with a drawstring neckline. The blouse was made of a paler fabric, ocean-teal shading to lavender. The amethyst-and-

chatkalite necklace I'd bought with the outfit hung with my
gold-nugget-and-puma-tooth necklace on its doubled gold
chain, between my cleavage. And that was something else new.
I had cleavage. Well, sorta. At least a valley, if not a crevasse,
thanks to all those extra pounds, a very tiny percentage of
which had landed as fat on my boobs. I slid my feet into a pair
of purple sandals, with ankle straps for dancing.

I tugged the purple and teal skirt lower on my hip bones,
pulling the peasant top lower on my breasts, the tie open with
a skin-toned jog bra beneath. Sexy, but showing nothing. The
skirt whispered around my calves with each step. I'd worn this
on the first night I'd heard Rick LaFleur play the saxophone in
the band at the Royal Mojo Blues Company. There had to be
a reason I'd chosen to wear this outfit tonight. Was it because
Rick was gone, but not totally gone, as in dead and buried?
Was it because he had texted me several times since he disappeared with Paka, his new were-black-panther girlfriend, as if
keeping in touch with me was important? Not that I had texted
back. I wasn't that stupid. Or was it something else?

I let my mind wander as I swished on a little bronzer to
brighten my skin, drew on some lips in a vamp red, and mas-
caraed my lashes. I didn't test the movement of my skirt in the
mirror, not like I had that first night. That first night dancing,
I'd worn a turban. But tonight, I French-braided my hair into
three short sections, secured them together at the crown of my
head, and let the rest of the hair fall in a straight sheen of midnight black to my hips. I was the same. And not the same. And
Rick was gone. I'd stopped mourning, though sometimes it
crept back in. Life sans boyfriend—any boyfriend—could be
unexpectedly lonely. I smiled at myself in the mirror, scarlet
lips and a dress that was sex on a stick. New beginnings often
started with the broken bits and shattered pieces of the old. I
was not the dumb girl I'd been a few months ago—that gal's
soul had been broken and put back together with bailing wire
and duct tape. And life went on. How corny was that?

But just because I'd grown up a bit didn't mean I'd grown
stupid. I strapped on a thigh sheath with a vamp-killer and two
stakes and stuck two more into my hair. I looked at myself in
the mirror again and let the skirt fall slowly over the weapons.
Yeah. I was still me. Maybe I was more me than ever.

The boys were talking when I opened my door, but the
chatter stopped when I entered the main room and paused in

the doorway. Alex nearly swallowed his tongue and managed, "Shhhh-oot," instead of what he'd started to say.

Feeling uncertain again, I bunched my skirt with my hands and said, "Thanks."

Eli's brows rose with a restrained reaction of some kind, and he said, "Babe. You planning to rock the house tonight? Or George's dreams?"

"*She's* got a date with *Bruiser*?" the Kid asked his brother.

I looked down at my dress. "Yeah. I'm pretty astounded too. I'm totally out of his league. You know? He's British. He was raised by a Lady, as in a capital *L* Lady. He dates vamps, some of whom are royalty. I mean, I was raised in a children's home."

"And you can hold your own anywhere with anyone, Janie," Alex said, staunchly.

"Yeah, but I bet she can't dance," Eli said.

"I can, too," I said, stung.

"Prove it," Eli said. "Music." I heard a faint *click*, and something African-inspired with drums and a low-pitched wind instrument and bells started playing. "No." The music changed to a Latin beat, horns and drums, hot, with a deep basso rhythm to it. Eli stood and held out his hand. "Yeah. That one, bro. Prove it, babe."

"How's that gonna make me feel better about a date with Bruiser?"

"Trust me."

When I didn't take his hand, Eli grabbed mine and whirled me into a rough dance I couldn't even begin to name. It had a six-beat dance pattern that cued as tri-ple step, tri-ple step, step, step, like a boogie-woogie, but the moves were all Latin, hips and shoulders and butt all acting independently of one another but managing to work. Somehow. Eli whirled me under his arm, out, and back in, with a snapping motion that would have put a lesser woman into a body cast. And suddenly I grinned.

"What is this?" I asked.

"The locals called it *'ha' dzuuy*,' which I think was translated as 'hard rain' in Mayan or some other dead language." He wasn't even breathing hard as he twirled me through a complicated set of moves that involved a lot of hip rotation, then slammed me into his side like a side of beef against a rock wall. "My unit was stationed in Mexico for a bit during a war between drug lords. We partied with the locals in our downtime.

"Try this." His feet continued the same pattern while his hips performed a sinuous, snaky move that could have come directly from my belly-dancing classes, all come-hither and keep-away at once. I followed the step and added a slight dip-and-bounce at the end, rolling my body back up to start the move all over again. Eli looked like I could have knocked him over with a feather—minimalist style—a twitch of lips that signified surprise.

The music ended midnote and I heard knocking on the front door. My date was here.

Oh crap. My *date*. But my nerves had dissipated somewhere in the dance, and I winked at the Kid as I swung out of Eli's arms and to the foyer, my feet and hips still moving as I tossed a tiny bag over my shoulder and opened the door on the late-day, May air.

Bruiser's scent swept in, smelling of citrus, gun oil, and male, riding along with the New Orleans' air—spring sunshine, heated concrete, and the wet of the Mississippi. It all mixed with the inside scents of flowers and catnip. Though I couldn't see the weapons, I knew he was wearing them. Bruiser always went armed. He was wearing casual clothes, dark brown slacks and a starched white shirt with the sleeves rolled up, a jacket hanging by a finger over his shoulder. Bruiser had great arms, muscular and tanned.

"Jane," he said. Just my name. And something lightened inside of me.

"Bruiser," I said back, and I smiled at him as Beast raised up and padded closer to the front of my mind, peering out through my eyes. *Mine,* she purred. Without looking over my shoulder, I said, "My gobag's in the foyer. See you at vamp HQ at nine sharp."

Eli said, "Roger that. Twenty-one hundred."

At the curb, a limo idled, the back door open in invitation. I knew this limo. I'd been in it before, more than once, the first time on my back on the floor with Bruiser on top of me. Not sex, but it had been close. I felt a faint flush, and to hide it, I turned and locked my front door behind me. Breathing deeply until the lock clicked and I had myself under control.

Bruiser touched my shoulder and guided me into the limo, then sat across from me, studying me. I felt awkward and foolish and I didn't know why. Bruiser said, "I always liked that outfit. I see the blood came out."

learned that Leo had a house in Malibu and shared one with the primo of California's MOC in Holmby Hills in L.A. Bruiser hadn't wasted the years he'd been granted as primo, with access to the blood that kept him young. He'd lived it, and I felt both like a kid at her grandpa's knee listening to stories, and like a seductive woman that men—this man, anyway— couldn't keep his eyes off of.

For the meal, we were served tiny portions of the speckled trout, prepared two ways: trout meunière and trout amandine, followed by sea bass from the Gulf, caught today, served two ways: filleted and sautéed, topped with fresh Louisiana crabmeat, and grilled fillet topped with fresh tomatoes, basil, extra-virgin olive oil, garlic, and kalamata olives. *To die for.* I think I said that aloud, maybe for the first time in my whole life. We had three pompano dishes: the pompano Duarte, which was sautéed fillet topped with Gulf shrimp and tomatoes, seasoned with garlic, fresh herbs, and crushed chili peppers; the pompano David—grilled, skin-on fillet brushed with extra-virgin olive oil, lemon, garlic, and fresh herbs—and pompano en croute. And baby pompano fillets and scallop mousse baked in flaky puff pastry, served on a bed of green peppercorn cream sauce. On a separate plate were the veggies, which were wild mushrooms, asparagus, some kind of soufflé, and potatoes, all with their own sauces. I didn't eat much in the way of plants, but these were enough to make me think about going vegetarian. The portions were tiny but I was stuffed even before the meats arrived.

Between food deliveries—I couldn't quite call them courses— Bruiser drew me out on my life in the children's home, and how I started into the security business, though he'd done a deep background on me before I was ever hired to work with the New Orleans' vamps. He sounded interested, as in *interested*, and it made me feel too warm, and all weird. He asked me about my weapons training and about my life in Asheville, before I'd come to work here. He made me feel important and . . . admirable, maybe. Which was a totally weird feeling.

There were two veal dishes, three filet mignon dishes, and sweetbreads, which were bull balls and I passed on them. Bruiser ate my portion with what looked like delight. The wines changed with every part of the meal. With my skin-walker metabolism, I could drink most humans under the table, but even I was feeling a little woozy by the time the meal ended. And full. And totally decadent. The food at Arnaud's was pricey. I snuck a peek at the menu when I went to the ladies' room, and figured that we could feed a whole house full of unwanted children at Bethel Nondenominational Christian Children's Home for a week for what we spent on one self-indulgent meal.

"Okay," I said afterward, as we weaved through the immaculate tables and the hoity-toity diners, Bruiser's hand warm on my spine through the thin blouse. "Next date, one week from now, in the Clover Grill, my treat." I grinned with delight. I loved getting what I wanted. "Followed by . . . *dancing*."

Bruiser leaned in and spoke next to my ear. "Only in the aisles, not on the tables." Which let me know he'd really been there. There was a sign printed somewhere in the diner proclaiming that. I smiled slowly as I got into the limo. *I can do this,* I thought. *I really can do this.* Not that I knew what *this* was. Yet.

We had talked through the sunset and into the dark of night. It was nearly nine when we braked in back of HQ, under the porte cochere, and alighted from the limo. That's what you did from a limo, though I'd never say the word aloud. *Alight.* I had a mental eye roll at the thought.

Eli met us there and handed me my bag of weapons, one hand holding Bruiser back. I left the men there, but my hearing was better than human, and I heard Eli say, "You hurt her and I'll skin you alive and feed your carcass to the wild boars in the swamps. You copy?"

"I do. And I'll break your arm if you ever accost me again. Civilized discourse is acceptable. Your hand upon my person is not."

"Be nice, boys," I called over my shoulder. "Be nice or I'll beat both your butts." *Yeah. That'll show them.* I changed clothes in the ladies' locker room, donning my second-best fighting leathers over Lycra undies—full-length leggings and a long-sleeved tight tee over the jogging bra. I now had two sets of black leathers, but this pair had already been repaired a time or two. Both sets were augmented by a thin layer of sterling silver–plated titanium chain mail, with hard plastic at the outer elbows and knees, the kind developed and worn by the Taiwanese military. *Star Wars* stuff. Bullet resistant all over. Fire resistant. The titanium chain-mail choker, I'd only recently discovered, was called a *gorget*. Who knew? This was my old fighting gear, soiled with blood and sweat and the smell of victory. The new gear was even better. And pretty, though I'd never say so aloud.

I slid into low combat boots with steel toes and rubber soles and a slit for a backup weapon in each boot shaft. Eli had packed no knives, so I assumed we were going for hand-to-hand fighting tonight, but I slid the stakes and blades I had worn under my skirt into my fighting clothes. I wasn't stupid.

My hair was braided by a blood-servant who plaited it like a horse's tail, into a club and then back up and into a bun bigger than my fist. I admired myself in the mirror over the sinks. I looked . . . yeah. Spiffy. Deadly, but spiffy.

I walked into the gym, which was, as usual, set for sparring practice. The scents were overwhelming for a moment—vamp, blood, humans. Sex. With vamps it was always blood and sex together. The big room had basketball goals and indentions intended to hold poles for a tennis net. Not that I'd ever seen them in use. It was weapons and fighting all the way in fanghead-land. As always, spectators lined the bleacher-style seating along one wall. Others clustered at the door on the far side, one I'd never been through. I made a mental note to check security there. The usual. However, one thing was new.

Weapons practice had never before included Grégoire or Girrard DiMercy. It had also never included swords. Two guys were in a sword ring fighting. Each man had two swords, and they were both bleeding through the padded white suits they were wearing. The smell of vamp blood and Gee's blood mingled in a magical miasma that half of me thought tasty and the other half thought a little terrifying.

Beast leaned forward into my eyes. *Long claws, steel and silver. Good claws. Want long claws.*

"No way am I using a sword," I muttered to her under my breath. It took years to master a sword. But Gee DiMercy and my Beast had other ideas and they didn't mesh with my own.

CHAPTER 7

LSD . . . Psilocybin Mushrooms and . . . Tequila

"En garde, little goddess!" he shouted, and tossed me a sword through the air, hilt first, the way he'd tossed a sword to Leo. Beast reared up in me, flooding me with adrenaline and strength. Time fractured, seeming to slow and thicken. The room went brighter and greener, sharper, Beast's sight meshing with my own.

As it flew through the air, I saw the way the hilt was made, the cross guard curving around to protect the wielder's hand; the hilt itself was braided with leather for a firm grip. A narrow, thin, flat blade, the double edge constructed of blunted steel, for teaching and practice — not sharp, with no silver plating that could accidently harm a vamp. But didn't classes usually start with wood swords?

Beast in charge, I stepped forward. My hand lifted into the air, moving with a languid ease, to slide fingers through the cross guard and around the hilt. The sword's weight shifted out of the air as gravity and momentum shoved it firmly into my palm. *Good claw. Fight with long claw,* Beast thought.

But I had no idea how. I was a knife fighter. What Beast called her steel claws. Or a knife thrower, Beast's flying claws. Not Beast's long claw. Time slapped me in the face as my fingers tightened on the hilt and I whirled, feeling the weight and length of the blade as I pirouetted with it. *Claw like long tail,* Beast thought at me. *Good for leaping. Good for balance.*

Good long claw. And I laughed. Around me, I felt the others, the onlookers, grow silent.

"Your Web page information suggested that you were 'unrated in swordplay.' Today we shall rate you."

That sounded ominous. I said, "I'm unrated because I don't know how to use a long sword at all. Only short swords, fourteen-inch vampire-killers. So can we skip this?"

"No."

That was short and sweet.

"*This* is the proper way to hold a long sword," Gee DiMercy said. "Feet thus, spine thus, knees and sword thusly."

I walked closer, out of sword range, but close enough to study his weight distribution and the exact position of his feet. I copied his posture. And felt like an idiot. The sword was too long, too unwieldy. And my leathers were too constricting. I held up a hand like a traffic cop to tell him to stop and kicked off the boots, pulled off the jacket and the pants, trying not to notice the reactions of the others as I did so. The sudden silence. The sound of a slow breath taken nearby. It might have been Leo but I didn't look to see. I didn't even look at Eli when he appeared at my side to take my clothes. Eli was my second. It felt right to have him there, and I relaxed, shaking out my arms. I was standing there in bare feet, a long length of tight black spandex, and a sword. I rolled my shoulders to loosen up.

Leo appeared at my side and gave me a second blade, this one also dull-edged, but shorter, with a groove on the back of the blade for hooking an opponent's weapon and pulling it away. This smaller blade felt good in my hand, nearly familiar, having the heft and balance of a vamp-killer. Leo smelled strange, his scent acrid and harsh, like rose thorns, but I didn't look at him. Not while I was trying to find the balance of the weapons. Though they were of differing lengths, they were of similar weights, so the balance that my mind insisted was not there, was actually present.

"You will begin lessons in La Destreza, also known as the Spanish Circle," Gee said. He spun his sword in a slow circle around him, behind him, left to right, always in an arc, the blade sketching and encompassing a sphere around his body. It sketched a cage of death anywhere his weapon reached. And then he sped it up. The blade moved faster and faster, until it was a flashing light all around him. I was going to be taught by the Obi-Wan of steel blades. Despite myself, my grin spread. I was either gonna hate it or love it.

"The books of history and books of teaching were incorrect," he said, his body not tensing or pausing. "There is nothing stiff or static about La Destreza. It is fluid, smooth, like the flow of water or oil across an object. I will teach you the forms. You will practice. Many, many hours each day. You will be challenged to *les Duels Sang* by the Enforcers of our visitors. You will be expected to comport yourself well on the field of battle."

"Okay. So I've got, like, three months to learn what the rest of them will have studied for centuries." I handed the short blade back to Leo. I figured one at a time was smart, and the unfamiliar one first was smarter. "What are the rules?"

"Other than proper etiquette, there are few *rules*," Gee said, his blade slowing. "One may fight with one blade or two, though two is more common. And most formal challenges are to first blood, though some few are to true-death. Deception and duplicity are looked upon with approval, as La Destreza—as the Mithrans practice it—is as much a mental game as a physical one."

"Sooo." I thought as I watched him dance with the sword, knowing I'd never get a cut through the circling blade. "Cheating is acceptable."

"Indeed. One may—"

Two-fingered, I pulled a throwing knife and flipped it at him. For once, I hit what I was aiming at. The steel blade embedded itself into Gee DiMercy's chest, slightly left of where a human's heart would be. If he had a heart.

Just like the last time I stabbed him, light sparkled out, downy blue mist, soft and bright. The mist had weight and texture. A blast of heat followed, stinking of cauterized blood and burned evergreen. Charred jasmine. Unlike the last time I stabbed him, when Gee had been asleep, no dark bloodred wings unfurled. I didn't get a glimpse of a dark-sapphire-feathered beast with crimson breast and wings, claws like spear points, glinting at wing tips and feet. His blood, trapped by the cloth of his gi, didn't splatter like liquid flowers, perfume like rainbows hitting the ground. No sparks shot up where the blossoms landed. There was none of that. But the air around his body flashed a faint shade of blue for a splintered moment. Had I not been watching so closely, I would have missed it.

The mist retreated, fast as a flinch, and the punch of power snapped at me, electric and solid. It hurt, even though I was

farther away this time, and was expecting the reaction. I felt/
heard a sharp, sizzling hiss. If he'd been human, I might have
killed him. But he wasn't. Gee was something else entirely.
Whatever he was, the layers of glamour around him reacted
negatively to steel. He had been expecting me this time. But he
hadn't expected exactly what he'd gotten.

"First blood. Cheating. With two blades," I said. "Like
that?"

"First blood to the Enforcer," Leo said, his voice coming
from the side, where the spectators sat, amusement in his voice.
"Does our Enforcer's methodology fit within the parameters
of the rules of etiquette?"

Gee pulled the weapon from his flesh and his padded suit.
With a flick of his wrist, he sent it back to me. Had Beast not
been so close in my mind, I might have gotten stuck. Instead, I
batted the flying claw out of the air and down to the ground.
With the new blade. Gee chortled, delighted. "Excellent. You
will learn quickly, my little goddess. Or not."

Crap. I was gonna learn how to fight with swords. And I
didn't know whether Gee's *or not* meant that I'd learn fast or
not, or that I was his goddess or not. Either way, I was *so* in
trouble.

Behind me I heard mocking laughter. Without turning, I
said, "I'll kick your butt for that one, Eli."

"You can try," my partner said, still taunting. "I'm just glad
I'm not the part-time Enforcer. Somebody's gonna be sore."

I was taught the positions for my feet for the Spanish Circle
and how to step into a lunge. I was not taught how to parry,
which I guessed was a move for wusses. And once I halfway
had the basic moves in my mind, if not in my muscle memory,
I was slapped half to death with the flat, beat with the dulled
edge, and stuck with the point of Gee's sword. I was disarmed,
tripped, elbowed, tapped numerous times—over a kidney
from the back or into my gut from the front—light blows and
shallow cuts that would have killed me had they been delivered with any intent. Gee made me pay for first blood with a
host of bruises and a little blood when I turned wrong and his
short sword caught my arm. Skinwalker blood added to the
vamp stench of the room. Once upon a time that had bothered
me. A lot. Now I had no reaction at all to the smell of my blood
in a room full of vamps.

As soon as I was warmed up—his words, *warmed up*, more like sweating like a horse—we sparred. The next six hours were a blur. Okay, maybe not really six hours, but it felt like it. I was dripping with sweat when the sparring-practice session was over, and yes, I was sore.

Beast was elated. *Beast likes long claw,* she murmured to me. *More.*

"No more," I gasped, wiping the sweat from my eyes. "I'm done."

"Accepted," Gee said, dropping his practice blades. "Tomorrow we will practice the same moves, study three more, and then spar for thirty minutes."

"Yeah?" I brightened. "I can do thirty."

"Excellent. Today you managed only twelve," Gee said, swatting me one last time across my butt. Hard.

"Owww. What was that for?" I asked, rubbing my backside.

"For being so very out of shape."

"*Me!* Bleeding and bruised all over, but not *out of shape.*" I pulled on my Beast and skinwalker magics, a small tug of gray energies, to help me get out the door. *I am not out of shape.*

Eli laughed. Evil man. But he took my weapons, which now weighed about forty pounds each, and carried them, along with my discarded leathers, toward the door. *Out of shape?* It had been a while since I lifted weights with the Youngers, but *out of shape?*

Just as we reached the hallway door, a prickle of danger danced along my skin, burning through the drying sweat on the damp, elastic fabric of my clothing. I stepped in front of Eli and grabbed the long sword from his lax grip. "Gun," I whispered.

He didn't argue or ask questions. He slapped a nine-mil into my hand and pulled his own weapons as I whipped my eyes across the gym. People were everywhere, three pairs on the sparring mats, Leo and Gee together, Grégoire and Bruiser together, Del and a young vamp named Liam, all with blades, sparring. What I was feeling wasn't coming from them.

"What?" Eli asked, his voice dropping low, his body tightening all over, the way an animal pulls inward just before the pounce.

Heat and light danced into the room, tingling on my skin. My body flooded with adrenaline, my eyes darting everywhere at once. Something was coming. Coming fast. "Magic!" I shouted. "Leo! Gee! Bruiser! Beware!"

There was a glint across the room, a glistening brilliance, yet no one looked up. At the back door, the light-being flowed through and into the room, snaking along the ceiling, a sparkling hint of rainbows and shadow. I pointed. "Lillilend," I said.

Eli grunted, not disagreeing, but not able to see it in the gray place of the change where energy and matter might be the same thing. Moving as one, we dashed back toward the center of the room. Eli holstered his gun and pulled blades. I realized he was right. You can't shoot something made of light. Or you could, the same way you could aim and pull the trigger at the sun. But you weren't gonna do it any damage.

I wasn't sure what good blades would do either, but between one step and the next, I shoved the useless gun into my waistband and accepted a vamp-killer from my always-armed second, fourteen inches of silver-plated, razor-edged steel to back up the practice weapon's blunted steel. Most magical beings had an aversion to some sort of metal, and I thought the lillilend's metal allergy was to steel.

The lillilend sped around the room, fast as an eyeblink, its body tight against the ceiling, hissing with anger. Eli released the useless bundle of my leathers and leaped over the pile it made without breaking stride.

Just ahead, the sparring partners raised weapons and bladed their bodies as if we were the danger. "Above!" I shouted, pointing.

Overhead, the light-being whipped around the vents and fixtures, wings spread, like something Disney might have envisioned if he'd taken a dose of LSD, backed up with a serving of psilocybin mushrooms, and a quart of tequila. It flashed into the visible range, a rippling of light and shadow, with human-shaped head, rows of shark teeth that glinted like pearls, transparent wings in all the colors of the rainbow, and a frill around its head in copper, brown, and pale white. Its body was vaguely snakelike, with iridescent scales the color of tinted glass and thick smoke and hints of copper. It smelled like green herbs burning over hot coals and the tang of fish and water plants. The thought came out of nowhere—*Dragon of Light* . . .

It dove. Snapped at Leo. He raised his weapons, executing one of the whirling moves Gee had used, his sword whipping and stabbing. Beside him, Gee stood still, his eyes and mouth open wide, his blades lowered, pointing at the floor. The lillilend dodged Leo's whirling blades as if they were stuck in park and bared its fangs. It struck. Biting down on Gee, fangs entering front and back across his left shoulder. Bruiser raced in, ramming the stunned Mercy Blade to the floor. The lightdragon released him and the small man landed on one knee, dropping his swords, still staring up. I caught a glimpse of his face in something like reverence or awe, his eyes a luminous blue with a funky, oily shimmer that moved, like heat rising. And blood on his chest that appeared iridescent, not red. Almost faster than I could follow, the magic light-thing reared back and dodged in again, this time extending a black tongue and flicking it at Gee. Tasting his blood.

At vamp speed, Bruiser and Leo went back-to-back, standing over Gee, as if they'd fought this way before, many times. Their blades sang and cut in perfect synchrony, holding the creature away.

"Jane," Bruiser shouted. "Do it! Change!"

For a span of heartbeats I had no idea what he meant; then I remembered. Bruiser had fought the light-dragon, or one similar to it, once before. In the gray place of the change, as I—as Beast—ran away. It was one of many things we hadn't talked about.

I pulled on Beast and she shoved me aside, sliding down my arms and legs in a move that was painful beyond anything I could remember, my flesh feeling as if it had turned inside out and spat my bones to the floor. *So fast.* A burning-cuttingboiling pain arced into the air, stole my breath, and shredded my skin. Eli yelped and leaped away. I screamed, the halfhuman, half-cat scream splitting the air. Everything around me slowed to a crawl as the gray of my skinwalker magics erupted from inside me. This was the battle timing that many soldiers report, where their senses go into overdrive and everything happens with an intensity and speed that isn't part of the normal human experience.

My arms sprouted tawny pelt; my fingers flashed with pain as they altered shape and claws pierced through the tips. Beast claws. My head whipped back, my face exploding outward, bones cracking.

A gray haze of energies whipped around me like a burning wind, a storm of power, just like the phase of unreality that the dragon operated in; blue and green and black motes of power swirled hotly in the place of the change. And I realized that I didn't enter the gray place—it originated from inside *me*. Had I noticed that before? The thought and the questions melted in the face of my agony. And then it was gone. But the light-dragon was looking at me, meeting my eyes, as if it saw me fully for the first time.

I stepped toward Bruiser, time still slightly out of sync. But moving through it all, the light-creature dodged me, dodged Bruiser, whipping so fast it was a rush of light and shadow, all teeth and snakelike tongue and spattered rainbows.

Time slammed back onto me, though I was still close to the gray energies, cold on my skin. Leo stabbed the creature, a single hard thrust, up through its belly, angled toward its head, his feet following as the thing rippled and tried to lash away.

Gee, still bleeding, fell to his backside, legs sprawled. In the same instant, Leo stabbed directly overhead with his short sword, into the creature's side, both blades buried in it. Something like liquid glass flooded down over Leo, and he murmured words that sounded like, "Lepree lumyear. Larcencel. Larcencel."

Faster than my eyes could follow, even in the gray place of the change, the creature curled back on itself, descended onto Leo, mouth open, teeth flashing. Striking. Biting. I could smell Leo's blood and something bitter as ashes and horehound ground together.

Leo went limp. I darted forward, Bruiser stepping into my magics, a shocking wash of electricity that burned my skin and prickled across my scalp, hot as flaming cactus. Together, we stabbed up at the thing. It released Leo, snapping jaws and clacking teeth. The creature shot up to the roof. Around us, everyone, everything, flowed into a blur, speeding up, or perhaps *we* sped up, our time matching with the time and the speed of the thing overhead.

As if we were suddenly the only things visible to it, the light-being focused on us, its eyes flashing like light through a stained-glass window. It curled tightly, its tail lashing into a coil, its wings snapping into a half furl. I slammed my back to Bruiser's, standing as he and Leo had stood only moments before. The thing dove at us.

Around us, everything vanished and we stood in the gray place of energy, Bruiser, the creature, and me. I screamed again, the sound more cat now than human. My toes dug into a mat beneath us, nails piercing the rubber.

Bruiser slid into the movements of La Destreza. My shoulders were against his, my backside just below his. My sword shadowed his; my feet mirrored his, following his lead. The swordplay was easy now, as Beast shared her power, her strength, and Bruiser led the way into the Spanish Circle of flashing, stabbing swords. A dance. I had always loved dancing with Bruiser.

Our blades connected with the creature. Bruiser's sword, sharp, not the blunted sword I had been given, sliced it, slashing up through its scaled hide, along its side, lifting as he rose to his toes. Light blasted out of the wound. More of the liquid glass spurted toward us, but the gray energies of the change repelled it, and it slid away, to puddle on the floor.

Pulling on Beast's strength, I rammed my blunt sword point up, beside Bruiser's, into the glare of light, through the scales of the light-dragon.

The creature screamed. It arched high and thrashed its tail. From the corner of my eye, I saw a wash of light and darkness. Heard a *pop* of displaced air, the sound a vamp makes when it rushes from one place to another. It was Bethany, red dress swirling around her legs, vamped out. She was scary in human guise; terrifying vamped out. She screamed words from a language I had never heard and leaped into the air. Her magics shot out and surrounded the creature like a net of power. She wrapped her arms around the light-dragon and latched on, as if to ride it.

The dragon-creature pulled itself free of our weapons. It knotted into a coil again, bucked to remove Bethany, who held on tighter. It flapped its wings once, and dove away, crashing through the closed door at the back of the practice room, breaking it into splinters as if the dragon was more than light.

And suddenly it was gone. Bethany landed on the floor and bounded back up. She raced to Bruiser's side and ran her hands up and down his body. Then she disappeared again with that little *pop* of air. I growled, the vibration filling the air in the gray place of the change with warning.

For a moment, Bruiser and I leaned against each other, our backs supporting our weight. Moving slowly, he stood and stepped away, pulling himself out of the gray energies that surrounded me, stepping with a shudder that looked like he'd been tased. Bruiser was breathing hard, dripping with sweat.

I/we sniffed him to check his health, nostrils spreading and puffing. Bruiser dropped to his knees near me, his image flickering and smudged on the other side of my magics. I/we watched him, waiting, not knowing what to do. He breathed, his motions smoother. He looked up at me and his mouth moved. "Jane. Come back."

I/we stared at him, brow furrowed, not understanding. He pointed at my hands. "Come back."

I/we looked down and saw my hands, still holding the weapons. My wrists, hands, and fingers were pelted and tawny, my knuckles large and rounded, stronger than anything human, nails curled and sharp. Looked lower and saw pelted and clawed feet, paw-like, except that they were far larger than Beast's—six inches across, claws extended and gripping the wood floor. Splinters came up around my Beast toes. Rubber gobbets from the practice mat littered the floor around me. I pulled into myself with an electric snap that tingled through me, and felt myself separate from Beast at some mental, almost spiritual level.

I dropped the practice sword and the vamp-killer and touched my face. The lower half of my face was outthrust. I had fangs, like small tusks at both my upper and lower jaw. My forehead and nose were human, or humanish. The pads of my fingers were thick and it was hard to feel, but I was pelted all over my face and down my neck. I pulled out my shirt and looked down. The pelt paled to cream and ended just above my breasts and my slim waist of solid muscle. The pelt ran down under my arms and across my shoulders, all the way to my fingers. I bent to my pants and pulled the ankles up. Pelt as far as I could pull the spandex. Bulky cat feet with huge knees and thighs. No way was I looking into my waistband. *Crap*. I was half-formed. Half Beast and half me. Without a mass change, my weight had been redistributed, my body cast in horror-movie mode.

But at least I was starting to think again, starting to think like a human, not the half-and-half I'd become. The first fully coherent thought was, *I'm a monster*. I managed a sound that might have been chuffing laughter. Even in the Party City of the South, I couldn't go outside without a mask or a deep hood to hide behind. I'd scare the locals.

Close to the front of my mind I heard Beast rumble, *Jane and big-cat are more than Jane and big-cat. I/we are Beast.*

She sounded contented and determined and satisfied. As if she wanted to stay this way. And I had no idea what to do about that.

CHAPTER 8

You Want Me to . . . Wash Your Back?

What strength and energy I had left drained out in a rush and I landed on my knees on the ruined floor. *Houston,* I thought. *We have a problem.*

What is Houston? Beast thought at me.

Never mind. Are we stuck like this? Last time it went away naturally. And fast. But it's worse this time. It feels . . . I don't know. Permanent?

Jane likes half-Beast form. Jane hurt light-predator-snake-that-flies.

I thought about that for a moment. *So I'm keeping myself like this? I'm doing it?*

I/we are Beast. I/we like this form too.

So, that's a yes. I thought about my human form, my Jane form. I reached deep inside of me into the memory of my human self, searching for the snake at the center of me, the double helix of DNA that made me both human and skinwalker. Instead, I found a jumbled mess.

My oddly shaped knees gave way and I sat hard on the splintered floor. It was cool beneath my backside. My peculiar-shaped hands folded, flaccid, in my lap, dangling from my too-big thighs. Hunger and weakness stabbed at me, striking deep into my middle, then twisting and clawing like the hand of a fanghead, talons extended. I groaned and gasped, panting to get enough air. But there wasn't enough. Not nearly. *Holy crap . . .*

I pushed past the pain and studied the mess that was my

current DNA. It no longer had just a double strand. It now had a triple strand in places, branching out and back in like a suspension bridge of weirdness. On the odd strands, the genes were doubled and tripled in places, genes totally missing in others.

"Jane." I heard a voice from far away. I waved a hand to show I'd heard but was a little busy just now. Then I flapped it to indicate I should be left alone.

It wasn't all the cells. Like, maybe half. Only half of my cells were cat. Made sense. My arms folded like a human, my feet like a cat. My flesh was half-pelted, half not. Feet were some weird paw shape; hands were more humanish. I zeroed in on one batch of cells, human cells, that made up my hip joints. All of that part of me was human. Totally human.

I exhaled in a rush, the panting growing faster. It had been a while since I'd needed to meditate to drop into the place of the change, to find the cellular structure and physiology that made me, me. Fortunately, I was halfway there.

Breathing deeply, holding the breath, I tried to calm my rapid heartbeat, tried to relax, to let the tension out of my shoulders and neck. Dropped my head and bowed my spine. Stretched back up, sitting straight, into a half lotus, funky hands on knobby knees. I released my breath until my lungs were empty. Fought the fear and the need to hyperventilate. Filled my chest with air slowly, exhaled, inhaled, breathing until my body was full of oxygen but the panic was under control. I exhaled one final time and let myself fall into the genetic structure that made me what I was. I had not left the gray place of the change completely and so, instantly, I felt my body twist and reshape. Bones snapping and popping.

Painpainpain! Beast screamed.

I opened my mouth on a breathless cry, one I hadn't planned on needing. And then the gray energies slid back into me. I was lying on the ruined floor, face on something smooth and hard, about the size of my hand. I slid a hand under my jaw, gripped the thing I was lying on, and pushed myself upright, legs splayed as vertigo whirled the room around me. I held the rounded thing as I forced my eyes open and focused on my hands. Normal. Human. Mine. I touched my face. Ditto. Looked down my shirt. No fur. I sniffed the thing I'd found on the floor; it had a scent like fish and water plants and the smoke from burning herbs. It was clear, like glass, but slightly pliable like plastic. Rounded on one side and torn-looking on the straight side. *Fingernail?* The thought intruded. *Maybe, but a big honking one, if so.* And then I knew what it was. A scale from the dragon's body. I pushed the scale into my shirt and bra, securing it. Though I had no idea why I'd need to hide it. Probably a leftover big-cat thought, but it just seemed right. And then the pain hit, that gripping, tearing agony, as if something inside me were being ripped apart.

I wrapped an arm around my middle as if to hold my guts in, but my outer flesh felt fine. The damage was inside and I pressed into my stomach to try to still the torture. The muscles there were rigid and tangled, and I pressed hard until the spasm eased and at least I could catch a breath. And *great*. Now I had done a half shift on multiple security cameras.

I looked around the room. The bleachers were empty. Quiet. But my hearing was still Beast-sharp and from behind me I heard breathing and the heartbeats of two people. I turned my head and saw Eli and Bruiser. And Grégoire. Yeah. Two heartbeats: two humans and one undead blood-sucker. Witnesses in addition to the footage.

"Hey, guys," I managed, my mouth drier than desert sands. "What's cooking?"

Eli released a breath. It was only slightly more pent than a normal one, but for him that meant he'd been really worried. I'd seen him fight off a werewolf with less change in his breathing. Bruiser moved to me and held down a hand. I let him pull me to my feet and held on as the room did a nauseating roll and spin. And then the hunger hit me, blossoming out from the pain in my stomach. My abdomen clenched and curled in on itself like a steel hand was kneading a batch of raw bread dough inside my gut. I gagged, a dry heave that left the room spinning. Okay, this was weird.

Bent in two, I got a glimpse of the floor and the workout mats and the coagulating blood and drying dragon gunk. It was crystallizing as it dried. On the edges there was nothing left but dust. A girl in hospital greens and sterile gloves was gathering some of the crystal dust into a sterile tube. *Good.* I croaked, "For workup in Leo's lab?"

She met my eyes and then dropped hers back to the floor. "Yes, ma'am."

"Get it messengered tonight." I tried to find a drop of moisture in my mouth, but there was nothing. I went on anyway, my voice raspy. "Full workup and DNA—if the gunk has any. Fast as you can."

"Yes, ma'am," she repeated.

Eli placed an open bottle of water in my hand and when I could breathe and stand upright at the same time, I drained it. Not sure I swallowed it, exactly, but the bottle was empty. Then another. And another. By the time I'd emptied four bottles, I could force my knees straight. "Steak?" Eli asked.

"Oatmeal," I grunted around the twisting in my guts. "It's faster to get into me."

Grégoire made a small motion to someone out of sight and Bruiser slid his arm around me, supporting me—okay, half carrying me—out of the gym and to the hallway. Grégoire fell in beside me and his scent wrapped around me, a near synesthesia I sometimes found when Beast was very close to the front of me—a pale green, the honey gold of spring flowers, a scent I'd always thought was luscious. The vamp smiled, not that slow smile they do when they're trying to charm, the one that transforms their faces into angelic beauty, but an uncertain one, which made him seem almost human. He took my arm, above the elbow, as if I was about to fall. And with the floor moving up and down like waves, and around like the water in a toilet bowl, maybe I was.

The four of us made it into the elevator before I threw up, all over the elevator floor, at least ninety percent of the water I'd guzzled. Grégoire stepped back quickly to protect his shoes, which were a wine-colored patent leather. If I hadn't been tossing my cookies, I'd have giggled. Eli was still in the hallway, out of the line of fire. Bruiser didn't react at all except to give me a clean hanky to wipe my mouth. "Sorry about your shoes," I croaked.

"They're just shoes, Jane," Bruiser replied. And the spare phrase made something turn over inside me. *Just shoes.* Not important. As if I was more important than the shoes.

The others stepped inside, onto a clean patch of floor, and the doors closed, leaving me in a tiny little cage that reeked of vamp scent, human scent, the heated warmth of Bruiser's sweat, which was no longer human but wasn't vamp either, and my own stink, both on my clothes and on the floor. Grégoire, holding something lacy to his nose, palmed the display with his other hand and activated the button panel on the elevator. It lurched gently into motion as Eli offered me another bottle of water. "Try it slow this time."

"Hindsight," I said, sounding more human. I sipped the water and looked up at the lights on the display. And I dropped the water, jerking my weapons out of Eli's arms. Once again he didn't question, just followed my lead.

"Jane?" Bruiser asked, warning in his voice. Beside him Grégoire vamped out at the sight of the guns and blades.

"We're going down. Way down," I said. I'd been so sick I hadn't noticed.

Grégoire hissed. Placed his hand over the biometric handprint reader and pressed a button. The elevator came to an abrupt stop, so fast I lost my precarious balance—still not back to normal. But Bruiser's arm tightened around me, and I let myself lean against him. Just a little. And then the lights in the elevator flickered, browned down to a dull glow, and went out, leaving us in the darkness. I think I growled, just enough of Beast left in me to manage that with a human throat.

The lightless interval didn't last long. Maybe five seconds. But it was enough time to make me see monsters in the dark. Which made me titter with a laugh because I *was* a monster. And I was in an elevator, stuck between floors, with another monster, one all vamped out and smelling of something sweet and flowery. And watery vomit. My life was so weird.

The lights came back on. Grégoire stood with his back to a corner, pupils black in bloody orbs, fangs snapped down, holding blades in both hands, talons extended. A monster. He hissed, his eyes on me. It was as if Grégoire had never been human.

"Grégoire. My friend," Bruiser added softly. "We are well. There is no need of battle. Jane, Eli, please put away the weapons."

"There's—" *A dark room with something in it. A monster.* Another *monster*. Right. Not saying that. I thumbed the safety back on and gave the gun to Eli. "There's one in the chamber." I remembered chambering a round when I grabbed the gun, but I wasn't sure how because I'd still held the open bottle of water. The elevator quivered, dropped an inch, and then started up again. Grégoire's eyes bled back to human so fast I would have missed it if I'd blinked.

No one spoke until the doors opened on the main floor, at

which point I pushed away from Bruiser, standing on my own two feet in my own vomit. *Ick.* But I needed to clear something up. To Grégoire, I asked, "You know about the dark room at the bottom of the elevator shaft?"

"There is no such room," Grégoire said stiffly. He sheathed his blades, yanked on the lace cuffs sticking out of the sleeves of his velvet coat—wine colored to match his shoes—and stalked off the elevator. *Liar, liar, pants on fire,* I thought. His *liar* pants were velvet too, which made me smile, though from the expression on Eli's face, it was more a grimace. And I had to wonder when Grégoire had found time to change out of his fighting leathers.

"Yeah," I murmured, "right." I stood as straight as I could with the clamped fist in my gut and thought over the last few minutes. To Eli I said, "I want every camera angle from the workout room downloaded, all the footage from the doorway where that dragon thing came into the room and back up to any surface opening or any subbasement opening. I want to know how it got in. Get Alex on it, and secure the footage. I don't want it appearing on YouTube." I meant footage of me changing but he seemed to know that too. He was Mr. Mind Reader tonight.

Eli nodded and pulled his cell to call Alex. To Bruiser, I said, "Food? And someone to clean the elevator?" My gut clenched again and I doubled over.

"I'll send housecleaning," Bruiser said, scooping me up in his arms like some oversized fairy-tale princess. He carried me to the green room just off the foyer, and dropped me on the couch, the door still open behind us for the guest cart I could hear squeaking down the hallway. The cart was stocked with guest goody bags for just such occasions—though usually for a vamp in need of a good sunscreen or a casket to sleep in. Not that I'd ever insult a sane vamp by suggesting aloud that he might really sleep in one. That was an old wives' tale and a terrible offense to suggest.

In short order I had brushed my teeth in the tiny unisex restroom and was drinking milk and eating oatmeal, or what passed for oatmeal in vamp central. It was instant, not stone ground, and had been cooked in such a way that the starch was activated. The oats had turned into a mushy gruel. It was topped with cinnamon and butter and brown sugar. *Gag.* Not the way I cooked oatmeal. I'd have to have a word with the cook, a thought that made me laugh like a madwoman deep inside, but not close to the surface where anyone could see or hear. I ate the vile stuff anyway, for the calories I'd used half shifting and fighting and then half shifting again. And I drank the milk, which was full fat and ice-cold and delicious.

As I ate, the room filled with security types, and the pain in my gut eased. I studied the room. Someone had rearranged and redecorated the odd room, and a mirror that used to hang on the end wall was gone, exposing the cracked and bowed plaster from the settling of the building and the constant humidity. It was cracked in the shape of a doorway. Huh. I looked up at the ceiling, putting the floor plan together in my mind. I wondered whether one of Leo's secret stairways, or maybe even an elevator, was behind the wall, a useless bit of trivia I'd never need.

When I was done, I flopped back on the couch and looked at the people in the room, all men, all armed, all staring at me. And caught a strong whiff of myself. My clothes stank of sweat and blood and lillilend slime and ticked-off cat. And vomit. *Ick.* My nose wrinkled. But before I could take care of my stench, I had to know other stuff. "How's Leo and Gee?"

"Alive," Bruiser said. "Both were bitten. Both are unwell. We brought in the priestesses." More gently, he added, "As you seem inclined to live, I'll look in on them now."

"Okay, yeah. I'm good. Keep me informed?"

Bruiser nodded and stepped out. Eli stepped in and gave one of his patented non-nods.

The security people in the room with us were armed to the teeth, taut with inaction and the need to do something. Anything physical. I rotated my shoulders and got to my feet, feeling a bit more steady than before the gaggy oatgruel, though my stomach ached as if I'd been kicked. "We have info to share and jobs to do," I said. "But can we wait until I've cleaned up before we do this?" I gestured around the room. "This debrief?"

"We need more space," Wrassler said. "Tables. Chairs. Doughnuts."

"Computer access," Eli said, his eyes hard.

Which was a clue to me that we had things to discuss. "Right. Okay," I said. "I'll get a fast shower and meet you in the conference room. We'll talk, cuss and discuss, and reach some preliminary conclusions. Because we have a problem,

people. A big one." I pointed to Wrassler. "Divide up your people. Two by two. No one alone until we figure this out. I want
the grounds walked over, every inch. I want the roofs looked
over. You're looking for any clear slime or any crystalline grit
from the attacking whatever-it-was. Plus which direction it
came from and if it was alone or with something or someone
else."

When no one moved, I said, "Now!" The room emptied
quickly of the ancillary people, which gave me more air to
breathe and fewer stress pheromones to struggle through. As
the door closed, I heard Wrassler giving orders and the sound
of feet moving off fast. Yeah. They'd needed jobs.

I pushed my own feet into motion, though they felt like
they weighed fifty pounds each, and moved toward the door. I
was sore. I really hoped I wouldn't need to fight again soon.
Usually when I changed back from Beast, everything was
healed, but this pain was new, as if I'd been put back together
wrong somehow. "Eli, you're with me."

I pushed through into the foyer, Eli calling after me, "You
want me to shower with you, babe?" he asked. "Wash your
back?"

I smiled, though it was more like a baring of teeth. He'd
choke on his tongue if I said yes. "*Watch* my back. Not wash it,"
I called to him. He was by my side in an instant and I continued, much softer. "We don't know how that thing got in and
I'm not quite myself yet." He looked me over in surprise and
I felt good that I had kept *something* from him, which means
that no one else had realized how worthless I was. "You're my
plus one until I'm better. I need to know how that thing managed to hurt Gee and Leo, and what effect it will have on them
long range." *And how it saw me in the gray place of the change,*
but I didn't say that. "And I need an update on the elevator
situation."

"Alex is already working on everything. He'll have an update in fifteen minutes."

"Good. Shower. Now."

"Yeah," Eli said, far too casually. "You really do stink,
babe."

I had been running around vamp HQ in my filthy Lycra and
bare feet, and no one had said a word about it. Except my
partner. He was such a good pal. Not.

Fortunately, the elevator had been cleaned, housecleaning

leaving behind a synthetic scent probably called Highlands Heather or Mystical Forest or some such stupid name. We were cleared for the gym floor, so I swiped my hand over the reader, punched a button, and soon I was standing, still clothed, under scalding hot water, letting it rinse away the stench of fighting.

Standing under the hard spray, I stripped, and something fell out of my shirt and jog bra. I caught the smooth, rounded, plastic-like thing before it hit the floor and set it aside to finish cleaning. When my hair was washed and combed, I was lotioned up, and was wrapped in one of the plush towels kept in the locker room, I called out to Eli, "I'm ready to dress now."

"Clear," came his response as he stepped out of sight of the curtained stalls. The towel covering me from shoulder to knees, I tossed my wet clothes into a sink and opened the locker assigned to me.

I never knew what clothes I'd find in my locker, provided by the HQ staff. Sometimes it was formal wear. Recently, I had found three pairs of dancing shoes—black, gold, and a silver pair that I was pretty sure had been put there by Del. Once, a pair of really nice formfitting pants and a gorgeous, black, cowl-necked sweater had been inside. Today, I found clean undies, a pair of black knit pants, a pair of black jeans, two sweaters, and several T-shirts. Leo was giving me a choice. That was a change. Underneath the clothes and tied up with a red bow was a brand-new, custom-made holster, a tactical SERPA carbon-fiber thigh holster, adjustable for various makes and models of guns. And my blades. And my stakes.

Had Leo given me this? He was a narcissistic, dictatorial, tyrannical, despotic, spoiled-as-a-child blood-sucker and he thought he could buy his way into my loyalty and my pants, so maybe, though guns didn't seem his style. And then I saw the card. It was handwritten on heavy card stock in black ink. No envelope. I lifted the card into the light and read.

"If a blade, tea, and catnip were not sufficient, perhaps I might woo you with a tactical, drop-thigh holster." It was signed with a simple script *G*.

A smile pulled at my lips. "Bruiser," I said. And, "*Woo*. What an odd little word." But the smile on my face lightened all through me.

I dressed quickly in the jeans, a leather belt, and the red, thin knit, cowl sweater. I liked the big loopy collars. They were great for sliding silver stakes through and making them look like jewelry. They were also loose enough that the odd pain remaining near my belly button didn't receive any unexpected pressure. I slid on the comfy slippers that were always in the locker. There must be a storeroom or closet somewhere that contained a stash, because I had taken several pairs home and there were always more here.

My fighting leathers and combat boots were on the long bench that divided the locker room, stuffed in a satchel that Eli had found somewhere, as if he'd known I wouldn't want to wear them. My weapons were in a neat row on the bench. Eli had cleaned the blades. "I'm decent," I said softly, knowing Eli would hear me.

Still geared up, he walked back into the main room and nodded to the weapons. It was Eli-speak for, *What weapons do you want? How do you want to weapon up? All of it? Or just some?* All that in a nod. We had learned to read each other's cues so quickly that it was sorta disturbing. And maybe awesome.

I held up the thigh holster and said, "Looky what Bruiser got me!"

Eli spread out the custom-made thigh holster on the bench, studying it with approval. "The man's got taste. And he seriously wants in your pants, babe."

A flash of warmth brightened my face and heated its way down my chest, so I thumped his arm with my fist. Hard. And took back the holster while he laughed and rubbed his biceps. I strapped the rig to my right thigh. A standard thigh holster was constructed with three straps, two around the thigh, one that went up and looped onto a belt. TV cops wore the rigs low on the thigh, which looked cool, but for close quarters fighting I liked my weapons a bit higher than the specs suggested. The upper thigh strap to my new rig went near my groin, the lower around the largest part of my thigh. The custom unit had a vertical strap that went to my belt, directly above the holster, and a longer, distinctive strap that went around my waist and back to the unit for stability. The holster was more complicated than a regular thigh rig, but because I was so slender the extra strap gave me more control and also allowed me to fasten on a holster for a backup weapon when I was wearing long coats or sweaters, like now. There was even a loop to secure my M4 harness. The shotgun hadn't gotten a lot of use lately, but it was my go-to weapon when facing large numbers of big-bad-uglies. It cleared a wide swath, when needed.

I holstered one of my matched Walther PK380s at my right thigh, and the other one at the small of my back for a left-hand draw. The semiautomatic handguns were lightweight and ambidextrous, with bloodred polymer grips that perfectly matched the red of the T-shirt. Which was a girly thought and one I didn't share with Eli, though I could imagine his expression if I did. The .380s offered less stopping power than nine-mils, but vamp central meant the possibility of collateral damage, and killing anyone or anything by accident was not on my schedule, now or ever. The .380 on my thigh, I pulled and holstered several times, testing the friction of the holster fabric, before I loaded it with standard rounds. The one at my spine was loaded with silver, just in case of vamp or were-animal attack. I liked to be prepared for both kinds of bad guys—human and supernatural big-bad-uglies.

There was a special sheath in the thigh rig for a fourteen-inch vamp-killer—steel with silver plating along the flat of the blade. Steel to cut flesh, silver to poison vamps or weres. The thigh holster had deep pockets for stakes, and I inserted silver-tipped ash stakes with little wooden buttons on the ends so I could shove them into a vamp without hurting the palm of my hand if needed, and also so that I could get a good grip if I ever wanted to pull one out. It had happened. The stakes were a new design and though they resembled knitting needles, they were easier to use than my old model. Into my calf holster went a six-round Kahr P380, a small semiautomatic with a matte black finish, loaded with standard ammo.

I stood and looked myself over in the long mirror and frowned. I looked long and lean and feminine, and even the gun strapped to my hip and thigh didn't fix that. "It's the cowl-neck," Eli said, reading my mind again. "Makes you look soft and sweet." He did that little lip-twitch thing he called a smile. "Good disguise, except for the gun. Which makes you look hot, in a deadly sort of way."

I shook my head at the left-handed insult and passed him the clear, rounded thing I'd found under me after the battle with the lillilend. Not wanting to steer him to my own result, I asked simply, "What do you think?"

"This that thing you tucked into your boobs after the fight?"

"Yeah. Who else saw?"

Eli shrugged. "Bruiser. No one else, I think." He ran his fingers over the curved side, which was blunt and smooth, and then over the opposite side, which was irregular, ripped-looking in spots, with longer fiber-like things hanging off. "Thin, clear, luminous, flexible, and slightly iridescent," he said, bending it to test its plasticity. It sprang back into shape. "What I could make out of the thing in the gym, it was vaguely snake-like. Scale? Like from a snake? Ripped out of the skin underneath?" He mimed pulling one off.

"I think so," I said. Weirdly, the spot on my chest where it had touched my skin continued to tingle. I rubbed my sternum, trying to stop the reaction. "I should send it to Leo's lab, in Texas, for DNA testing, but they already have the gunk off the floor." I bent it and held it to the light, where the surface swam with color like the surface of a pearl. "I don't know. Maybe I'll keep it." I tucked it into a slit in the thigh holster that buttoned shut, discovering as I did that there was even a small pocket in the rig, holding a tourniquet and sterile bandages. Bruiser had thought of everything. I liked that in a man. "Let's get this debrief on the road."

We were walking into the security/conference room when Eli's cell did that little jangle-buzz that let him know he had a text. "Alex has everything secure," he said, "and all non-Jane footage ready for viewing."

The air of the conference room was redolent of scorched coffee, fresh Krispy Kreme doughnuts, the heated scent of Onorio, to tell me that Bruiser was present, Grégoire's intense personal vamp scent, gun oil, the reek of fired weapons, and testosterone. In other words, it smelled wonderful. The underground room had a security console, a huge monitor/TV screen, a massive table, and comfortable rolling desk chairs.

The primo, Adelaide Mooney, opened the meeting with the info that Leo and Gee were being treated by the priestesses. She assured us that they would both be okay, but it would be tomorrow night before we'd see them again. With the fast healing of vampires and whatever species an Anzû was, that sounded pretty ominous. Del looked haggard but elegant, dressed in a monochrome blend of blond tones that matched her hair, which was down and curling on her shoulders. I remembered seeing her at some point in the gym, sword raised. It had been only a glimpse, but it looked as if Del knew her way around sharp objects.

When she finished her report, I asked, "Can you tell us what Leo was saying when the thing flew into the room? It sounded like, *Lepree lumyear. Larcencel. Larcencel.*"

Del's eyes flicked down and back to me. I wasn't sure what the reaction meant, other than she wanted to be done and outta here. She stood and said, "The Master of the City said to give you this." She passed a folded scrap of paper to me. On it was written in a shaky hand, with what looked like a ballpoint pen, the words, *Grand danger, mon cour. L'esprit lumière. L'arcenciel.*

It wasn't Leo's usual fancy, calligraphy-like script, and I'd never seen him use a ballpoint pen or write on a torn piece of paper, but the words on it had the right *L*s in them to be his handwriting. "Okay. What's it say?"

Toneless, she replied. "It says, 'Great danger, my heart. The light spirit. The rainbow.'"

"What's wrong with his heart? Did the bite damage it?" For that matter, did Leo even have a heart? Fortunately I got my mouth closed before I said those words.

"I believe that Leo is calling *you* his heart," Bruiser said, his tone droll.

"Oh. Okay. No." I looked at Del and finally was able to deduce her expression as an unwilling possessiveness. Del and Leo had begun a relationship that included more than just blood sharing, and this read like I was poaching on her territory. Though how that all worked when Leo was still sleeping with Grégoire, I had no idea. "I'm not his heart. He just calls me that to tick me off."

"I see. Well . . . if you need me, I'll have my cell and in-house radio." She turned on her expensive two-inch heels and left the room. I followed her into the hallway, but she cut me off with a terse, "I don't have time now, Jane."

I stepped back fast at her abrupt words. An embarrassed flush shocked through me. I don't make friends easily and—

"Sorry," Del said. Her shoulders slumped and she rubbed her forehead. I didn't get headaches much but Del looked like she was in pain. "It's been a difficult week."

Tentatively, I said, "Leo giving you a hard time?"

She dropped her hand. "I'm not the primo he's used to working with," she said stiffly, as if she had heard the words once too often recently. "He's still grieving for George, and there's nothing I can do to take away the fact that he's lost his right-hand man. It's also taking me a while to get up to speed. I don't know where things are located, filed, or stored. I made a mistake ordering wine for a small gala Leo has planned. We got a delivery of 'substandard, even for American swill,' wine that I liked and that cost a small fortune. He broke every bottle. Every single one. Quesnel was horrified."

Which sounded like underling-speak for the boss was being a pain in the butt. Was the jealousy a misread on my part? I said, "Ouch. Sooo, because you don't have instant recall and superpsychic powers of vamp-omniscience, Leo bites your head off?"

She smiled slightly. "Metaphorically speaking."

"Want me to stake him for you?"

Del spluttered with laughter, which was what I had hoped for, her pale complexion brightening. "I think not. Job security, you know."

"Yeah. I bet it'd be hard to find a new position as primo in today's job market." The words felt familiar, as if I'd said them before. To Del? To Bruiser? Both had changed jobs recently.

Still chuckling, Del stretched her shoulders back and then let them relax. She said, "I'm sorry about my tone in there. Girls' day out soon? I know this town has excellent spas and I'm dying to try one out."

I didn't do girlie stuff, manis and pedis and facials, but I'd had a massage once and it had been fantastic. "Soon," I promised her with a nod, and then added, "Leo doesn't understand the concept of monogamous. He'll protect you with his life and give you anything you want except that." Without watching for her reaction, I opened the conference room door and slipped back inside.

The lights were off in the room, security footage up on the oversized central monitor screen. A voice in the darkness said, "Legs, I'll look over the footage again later for anything we might have missed, but so far, nothing shows on the cameras until the rainbow thing, whatever Leo called it, entered the gym."

"Okay," I said as I slid into a chair at the head of the table. Belatedly I identified the voice as Angel Tit, one of Derek's men, a former active-duty marine and IT security specialist. And the scent beside me was Bruiser, silent, watching. He must have come back in through the other entrance. I could feel his eyes on me in the dark. "What?"

"That," he said. *That* was digital footage from four cameras, taking up half of the screen, two by two. I'd installed the cameras to cover all aspects of the workout room and its two entrances. The screens showed footage that had been aligned by time stamp to show the moment the creature entered the gym in a flash of light. Instantly, all the cameras had splotches of white-out and partial white-out, in the blocky shapes of ruined digital feed.

Angel said, "I'm piecing together sections of footage that are still okay, so we can get a view of the fight. This is all I got at this time."

A fifth screen appeared on the far right of the TV and showed the creature entering the room. It was a blister of light, a halo of nothingness with glistening movement to the side that could have been wings, followed by a smoky cloud of out-of-focus, thrashing tail. The camera angle changed, and changed again as it flew across the room. It whipped to Gee and bit him.

"It went straight to Gee," I said. "I thought it was angling for Leo and got Gee instead. But it targeted Gee DiMercy first. Anybody have any ideas about that?" No one answered, but I could feel a growing discomfort in the room as the snake thing attacked Leo, fought, and finally flew away, then did it again, and again, as Angel replayed the footage. The uneasiness might have been the result of the appearance of what would have passed for a dragon in mythology, or maybe the part where Bruiser and I both vanished from the screen into a haze of gray energies, but whatever caused it, the humans in the room were not happy campers. Fortunately, no footage appeared showing me in half-cat form, and though it was strange that no one brought that up, I decided not to mention it. Discretion being the better part of valor, or I am a scaredy cat, or something like that.

We watched the footage several more times before I said, "Okay. Stop. Is it just me or does anyone else get a different impression of the action from what we saw in the room at the time it happened?"

"I thought my eyes were going bad," a voice said from the front of the room.

"Nothing I see now is what I saw at the time," Bruiser agreed. His voice wasn't worried, but it was far more bland than usual, which was telling in its own way.

"Me neither. That's not what I saw," another voice said. Others murmured what they had seen.

"I saw a buncha bats. Nearly crapped my pants."

"I saw bees, dude. Killer bees. Heard 'em too. Scared the shi— Ooof. Whadju do that for?"

"No cussing around Janie," Angel Tit said, making it sound like a law.

"I just got dizzy, like someone spiked my drink."

"I started itching. I got outta there." Others agreed. The spectators to the sparring had cleared the room fast. Few witnesses had been left to see my partial shift. "Interesting," I said, feeling a weight lift off of me. "So it makes humans forget they ever saw it. Pretty good survival mechanism. Everyone write up a report and send it to my e-mail."

There were groans from around the room, the soldier's universal hatred of after-action reports. Beside me, Bruiser chuckled under his breath. I said, "We need to know if it's messing with our minds, our eyesight, or our memories." That shut them up. No one human liked to think their minds might be an open book to some supernat.

I said, "I want to know what everyone saw at the time, versus what we just saw on the footage. Keep the reports brief and get them to me by nightfall. Angel, see if you can sharpen the images or fix the interference or whatever you call the blocky white-out sections. Send it to me ASAP."

"Yeah, I'll get right on that. Nice work with the tech lingo, Legs," he said with unrestrained sarcasm. The men laughed, and some of the tension that had been generated by the meeting dissipated. "Just kiddin', Janie. I'll let you know what I find and send the Kid a copy."

"Good. Lights, please." We all blinked as our eyes adjusted and someone passed around a mega-sized coffee carafe and a tray full of mugs. Boxes of Krispy Kreme doughnuts followed. I wasn't interested in the coffee but took a vanilla-cream-filled doughnut and bit into it, the sugary, doughy goodness practically exploding in my mouth. Vanilla cream squished out the small hole and I caught it on a finger and licked it clean. I had to wonder whether the local witches had ever heard of light-dragons, and I pulled my cell to text my best friend, Molly, to ask for me. Eventually, I'd have to meet the local witches myself, but so far, I hadn't had to add that to my supernatural plate.

Mouth still full, I went on. "Okay. Last thing. Everyone knows about the elevator problems. The Otis people did the online diagnostic and pretty much got what Alex did, so they're sending out repair people, ones who have worked in a vamp's household before. They'll be here at eight in the morning, in"—I looked at the time stamp on the monitor—"just a few hours. There will be two of them, and Alex has done preliminary background and social media checks on both. Neither seem to have overt anti-vamp prejudice, but I don't want our guests wandering around alone. Eli will oversee their activities if they need to go into the shaft itself. Derek, if you'll coordinate with him and position a couple more people to keep them in sight at all times?" Leo's new Enforcer nodded, and I was happy to see him looking more confident about his position. Maybe our little chat at the clan home construction site had helped.

I addressed my next question to Angel Tit at the security console. "Angel? Who has day shift on the cameras?"

"That would still be me. I'm on till noon. I'll stay over until the repair people are done."

"Thanks," I said. "I want them in sight at all times."

"Yes, ma'am."

"What do we do if the rainbow-snake-thing comes back?" Derek asked. The room went dead silent at the disquiet in his voice. I leaned back in my chair as if thinking about his question. When I replied I kept my tone dry and amused. "Try to keep it from eating anyone."

The laughter in the room was quick and a hair uncertain, but Derek smiled and shook his head. "Ask a dumb question."

"If there are no undumb questions, meeting adjourned."

CHAPTER 9

It Was a Girly Scream

Eli drove home slowly, watching behind us and up and down the streets we passed. "Problems?" I asked.

"We're being followed. Three vehicles—two black or charcoal SUVs and one black four-door coupe. They're playing ABC with cars." ABC was a method of tailing a subject using a three-man team. In cars it meant each vehicle altered its position according to a prearranged system. The method was difficult to detect because the target subject was never given long enough to recognize any team member. It was hard enough to detect on foot. In cars, with traffic, it was near impossible. Eli was better than impossible. In the ABC system, the A vehicle followed the subject car. B followed A, and C paralleled either A or B. When the parade reached an intersection, C would speed up and cross or turn ahead of the target. This allowed the C vehicle to keep the subject vehicle in view in case it turned unexpectedly.

As C turned the corner, A would slow down, while B sped up to take A's place. After a decent interval, A would pull out, find B's back, and tail him. It could get complicated. "Cars?" I asked.

"A is behind us. B is the charcoal SUV a block back, and C is on Royal. You want me to lose them?"

I remembered the black SUV I had thought might be tailing me earlier and grinned. "Nah. Let's play with them."

Eli chuckled and made several fast turns, which had us going back the way we had come, the C car, which had tried to keep up with the turns, in front of us. I took down the tag number. Moments later, the *C* car pulled away and down a side street at speed. The two other cars veered off as well, knowing they had been made. Meanwhile, I texted the Kid with the license number and Eli turned back toward home.

Fun, Beast murmured deep inside, *to hunt prey with metal bones and bad-tasting blood. Hunt prey now with blood and flesh to tear and eat?*

"Yeah," I said aloud. "Keep the engine running when we get home. I'm going hunting."

Eli pulled up in front of the house and got out, grabbing an armful of my fighting leathers from the backseat as he did. "Be safe," he said as I slid over the gear console and into the driver's seat. I waved my agreement and took off. After a complicated set of turns to make sure I hadn't been tailed again, I headed across the river. I had three hours, more or less, until dawn. Beast needed to hunt.

I woke on path with dirt under belly and paws. Studied place. Jane had picked good spot to change. Tall grasses and deep shadows. Strange bent and stunted swamp trees. No standing water fallen from sky—from rain. Smelled of fish and rotten things and snake and skunk and opossum and scat of bobcat. Wesa, bobcat, had marked territory on tree. I chuffed with laughter. Jane had been Wesa when she took big-cat's form and soul. Jane as Wesa had been strong, good fighter.

Looked for Jane in den of mind. She slept. I, Beast, pressed paw onto her and forced her deeper into sleep. Jane did not know Beast could do this. There was much that Jane did not know. Beast could not decide what to tell her. How to tell her. Was confusing. Jane was like Wesa. And not. Jane could need to know much of what Beast knew. But much would hurt her. Chuffed out breath. *Confused.* Did not like *confused.*

Hunger gripped belly like Wesa claws. Was not confused at *hunger.* Understood *hunger.* Stood and stepped over pile of Jane clothes on ground. Stopped. Looked back at thing on top of Jane-shirt. Was supposed to smell thing from fight, thing like scale of fish. Lowered head and snuffled, nostrils fluttering. Opened mouth and pulled in air over tongue and roof of mouth in soft *scree* of sound, taking scent deep.

Strange thing smelled of fish and snake and water of Mississippi. Smelled of burning green things. Knew this creature.

Had smelled one before, many years in past, during start of hunger times, when white man had killed off all animals and cut down all trees, and land itself washed away in rains. Beast had wanted hunter out of territory. Wanted snake/fish/winged-like bat hunter of prey gone. Wanted it dead. But it was too big to fight. Fangs were full of bad things, smelled of danger.

Beast had thought like Jane. Had shared part of kill with creature. It crawled from small pool of water and ate deer. Then flashed with light, like sun. When light went dark, it was standing on two legs, upright, like human. But creature did not smell like human. Smelled like this, fish, snake, water, and fire-burning-grass.

Beast had taken thing-of-light to mouth of river, to show it water-path to bigger water and safety, far away from Beast hunting territory. Beast was not being-doing-thinking emotion that Jane called *kind*. Just wanted thing-of-light-that-ate-prey gone.

Creature was happy and swam away, leaving Beast's hunting territory. Should remind Jane of this. Thing had scales like fish. Like snake. Like *this*. But could change shape. Like Jane. But was not like Jane. Did not smell like skinwalker.

With teeth, Beast pulled shirt over scale. Hiding it. Patted it with paw.

Yawned. Stretched hard, pulling on front legs and chest and down belly. Felt good, except for Jane gobag on Beast-neck. Did not like bag, but bag held Jane-clothes. Did not understand Jane. Jane could grow pelt but would not. Jane did not like pelt. Jane liked clothes.

Silent, moving with night wind, I, Beast, trotted into darkness.

Later, lay on bank of small pond, water still and unmoving. Not creek, fast and falling through mountains, not bayou, slow and crawling through swamp. But still and muddy and deep. Good place to catch and kill sleeping alli-gator. Alli-gator. Jane-word for big predator in water. But Beast was smart. Did not hunt and try to catch *big* alli-gator. Leaped on small one and caught it in jaws. Fought it. Dragged it to shore by back leg. When Beast let go, little gator whipped back and bit Beast. Took bite of Beast skin from Beast, at place where leg met belly. Now smelled Beast blood on air. Licked wound. Hurt. But had learned how to hunt predator with many killing teeth.

Should not grab leg. Would be smarter to grab gator-face and jaw and muzzle when gator-mouth was closed. And bite down. Hard. Breaking gator-jaw. Pull snake with legs and many teeth to shore. Then could play with injured gator like playing with rabbits.

But did not think *big* gator would be so easy. If *big* alli-gator bit Beast, Beast would die. Did not want to die in many pieces in gator-belly. *Chuffed.* Wanted to live. Did not want to hunt gator again. Small one was enough. It was long as Beast and tail. I pawed gator-foot. Lowered head and bit it. Crunch of claws and bone and thick skin and scales. Tasted like frog-fish-snake. Beast belly was full, and all good meat gone. Buzzards would eat rest. Buzzards and big rats called nutria.

Beast rose and pawed rest of dead alli-gator. Moved its teeth into moonlight. Was good predator, good hunter. But Beast was best hunter.

Felt magic, like Jane's magic, but not Jane's. It tingled through air, foreign, strange magic, full of green lights and good smells of blood. It smoothed along pelt. Beast looked up, into night, saw lights, like Jane's light, but not Jane's light. Light reached into Beast, to touch Jane's gray place of change. It wanted gray place, full of power. Beast leaped, high into air and away from light-thing. Growled. Light-thing pulled away, watching Beast. Was same light-thing that bit Leo and Gee. Light-thing had followed Jane and Beast. Had been watching. Like hunter of prey. *Beast is not prey!* Beast raised head and screamed. *Go away! Go away, magic snake. This is Beast's place. Go away!*

Magic coiled back, like rattlesnake on rock, faded like moon-light into fog. Was gone.

Beast padded along pond and lay down facing water. Facing sunrise. Lay down and thought of Jane. But did not know if Beast should tell Jane of magic. Was better that Jane did not know? Was better to keep Jane like kit, safe in den? Jane did not know many things. Must think like Jane. Must decide.

I woke facing a pond and a pair of gator eyes. I jumped back-ward from prone to standing in one move. I hadn't even known I could do that. I screamed a little when I landed. I was pretty sure it was a girly scream and I was really glad Eli hadn't heard it. He'd razz me forever.

The gator was huge and staring right at me. Tiny bumps

broke the water for twelve feet behind it. "Holy crap," I whispered. "Beast, I'll freaking kill you." At the sound of my voice, the gator's long tail twitched slightly, sending ripples over the smooth, muddy surface.

Deep inside, my Beast chuffed and rolled over. And closed her eyes.

"Faker," I muttered.

I unsnapped the gobag and pulled out a pair of pants made of thin material, a soft T-shirt, flip-flops, and a hoodie. I had forgotten to pack panties, which I didn't need but which made me more comfortable. As I moved, I felt the odd place on my chest where the light-dragon scale had rested. The tingling was gone, as was the lingering pain of abdominal muscles twisted out of shape, into a half-cat form. All good and normal, including the hunger that gripped me. I dressed and nudged Beast when I saw the remains of the small gator. *Did you kill that?*

Beast yawned and showed me her canines. *Beast is best hunter.*

Uh-huh. I smell your blood. How badly were you hurt?

Beast turned away and ignored me. Dang cat.

Am not dang cat. Am Beast.

I looked at the pond. *And that is an alligator. A huge alligator.*

Know alli-gator. Alli-gator is not important. Know creature of light. Creature is important. Creature was shape-changer, like Jane but not like Jane. Not skinwalker. A memory of a denuded world, rock, bare earth, and withered tree limbs appeared in Beast's memory. It was familiar but distant, like a scene from a book I read long ago. I was inside Beast's head, watching a light-dragon eat a hank of raw deer, its energies coruscating and shadowed both, its snake tail whipping a small, tree-choked pond as it ate. It was summer, and in the memory I could smell the deer, ripe and going bad. Beast shared her memories as the thing, the rainbow thing, emitted a burst of white light and changed shape. It took on the form of a two-legged female. Almost human. Almost.

"Son of a gun," I muttered. "I remember that. I remember you feeding it. How many of those things are there?" I asked her.

Beast knows many things, she thought at me. *Have thought like Jane. Have decided like Jane. Jane must know.*

Okay. Confusion melted along my bones, feeling like the

aftereffect of magic, or maybe like worry. Just how much was Beast hiding from me?

Before hunger times, were many light-beings, Beast thought. *Before white man dumped his waste into rivers and creeks, were many. Before white man cut and killed forest, were many. Before white man stopped rivers and creeks and made lakes, were many. Light-creatures lived in waterfalls, in fast streams that raced over rocks. Most humans did not see, but shamans and magic users could see. Big-cats could see. Pack hunters could see. Deer, fox, bison could see. Light-beings lived in water, played in water. Did not hurt Beast. Beast did not hurt them.*

Softly I said, "When the white man came, he brought changes and disease and death to the people and the landscape and the environment. Everything the white man touched was ruined or damaged or killed or wiped off the face of the Earth. And that included the magical beings, the beings of mythology that died or went into hiding. Beings that used to share the Earth were destroyed and vanished into the oral tradition."

When Beast didn't answer, I finished dressing and headed back to my clothes and the car. Beast had wandered for a while, and I was well chewed by mosquitoes and had splinters and thorns in my feet when I finally spotted the clothes and, just beyond them, the SUV Leo had loaned me. Beast, paying attention to me for the first time since she revealed the light-being memory, thought my sore feet were sad. *Should have paws and claws and killing teeth,* she thought. *Jane is stupid kit.*

Hunting in the brushy, marshy, swampy land west of the Mississippi was easier now that I knew the terrain and knew where I could leave my vehicle without the locals wondering what was up. Some of the back roads in Louisiana, especially this far south, were little used, not much more than sinking tracks in the wet ground. Others were already underwater by as much as two feet. According to reports by the Army Corps of Engineers and any other government agency that cared to comment, South Louisiana was sinking fast, thanks to man changing how the rivers flowed, keeping their waters in place behind levees. With rising sea levels, most of the coastal regions would be underwater in a century, unless something drastic changed. Which wasn't likely.

As usual, my vehicle had remained safe overnight, except for the fact that it was now mired down in the mud. Fortunately, the armored vehicle came with a heavy-duty winch, which I knew how to use. However, I was covered in mud and irritated beyond measure, both of which Beast found highly amusing, by the time I had the SUV free.

Mad at the world, not knowing what to do with what I knew, I stopped at a mom-and-pop grocery and glared down the aging couple's stares at my filthy condition, as I bought most of the breakfast sandwiches they had made. I ate all ten egg-and–Andouille sausage rolls on the way home. Traffic was light. One good thing out of the morning.

I was home, stripped, cleaned up, and in bed, flopping onto the mattress in a boneless heap. The smell of catnip was everywhere in the house, a thick, heavy scent that had both of my souls purring. Every breath a sensual indulgence, I slid into sleep.

I woke tangled in my own hair, my head pulled back and pinned beneath me, the bane of hair that had never been cut. I had forgotten to braid it before I plopped on the bed. Yanking on my scalp, I managed to roll over and out of bed and to the bedroom door, where Alex was knocking. I could tell it was him by the tentative taps and the stench wafting under the door. I double-checked to make sure I was dressed—and saw a pair of new sleep shorts and an old tee. I was sorta presentable. Sleeping in clothes had become mandatory since the guys moved in.

I twisted the knob and said, "What's up, Stinky?"

The Kid, standing there with three tablets in hand, lifted an arm and sniffed. Sounding guilty and defensive, he said, "I bathed."

"Day before yesterday, maybe." Eli and I were trying to teach the brilliant but late-blooming teenager to take regular showers. We had been doing pretty well until now. "No pizza this week. Now whaddaya want?"

"Two things. I got the video of the light-thing attacking your SUV, and the video of it and you guys fighting at fanghead HQ. Where do you want it to go?"

"Send it to my e-mail and to Soul at PsyLED." When he looked at me in shock, I said, "Soul knows stuff about them. I want her input." I'd rather have her input here, now, but I figured her arrival was going to be a waiting game. Meanwhile, I'd play bait and hook, offer a bit and tease with more to get her here sooner, whet her appetite. "What else?"

"The Otis people are certifying that the mechanical parts of the elevator itself are working perfectly, but because of the electrical surges and brownouts from the building's electrical system, which is misdirecting the cage, they've shut down the elevator until they can figure out what's going wrong. Eli said he's been down the shaft and he smells ozone and something burning on the lower levels, like wires and bad meat. He didn't go exploring where he shouldn't, but he wants security to check all the wiring in the basements, including the deepest subbasements where no one goes. His descent proved that there are five, by the way. But Leo said no."

"They woke him up to ask that? In the middle of his night? After he'd been bitten by a giant dragon? And he said no? Gee, wonder why?"

"You wake up snarky."

I raked my fingers across my scalp and through my hair, catching on snarls, which hurt. But it was marginally better than belting the Kid. "Tell Eli to get the security team to walk around the lower levels that are accessible to them. If they spot something, Derek can deal with it. And tell Eli to get home and get some sleep. We'll ask Leo about the subbasements tonight." I started to push the door closed but the Kid stuck his hand in the way. "What?"

"You got a text." He handed my cell through the crack in the door. "It's from Rick."

I froze, holding the official cell, the bullet-resistant one, with the titanium lid and Kevlar cover. I could feel the tiny devices the Kid had loaded into the fancy cover. Stuff I had never used. They were hard and rounded beneath my fingertips.

"I know it's none of my business, but Bruiser loves you," Alex said, sounding terrified but determined. "He sends you presents. He waited on you when you wouldn't let Rick go."

Cold, air-conditioned air hurt the back of my throat. My fingers closed on the cell phone. It was frigid, and I remembered dropping some of my clothes in a heap in the foyer, beside the air-conditioning vent, the cell on top.

"You *need* to let Rick go," Alex said, his voice a distant, muffled roar inside my skull. "I know broken hearts take time to heal and all that sh—crap, but you've waited long enough. You need to start living again. And stop being such a little *girl*." The door closed in my face and I stood there holding the cell. The cover was open, the blinking red light telling me that I had a text.

"There's nothing wrong with being a little girl," I said to the closed door. "Sometimes it keeps me safe. I know a lot of big macho men who'd still be alive if they'd been a little more like a little girl." That didn't seem like enough, so I shouted, "That was sexist!"

"Deal with it!" Alex shouted back.

Holding the cell as if it were a bomb—and maybe it was—I crossed to the bed and sat in the pile of tangled sheets. After a moment I activated the screen and opened the text. *Hey, darlin'. Checking in. I'm on sabbatical from PsyLED. Am in mountains in national park. Am okay. Will call you soon.*

On *sabbatical*. In the *mountains*, where his black wereleopard *mate* could hunt and roam in cat shape. Where he could do the same if she had managed to free him of the magic that kept him in human form, unable to shift into his were-cat. His *mate* . . . And he had called me *Darlin'*. Again. So much in that short text, and so little. And . . . why would Rick even think I'd care where he was? Rick had always been a player, too good-looking for his own good. A chick magnet. And he likely always would be. I considered my heart, my once-*broken* heart. And it was fine. Not broken anymore. How 'bout that?

Fingers cold, I deleted the text and closed the cell. Set it on the bedside table. I rolled back on the mattress and closed my eyes. Overhead I heard the shower start, Stinky/Kid/Alex taking a shower. He was growing up, and his advice, while unwelcome, was on target.

Sunset was only two hours away when I woke again. I lay on the bed, looking out through the cracks in the blinds, seeing a tourist couple walk by hand in hand. I got only fractured glimpses, but her head was on his shoulder. Their quiet laughter came through the window. They sounded happy.

A spike of jealousy shafted through me. I wasn't sure what happy felt like. I knew for sure I had never wandered through a tourist town with my head on a man's shoulder.

Tourists . . .

Not many tourists rambled this far away from Bourbon Street except during Mardi Gras and New Year's, when they roamed drunkenly all over the French Quarter. And the Garden District. And most of the rest of New Orleans. They relieved themselves on every street corner and passed out in every alleyway and threw up everywhere. They had sex on street corners and in bars and in bathrooms. Most of the locals made a point to be out of town during the holidays and I had heard it was often dirty and stinky and horrible, but I had never spent the holiday in town, despite some intense dream sequences that suggested otherwise. I had taken a vacation of sorts while Fat Tuesday took place this year; during New Year's—the next-biggest shindig—I'd been working a case, and through a case of depression. I lived in the party town of the nation and I'd never participated. Go figure.

And now I had Bruiser. And I didn't know what to do about him.

I rolled over, trapping my hair, again, and checked my cell. I had more text messages, including one from Derek. *Electrical system. Scorched places on walls on all accessible lower levels. Opened wall with hammer. Old copper wires shorting out. Have called in electrical service, owned by blood-servant family. Security will stay on them, same method, Otis people.*

I texted back a short reply and rolled out of bed—again—feeling stiff and sore, and spent half an hour stretching and pulling at muscles that felt tense and all wrong. Odd, considering that I'd been in my Beast form before dawn and that usually left me feeling smooth and toned and svelte, like a cat. It couldn't be from keeping vamp hours (up all night and sleeping all day) because that was Beast's natural state, and I'd lived that way for decades at a time. But it could be because I wasn't getting enough sleep, period. I wasn't Superwoman. I checked my sternum, and at least that part of me felt good.

I dressed for HQ, with more insight than I'd used the night before. I wore leggings, a tank over a jog bra, and a hoodie over that.

In the main room, I found the Kid bent over his tablets, hair straggling over his eyes, shoulders hunched, making a point not to look up at me. "Hey, Kid," I said, trying for offhand and casual. "You smell better. And thanks for the boyfriend pep talk. Skip what I said about no pizza; I'm sending out for Mona's. You want something?"

Mona Lisa's on Royal Street was, arguably, the best Italian place in the Quarter. And they delivered. Alex relaxed his shoulders. "Deep-dish meat lover's?" he asked.

"Sounds good." I called it in and added the eggplant parmesan for Eli. He was a meat lover, but not one of high-fat, pork-based foods.

When I got off the phone, Alex, said, "Check the door, wouldja? Someone knocked a few minutes ago, but I haven't had time to see what it was. Delivery of some kind."

I opened the door to find a box with a USPS mailing label. I bent to pick it up and stopped, my hands just above the cardboard. The scent was wrong. All wrong. *Wrong!* I stood and backed slowly away, easing the door closed. "Kid, call nine-one-one. Tell them we have a possible bomb on the front porch. And get your brother here. Now!"

The NOPD Bomb Squad, the FBI, the ATF, and a few other initial-agencies took over my house, my yard, and my life. They had insisted the entire street evacuate, but I had refused to go. No way was I going to leave my home with a bunch of cops in it. Not with all the toys in the hidden room. I hadn't checked it lately, but I had a feeling that Eli had begun keeping bigger and better weapons in there, weapons that the ATF might have been unhappy for us civilians to have. Somebody had to guard the place. The Younger brothers were human and a bomb would kill them, so they had to go; I wasn't and didn't, not that the cops knew that. The token firefighter in boots and heavy gear looked over at me, measuring the level of what he thought was my stupidity. Okay. Maybe I couldn't survive a bomb blast. I wasn't leaving until I had to.

I sat, alone, at the back of the living room, Bruiser's huge bouquet in my line of sight, watching the activity in the front part of the house, eating a stick of Eli's beef jerky, which reeked of spices I usually didn't ingest, and drinking iced tea. Fingering the business card given to me by the officer in charge. Wanting to rip it into small pieces, except I might need the contact info later on. I was mad, and, well, mad.

The firefighter glanced at me again, and I saluted him with the stick of jerky, ripped off another bite, smiling, or maybe snarling, from the way he reacted. I chewed and swallowed and ate another chomp.

The Kid had called me several times, explaining that the pizza delivery had been rerouted and was delicious, and updating me on law enforcement's progress. Not that he was supposed to know. He had hacked their communication systems, which (according to him) had only basic, elementary firewalls and protection. He was in heaven; his brother was torn between the need for intel and the need to keep Alex out of jail;

I was ticked off that someone had sent me a bomb. A bomb. *Really?* Couldn't they do something inventive? Something creative? Like an attack by mutant blood-sucking mosquitoes, a rogue-vamp attack, or even a drone attack? One with a bomb in its fuselage. No. They had to send me a *letter bomb*. A *package bomb*. I was too busy for this crap.

My cell rang again. "Yeah?"

"A robotic bomb detection and defusing device is rolling down your street," Alex said, his inner geek turned up to max. "Can you see it?"

"Not from here. They won't let me near the front of my house." But the padded fireman was nowhere in sight at the moment. "Hold on," I whispered into the cell. I raced to the kitchen window and looked out. Streetlights meant I could see about fifty feet to either side in both directions. The street was lined with marked and unmarked cop vans, cop cars, fire trucks, and sundry emergency vehicles with flashing lights. There wasn't a single POV—personally owned vehicle—anywhere. Placing my face to the window glass, I could see farther down the block where news vans were blocking the street both ways, and overhead I could hear the steady *thump-thump-thump* of a helicopter. From the far left, in the middle of the street, something moved.

The robot could have been designed by Caterpillar Inc. in miniature, a long, lean, low, bright orange body with tanklike track wheels. It had a single long arm mounted on the deck, with four tweezer-type fingers on the end, and a tall, slender black box mounted higher, housing a camera and the remote controls and a mini flashlight. The robot was maybe three feet long and a little more than a foot wide, and looked like something a kid would love to get for Christmas. "Cooool," I whispered, drawing out the word.

"Ma'am. You said you'd stay—" I jolted, guilty, and whirled on the firefighter who had managed to get back in the living room without me seeing him, smelling him, or hearing him. He heaved a disgusted breath. "Never mind. You have to leave now."

I said, "Are *you* leaving?"

He made this gesture that probably involved his whole body under the firefighting gear, and though I saw only his hands and shoulders, I could tell he was annoyed. "Yes, ma'am. I'm heading out that side door"—he pointed to my kitchen door — "with you, walking on your own feet, or tossed over my shoulder, however you want it."

I narrowed my eyes at him, daring him to try, and then heard Eli over the cell. "Jane, you're acting like a civilian. Get out and let them do their job." *Civilian* was an insult from Eli. I frowned, closed the cell, and walked to the side door and out into the backyard. The padded firefighter followed, leaving the door open behind us as he went out the narrow side drive to the street. Open door . . . to help equalize the pressure should the bomb blow? I took a last look at my house. Replacing windows was getting expensive. I hoped that was all I would need to do before the night was over.

CHAPTER 10

HOT Spelled Out Across His Rump

No one was looking at the back of the house, so I half climbed, half jumped the brick fence to Katie's. I could hear the sounds of hammers, electric skill saws, and other noisy equipment from nearby, and tracked the sounds to the house near Katie's. Renovation had started in the old building, and the back attic window was cracked open. The smell of sawdust and old plaster filtered out into the night. Hoping that the new owners knew about Katie and wouldn't later cry foul about living or having a business next to hers, I went on to the back door and waved at the security camera.

Katie's Ladies was the oldest continuously operating whorehouse in New Orleans, catering to both humans and vamps. The owner was Leo's heir, was scary powerful, and wasn't totally sane—even as far as sane vampires went. Katie was also my former landlady, before I was given the deed to the house. And if I was honest, Katie didn't like me much.

When Troll let me in, I joined the Youngers. The guys were at the big bar in the huge kitchen, watching raw footage from different vantage points, on several screens, as the robot approached the box on my front porch. I smelled food and tea and coffee and liquor and perfume. Way too much perfume.

"Civilian?" I demanded, as I took one of the tall stools and stuffed a nigiri sushi into my mouth.

Eli gave a one-tenths smile, more a twitch than an indication of amusement as Deon, Katie's chef, placed a Coke in my hand. "Eat. You bein' starved, Tartlet, in that house with all that military eatin'," he said, in his lovely island accent. Eli's smile widened at the nickname. I pretended to not see it and ate another sushi piece, a ball of rice with a strip of raw salmon on top. Deep inside, Beast chuffed happily at the raw meat. It wasn't Mona Lisa's pizza—the box was, not surprisingly, empty—but it was totally delicious in its own raw-meat way.

The slight, dark-skinned chef shoved a full plate at me and batted his eyes. Deon was wearing mascara and some kind of glitter eyeliner. His hair was swept back and around in an Elvis Presley swirl, with little pink bows at the sides that matched his skintight pink tee. "What are you all gussied up for, Deon?" I asked. "You been taking lessons from HBO reruns of *True Blood*?"

"Lafayette Reynolds is my idol, Tartlet. He be frisky and outrageous. Like me."

I shook my head and ate another sushi piece as he answered my original question. "These lovely tasteful pants is in case some reporter-man want a 'hot man on the street' interview after your house blow up." He pranced away, showing off his glitter shorts with the word HOT spelled out across his rump. Matching pink sneakers did a dance move, accompanied by a come-hither gesture directed at Eli.

The former Ranger backed almost into the next room. Fast.

I burst out laughing. Deon was more flamboyant than a Bourbon Street cross-dressing stripper, and no way was the local news going to interview him for their Bible Belt viewers. Most of the citizens liked to pretend that the steamy side of the city, with its strip clubs, nudie bars, and cross-dressing musical revues, didn't exist. As Deon would say, *Au contraire, sweetie*. Deon's outrageous antics and excellent hors d'oeuvres were perfect for Katie's Ladies. Some of the city's most upright, Bible-thumping leaders and media moguls were regular customers here, and, in private, many of them thought the three-star chef and, um, *entertainer*, was delightful.

Eli, not so much. I wasn't sure whether Deon really had the hots for my partner, or just liked yanking his chain. Maybe both. Eli wasn't generally homophobic, but the recent zealous attention had made him a little gun-shy.

"Civilian," I muttered the insult to Eli. "Big man can't take a little honest adoration?"

Eli shook it off and retook his stool, to focus on the screens. Deon turned his attention to making more sushi as some of the girls came down from their rooms upstairs to see what was going on. The set of Eli's shoulders relaxed as scantily clad females joined the mix, and the scents of lotions, perfumes, hair products, and sex pheromones filled the room. By their scents, I recognized Christie, Ipsita, and Tia, who started to drape herself all over Alex until I cleared my throat. She halted mid-drape and sat instead on a stool, arranging her body over the bar in a languid pose. Alex gave me a nasty glare, which I also pretended not to see.

We had some rules in our little family group. One was no cussing. The other was no hookers, no matter how refined and smart and expensive, until Alex was of legal age, cleared of his legal troubles, and could afford their rates. At that point, any ensuing diseases and emotional and legal fallout were the responsibility of the Kid. Until then, the girls were off-limits.

On the central screen, the robot was nearly at the porch, casting long and tangled shadows from the lighting set up by the emergency workers. Some helpful bomb squad member had placed a six-foot-long ramp from the street to the porch, and the robot made a ninety-degree turn, rolling up to the bomb box. I shifted my attention to the screen whose footage originated from on top of the robot. The black-and-white picture showed the box clearly, an ordinary cardboard box, totally taped up. Innocuous looking to the eye. I'd have picked it up and carried it inside except for the smell of things that shouldn't have been there. Though ordinary humans wouldn't have detected it, C4 plastic explosives had a faint but peculiar scent, one that stayed in Beast's memory.

On one side of his body, the robot carried a miniature X-ray camera and the footage went all shaky as the handler turned the robot, vibrating the top-mounted camera. Moments later digital images appeared on a different screen. Eli sighed, a faint breath of sound, but even without it, I knew it was bad. Eli launched into instructor mode. "C4 is composed of explosives, chemicals used as a plastic binder, a plasticizer, and usually an odorizing taggant to help detect the explosive and identify its source, chemicals such as DMDNB." I didn't ask what that was and fortunately Eli saw no reason to educate us. "The explosive in C4 is RDX, also known by the boom jockeys as cyclonite or cyclotrimethylene trinitramine."

I thought a moment and then let my mouth relax into a

smile. Boom jockeys. People who rode the boom of an explosion. "Funny, funny man," I muttered.

"It looks like you might have four ounces in there, which is enough to do a lot of damage to your house all by itself if you'd brought it inside before it detonated, but the big package of nails inside is the real bad news."

I felt cold all over. If the bomb had gone off inside, everyone within projectile range would have been injured. Maimed, scarred, possibly dead.

Eli leaned forward, pointed at a shadow on the screen, and added, "That might be a cell phone. If so, then a cell call to the device would be the trigger mechanism." He pointed to another shadow. "However, this might be tied to a detonator . . . here"—he moved his finger higher—"to go off if you ripped the tape and opened it."

"Wait a minute. Someone sent a bomb to Jane?" Christie asked, finally waking up enough to understand what was going on. There was near reverence in her voice, as if getting a bomb delivered was cool or something. In her world, maybe it was.

Today, Christie was decked out in yoga pants and a near-transparent tank top. No bra, but spiked matching nipple rings that looked downright painful. She wore her usual metal-studded dog collar, one only a vampire dominatrix would have worn. In the human BDSM community, a dog collar was usually worn by submissives, but in the vamp BDSM community, the dominatrix wore one. Because when a vamp tried to drink her down, it hurt. A lot. Ditto for the nipple rings. There were tiny little barbs on the ends, turned so they wouldn't hurt her but would hurt anyone getting too close. Part of me felt, *Ewww*. A second part of me just thought people were weird. And yet a third part was horrified that I had learned so much about stuff like this—and that it didn't bother me that I had.

Christie had one foot up tight against her butt on the stool and the other out to her side and up on the bar in what looked like a stretch capable of ripping the average person's pelvis apart. "A bomb! That is so cool!" she said.

"It's not something to be proud of," I said mildly.

"It means that somebody thinks you're important enough to try to commit a federal crime over," she said. She had a point. And that should bother me. A lot.

"What's it doing now?" the Kid asked his brother.

"It's looking to see if there's a third trigger beneath the box. So far, so good."

This looked like a long, drawn-out procedure, so I opened my phone when it buzzed, saw the name, and tapped the Kid's shoulder. "Trace this." I showed him the Darth Vader happy face on the screen. It was Reach's icon, and Reach—the best-known research guy in the paranormal hunting business—had proven to be an inconstant ally, and a sometime enemy.

The Kid nodded, shushed the girl's conversation, removed one screen from among the pile, and started tracing the call. He nodded for me to go. I hit the call button and said, "Hey, frenemy. You gonna tell me something good today or stab me in the back?"

"Just a word of warning."

I wasn't sure the croak was Reach's voice and trepidation cascaded through me. I put him on speaker and asked, "Reach?"

His breathy laugh sounded like something broken. "Yeah. What's left of me. They found me. And they took me out."

Eli stepped to the side where he could watch the screens and me too. One hand had already found his weapon.

"Who took you out?" I asked.

"A human. Might have been a woman. Tall. Spoke English like a foreigner, talking with whispery, sliding sounds. Accompanied by two vamps, male and female. The male never spoke. The female vamp had a Middle Eastern accent. The human and the vamps were tattooed with wristbands of falcons. Or hawks. Raptors, anyway. Don't know."

Vamps did not tattoo themselves very often, which made these vamps unusual, and therefore interesting. The Reach I knew would have found out any unknown info before his attacker got out the door good. Now, not only did he not know the gender of an attacker (which seemed impossible), he also didn't know what kind of bird was in a tattoo. This was not the Reach I knew. The sense of dread deepened, making my palms ache. "How bad are you hurt?" I asked, my throat tight.

He gave that broken, breathy laugh again. "Well, I won't type two-handed ever again."

"Reach," I whispered.

"Don't," he said. "Save it for yourself. They were here for information about Leo, but they also were looking for you. Not just where you lived. They had that." I turned and looked at the video screens. Reach's torturers knew where I lived? "They wanted *everything*," he said. "And I gave them everything I had. Not that it did me any good. They left me in pieces anyway. This was a week ago. I couldn't call until now. The lead vamp made sure of that. He's coming for you, for the icons you have. The something Leo has, or might have. But more important, he wants someone he called . . . I don't know. It sounded something like *E-sen-do Lucy*. I don't know who it is, but they want her—or him—bad. Be careful, Jane. Make sure your family is safe." The call disconnected.

The Kid said, "Got him. He's moving west. Right here." The Kid showed us a map, and Reach was at the bottom of one of the Great Lakes, the one that looks like Florida, or a body part—and not a mitten. "GPS puts him coming into Chicago, could be a train."

A moment later, Alex said, "There are train tracks at his location . . ." His voice trailed away, his fingers flying over the tablet.

Moments passed, and I studied the tablet screens with the robot on them. Nothing was happening. A lot of hurry up and wait as the night shadows lengthened.

"Yeah. He's on a train," the Kid said, "or his cell is. Train route originated in Boston, but made multiple stops on the way. No Amtrak ticket in the name of Reach, first or last. Chicago is the biggest passenger train hub in the country, and if he stays on an Amtrak route, he can go in one of nine general directions. If he gets a car, he can go anywhere." Moments later Alex said, "GPS stopped. Cell has been turned off."

"Assume he dumped the phone," Eli said.

"He can't type two-handed," I said, my voice numb. "And they left him in pieces." It sounded selfish to speak of myself in the midst of someone else's pain, but I added, "And someone's had my info for a week. Bomb. Tail cars. Someone's after me."

Eli set a hand on my shoulder, took the cell phone away, and guided me back to my stool. Deon put a mug of hot tea in front of me. I took it up, holding the cup in icy fingers. Reach had been with me for years. Never in person, but always there with info when I needed it. Yeah, he'd turned on me a time or two, but Reach had never been reticent about admitting that he sold his services to the highest bidder. This time the price had come from him.

"Drink up, Tartlet," Deon said gently. "I put a little tequila in yo' cup." He placed a blanket around my shoulders, and when I didn't drink, he cupped his hands around mine and lifted the mug to my mouth. I drank—it was that or drown in tea.

It burned all the way down and I coughed, pushing him away. "Holy moly. A *little* tequila?" I spluttered and the burning continued all the way down to my toes.

"Drink or I be making sure you regret it."

I sipped and withstood the pain as the alcohol scorched through my gut.

"I'm changing all the passwords into the security system here, at home, and at vamp HQ, and looking for any sign they've been compromised," Alex said. "But you'd better call Molly and Evan and tell them about the threat. And anyone else you know." He looked up under his too-long, spiraled-kinky hair. "Maybe that Christian school you grew up in. The security firm you interned in. And"—his mouth twisted in distaste at what he was about to say—"Rick needs to know too."

The dread spread through me like a virus, eating away at my viscera. "We need to know who we're fighting and why and what resources he has. Find out who that person is, the Lucy person, or what the words mean if it isn't a name." To Eli, I said, "I'll be calling Adelaide to initiate the next security protocol upgrade." Eli reacted with a slight tightening of his eyelids as he remembered the one I was talking about. "Work with her to tighten HQ security. I want it so tight no one can take a breath without being on camera somewhere. Privacy issues are currently of no importance whatsoever," I said. Eli nodded.

I dialed Evan Trueblood, Molly's husband, and got him on the first try. I explained about Reach and the danger. Evan was silent through the whole thing, then said, "I've got a place. Don't call us; we'll call you." The call ended. I dialed Aggie One Feather, the Cherokee elder who was guiding me into healing and recovery of my lost past. When I told her about the situation, her reply was short and stiff, as if my problems were nothing to worry over. I hoped she was right. Rather than call the children's home where I was raised, I dialed the number on the card of the ATF OIC—the Alcohol, Tobacco, and Firearms officer in charge—outside.

"Special Agent Stanley." He sounded calm, that remote and reserved calm of people who had high-stress jobs but kept all the reactions internalized. They either found a way to breathe through the stress—meditation or yoga or prayer or drug of choice—or they died early of heart attack, stroke, or eating their weapons.

"Stanley, we may have info about who put the bomb on the porch, or who hired it done. A friend of mine just called and told me he had been tor-"—I stopped, took a slow breath, and went on—"tortured for information about Leo Pellissier and about me. We don't have a name yet." I gave him the descriptions of the three who had hurt Reach. "My friend is a researcher so he had everything on Leo. And everything on me back to the first time I appeared in the world. Leo can take care of himself, but my people can't. If I give you a list of names, places, and addresses, can you send local law enforcement to each and check for problems?"

"Does your friend need protective custody?"

"Too late for that," I said, my chest hurting. I pressed a fist to my sternum, rubbing hard. "He's gone underground." *I hope.*

"Text the names and contact info to me."

"Yes. I will. And thank you."

"Part of my job, Miz Yellowrock." He disconnected.

I told Alex to text the OIC all pertinent contact info on my address book. We discussed who was to be included and then I dialed Del. She sounded cool and collected when she answered, but I was getting ready to ruin that. "Jane here. Get Derek and Wrassler. Tell them Protocol Aardvark. They'll know what to do. Eli will be joining you."

"Aardvark?"

"Yeah. It used to be Groundhog, but it got activated on Groundhog Day one year and— Never mind. Just tell them. I put the updated security protocol handbook in the primo's office in the file cabinet under *S* for security. Hard copy only. Initiate Aardvark immediately. Under Aardvark, everyone on security goes armed at all times."

Del made a soft harrumphing sound. "If this is a practical joke, I will not be amused."

"I know. It's not. There's a bomb at my house." Which sounded so weird just saying it. "It's probably on the local news."

"A bomb?" There was a moment of silence before Del said, "I'll make sure that all necessary protocols are instituted."

"Thanks. Meanwhile, are any vamps and followers known to wear bird tattoos?"

I could hear her tapping on a tablet or keyboard. "Blood-servants and followers of a vampire called Peregrinus," she said after only a moment. "Why?"

"A human wearing bird wristband tattoos and a female vamp tortured Reach to get my info. A male vamp watched."

"Dear God." The words came out as a gasp. "The Devil and Batildis are here." And then she added on the fragments of a breath, "Peregrinus." The last word was whispered, as if to speak the name aloud was to summon the vamp.

"Does this mean the EuroVamps are here early?"

"No. The Three have never followed the lead of the European Council. They are outlaws. And they are utterly and totally vile." The call ended. Del had sounded horrified. Or maybe terrified, if that was worse.

That was me, spreading good cheer everywhere I go. *The Devil, Batildis, and Peregrinus,* I thought. I'd heard the name Batildis recently. Leo had mentioned the name when talking to Grégoire. *"Your brother and your sister Batildis have begun to rally their supporters to this end. And yes, that might eventually mean the interest of Le Bâtard, though he is not scheduled to travel to these shores . . ."* I could guess that Le Bâtard was Grégoire's sire, his brother was Peregrinus, his sister was Batildis, and the Devil was their human blood-servant. How evil and twisted did you have to be to have the nickname of *the Devil* among vamps and blood-servants?

"Alex, followers of a vamp named Peregrinus wear bird jewelry. He and people named the Devil and Batildis are likely in town." I told him what I knew and guessed about the vamps, which wasn't much.

"On it. The Devil, Batildis, and Peregrinus. Gotta love vamp names and their flair for the dramatic," he grumbled. "Why can't they just be John Smith or Sally Jones?"

I dialed Bruiser and he answered, "I am delighted to hear you're in one piece, Jane."

Instantly I flushed and walked away from the group. "You know about the bomb?"

"I do. I was assured you're safe."

His tone was odd, like maybe I should have called him first. I wasn't sure. "Yeah. So far," I said. And decided to pretend that I hadn't maybe done something wrong by not calling him immediately, and concentrate on the important stuff taking place. "People who sound like the Devil, Batildis, and Peregrinus tortured Reach a week ago. Seven days." I was proud that my voice sounded calm and sane, though the words themselves were enough to send me screaming into the night. "He just called and told me. He gave me up. He gave up Leo and probably you and Katie and Grégoire. Everything in his database has to be considered compromised. I'm instituting Protocol Aardvark. Del, Wrassler, and Derek will bring in all the outlying vamps and servants, and get them settled at HQ. They're good at their jobs, but they aren't you."

"No, they aren't. I'm on the council house premises. I'll get with them. You should consider bringing your people to the council house until this is resolved. Satan's Three are dangerous, Jane, more so than any other ménage à trois in all of Mithrandom."

Satan's Three. Wow, the people after me even had a title. Moving to HQ sounded like a pretty good idea on the surface. Nothing short of a rocket launcher was getting inside the place now. Of course, anything that went in might have trouble getting out. Like me, if Leo actually got his talons on me in his lair. And there was that saying about putting all one's eggs in one basket. If we were all in one spot, then we'd be easy to find. "I'll think about it."

I could hear the smile in Bruiser's voice when he said, "We're short on space at the moment, and things will only get tighter with Aardvark in place. You might have to bunk in with someone."

Heat exploded through me, tightening things low in my belly. And suddenly I didn't feel so worried or dark. "Yeah?" *Oh. Pithy comeback, Jane.*

"Yes. Too few beds, too many warm bodies."

"That sounds . . . like a good idea. And fun," I said. Bruiser's breath hitched. "Tell Del we might be roomies. We can have a slumber party, make s'mores, do each other's nails." *Yeah. That was better.*

"You wound me." But I could hear the laughter in his voice, and thanked all that was holy that Eli had spent so much time teaching me to flirt when we first met. It was coming in handy.

"Later." Smiling what I knew was a silly smile, and keeping my back to the room, I disconnected and pulled Rick's number up on my cell. I had to warn him that someone was gunning for everyone who'd ever meant something to me. My smile died. Rick, who was no longer on speed dial. My onetime boyfriend.

I dialed the number. When he answered, it was with a simple, "Jane." Not Jane, darlin'. Not babe. Just Jane. Paka was standing right next to him. Or lying next to him. I knew it. I recited the problem, talking steadily, not fast enough that would suggest I was hurting, not slow enough for him to be able to interrupt.

When I was finished, he said, "Thank you. I'll be heading in-country. You won't be able to contact me. I'll check back with you in a few days for updates."

I said, "Good," and ended the call. And stared at the blue screen. "Really good." It was totally inadequate. And it was all I'd ever get. And I was fine. A slow smile softened my face. I really was okay.

"We got action," Eli said.

I tucked the oversized cell into a pocket and moved back to the sushi and the horrible tequila tea and the tablets. I tossed back two nigiri pieces and watched as a new robot, this one matte black, short, stubby, and sturdy, running on tracked wheels, replaced the more linear orange robot. The black robot was carrying two tan bags, one in each heavy-duty pincer-like hand. "What's that?" I asked.

"Sandbags," Eli said.

"Wait. They're gonna blow it up on my porch?"

"You want they should risk their lives carting it off to la-la land first?"

"But I just got a new front door!"

Eli laughed evilly. "Face it, babe, your insurance is going through the roof."

"Aw, man. No!" I put my hands to the top of my head, trying to think of a way to stop this. But short of running over, grabbing the bomb, and tossing it away, risking it exploding me into a pile of meat and puddles of blood, there wasn't anything I could do. "Nooo."

Eli laughed again. This time the Kid and Christie joined him.

The squat robot set both bags down carefully and went back for more. The bomb box wasn't that big, maybe a foot long, ten inches wide, and eight inches deep. Eight bags of sand and one heavy cloth blanket of some kind later, the stout little robot rolled away, leaving the bomb box covered. The street had been evacuated; this time even the experts were gone, undercover, as we watched on remote cameras.

Nothing happened as seconds turned into minutes. Then there was a *poof*. On the hijacked video screen, dust and sand flew. All I heard from my house was a muffled *whomp*. The bomb was detonated. On the screen, my front door shuddered. The glass in its window tinkled around the remains of the bomb. Broken. Again.

"Well, your door survived," Eli observed.

"Your window didn't," Alex said, snarky.

I swallowed the rest of the rocket-fueled tea and left the house, jogging back home.

Hours later, they hadn't let me see anything that had been left of the bomb. They hadn't let me see anything at all except my damaged front door and busted door window. I had made a stink about it, and still they wouldn't let me see. Dang bureaucrats. However, they hadn't questioned me much, my position attached to the Master of the City of New Orleans and the greater Southeast having protected me from anything in the way of legal harassment.

Conversely, it didn't protect me from media harassment. If anything, my position as Leo's Enforcer only made that worse. According to NBC and their repeated phone call messages, I was "newsworthy," whatever that meant. ABC made my house continuous "breaking news," and the local cable channel had camped outside my house for all the hours of the emergency. They were all still there now.

While the legal scientific types ran tests, hauled off the debris for examination, removed their equipment, and had a press conference in front of my broken door, I made calls and Eli took care of the house. He ordered a replacement door and window from the big-box-home-repair store, asking for the model number from memory, which was an indication of the level of violence in my life. He hammered a piece of plywood over the window opening and hammered the damaged door shut, which made the evening news.

Ten minutes after his toned body and stern face appeared on camera, a locally famous anchorwoman called him personally for an interview. He turned her down, but it was clear that she had called because she found him *interesting*, because she flirted with him the whole phone call. Not that Eli flirted back. He was madly in love with the sheriff of Natchez, Syl.

My time was much less profitable. No one I wanted to talk to called me back.

By the time most of the cops were gone and the news agencies had packed up their equipment, it was way after midnight. Alex hadn't located Reach. Bruiser hadn't called. Rick was gone. I had spent the evening at a whorehouse. The only good thing was that I had pigged out on sushi. Now I was expected to show up at vamp HQ and get cut up with a sword. My life was not normal.

CHAPTER 11

Testicle Stretchers

I had tried calling Leo about Reach and the three who had tortured the research specialist, but the MOC wasn't taking calls—or it might be more likely to say that he wasn't taking calls from me. He had surely been notified about Protocol Aardvark, and had his freedom restricted by its stringent demands, but the chief fanghead had signed off on the policy himself, so he had no one to blame but himself and me.

On the way in to HQ, where we had to list our weapons and go through a thorough pat-down, I remembered the "small gala" Leo had planned, the one about which he'd thrown a wine tantrum. I hoped he'd had to send out a couple dozen "change of plans" letters. It would serve the spoiled-brat-of-a-vamp right.

We took the fire stairs down to the gym, as the elevator had been turned off by the Otis people. I wondered how vamps liked taking the stairs—a plebeian occupation so far beneath them, or a delightful romp into the past? I made a note of the darkened stairs that wended on down, into levels I hadn't visited yet, at least not on purpose. One level below the gym, I saw a dynamic camera, the make and model I had installed in the council house, but I hadn't installed this one; nor was it part of the upgraded security system that Eli, Alex, and I had designed. Which meant that there was a second monitoring system somewhere based on my work too. This wasn't the first time Leo had gone around me on security. I made a mental note to ask when I was getting paid for my design. I also made a mental note that if I went skulking below stairs, I'd surely be caught on tape somewhere.

In the girls' locker room I was met by frowning female blood-servants, ones I hadn't encountered before but whose names I recognized on the personnel list as being *fonctionnaires des Duels Sang*. Which I now understood as blood-servants who served at blood-duels. They were older, actually gray-haired, which is not common for blood-servants, and had severe expressions and stocky builds. They looked like weight lifters, broad and muscular Titans. They were also crotchety, harsh, unyielding, and dressed in matching outfits that looked like catcher uniforms at a baseball game. And though they tried to hide it, they were horrified at my total ignorance of their purpose.

As if I were a rag doll, the women stripped me. I nearly decked them until I realized that they were playing the role of lady's maid or valet or squire. But it was a near thing. When I was down to the Lycra, they stuffed me into a pair of white knickers with built-in suspenders that they called braces. Socks that went to my thighs. Flat-soled shoes that were reinforced oddly, one shoe with extra padding in front and the other with the padding in back and were impossible to walk in without a slight duck waddle.

Over the stupid knickers and my T-shirt went a plastic chest protector. Think Roman gladiator chest protector, but of heavy-duty plastic with boob shapes. Over that went a white, long-sleeved shirt that sealed up the back, lightly padded with Dyneema, a new puncture-resistant material. It was reinforced with a heavier layer of plastic foam. I was informed that this was the Mithran blood-duel version of a plastron—the under-arm protector used in fencing. To which I nodded as if that meant something to me. It didn't. Titan One told me that in Olympic fencing, it would only cover the right side. Again I nodded, though that made no sense at all. *Half a shirt?*

All I knew was that the layers made fluid movement difficult. The shirt collar was a doubled length of Dyneema, secured with Velcro as a gorget. I looked like a too-tall, scrawny image of the Pillsbury Doughboy.

And then the two Titans held out another shirt with a strap at the bottom hem. They made me step through the strap and pulled the shirt up my body. The strap was a thong. Seriously. The female blood-servants dressing me called it a *croissard*, but it was a thong. It went on top of my knickers, attaching the front of the overshirt to the back. And the thong moved. Into the most uncomfortable places. I pulled at it, trying to find a comfortable spot for the thong, but there wasn't one until Titan Two loosened it. I was pretty sure she thought I was hilarious.

The gloves were made of Dyneema, covered with suede, and had rubberized grips. They, like the outfit, were specialized for *le Duel Sang*, gloves the European vamps insisted upon, as their duels tended to be much bloodier than historical duels or Olympic fencing. The gloves I liked, the rest, not so much. My only peace of mind came from the addition of a few surprises I tucked into my sleeves when the Titans weren't looking.

While one of the Titans braided my hair and tucked it up under my head shield, I studied myself in the mirror. I looked like an idiot. The Titans thought I looked great as they led me to the workout room.

If Eli laughed, I'd stab him.

In that garb I stood in the doorway of the workout room and glared, but no one laughed or even appeared to think I was dressed oddly. The crowd in the underground gym was bigger than normal, whether because everyone hoped to see a rainbow dragon again or they wanted to see me get sliced to ribbons while wearing a padded, thonged monkey suit, I didn't know.

Eli, similarly dressed, stepped to my side and muttered to me, "I've worn most every kind of military and paramilitary uniform currently in use anywhere. And not one has . . . um, testicle stretchers."

I snorted in reaction and relaxed enough that the scents in the room filled my head, clamoring for attention. Blood, vamps, humans, and from somewhere the smell of fresh baking bread. I closed my eyes and let the odors take me over for a moment, only a few heartbeats, but those seconds were enough, and the perfume of the room and the beings in it brought me to the edge of an odd tranquility. The room went quiet, as I stood there, the silence of expectancy and potential violence. My shoulders dropped and I took deep breaths of the wealth of scent patterns. I opened my eyes, feeling comfortable in my own skin for the first time since the bomb.

A form dressed in black from head to toe gestured for me to join him on the fighting floor, and I was able to move as if the thong wasn't cutting me in half. My instructor was slight, short, and graceful, his head hidden beneath a mask like mine, but his black garb was a much cooler color than my student whites. He looked good in the outfit, even the thong part, which had two straps that divided around an athletic cup of prodigious proportions. Mithrans must believe in hitting below the belt.

My partner might have been Gee DiMercy, but Gee had been bitten by the flying light-dragon, so I was betting on Grégoire, the best fighter the Americas boasted. Better than Gee DiMercy. Better than Leo. The best. Against me. And the weapons he held to his sides were not blunted practice weapons. They were sharp enough to make the air bleed.

They looked like a death threat in steel. Like *my* death. Beast glared out at him through my eyes, and I heard her snarl, *Steel claws. Claws in hand of predator. In hand of hunter-killer.*

I knew better than to let my reactions turn to fear. Vamps can smell fear. So I let Beast's emotions roll over into anger and insult. Loudly, I said, "I've had too little sleep, too little food, my house has been targeted by a bomber, and this thong is miserable. You really think that oversized pig sticker is gonna scare me?"

"No, little kitten. I think it will cut you and make you bleed if you do not learn quickly enough." *Yeah. Grégoire.* I wanted to ask him about his siblings, but not while he carried a sword. Later. I accepted my blunted practice weapons from Titan Two, who had followed me out onto the fighting floor. Maybe she was acting as my second now. Made sense. Eli usually had that job, but he was flat on his back on the mat beside me, put there by Wrassler. Wrassler was wearing practice blacks, with a sword at my partner's throat. I wished I had a camera. Titan Two put the shorter sword, the one with the notch in the blade, in my left hand and adjusted my grip on both weapons.

"That," Grégoire said, "and this"—he held up the longer weapon—"are flat swords." Next he indicated our short swords. Our *cajas cortas*, loosely translated as *short box* or *short trap*. "You will not see the like of such weapons in the human world. They are made for *le Duel Sang*. They are made for killing Mithrans."

Which meant I'd better get used to them. Killing Mithrans was how I made my money.

The mat where I had practiced last night was gone and the floor, damaged by my claws, had been sanded. Someone had taped a large fighting circle on the polished wood away from the scratched area. Grégoire stood inside the taped circle, waiting. Not impatiently. Calmly. But somehow there was a big evil grin about his whole stance, as if he was itching for the chance to hurt me. *Oh goody.*

"Let us see what you remember from your last session," he said, stepping out of the fighting circle. He pointed with his long sword. "Begin with your feet."

I placed my feet in the proper positions, straightened my back, bent my knees as if I were sitting on a tall stool, and held my weapons in the first form. With his sword tip, Grégoire lifted my long sword and moved it closer in front of my body, making my body angle sharper, bladed, so as to make a smaller target. His sword tapped my arm holding the short sword and altered the angle of my elbow.

"Better," he said. "La Destreza, the Mithran version, is fluid, flowing like water over rounded stones, liquid and graceful." He moved his sword in a full circle, from pointing at me to his left, across his body, up even with his head, down to his right, farther down, around again at knee level, up to his left again, and back to his starting point. If it had been a bare-handed move, it would have defended against two punches, a kick, and a third punch. His sword indicated that I should try.

As best I could, I mimicked his moves. "Again," he said. And then, "Again, right elbow not locked, but loose"—he demonstrated—"thusly." He watched me and said, "Better. Again. Faster."

From there, we moved into another movement. And I started to sweat.

Grégoire slapped my butt with the flat of his blade as I turned in the second movement, and at the same moment, as if he had three hands, Grégoire tossed his mask to the side. His golden hair flowed out, long and loose and glistening in the too-bright overhead lights. "Elbow out," he demanded, blue eyes dancing in what looked like delight. "Feet move thusly. No, no, no. *Thus*ly." A perpetually fifteen-year-old, utterly beautiful, sword master and sadist. "Yes, now faster. Turn and turn and sweep and cut and lunge and lunge and lunge . . ."

Until I was so tired I could barely lift my arms, even with Beast adding speed and strength to my human limbs. Finally, when my breath was fast and painful and loud in the room and the audience had dwindled at the lack of blood spilled, Grégoire yawned.

Bored.

Sleepy.

In the middle of his yawn I dropped the short sword and pulled the throwing knife in my sleeve. Flipped it at Grégoire. While it was still in the air, I spun another at him. And the third. With his sword he batted each away with a *ting-ting-ting*. And finished the yawn with a grin that let me see why this vampire was the best fighter in the entire U.S. He had been nothing like bored. The yawn was to tempt me, to lure me in. Grégoire was having *fun*. Vicious, venomous, nasty *fun*.

Inside me, Beast growled, the sound coming from my mouth. She rose in me fast, staring out at him. In a single heartbeat, the orbs of his eyes went scarlet, centered with wide, black pupils. He attacked. Lunging, lunging, lunging, his sword circling like the blades of a fan, razor-sharp, cutting at me. His fangs dropped down; his talons pierced through the fingertips of his gloves. He was totally vamped out. Lunging, cutting, lunging, his long sword a spinning blade of death.

I had only the long sword, the short sword still at my feet. I danced back from him fastfastfast, my blade circling through his, my feet finding balance only after my padded white uniform had three scarlet, bloody rents in them. I felt no pain, not yet. But the stink of my blood and anger filled the air. I growled again. And I lunged back. Again and again, faster, drawing on Beast's power and speed. Circling my blade, my dull club of a blade.

The words of my very first sensei came back to me. *"Everything is a weapon, Jane. Your fingers, your forehead, a pencil behind your ear, a paper clip. Everything can be used to defend and attack."*

I drew on Beast's power and let my body slide into the fluid motions of the Spanish Circle. As if I had all the time in the world, I reversed my motions, taking the second movement to a backhand, both of my hands finding the hilt. Whirling. I slammed the dull edge of the sword against Grégoire's shoulder with everything I had in me. Stepped back and lunged again, while he staggered. I swung the weapon like a baseball bat, letting the weight of the dull sword pull itself around. And smashed it against Grégoire's knee. The joint buckled. Up, over, I let the momentum of the non-weapon carry itself around and against his neck, deliberately above the gorget. I heard the thump of the weapon hitting and a snapping crack.

Grégoire's head knocked to the side at a sharp angle and he followed it, flying across the floor to the side and crumpling.

I stood over him, watching him on the floor, my breath heaving. "Like that?"

"Yes, my Enforcer." Leo's liquid tones came from behind me. "Exactly like that."

I had actually hurt Grégoire. Hadn't killed him, not with the battering of a dull blade. But I had broken *something*. Something important. With a terrible sinking feeling, I realized that I had, maybe, broken Grégoire's cervical spine with my practice blade. Beast's power drained out of me and out of my eyes, leaving me weak. I stepped back, away from the fighting circle, and tossed the head shield to the floor.

Leo had gathered him up, and now Grégoire's head was resting on Leo's lap, his golden hair spread over Leo's legs and across the wood floor. His limbs were unmoving and limp, his black shirt ripped open to reveal his pale chest. Grégoire was gasping like a human, his eyes filled with bloody tears, yet his eyes had bled back to human blue irises. Leo was bending over his friend, his black hair hanging down over Grégoire's golden blond, the strands mixing. Leo looked pale, his skin with a slightly bluish tinge, and I remembered that he had been bitten by the light-creature. Leo hadn't healed as quickly as Gee DiMercy. And Grégoire didn't appear to be healing at all.

I had wanted to prove something. I didn't like what I'd proven. The bruise on Grégoire's neck was spectacular, totally unlike any bruise I had ever seen on anyone, human or vamp. It was purple in the center, a long, narrow, deep purple indentation just below where the skull and neck came together, in the shape of my weapon's blunt edge. The bruise around it was swelling, spreading, blooming like a scarlet flower, the blood beneath his skin flooding like petals. Like a fuchsia flower beneath the white, white skin.

Soft words filled the air in the gym. I didn't understand a single one, but I knew Grégoire was cursing fluently under his breath, the syllables French-sounding, and Leo was whispering back in the same language. I heard a faint snicking sound and the Master of the City lifted his wrist, biting the flesh on the inside of his own lower arm. Blood rolled out and Leo placed the wound to Grégoire's lips, cradling his friend's head with his palm. Grégoire sealed his lips around the bite and sucked.

Bethany appeared with a small *pop* of air and settled to the floor with them. The priestess extended her fangs and bit into Grégoire's arm near the brachial artery. Her hair, as always, was knotted and twisted into locks, worked with hundreds of gold and stone beads, the mass pulled to the nape of her neck, hiding her ears, but showing the many hoops and studs that hung there. Bethany Salazar y Medina was African. Unlike most vamps, whose skin paled after long years without the sun, her flesh had remained blue black, her lips like storm clouds at night. Her sclera were brownish, her irises blacker than that dark, stormy night. As she sucked, she lifted her head to me and stared.

Bethany was crazy, and not in a fun, party-girl kinda way. Bethany was scary. I took a step back as her power began to rise and tingle across my skin like needles. She poured her magic into Grégoire, healing magic that the others didn't seem to feel, dancing on their skin, nearly as much as I did.

A small crowd had begun to gather, standing apart from me, except for Eli, and no one was looking at us. Eli murmured, "How badly are you hurt?" I turned from Bethany to him and then looked down, where his eyes rested on my bloody clothes.

"I don't know." I looked back to my opponent and Leo and the priestess. It occurred to me that she was around an awful lot lately. Or, rather, that she lived here and I was the one who was around a lot lately. I wondered who she was feeding off of to keep her relatively sane. I was pretty sure it used to be Bruiser. I shook my head to clear it of the effects of her magics, and took yet another step away. "How bad is Grégoire hurt?"

"He's undead. How bad can it be?"

I spluttered with laughter that I turned into a cough as Eli took my elbow and led me from the room, to a small windowless space just off the women's locker room. It was about ten by twelve, with two small sofas, two small chairs, and tiny tables covered with magazines. I had never been in it. Eli had been exploring, which was good. We needed to know this place much better than we now did. The room looked like a waiting area off a surgery suite, or off a courtroom, with dull brown and blue plaid stain-resistant furniture and industrial carpet. Eli quickly loosened his own white gear and then started helping me to remove mine.

I was hurt quite a bit worse than I had thought, with the skin sliced deeply into the muscle beneath, and the clotting blood sealing itself to the fabric over the wounds. There had been no pain until I saw gashes, and then they started throbbing, a steady, pounding misery. I sat down fast, onto the unyielding surface of the hard sofa. Eli slipped out of the room, and with him gone, I pushed on the cut along the bottom of my ribs. Lightning pain flashed along my nerves and the breath I took sounded like a string of *S*'s. Blood flooded out across my side and belly, under my ruined undershirt.

From the hallway, I heard Eli say to someone, "Ask him to come now." Closing the door softly behind him, Eli reentered, carrying a basket of rolled towels. He pressed one to the newly opened wound. Quietly, he asked, "Do you need to shift? Do you have time?"

"No. I don't want to do that again. Not here. Not ever. Not near—" I stopped.

"Not near fangheads. Especially not near Leo. Who wants to own you enough anyway, without making him more covetous of you."

My eyes found his face and I shuddered with a tiny laugh. He understood. Without my telling him, Eli understood. "Yeah. That."

"I've asked Edmund to help. Okay?"

I nodded. Edmund Hartley had healed me before, and the unassuming but powerful vamp had been good. And helpful. And hadn't tried to roll me with compulsion. I heard a knock and Edmund entered. He was five foot seven or eight, brown haired, hazel eyed, and he seemed kind, nonthreatening. Mild-mannered was a good term for him, until he turned up the vamp-o-meter.

He might look like a pushover, but Edmund was old and powerful. As he closed the door behind him, I could feel his power as he pulled it up and around himself, icy prickles, like spikes of frozen air. Yet, despite his dazzling magics, now lifting the hairs along the back of my neck, he'd lost blood-master status of Clan Laurent—a story I thought had a lot more going on than had been reported—to a vamp named Bettina and ended up as a slave to Leo for the next twenty years. When vamps lost, they lost big.

"I smell your blood. Again," he said. Eli stepped aside and Edmund knelt near me. He breathed in and held the scent of my blood the way a wine connoisseur might inhale the perfume of a really good vintage. When he exhaled he said, "I heard about the sparring match. No one mentioned that you had been injured as well."

"Isn't that just like the fangheads?"

Edmund smiled at the insult and leaned close to my side. I felt his cold breath against my skin. "Your clothing must come away," he said, sadly. "Fast or slow?"

"Do it."

Edmund didn't give me a chance to change my mind. He gripped the hem of my undershirt in both hands and yanked. It ripped up the middle and out of the wounds. I hissed with pain and said something I didn't usually. Eli chuckled and I speared him with a look just as Edmund put his mouth onto my side and his chill tongue slicked the blood away. Heat followed in its wake, heat that danced along my nerves and then dove deep inside as his tongue delved into the cut.

I closed my eyes and steeled my face to show nothing. Absolutely nothing. I worked to keep my breathing steady and slow, and managed to keep my heart rate slower than a speeding bullet. Maybe. For about half a minute. And then the heat ricocheted out of the slice and right to my core. I knew it was bad when Eli left the room. "Coward," I hissed to his retreating back. And then moaned as the healing energies bent my head back and arched up my spine. Healing and desire, two halves of vamp magic.

Edmund laughed gently against my flesh; the vibrations of his laughter rebounded through me, and his arms circled my waist, pulling me against his body. I felt another moan rising and swallowed it down. No way was I gonna moan again. Not. Gonna. Happen.

He could have had me right there, on the small couch in the small room. But Edmund was a gentleman. Either that or Leo's proscription against any vamp seducing me made him refrain. I was betting on the latter, and couldn't decide whether I should thank Leo or stake him when, much later, Edmund rose from the floor beside the couch and pulled a knitted afghan from somewhere and covered me with it.

"You are well."

I swallowed and said, "Thanks, Ed. And thanks for not, um, you know."

"I like my head where it is," he said, confirming my guess. "But the moment you no longer work for my master, I will come to you. If you are willing, then I will give you all the pleasure that I am able." He leaned in, close to my face. "And I am very, very able."

"Oh," I said, keeping my eyes closed like the fraidy-cat that I was. I waved a hand in what might have been agreement or might have been waving him away from me. "I'll keep that in mind. And, ummm . . . thanks." I dropped the hand over my face. "And, yeah. Thanks." The door opened and closed behind him. I smelled Eli and I said, "If you say anything, even one single word, I'll cut you and feed your lifeless body to the dogs."

"We don't have dogs." That didn't stop him from laughing, however, and somehow, the wordless laughter, low and mocking, was even worse than anything he might have said. Without looking at him, I gathered my torn clothes and the afghan and went to the ladies' locker room, where I rinsed off Edmund's healing-induced desire beneath a stream of cool water. And cursed the fact that New Orleans never had really cold water.

The meeting was held in the downstairs conference room, necessitating only a short walk through the corridors. I had put on a pair of slim pants, my thigh rig, and a short-sleeved, dark copper sweater I found in my locker, which looked pretty good against my lighter copper skin tone. Black slippers. With my slicked-back hair and red lipstick, I looked striking. Not beautiful—I'd never be beautiful—but striking I could do. Striking was easy for tall, slender women.

When I entered the room, the chatter, heard through the door, stopped instantly. I moved to my place, Eli to my left, this time, and looked around the room, searching faces. Leo, Gee, and Grégoire were all missing. My heart stuttered painfully. The rest of the gathered were seated and wore remarkable expressions: a third of them looked expectant; the others looked either furious or gloomy, or a combo of the two.

I pushed my rolling chair away and stayed standing, leaning forward to balance some of my weight on my balled fists, a little like Leo had stood not so long ago. My gold double chain swung forward, the gold nugget and the wired lion tooth focals catching the light as they swung. I looked at Wrassler. "Update on Leo, Gee, and Grégoire."

Wrassler leaned back in his chair and crossed his hands over his muscle-bound midsection. His face took an expression I didn't know how to read, and his body was too far away from me to read his pheromones. "You broke Grégoire's neck."

I didn't blink. I didn't move. I didn't even breathe. To my side, Eli still stood as well, and I could hear his breath tighten, but he didn't move either.

"He's never had his neck broken before," Wrassler said, "and he's unhappy."

I still didn't react.

"He's also impressed. He says, and I translate his quote, 'Our Jane fights well. She will not be killed in an Enforcer blood duel.'" Wrassler smiled, and now I could smell his satisfaction. "Word went out on Mithran social media that you brought down our best fighter. Now almost all the European Mithrans who had queued to fight you have backed down."

A little zing of surprise shot through me. "Vamps wanted to fight me?" I asked.

"Ernestine was keeping a list of interested parties—blood-servants, and Mithrans—to be allowed to challenge you when the Europeans arrived. Ten of our own swordsmen wanted to test themselves against you in nonlethal matches. Five of our expected guests in Blood Challenge. Only the European Enforcers' names remain on the list."

"Rais—" I stopped in time. Raisin was my nickname for her, but might be interpreted as lacking in respect. "Ernestine was keeping a list of people who wanted to fight me?"

"Ernestine keeps all the lists," Wrassler said. "And the pools."

I shook my head in confusion. Beside me Eli asked, "So how many of you lost money when Janie kicked Grégoire's butt just now?"

"About ninety percent of the people gathered here and about ninety-five percent of the city's blood-servants and Mithrans." There was a lot of satisfaction in Wrassler's tone.

Eli said, "I'm guessing you were one of the few who were betting on Jane."

Betting on me? Holy crap. These crazy people were betting on who would get hurt? A hot flush that had nothing to do with vamp healing went through me like a brush fire in a high wind. Trying to sound mild and not angry, I said, "How long before Grégoire's spine is a hundred percent?"

Wrassler shrugged, evaluated my expression, and apparently found something there he hadn't expected. He sat up in his chair and laced his fingers together on the large table. The springs in his chair squeaked. "Couple of days. Between them,

Leo and Bethany can heal most anything. And if they can't, then Katie can."

I never thought much about Katie and healing. She had special blood since she'd been buried in a coffin full of mixed vamp blood. "Huh." The sound was full of challenge. "And Leo? How long before he's fully back to himself after the bite by the light-dragon thing? Just asking because he looked a little pale tonight."

Wrassler, his tone now all business, sat straight and dropped his arms to the chair arms. The pheromones in the room changed too, all jocularity vanishing under the weight of my expression—whatever that was. "The priestess Sabina spent the last day with him," Wrassler said. "He was pretty close to ninety percent until he fed Grégoire."

"And Gee? He seemed fine on the gym floor beating my partner's butt. Is the Mercy Blade the *only* one in a position of authority who's up and at his best?"

"Gee's fine," Wrassler said shortly. Beside him, Derek sat straighter too, his face thoughtful. Across the table Adelaide Mooney shifted position as well.

"Del, are Leo and Grégoire up to speed on Satan's Three? That they may be in town?"

"Yes," she said simply. "They have not presented themselves to Leo, according to the Vampira Carta; therefore they are interlopers in his hunting territory," she said formally, as if handing down a sentence against a lawbreaker. "You have carte blanche in any dealings with them."

"Good. As part of Protocol Aardvark, I want Katie here on-site until Leo is fully recuperated. Once everyone is on-site, all travel is to be curtailed, and any travel that the vamps insist upon is to be by armored vehicle with standard three-vehicle precautions, a definite itinerary, and no deviation. And if you can distract them from travel, all the better." We all knew that *distract* meant blood or sex. It didn't have to be said. "Bethany is with Grégoire. I want blood-meals—the strongest blood we have in the city—for Leo and Grégoire until they're fully healed and a hundred and ten percent. And whatever they need to be made totally well. If that means dragging the clan blood-masters to help, then that's want I want to happen. I want this city's vamps at full power in two days, without giving up the protection of Protocol Aardvark. I also need a private audience with Grégoire. ASAP. You have an hour before dawn to see that my orders—the orders of the *Enforcer*," I corrected, "are carried out. Take whoever you need to get the people in place. Then get back in here."

"Yes, ma'am," Wrassler said, standing and motioning to three others at the table.

As they left the room, I went on. "The next person who wants to bet on me in a fight gets to fight me him- or herself. Personally." I looked around the room. "In case you didn't get it, a foreign creature got in to va—Mithran HQ and *bit Leo*. It messed with our minds and our memories. We have a parley with European Mithrans to plan for. The electrical system isn't working properly. The elevator's screwy. And we have some-one in town targeting me, who I think is a rogue EuroVamp named Peregrinus." That made them sit up and take notice. I could have added, *And there's something scary on the bottom basement level*. But I didn't say that, not until I asked some questions of the powers that be. There was a time for every-thing, and the thing in the basement wasn't for now. "Peregri-nus is Grégoire's brother and we don't have much data on him yet. I'll be talking to Grégoire and others in HQ and will up-date those who need to know as I obtain info.

"For the record, I screwed up when I hurt Grégoire. Not because it was wrong to do my best, not because I should have let him win to be *nice*, but because timing is everything and this is not the time. We have a lot of crap going down, and while I don't give a rat's fuzzy behind what you *bet on* in down-times, this is not that time."

Del said softly, "Betting is expected among the Europeans."

"Fine. When we get everything and everyone back into top shape, when the Europeans arrive on American soil, I'll re-scind my orders. Until then, I want you all to turn that excite-ment and energy to figuring out why we're having brownouts and why the elevator is wonky. And if you have enough energy left after that, I want you feeding the Mithrans. Got it?"

Heads nodded. To my side, Wrassler reentered and gave me a thumbs-up. "Grégoire will see you at any point before dawn this morning."

I nodded back, a tiny inclination of my head that would have done Eli proud. "Wrassler, update me on the European parley. What's new?"

"Our ambassadorial team has been negotiating under the direction of Grégoire and Adelaide Mooney." He paused, as if just realizing what it might mean to have Grégoire out of commission for even a day. And my own guilt, which I had done a good job of hiding, shot deeply into my core. I'd screwed up when I hurt Grégoire. Pride goeth before a fall and all that. *Crap.*

Wrassler said, "The agreements to this point are: Three European Mithrans will arrive, on a date yet to be determined, with twelve human blood-servants, three of them primos, and two aligned Onorios, for a total of seventeen guests. All will be housed here, in the council house. By then, Leo will be back in his clan home, which will be ready for a certificate of occupancy in about ten weeks." He looked at me and I did that little head tilt again.

He continued. "Grégoire asked me to tell Jane that he came into possession of certain historical papers pertaining to the witches and Mithrans in the Middle East, Europe, and the Americas, and the history of animosity between them." Which sounded like a direct quote from Grégoire. "He and Leo have agreed that Jane needs previously proscribed information to understand what she's dealing with in regard to issues with the witches' magical artifacts." Wrassler glanced down the table and pointed from one of Derek's men, to the corner where a metal box sat on the floor, and to me. "Grégoire wanted to give you the documents himself." Wrassler's lips twitched as he restrained a smile. "However, since he's indisposed, he asked me to present them."

One of Derek's men from Team Tequila, who went by the moniker Jolly Green Giant, stood and carried the metal box to me. With a heavy *thud*, he set it on the table in front of me, and I opened the lid. It was full of documents, some so old they were crumbling. I lifted one out only to see it was written in some kind of fancy old script, in a language I couldn't read. "Thanks. This means a lot." I pulled on the manners pounded into me by the housemothers in the children's home and said to Wrassler, "I'll, uh, convey my thanks to Grégoire for his generosity. And I'll take good care of the documents."

I sat down and Eli placed the box in an empty chair, then took the seat next to me. His timing suggested that he sat only after I did. That when I stood, he stood. That he was my, what? My right arm? Whatever the psychology of it, it worked. There was something different in the room tonight, and it had to do with what I was. Who I was. It gave me strength and authority I hadn't known or used before. It terrified me.

But I could run screaming into the day later. I dropped my shoulders, lifted my head, and sat easy in my chair as if I had it all under control. Liar me. "I want any and all info about the EuroVamps known as Peregrinus, Batildis, and a human known as the Devil. Anyone?"

CHAPTER 12

I Haven't Slept with You Yet

Del opened a pink file on the table in front of her. "Since you told me about the raptor tattoos, I've been refreshing myself on the Mithran named Peregrinus, and will begin with his sire, Le Bâtard.

"Le Bâtard is a third-generation Mithran, making him powerful and dangerous. He is on the European Council of Mithrans, and while he verbally adheres to the Vampira Carta, it is rumored that he still practices the worst of slavery, buying children and drinking from them. Until recently, most of his scions were younger than fifteen when they were turned."

I smelled the reaction of the people in the room. Le Bâtard already had enemies. Good.

Her voice pedantic, Adelaide continued. "Le Bâtard turned Peregrinus, Batildis, and our Grégoire, and while Grégoire walked away from his maker's cruelty, Peregrinus did not. It is said that he emulates his sire and still serves him. Le Bâtard seldom leaves France. Peregrinus and his sister—sister in the Mithran manner, being the children of a common sire, but partners and lovers—travel often, and are accompanied by the Devil, their primo blood-servant, and a swordswoman who has never been defeated in Blood Challenge. Wherever they travel, they leave in their wake a swath of death and destruction, and always a number of missing children." I frowned and so did lots of others at the table. "They have come to be known as Satan's Three. They have, purportedly, been looking for magical items for years, all over the world," Del said.

I looked up at that one as quick thoughts tumbled over in my mind. Now it all made sense. I had magical items in a bank vault, which Reach would have known. I had thought about moving in here, but maybe that wasn't such a good way to protect my client. If I was here, then all the attacks would be here. If I was out there, then Satan's Three would come to me first, thinking me the easier nut to crack.

Del said, "After recent events, it is no surprise that seekers of the magical would show up here, in the States."

I said, "We believe that Peregrinus and his cronies are here in Louisiana now, without Leo's leave. We also believe that it was the human blood-servant known as the Devil who kidnapped and tortured the world's best researcher on vamps while two vamps, a male and a female, looked on. Reach disconnected before I was able to get a description of the torturer, except it might have been female and it had birds tattooed on its arms. Her arms. Whatever." Electricity seemed to race through the room as the words penetrated and they realized the importance of it all.

"Our best guess is that while the Devil worked on Reach, he or she got everything in Reach's databases. That means my file, Leo's file, and probably the file on everyone here at HQ. Reach was nosy and I don't doubt that he had the security protocols, which is why Aardvark was only in hard copy. We've changed passwords and set up the one protocol that Reach couldn't have, but it may be a case of too little, too late. The Three want something that they think I have or that Leo has."

I continued. "Next item is the brownouts. We've had people all over checking the HQ wiring and making replacements. It's taking forever, because some of the wiring is decades old and not in use or hidden inside walls, which then have to be torn out and repaired. Frankly, we need all the wiring torn out and new wiring installed from top to bottom, but there's not enough time between now and the Europeans' arrival to do that, so we're stuck with making jury-rigged repairs while looking for the causative factor for the events.

"The Otis repair people and the electrical wiring company people have been in and out. They'll continue to be on the buddy system with our people. Let's make sure the workers are always—and I mean always—with someone from security. You need to take a bathroom break, you call for backup. The workers need a break, you get someone to go in with them.

Most of the repair people are related by blood-servant status, but any one of them could have hidden connections to one of the groups who hate nonhumans. No outsiders go alone at all, and if they have any kind of electronic devices on their person, they leave them in your hands when they go to restrooms. Understood?"

There were nods around the table, but I felt an itch between my shoulder blades. I had done deep background on all of these guys and gals. But it was very possible that I'd missed something. It only took one ticked-off human with a hand grenade or a pipe bomb.

"Del, our greatest concerns are rewiring security, food service, and emergency lighting, in that order."

Del nodded and made a note to herself.

"Okay, folks. Let's talk about the rainbow light-dragon. Leo called it a '*Grand danger. L'esprit lumière. L'arcenciel.*'" I stumbled over the French. "Anyone know what that is?" When no one volunteered, I said, "I'll be finding out. Meeting adjourned."

Wrassler led me to Grégoire's boudoir. That was the only thing I could call it. *Bedroom* was too plain; *suite* was too business-like; *quarters* was too military, though there were parts to all of those in the three small rooms. The woodwork at the ceiling was heavily carved, coated with gilt, and the walls had been painted in shades of blue that would complement the color of Grégoire's eyes. I knew that because there was a life-sized painting of Grégoire just inside the door, his eyes matching his velvet clothes, gold lace at his wrists.

The entrance was wide with cabinets on either side of the door. I could smell steel and lemon oil, baby oil, lacquer or varnish—something to coat wood—and leather. The scents were different from the smells a gun cabinet would have held. These cabinets held swords. Metal weapons. Probably lots of different blades. My hands itched to open the doors and sniff through them. Wrassler led me on inside.

To the left of the door was a tiny room with one whole wall dedicated to wines, most with dusty labels. There was a narrow bar with crystal decanters and crystal glasses for decanting and drinking wine. The rest of the room was taken up by a delicate sofa, a tiny table, and two small chairs, all looking like something a French king might have used. And maybe had.

To the right was a closed door and I knew better than to open it uninvited, but I guessed it was a closet and dressing room. Grégoire was a dandy and his closet probably took up the biggest room in the boudoir suite.

Directly ahead was the bedroom, most of it blocked by Wrassler's broad back. The room was like something out of a French castle. Silks and tapestries and rugs piled on top of rugs and art stacked several deep against the walls. In most of the artwork a female was front and center. Batildis. Batildis in velvets and silks and lace, posed in fields and libraries and fancy salons. And in others wearing nothing, posed on beds and horses and . . . with Grégoire.

This discussion was going to be harder than I had expected. He had been in love with Batildis. And if vamp emotions were anything to go on, he likely still was. Wrassler said something French that had my name in the middle, and Grégoire said something back. Wrassler nodded me to the chair by the bed and stepped out of the way, allowing me to see the rest of the room, which was filled with tables and chairs and knickknacks and art from centuries of living.

Grégoire, wearing a blue silk dressing gown, was on the huge wrought-iron bed. The frame was shaped with fleurs-de-lis at every angle, an ornate, exotic structure that made the iron look like lace. He was lying back against a stack of pillows, blue silk linens over him and beneath him. Curled up beside him, a happy smile on her face and a smear of blood on her throat, was Amy Lynn Brown, a new scion who had come from Asheville along with Adelaide Mooney. Amy was the kind of person who would disappear into a crowd in a heartbeat, nondescript, brown everything, and on the surface, mousy. But Amy was famous. Her blood brought scions back from the devoveo in record time. It was brilliant to have the injured vamps drink from her, and from the smile on her face she wasn't averse to helping out in any way required.

Grégoire was vamped out from feeding but as Wrassler moved toward the doorway, his fangs clicked up into the roof of his mouth and his eyes bled back into the famous blue irises. His skin was pink from the blood he had taken and he licked his lips. "Thank you, Amy," he said. "When I am more myself, I shall court you and shower you with gifts. You are a treasure to drink from, your blood like the finest wines of my home country."

Amy blushed, bobbed her head, and skedaddled. Grégoire didn't move, which was not a good thing; nor were the cold eyes he turned to me. His scent was flowery and soft, like the seashore and spring blossoms, but underneath it was a trace of frustration, like creosote in the sun. Grégoire looked like a fifteen-year-old human kid in the big bed, but the vamp had fought and debauched his way all through Europe for centuries. He was not a fanghead to take lightly or to treat as anything less than a dangerous predator.

"Um . . . are you still paralyzed?" I asked. *Great. Fantastic greeting, Jane.*

He let a silence build between us, as he scrutinized me, his face neither soft nor forgiving, his body unmoving and more dead than usual. "I can move my head," he said at last, and I flinched at the words. He slid across the pillow, mussing his long blond hair against the blue silk. "I am able to move my left foot and toes," he said, the covers wiggling in demonstration, but his gaze not wavering. "My left hand is also much improved." His fingers wiggled. "And other bodily functions have returned in full. But I am still paralyzed, yes."

"Sorry about that," I said. "I didn't intend to hurt you so bad."

"You were perhaps planning a love tap?"

"Ummm . . ."

"I know you are not human, Jane, but I was not aware of your speed, nor your strength. They are secrets worth hiding, and will be of use when you face the Europeans. And my kin," he finished, emphasizing the last three words.

"Yeah." I took a breath. "About your fam—"

"Sadly, you will face them alone," he interrupted, "if I am not well recovered. And even with your speed and trickery, you will not survive, not against Peregrinus and his Devil." I wasn't adept at reading Grégoire, but I thought I detected a bit of satisfaction in his tone at the thought of me dying. "It would have been better had you shared your secrets with Leo and with me, that you might be better trained and your gifts better utilized. You have kept a great weapon from us. Why?"

"I said I'm sorry."

"Remorseful enough to share your blood that I might heal the faster?" I didn't reply and Grégoire gave me a smile that contained stony gratification. "Sorrow is a wasted emotion when not supported with actions to repair the wrong. You did not answer my question. Why did you hide this when you know we face such a danger?"

I shrugged and sighed. "Would you believe me if I said I just discovered I could move so fast?" His expression said he wouldn't. "It's true. I was raised alone from the time I was five years old. I didn't have teachers. I don't know how to use all the abilities of my kind. I'm still learning. And while I knew I could move fast, I seem to be getting"—I lifted a shoulder— "faster." Which sounded woefully inadequate. Because, even if I knew all that another skinwalker could teach me, I'd still be floundering with the abilities that my Beast gave me. Couldn't share that. *Nope.*

"A singularity? You have never met another of your kind?"

I looked at the doorway. Wrassler had left us alone but the door was open. I stepped to the entry and closed the door. Grégoire's eyes were narrowed when I turned back, and he held a long, slender knife in his left fingers. I figured knives were never far from the vamp's hand, even a hand that only partly worked. "I'm not gonna hurt you," I said, sounding cross. "But I don't want this getting back to Leo."

Grégoire's pale blond eyebrows went up. "You think I would keep something from my master?"

"Only if it was necessary. And this is necessary." I sat on one of the small chairs, one made when humans were Grégoire's size, not my six feet in height. My knees rose high and I felt ridiculous, but the position made Grégoire pause, and he flipped the knife, holding it in such a way that he couldn't throw it in a single move. But he didn't put it away either. I smelled a fresh scent in the room, overriding the smell of vamp blood, slightly acrid, and I eyed the blade. *Poison? That was ducky.*

"Leo knows that Immanuel was killed and eaten by a black-magic user. The thing that posed as Leo's son and heir for decades was a skinwalker, like me. But he had gone off the deep end." At the confusion on Grégoire's face, I said, "He'd gone crazy. When skinwalkers get old they lose mental stability and do what Immanuel did. They eat humans. Immanuel is the only other skinwalker I've seen in"—I shrugged, not knowing how to finish this—"in ever."

"Leo knows this?"

"He knows some of it. He sent me the bones Immanuel collected. But he doesn't know everything. Like how fast I am.

Or how strong." *Or that I can now bend time. Yeah. Not that either*.

Grégoire took a breath he didn't need and blew it out in a sound that was all French, a *pah* of disgust. "Leo still grieves. Perhaps it is wise to let sleeping dogs lie, as you Americans say." He shifted his head on the pillow and smiled. "I moved my right big toe. I can feel the sheets."

"I'm glad," I said. "Because I have to ask about your Mithran family." Grégoire frowned, the expression looking hard and remote and *wrong* on his young face. I kept my eyes on the knife in his hand. I could shift and heal from most wounds, but a poisoned blade might have unexpected consequences. "Is there something here in the Council Chambers that Reach might have discovered? Something that Satan's Three might want?"

Grégoire's eyes shifted slightly before meeting mine. If I hadn't been living with Mr. Minimalist in all things emotional, I might have missed it. I'd have to remember to thank Eli. "What does Leo have that they might want?" I whispered.

"Should I speak of my master's secrets? Of the weapons that keep us safe?" he asked. "I have not forgotten that you once saved my life and my clan. For this, I will not kill you. I will think on what you seek to learn and the dark things hidden here."

I frowned, but I'd heard that tone in vamps' voices before. I was about to be kicked out. Before he could, I said, "Thank you for the box of papers."

Grégoire didn't reply. "If you will not feed me, you are dismissed. And tell the next blood-servant to enter." Grégoire turned his head, but he didn't let go of the knife he still held. I stood and left the boudoir, leaving the door open for Katie, who looked me over with cool disdain as she entered. Or rather, she looked me over the way she might something icky she found on the bottom of her shoe.

My attempts to see Leo were thwarted by Derek himself, standing in front of Leo's door. "Per the MOC. You can come back at dusk," the former marine said. "Not before." And from the look on his face, Derek was ready and willing to enforce the edict: it wasn't worth fighting for. So I headed out.

It was two hours after dawn when I finally made it back to my house, and in through the door on the back porch. The front was still sealed off with crime scene tape, and if I'd been someone not connected to the household of the Blood Master of the City, I'd be in a hotel. I needed to sleep, but my body was too wired, and my mind was too busy making lists of things I needed to do. Eli headed upstairs to repack his gobag and then to crash for an hour or two. Even Uncle Sam's finest needed to sleep sometime.

I was brewing a pot of tea when my cell rang with a familiar local number and I answered it with the name of my business, just in case it wasn't who I thought it might be. "Yellowrock Securities."

"Jodi here."

I smiled into the cell. "Long time, no see."

"Yeah, well, if you'd keep people from leaving bombs on your doorstep, you might get some social time."

"Ouch. Did you catch that?"

"I got dragged into the paperwork, liaison, and media side of things. Thanks in great part to the general knowledge at NOPD that I know you."

Jodi was the head of the woo-woo department, working to solve new and cold paranormal cases. She had been given the promotion as a way to punish her for knowing the wrong people, supernatural people, but it hadn't worked out quite the way her superiors expected. Instead of sitting forever in her basement cubicle, Jodi had been thrust into cases with the vamps and the three-initial law enforcement departments. The ATF, the DEA, the FBI, and the longer acronym, PsyLED, to name a few. Jodi was making waves in state and national law enforcement and rubbing elbows with the rich and fangy. She now had media power, enough that her superiors' intent to ruin her career had backfired. She was fast-tracking up toward a glass ceiling that the family of known witches had never made before, or at least not in Louisiana law enforcement.

"So what did they discover about my bomber?" I asked, hoping she'd share things most victims didn't have access to.

"He's had a long-running career. Like well over thirty years. His fingerprints were found through Interpol, on another bomb in Russia."

"Yeah, about that timeline. I may have an enemy or three in town. Some who were alive four hundred years ago," I said. "They go by the names of Peregrinus, Batildis, and the Devil. The vamps call them Satan's Three."

Jodi cursed softly under her breath.

"My feelings exactly. They have to be really bad to get such cute nicknames among vamps. Do some checking on them, would you? The vamps are children of a vamp named François Le Bâtard. You may have something in your files that I don't. I'll show you mine if you'll show me yours. Ummm. Totally in a platonic way," I said.

"That rings a bell somewhere. Later." Jodi disconnected.

I ended the call on my end and took the metal box of ancient papers gifted to me by Grégoire to the kitchen table, and started a good strong black tea. When I had it steeping, I opened the box.

The scent of age wafted up from the papers, to mix with the bouquet of George's flowers. Pollen and catnip blended with the scents of old inks, old heavy-cloth paper, old flax paper, old vellum, and older papyrus, each in fancy manila folders, probably made of acid-free paper to protect the contents. I lifted out the topmost file and opened it, without touching the pages within. The writing on the loose pages inside was an ancient script with lots of flourishes and sweeps, like most vamp calligraphy, but more spidery and uncertain. I thought it might be Latin. Or an archaic version of one the Romance Languages. Spanish? Italian?

I heard a soft knock at the side door and knew it was Bruiser. Just knew. I set down the file. Swiveled in my seat and stared at the side door, into the shadows there. I walked to the door, my slippered feet silent on the wood floors.

I placed a hand on the door, not sure I wanted to open it. Not sure why I wouldn't open it—except fear. *Am not afraid,* Beast thought, rising up in my mind. *Want. Want mate.* I opened the door, letting in the heated morning light, and looked up into Bruiser's brown eyes, studying him. He studied me back, his expression both calm and captivating, a warm snare of possibility. Beast, and something else, something of myself, moved deep within me, questing. *Want this one,* Beast thought at me. *Strong, good mate.* She sent claws into my mind, just pinpricks, for now, and I held her back.

"What do you want?" I asked Bruiser, curious, not sure I wanted to know what he might say. "What do you really want?"

"You."

I felt my flush, felt my heart race, out of control. Knew he could sense those things now that he was Onorio.

"Eventually," he added. "When you're ready."

Beast sank her claws deeper, kneading my heart this time, a measured, pricking, painful pad . . . pad . . . pad. She purred deep inside me, peering through my eyes. I could see the golden reflection of her in his.

He didn't comment on my eyes, on the proof that I wasn't human. But then, he had been a blood-servant and primo of a master vamp for decades. He hadn't been truly human for a long while, so proof of my lack of humanity might not bother him at all. I took a breath that hurt as my ribs moved, recently healed flesh tingling, that sharp pain blending with Beast's claws, pressing in on me. I remembered the feel of the scale of the light-dragon, and the magic that it left prickling on my flesh. "You keep saying that."

"Yes. I do." He gave a small smile. Stepped inside the door without my asking him in, and closed the door behind himself. The kitchen was shadowed and still. Intimate. Slowly, Bruiser lifted his right hand and cupped my face, his flesh warmer than human. Fevered. I tilted my head into his palm, not sure. Not sure of anything. So *very* not sure.

Am not afraid, Beast thought. *Want. Want this one. Want mate.* She pushed back at me, fighting my control. My breath quickened as I/we stared into Bruiser's eyes.

He tilted my head back, his gaze holding me. Odd, that angle up to see a taller man. Brown eyes with yellow streaks in them, pale amber, brightened by Beast's glow, heated, like banked fires. He stepped closer. His mouth came down to mine. A bare brush of lips. The heated taste of Onorio, as if he might burn me. His breath a warm wisp. Another graze of lips. Slow. My eyes closed. The tension I hadn't noted fell away. His lips sealed over mine. And I sighed into his mouth. Liquid warmth, like melting chocolate and heavy cream, swirled and merged deep inside me, spreading through me and out, to slide along my skin, a sweet burning.

Want, Beast thought. *Want this. This mate.* I breathed in, and Bruiser's scent was searing and honeyed, like caramelized sugar, scorching in the pan. *Want,* she purred, the sensation like velvet sliding through me, shredding the endings of nerves in my palms and breasts and puddling between my thighs.

But you wanted Rick. And he failed us, I thought at Beast. The old hurt rose up, and I saw again his face, suffused with desire and magic as he walked away from us and toward Paka.

I no longer wanted Rick. I didn't. But the pain was still raw.

Mine. Now! Beast thought. But I was caught between two needs, protection and desire.

Bruiser's hand soothed my cheek, down along my neck, and cupped my head, tilting my face farther upward. His other arm slipped around me, drawing me close. Moving slowly, as if I might leap away, like a wild animal, caught delicately in his hands. His body like a furnace, like an oaken fire in the midst of winter, melded to mine.

This not Rick. This is mate. Beast struggled, wanting free. Pain raced along my nerves and through my fingertips as her claws threatened to pierce my flesh.

I raised my hands and placed my palms on his upper arms, feeling the corded muscle hidden beneath the inhumanly warm flesh. I tightened my fingers over his arms, careful of the pain in my fingertips. Not pulling him closer. But not pushing him away either. His lips brushed warmth through me and I closed my eyes, scenting, tasting, feeling, knowing. Heat spread out from the center of me, bright and painful and needing.

Jane wants. Jane wants mate. Jane is foolish kit not to take. Stupid, Beast hissed.

His arms tightened, pulling me closer. One hand slid low and cupped me in, toward the center of him. His tongue brushed against my teeth and my breath hitched, feeling-seeing-tasting the thought of Bruiser and me in my bed. Beast swiped claws of desire through me. Heat billowed up from the center of me to throb, low in my belly. Electric pulses thrummed through me, burning with need. And yet I held back, seeing, hearing all those unanswered questions between us. All that depth of the unknown. I didn't want to take a man to my bed again without honesty between us. Yet, my arm slid up, one hand cupping his head, the other riding low, one thumb on the edge of the waistband of his slacks.

At that thought, Beast paused. *Bruiser would know the I/we of Beast,* she murmured.

As if he sensed both my need and my pliant uncertainty, Bruiser's lips curled up and he chuckled into my mouth, his laughter a rumble of delight, a vibration that met and merged with Beast's laughing purr. Settled low in me, throbbing.

Bruiser would take the I/we of Beast as mate. Want this. Like hunting, slow stalk and wait in sun for perfect prey.

Bruiser pulled away, ending the kiss slowly, his lips clinging and withdrawing all at once. I opened my eyes to see his, watching me. So close. The heat of his kiss made my knees weak. I wanted more. I *wanted*. And he knew it. His eyes shifted to my mouth, his own still holding that half smile.

Beast pulled back. *Mate. Mate the I/we of Beast. Mate all of what we are.*

Yes. That, I thought. I licked my lips and said the first thing that popped into my head. "Do you read Latin?" And then blushed like a schoolgirl. *Idiot. Stupid. I am so stupid!*

Bruiser laughed, the vibrations rushing up through my chest, pressed against his. "You are a never-ending source of delight," he said. He kissed my forehead as if I were a favored child, released me, and walked away, taking with him that extraordinary warmth. Leaving me feeling abnormally chilled in the May-warm house.

Not knowing what else to do, not sure what had just happened, I crossed my arms over my chest, thinking, *Holy crap on crackers with cheese*, and followed him into the kitchen.

"I assume you are talking about the papers Grégoire gave to you," he said, stopping in front of the box in question. "Make me some coffee and I'll see if I can help."

It wasn't what I wanted, not at all, but it also seemed like a fair trade, and perhaps a chance to ask of the former primo what I had asked of Grégoire. I used the semi-new coffee machine to brew Bruiser a perfect cup of golden roast and poured myself a mug of vanilla-flavored tea, with hazelnut creamer and a half teaspoon of sugar, keeping my hands busy so I didn't have to look at Bruiser as I served him. Keeping my head down, thinking. Feeling his lips on mine again. It had been a chaste kiss. Not much tongue. No grinding body to body. The warmth cached within me flared at the thought and I swallowed a soft gasp. Drank the hot tea to cover my reaction. And burned my tongue, which served me right.

Bruiser sat at the table and took a smaller pasteboard box from inside the metal one. Within it were several pairs of white gloves, and I figured they were intended to keep finger oil off the papers. He put on a pair, though they were tight and the fingers too short for his long, slender hands. Beautiful hands, with well-shaped knuckles and long phalanges. Hands I wanted to touch. I gripped the mug tighter.

Handling the papers carefully, he scanned the pages I had left open. "Italian," he said, musingly, "like all of the Romance languages, has roots in Latin, but Italian is closest to the ancient

tongue. Its poetic and literary origins became more standard-
ized in the twelfth century, and this was written much later than
that. It's dated the tenth of July, in the year of our Lord, 1593."

I knew a lot of that, but the professorial tone relaxed me, as
it was undoubtedly intended to. I slid his coffee cup closer to
him and Bruiser picked it up, sipped, eyes on the paper. "This
is a letter, signed Pope Clement VIII." He raised his brows and
looked at me over the lip of the cup. "This should be in the archives of the Vatican. In a museum somewhere. And Grégoire
just gave it to you?" Bruiser smiled, shaking his head. "You do
have an effect on people, Jane Yellowrock."

Bruiser started reading aloud, in English, translating from
the letter as he went. It wasn't a smooth and effortless translation, but it was way better than me trying to key the letters and
words into an online translation site. I took a chair across from
him and watched his mouth as he read, half listening to the
minutiae of church politics that had nothing to do with witches.
Until he read, "'As to the workers of the *magickal*, my dear
Paulinus, they are a hindrance to the church, and much as the
Christ killers . . .'" He glanced up at me. "He's talking about
the Jews. The Roman Church declared them Christ killers so
they could take their property under religious law, even though
the Romans themselves actually killed him."

I nodded. I knew that.

"'. . . and the Mohammedan troubles, the *magickal* must be
sought out with a firm and thorough hand. Our dealings with
them must be meticulous to reduce their numbers comprehen-
sively and quickly.'"

"That's horrible," I said. "That sounds like genocide."

"It was exactly like genocide. Religion as a political entity
is always horrible," Bruiser said, his tone final.

"But—" I stopped. My religion wasn't supposed to be horrible. It was supposed to be based on love and generosity and
forgiveness. But history had always suggested otherwise. And
my other spirituality, the Cherokee, had a bloody and violent
historical aspect that made the old pope's comments seem con-
ventional. How was I supposed to look at the mores of history
and compare them to today's violence and judgment? Current
events suggested that humanity was no better today than it
had ever been, that we had learned nothing. And my own job
description suggested just the same. Vampire hunter. Vampire
killer. My throat clogged on the implications, I said, "Go on."

"That's all. The rest of the pages in this folder appear to be from the same era and written by the same hand. Politics. Purchases of land. Taking of property and holdings from the people 'disappeared' by the Church."

He shifted through the papers, pausing to read here and there. I refreshed his coffee, feeling disturbed for lots of reasons. He closed the file and stood, returning it to the box, his fingers moving through the pages and files. He reached deeper in and pulled out a very old book. "Ah, this is what you've been hoping for, I think. *Treatise of the Magikal.*" Bruiser opened the book and paged through the front; looked at me from under his eyebrows. "Shall we take this to the other room?"

"Yeah. Okay." I started him a fresh cup and followed him to the living room. Overhead, I heard stirring, as Alex got up for the day and went to the bathroom. Soon he would bring me info on Satan's Three, and my quiet time would be over. And I'd go back to being what I was and doing what I did. Bruiser sat on the couch, and after a moment, I curled up on the other end.

"This book is from the seventeen hundreds, printed in Germany. My familiarity with the tongue is limited, so I'll read, translate, and then summarize it for you."

"How do you know all this stuff? Languages and all. I mean, I know you're old, but—" I stopped myself. "I mean you're not *old* old, but you're . . . just . . ."

"Old?" he asked, that same warm laughter in his tone. I shrugged uncomfortably, and he asked, "How old are you, Jane?"

I jerked my eyes from my tea mug to his face. Chills snaked along my limbs, any remaining warmth from our kiss chased away by the question.

"Are you as old as I? I was born in nineteen hundred and three." His eyes were crinkled slightly as he watched me struggle with the question. "Until we emigrated to the colonies, I had a classical education, learning Latin, Greek, French, mathematics, philosophy, and history. Once I entered Leo's household, I was tutored by a variety of Mithrans in numerous subjects. I like languages, their histories and mutability, the cultures they reference and revive from the ashes of time."

"I don't know," I blurted. A weight lifted from my shoulders when he didn't react. "Found in the woods when I was twelvish. No memories. Raised by wolves. All that nonsense. It made the papers."

Mate to know all of I/we, Beast thought at me.

Bruiser raised his eyebrows politely, asking silently for more. For no reason I understood, I answered. "I was about five on the Trail of Tears."

"The *nunahi-duna-dlo-hilu-i*," Bruiser said softly, his voice holding no nuance at all.

Shock that he pronounced it perfectly went through me and my heart rate sped. "Yes."

"The trail lasted from 1831 to 1838, and involved many tribes in the eastern part of the States. The Cherokees were the last tribe moved. Forcefully. Brutally. So you might have been born anytime from eighteen thirty to eighteen thirty-three."

He didn't look like he was about to freak out so I nodded once, a jerk of my head.

"You're robbing the cradle, then," he said. Humor filled his face. "You're a cougar."

Laughter burbled out of me, part of it relieved nerves, the other part surprise at the play on words. "I'm not that kind of cougar," I said, my tone lofty. Unthinking, I added, "I haven't slept with you yet." A hot blush followed the shock through me like lightning when I heard that last word come out of my mouth.

"No. Not yet," he agreed, but his words were no longer smooth, or amused. He sounded something else, something heated and waiting. Bruiser returned his eyes to the old book and started reading, his eyes going back and forth across the page.

I managed to keep my breath from whooshing out with relief, but my skin felt hot and prickly. Beast purred inside of me, oddly satisfied. Upstairs, Alex started a shower and thumped around in the bathroom.

Long minutes later Bruiser said, "The magical beings have existed for thousands of years. There are numerous kinds, and they appear to be divided along racial, ethnic, and familial lines, though that is thought to be due to travel restrictions and inbreeding in prehistoric tribal times, not an actual genetic or racial difference that denotes ability or power levels. The writer seems to be saying that all witches are equal. But not really."

"Helpful. Not."

"Mmmm. The persecution of the magical began after the fall of Atlantis"—his eyebrows went up together—"in the year 5,000 BC, following a great worldwide flood. That makes it seven thousand years ago. A flood that killed off The People of the Straight Ways."

"Say that again."

Bruiser looked up at me. "The People of the Straight Ways?"

"Yeah. That could tie back with the *l'arcenciel*—the light-dragon that bit Leo and Gee. Back with stuff I heard when I was working south of Chauvin, hunting that escaped prisoner." Bruiser inclined his head. "I was told that they built lots of the ancient canals found in Louisiana, Mississippi, Florida, New England, and all over the world. Do you know about them?"

"*L'arcenciel*, or the *arcenciel*. The *L* is the article." I gave a nod of understanding, and he went on. "I've come across the term once or twice, but not with any particular emphasis or related to any flood. Or related to *the* flood." He closed the book and pulled off the white gloves. "You look tired. When did you last sleep?"

I thought about that for a while and sipped my cold tea. "I don't remember when I last slept for a whole night. I've been on vamp hours. And then my house was targeted by a bomb maker. And then I got cut up by a master swordsman."

"And broke his neck."

"Yeah. That too. So I don't know." I added, by way of ambush, "What do Satan's Three want with Leo? And me?"

With a faint smile, he said, "You'll have to ask Leo that." Bruiser held up the book and asked, "May I take this with me? I'll read and summarize it for you as I go and send it to you via e-mail. The contents don't sound as if they need immediate attention."

So much for verbal surprise attacks. I flipped my hand in a modified shrug. "Sure. If you find anything out about the iron spike of Golgotha or any of the other magical items, let me know."

Bruiser took my mug and carried both empties back to the kitchen. I watched as he washed the cup and mug. I had watched Eli and Alex doing that for months, but this felt different. Weirdly domestic. Bruiser placed the cleaned stoneware upside down on a dish towel to drain and placed the book and gloves by the side door before returning to me. He bent over my chair and placed his head near mine, the heat of his skin a furnace on my cheek. Breathing into my ear, he whispered the words, "I should not suggest this to you, but—" He placed a kiss on my ear, and shivers thundered through me. I pulled in a breath that smelled of him, *Bruiser*. My hands tight-ened on the edge of the couch cushion.

His lips moved on my ear as he said, "All magical items that interest the Mithrans go back to the Sons of Darkness, one of whom disappeared here, in New Orleans, long ago." My confu-sion must have shown on my face because Bruiser said, "The makers of all vampire-kind, the sons of Judas Iscariot." With no warning at all, he bent, slid his arms under my knees and around my back, and picked me up.

My heart did a major stutter stop-and-go and I gasped. He carried me through the foyer and pushed open my bedroom door. My bed was unmade. My room was a disaster. This was not the way I wanted this to play out. "Bruiser. What—?" He dropped me on my bed. I bounced. I'm pretty sure I squealed.

Bruiser turned on a heel and left me there, amid the twisted, unwashed sheets and squished pillows. "Get some sleep." He shut my door.

"Wh— Get some sleep? No fair!" I shouted through the door.

I heard him chuckle as he let himself out the kitchen side door.

"So totally not fair." I punched my pillow. Not that I had indicated to him that I'd welcome any romantic overtures. Well, except for the kiss at the door. And maybe a hot make-out session in my shower once. And on a limo floor. But then there had been Rick, who had torn a raw, painful wound inside me. Maybe that was what Bruiser had been waiting for? For me to heal?

Jane is silly kit, Beast murmured at me.

I pulled off my clothes, dropped them on the floor, and smoothed the covers over me. Even with the sounds of ham-mers and skill saws in the background, where the house next to Katie's was being renovated, I was asleep in an instant. But his words hung in my mind, part spoken in Bruiser's voice, part from a fragmented memory. *A Son of Darkness disappeared here.*

CHAPTER 13

Who Was That Masked Man?

I woke with a jolt, the dream slipping away. Which totally sucked, because when a dream-thought slipped away, it was always vitally important. All I could remember was Jodi saying something about penguins. No. Wait. It was *Peregrinus*. The old vamp in town, along with his partner, Batildis, and the blood-servant the Devil. The blood-servant who had hurt Reach.

If Reach was telling the truth. Was Reach really hurt? Would he have made up something like being tortured by the Devil? The dream was about the vamp and the Devil—a blood-servant so terrifying she had no name, only a title, who had built a bomb and put it at my door. Maybe. Or perhaps it had been her master, Batildis. Where were the Devil and her vamps? In New Orleans? Was the Devil acting alone or with the help of other human followers, other blood-servants? What the heck had they gotten from Reach? I was having a hard time putting things together, because the bad guys had all the intel.

These bad guys were vamps, so being here in New Orleans probably wasn't because of just one reason, but many reasons, multilayered and overlapping. That felt right, but logic wasn't pulling the dream any closer; rather, it was tearing at the dream like talons until there was nothing left but a feeling of disquiet. A feeling that I was missing something important, some instigating event that brought the attention of Satan's Three to New Orleans. Unless that event had been publicized all over the world on TV. Yeah. I gave a mental sigh. It was looking more and more like this was all my fault. Again.

My cell buzzed and I rolled over in bed to grab up the phone. It was a text from Soul, saying she was clearing her calendar. It was about time. I closed my heavy cell, staring up at the ceiling as the overhead fan twirled lazily above me.

I heard footsteps in the foyer and a soft tap on my door. "Hold on," I said. I flipped the covers away and looked for my black robe, which was nowhere to be seen, so I pulled on the wrinkled clothes I'd dropped to the floor. When I opened the door, Eli stood there, his dark skin appearing even darker in the shadowed foyer. He was wearing his business face, which meant even less emotional expression than usual.

"Someone's watching the house," he said.

The gnawing worry ramped up. "Again?"

"You're popular in the whacked-out fangy crowd."

"Thanks, I'm sure. But it's daylight. Not a vamp."

"Okay. But my money's on the vamps anyway. Maybe a vamp's blood-meal, but still a vamp."

"No argument." I slipped my bedroom shoes back on my feet and left my room, following Eli. "Where?"

"Not the usual place." The usual place was the house cater-cornered, across the street. It had a small nook at the door and low, wide porch walls supporting the posts holding up the porch roof, making it perfect for pots of plants or for a watcher to sit and observe. I'd found more than one spy there. "This one is actually *in* a house. Directly across the street." He stopped to the side of the kitchen window, which was small and obscure, but looked out over the front street. I leaned over to get a better view.

"See the window to the left of the door, second story?" he asked. "That curtain's never been open before. It's just a crack, but there's a small round object, like the end of a scope, in the opening." Eli handed me a pair of binoculars and I reshaped them to my face.

I found the window and the corner of the drapery that had been folded back. Sure enough, there was a round thing in it, pointed directly at my house. "Who owns the property?"

"Alex is checking now."

With very few exceptions, like me, few people lived in the houses in the French Quarter. The property values were so high and the tourist attention was so acute, that the buildings and houses were often rented out as artist's studios, small shops, bars, and restaurants rather than used as homes. I handed Eli the eyes and went back to my room, saying, "I need a shower and a few minutes to think."

Behind closed doors, I stripped, dropping the clothes again as I made my way to the shower. I wasn't dirty, but I was sleepy, my brain was sluggish, and all I could think to do about the spy was to go over there and slap him silly. Physical force might be my specialty, but it wasn't always the most effective means of problem solving.

Ten minutes later I turned off the cold water and stepped out of the bathroom. Five minutes after that, I was dressed in jeans and a T-shirt with a jean jacket over it all to hide my weapons. I yanked on an old pair of scuffed and worn Lucchese Western boots and left my room. To Alex, who was sitting at his small desk, surrounded by electronic tablets, I asked, "Who owns the house?"

"A woman named Margery Thibodaux. According to records, she's lived there for sixty years. Recluse, drives a 1972 Ford Galaxie, has a net worth of two million, some of it in conservative stocks and bonds. Her husband and she bought into Walmart the same year they bought the Ford, and that's where most of the money came from. She has a daughter in Dallas and a son in Connecticut. I found contact numbers and neither adult child has seen or heard from her in forty-eight hours. Both have, by now, called the police."

I dropped on the couch and let a tired grin on my face. "The police. Now, why didn't I think of that?"

From the kitchen window, Eli said, "A marked car just pulled up. Female officer, going to the door."

I closed my eyes and let my head fall back. "I coulda stayed in bed."

The sound of automatic gunfire shot me to my feet. I made the side door and was outside before Eli finished his turn. Beast butted in close, sharing her speed and strength. Behind me, I heard the Kid shouting into his cell phone, "Officer down, Officer down! Automatic gunfire! Request backup and medic!" He started shouting the address as I rounded the house.

I didn't bother with the wrought-iron gate. There wasn't time. I leaped, grabbed the horizontal bar to the side of the fleur-de-lis at the gate top, and vaulted over, landing in a crouch. Behind me, Eli cursed and rattled the gate lock. Another burst of gunfire erupted from across the street.

I leaned into the side of the house and looked around the

corner. The officer was lying in the street, bloody, but crawling for the protection of her unit. She had her service weapon in one hand and from her body came the sound of a steady beep—the "officer in trouble" alarm and GPS that cops pressed when they were in danger. Already I could hear sirens from all around.

I looked up at the window where we had spotted the surveillance and saw the glass was busted out. The barrel of a weapon was trained down, directly at the cop. With no thought at all, I raced across the street, seeing the barrel rise toward me. And realized that was exactly what the shooter had been trying for—me in the line of fire.

Time did that weird slow-down thing that happened often when I was in danger of getting dead. I jerked my body left, then right, the barrel in the window following. Behind me I heard the distinctive sound of a nine-mil as Eli laid down cover fire. Puny shots in the aftermath of the automatic weapon fire.

The shooter fired again, rounds hitting the street just behind me. I dove for the cop, grabbed her as I landed, and rolled her behind the car. I lay atop her as the cop car was riddled with bullets. What hearing I had was lost to the concussive battering.

NOPD units started to arrive, sirens and lights flashing. A car swerved up to me and screeched to a halt. Suddenly I was surrounded by three cops, all with their weapons pointed at me. "Not me!" I screamed and pointed, deafened. "The window!"

Two cops fell, hit by the shooter before they could take cover. One was dead before he hit the street, the back of his head gone. The unwounded cop pulled him and the other officer out of the line of fire. He started doing CPR on the dead guy. I rolled off the female officer and applied pressure to the bloody place in her left shoulder. The blood was pouring, not spurting, but no telling what was happening inside her.

More cop cars arrived. "Around back!" the officer shouted, and pointed at the house. "Seal off the streets!"

"Got him!" someone screamed. "Down on your knees! Down on your knees. Hands behind your head!"

Eli. They had Eli. Cops in a panic, three of their own down. "He's with me!" I shouted.

The cop beneath me added her voice to mine. "Not him! Not him! The house." She pointed, and coughed blood. I knew instantly what that meant. A round had hit a lung. The lung was collapsing and her chest cavity was filling up with blood. The officer was drowning in her own blood. My emergency medical training was years old, but it came back to me now with absolute clarity.

I angled the cop against the cruiser door. Looked up into the eyes of a paramedic who dropped to his knees beside me. "GSW," I said. "Left lung. Probable hemothorax."

The medic stuck his ear pieces in and listened to her chest with his stethoscope. "Yeah. Lung is down," he said, already cutting through her uniform shirt. "We have to get her transferred stat." He started removing the Kevlar vest that hadn't protected the officer. The bullet had gone in just above the vest at a downward angle.

The cop coughed and sucked blood and coughed again. Blood splattered over all of us. She was wearing a T-shirt under the vest. It was scarlet and sopping. I felt her heart stutter under my hands. If my hearing hadn't been compromised by the concussive gunfire, I knew I could have heard the heart in distress. Beast's hearing is that good, even over the sirens squalling.

"She needs a chest tube. She won't make it to the hospital," I said. Paramedics weren't certified to insert chest tubes in the field. Only doctors could do that. Meaning that this cop was dead. I looked at her for the first time. She was brown haired, brown-but-pasty-skinned, brown eyed. Maybe Latina. Maybe one of the mixed races found so commonly in the Deep South. And she was seeing her death, her eyes wide and panicked and knowing.

With a pair of scissors, the paramedic cut her T-shirt open. The wound was bad.

Eli dropped to his knees beside me. Eli. He was a Ranger. Rangers have to do all sorts of things in the field. Like save one another, or themselves. I asked the paramedic, "If you were to stick a large bore needle into her chest beneath her left arm, well around her chest wall from the bleeding bullet hole, where exactly would you stick it?"

The paramedic looked back and forth between us, understanding what I was asking. He couldn't help her, but a bystander could. "I'd stick it right here." He touched the cop's skin. It was icy, sweating. She was going into shock.

I slapped her face, and she looked at me, pulling back from

the brink. "We can try to save you, or we can be smart and avoid a lawsuit and let you die. You want us to try to save you? Nod once for yes."

The cop nodded once, then again, and again. Coughing. Blood going everywhere.

Eli handed me an oversized Betadine swab. I swiped her chest at the site the paramedic had pointed to. Eli tore a paper-and-plastic package and removed the plastic top from a needle. It looked like a ten-penny nail with a hole bored through. It was huge. There wasn't time for gloves or better cleaning. There wasn't time for anything.

Eli's fingers pushed between two of the cop's ribs, pressing into the . . . intercostal space. I remembered the word. Useless now, that memory. He jammed the needle through the flesh. The injured cop didn't even flinch. Blood flushed through the needle end and out into the street. Eli secured the needle in place with a wad of gauze and taped it down.

I looked at him and said, "Get outta here." He understood. So did the paramedic and the cops around us. Civilians don't do stuff like this. The official types all looked away. Eli grabbed a blue absorbent pad, stood, and walked away, head down, wiping his hands and hiding the blood all at once. He moved down the street away from my house, away from the shooting.

I looked at the cop and saw her badge. Her name was Officer Swelling. She was maybe twenty-five. Was wearing a wedding ring. She took a breath and exhaled, the sound of air gargling and thick, her eyes on me. She didn't cough, but it was a near thing. She mouthed the words, *Thank you.* I shrugged at her and she added, her words a whisper, "Who was that masked man?"

I laughed. So did Swelling, as well as she was able. Moments later, the cop was inside an ambulance, hooked up to fluids and being transported down the street toward the nearest hospital. A second ambulance was departing with the other injured cop. The coroner was standing over the third one. The paramedics were still doing CPR but everyone knew it was just a formality. The officer was familiar, but I couldn't think of his name at the moment. A face I'd seen at NOPD or on a scene. An older guy, midfifties, one who'd eaten one too many beignets and sipped one too many sugared drinks. White guy. Dead white guy.

I looked up at the broken window pane where the shots had come from. Other panes were busted out from where Eli had fired back. I looked down at myself. I was covered in sticky, drying blood. I opened and closed my hands; the blood was tacky and cold in the warm air.

I had blood on my hands. Again. Maybe this time I should have felt good about it, good because I'd maybe saved an officer's life. But I had a feeling that Swelling would be uninjured and going about her life just fine had I not lived across the street from the house.

I might be War Woman, but my past was still alive and well inside me. My old enemy guilt rose up and wrapped cold, slimy arms around me, a death stench rising from inside me.

Around us all, a breeze gusted, cooler than the midday air. Overhead, clouds were moving in. Rain on the wind and the threat of lightning in the ozone scent.

I felt a tap and looked down at Jodi, my friend on NOPD. The vamps' best friend at cop central. "He fired from up there," I said, nodding to the busted window. "Did the unknown person who offered me cover while I pulled Swelling to safety hit him?"

"Blood at the scene," Jodi said. "No one there. Trail out the back door, across the alley and the garden behind the house, through the next alley to the street; then it stops. Shooter got into a vehicle and disappeared."

"The old lady?" The name came to me. "Margery Thibodaux? Is she okay?"

"Dead. Single GSW to the head. Maybe two days ago. Before the bomb incident." Her voice lowered. "What are you mixed up in, Jane?"

My ears hadn't returned to normal. There was a hum of damaged eardrums that made her voice sound tinny. And then I realized that her voice also sounded odd because of the dead cop. There was horror and anger on the faces all around me. Explosive anger, needing only a spark to set them all off.

"I don't know," I said. "I really don't know. Except there's this vamp, looking for trouble, and an old friend sent him to me."

"Friend?" The word was skeptical. "This friend have a name?"

"Yeah. Reach. That's all I know him by. The vamp tortured him to get to me. Supposedly. And no, I don't have an address; our only contact was through e-mail and cell." I gave her both his e-mail addy and his cell number. "But don't expect to find him. He's gone to ground."

She grunted, unimpressed, taking down the info on her tablet. "You're part of a crime scene. I need your clothes and a statement." Jodi pointed me at an unmarked cop car. "Sit there and wait until Crime Scene can get to you. Don't touch anything. Preserve the trace evidence."

That meant sitting in drying blood, no shower, no breakfast, no water, probably all day. I didn't complain. Not with a dead cop at my feet.

It started to rain an hour later and I ended up back at cop central, in a small room where a female crime scene tech removed trace evidence from me, took samples of the cracked and dried blood all over me, did a trace-gunshot residue test, which came back negative, clearing me of being the person who fired the shots back at the shooter. She took my clothes but let me wash up and put on fresh clothing delivered by Alex, who had nothing to add, saying that he had been playing video games when the shooting started. He hadn't seen anyone fire back. Neither had I. All truth. I didn't volunteer that the person who returned fire was my partner, Eli Younger, nor that he had gone after the suspect. I hadn't seen him do any of that.

I finally got to head home before sunset, a cloudy, rainy afternoon leading into a cooler, wet evening, taking a cab back to the house. I was so tired I was swaying on my feet, standing on my front porch as I watched the cab roll away. I remembered only then that I had a cabdriver friend of sorts, and I hadn't called Rinaldo recently. So many things I needed to do, including sleeping and eating and maybe drinking water. I'd taken nothing in me all day. But I stood at the side gate in a puddle of rain and stared out at the world.

The front door across from my house was sealed by crime scene tape. I could get in, if I was willing to cut the tape or go around back for a little B&E. I needed to sniff the shooter's blood to see whether I recognized it. But I just couldn't make myself.

The street between our houses had been scrubbed free of blood, any final traces washed away by rain. I swiveled and looked at my house. The wood was pocked in several places, holes that had been enlarged by CSI retrieving evidence.

On the cooling evening breeze, I smelled exhaust, steak from inside my house, water from the Mississippi, blooming flowers, Creole and Cajun restaurant cooking with a high percentage of seafood, coffee—the usual French Quarter smells, rich and layered and intense. A spatter of rain pounded down, pebbling the water on the street. Because of the heavy clouds, the streetlights came on early, the sensors claiming night was falling. The old-fashioned globes cast homey yellowed light into the false dusk, but I didn't feel homey. I felt numb and worn. Tired beyond anything I'd felt in recent months. It would be smarter to move my partners to vamp HQ, and leave myself out as bait. I wondered whether I'd be able to talk them into it.

Our hunting territory, Beast thought at me. *We will not run. We will fight.*

Neither one of us is very bright, I thought back.

I went inside.

Over a steak and a beer—which made me feel a little better—I made the suggestion that the boys go to HQ, "to keep Leo safer," I said, trying for nonchalant.

Eli paused, a bite halfway to his mouth. "So you can be bait and fight Satan's Three alone?" Eli said, his tone so mild that I instantly realized I had insulted him. Carefully, as if his fork and steak knife were made of glass, he set them onto the plate, the bite of steak forgotten. "No."

"Not even Alex?"

"That would be up to him," my partner said, his words measured and precise, his tone and expression giving nothing at all away. "He's over eighteen."

"No," Alex said shortly.

"Okay. It's what I expected. But I had to ask. It's"—I shrugged—"polite."

"Bugger polite," Eli said. And with that he picked up his fork and shoved the bite into his mouth.

"What my brother said," Alex said.

I decided this was not the time to discuss house rules and, after a moment, nodded. "Okay. Let's compare stories."

I learned that Eli had shown up at NOPD and been taken in to give a statement. He had gunshot residue on his hands, but no blood on his clothes because he had managed to change before he appeared at NOPD. He had admitted that he was the one who returned fire and had turned over the weapon that he'd used. He had been questioned to within an inch of his life before being released with the usual order not to leave town.

I told them all about my day at cop central. Eli shared a few details about his time there too. His Q&A had included Jodi and lunch with the cops—who wanted to say thank you to the man who had saved a cop's life.

Alex told us about his research and about the dead cop. Everett Semer had been fifty-five and heading to retirement in a little more than a year, with a wife and two kids and grandkids. We watched the coverage on TV and social media and sent a donation in to help the family. And we were relieved to learn that the injured cops were expected to survive.

Sobered, Eli turned off the news and called vamp HQ. I listened, silent and feeling a bit managed and outmaneuvered as he told someone that we would not be in tonight. I stared at him, surprised but not stopping him. When he hung up, he raised his eyebrows. "What? We need to figure out who's targeting us. And we need a day off from fangheads, which you never take."

I gave him a dismal smile. "What's this of which you speak, 'day off'?"

Instead of answering, he said, "Coke floats for dessert," which cheered me considerably. Sweets were not Eli's drug of choice. Eli had no drugs of choice—it was an all-healthy lifestyle for the Ranger.

Over dessert, served in tall glasses with vanilla ice cream and Coke and lots of the resulting foam, Eli turned the conversation to the shooter. "According to what I learned through Jodi, the FBI's Integrated Automated Fingerprint Identification System, the bomb builder and the shooter were the same person. Fingerprints match."

"No way," Alex said. "Bomb makers and shooters have distinct and different personalities."

Eli settled hard eyes on his brother, which had to be uncomfortable. Alex jutted out his jaw and stared back. "You're a shooter," the Kid said. "You've got all the personality markers for a shooter, including high markers for survival, tenacity, independent action, and patience. Bomb makers have different personalities, with lower markers for survival and independence, but higher markers for single-mindedness."

"You've been playing shrink on me?" The question contained no overt emotions, but Eli's scent changed, with aggressive pheromones tainting the air.

"I have an IQ considerably higher than yours," Alex said

seriously, "with personality markers for insatiable curiosity. It isn't my fault."

"Everyone has to take responsibility for our own decisions, actions, and inactions, Kid."

"Stop," I said. "We're not talking about your pasts. We're talking about the shooter and bomb maker who targeted this house. If it's a blood-servant, and we think it is, he's had a lot of years to learn all sorts of things, including how to beat any personality test or even grow a new personality if he needs one. You live long enough, you can overcome most anything, including your own disposition."

"That from personal experience?" Eli asked.

I stabbed him with a look and let Beast rise in my eyes, just a bit. "You got questions about me, Eli? 'Cause if we start asking questions, we're all gonna have to answer them." I let my eyes fall to his collarbone and the scarring there, scarring he had never talked about, scarring that had ended his military career, or had been the impetus for his voluntary honorable discharge, or whatever they called it.

"Maybe it's time to clear the air," Eli said, and my heart jumped in surprise before he went on. "But not until after we catch this guy. Then I'll tell you mine if you'll tell me yours."

It was a challenge that Eli clearly didn't expect me to accept. So I did. "Okeydokey." He didn't gape like a fish on land, but it was a near thing, and I grinned at him to show I knew I had scored a point. To drive it home, I licked my fingertip and drew a vertical line in the air. "Until then, you got any of the shooter's blood for me to sniff?"

Eli frowned, actually had a tiny line form between his brows. "Yeah. How'd you know I collected some of the blood?"

"You were too quick to disappear. I figured you followed him and collected some spatter for me."

"I did."

I held out my hand. "That blood spatter, please?"

Eli retrieved a plastic Ziploc bag from the counter and opened it before handing it to me. I bent my nose over the opening and sniffed. And rocked my head back in surprise.

"What?" Eli said, knees in a crouch, one hand behind him, going for his weapon. Eli always had a weapon on him, and drawing one was his first action of choice.

I waved away his gun and the stink at the same time. "Nothing. Just, I never smelled a blood-servant like this one. I don't even need to shift." I took another sniff and wrinkled my nose. "*Ick*. Angry, cold and purposed, been drinking from a very old vamp for a lot of years. Old blood-servant, maybe the oldest I've ever smelled." I raised my eyes to Eli as he settled back into his chair. "And our shooter is a she."

Eli didn't seem terribly surprised. "Women make good shooters: steady, dependable, and reliable. Good hand-to-eye. Until they have families. Then different instincts kick in and they have a harder time following orders. They think too much."

My feminist side wanted to stick up her head and disagree, but maybe he had a point. What did I know? I took another sniff. The blood was starting to break down and smelled a bit rank, but I caught a whiff of something else. Something almost familiar, but not quite there, not quite envisioned. But whatever it was, little alarm bells went off inside my brain. I resealed the baggie, thinking.

"Are you going to change shape to sniff it?" Alex blurted. "I want to watch!"

"No," Eli said.

"Yes, I'm going to change. And it's the same answer you will always get to that question. No, you can't watch. It's private," I said. "Sorry." But I wasn't really sorry. Changing, even in extremis, always involved a certain amount of nudity, and no way was I willing to share that with a nineteen-year-old boy/man, no matter how high his IQ was. "I'll be right back."

I went to my room and closed the door.

I took my box of fetishes from the top shelf of the closet and removed the one I wanted, bones and teeth strung on a length of jewelry wire. I stripped, sat on my bed, and held the necklace in my lap. Beast had been unusually quiet until I settled down to meditate; then she said, *Good nose. Ugly dog.*

"Yeah. I know. Sorry." And I entered the gray place of the change.

CHAPTER 14

Talk to Big Bird

As soon as the dizziness cleared and my head stopped being filled with images and scents, I stepped down from the bed. I had to change the sheets. Buy a new bed. Scrub the bathroom. Good oogly moogly, this place stank.

I made it to the door and scratched on it with my paw. Then, just for fun, I barked, a long *arrrooooo* of sound. Alex, smelling of garlic, onions, sweat, deodorant, and growing boy—a toxic mixture—opened the door and stared down at me, his eyes big as always when he saw me in a different shape. I considered letting go some gas—a doggie way of stating an opinion on any number of things, but I thought better of it. I walked into the kitchen and ate the raw hamburger that Eli put on a plate for me. The energy required by shifting always left me starving and I hadn't had to tell my partner. I butted his leg in thanks and he scratched my ears, a familiarity I'd never have permitted in human form but which felt perfect in dog form.

Back in the living room, I stepped up on the sofa and sat, my tail thumping, staring at Eli. Who smelled wonderful to my dog nose, and made me wonder how Bruiser might smell, which nearly made me drool. Associations in bloodhound form were so totally different from human or Beast shape. All the senses were closer together, interwoven, more intricate, and so much more intense, that I could see how easy it might be to let them take over and to lose myself in the textures and blends of scent patterns. I realized that Eli was talking and I woofed to show I was ready for a sniff test.

Inside me, Beast growled. *Ugly dog. Good nose, on ugly dog.* She thought a moment, and added, *All dogs ugly.*

Eli came at me with the sealed baggie and I pulled my head away for a moment, already almost overcome by the smells as he pulled the Ziploc open. I shook my head, my ears flapping, and gave a little sneeze to clear my nose before sticking my head forward and my snout into the baggie. I took a small sniff. Then another. And another, breathing deeply as the smells found new places in my doggie brain, forming associations with other scents from the last time I was in this form, from times I took other forms with good scent noses, and also from when I was human—nose-blind, I understood. Humans had so little understanding of the smells of the world around us that if we were sightless, deaf, and unable to touch at all, that isolation *might* show the difference between a human's ability to smell and a bloodhound's ability.

I learned all I could from the bloody cloth, lifted my head from the baggie, and trotted back to my room, closing the door with my nose.

I was sitting on the bed, firmly in the gray place of the change, when I felt the magics. Like mine, but different. In the location of mine, yet not. *L'arcenciel* magics. Close. I reached in to the deeps of me and found the genetic form that was mine, that was all Jane, all human, and I ripped it up and out through me, through the energies that glowed with zooming lights, that sparkled like stars, and blazed like comets, through the flesh that needed to become my own. I rolled from the bed to the floor.

And I screamed. Pain like being burned to the bone, being branded, being dipped in molten iron. I threw back my head and found the genetic structure that could weld a sword and shoot a gun. I found myself, my human form. Gasping, I rolled to my backside and to a sitting position, twisted in sheets. Eli stood over me, weapons drawn. Overhead the light shined into the formerly dark room. I grabbed up the sheets and tried to stand but my legs collapsed and I fell.

"Magics," I gasped. "The light-dragon is here."

Eli stepped, balanced, lifting his feet one at a time, setting them down in stable position, rooted, as he slowly turned. "Where?"

That's right. Humans can't see it in every form. "Close," I managed. I pulled on my jeans and tee and grabbed my weapons, a little-used eighteen-inch, steel-bladed vamp-killer that hung in a sling on the back of the bed frame and a nine-millimeter semiautomatic handgun. I chambered a round, pointed to the front of the house, and followed Eli out of the room.

He forced open the front door and we broke through the crime scene tape and out into the street. The smell of a flash rain was in the air, the stink of lightning. The street ran with water, warm on the asphalt beneath my feet. But the magics faded and disappeared.

"I don't believe in coincidence," I said, as I stuffed my face with the rare steak that Eli had cooked (if a steak this rare can be called cooked) while I shifted back. "But I smelled something in the blood that I've smelled before. Or nearly. The shooter smells like one of The People. I need to get another look at the paintings on one of the lower levels of vamp HQ."

Eli's mouth pursed. "What does Leo have in all his basements? Sounds more and more like we need to recon down there."

Remembering the breath-freezing fear response I'd had standing in the elevator in the dark, I said, "Bring flashlights. Maybe that bazooka you keep talking about."

The look on Eli's face said I was a scaredy-cat girl. Inside, Beast hissed at the insult, but I didn't correct him, stuffing my face instead. He'd find out soon enough if he followed through on his recon idea. The bogeyman was in the basement? A scion so special—or so old? One of the long-chained ones?—that he or she was kept alone and out of sight, hidden away until its existence had faded into myth? I said, "There're cameras in the stairwells. You'll never get downstairs."

"Whoa," Alex said. "We didn't install cameras there. What kind of cameras?"

"Same make and model we used in the rest of the place." I flashed him a grin that was all teeth. "I'll be taking up the need for payment on that design with Raisin and Del. Someone cheated us."

"More important than that," Alex said, a look of triumph on his face. "Those cameras have to be monitored somewhere."

"Nice," Eli said. "Meaning that we can gain access, take it over, and use it. We can see what's below stairs."

I pointed a fork at the Kid. "Make it so, Number Two."

Alex chuckled once at the old order given by the *Next Generation, Star Trek*'s captain. It was a single huff of sound, much like one of his brother's restrained laughs, or Beast's, and he headed back to his work area, his head already bowed over a tablet.

"If we can get into the system, we can manage an unobserved basement visit," Eli said. "Until then, I have an update. I just finished the reports of all the eyewitnesses who saw the *arcenciel* attack in the sparring room." At my polite but incomprehensible, steak-choked interrogative he said, "None of them match. In fact, none of the descriptions of the *arcenciel* match, beyond a glittery, shadowy creature."

I made a circular motion with my fork to indicate he should continue, before stabbing it into a morsel of meat.

Eli said, "I don't think it's mind control. But how about something the snake releases from its body?"

I paused in my chewing and thought about the feel of the scale on my chest, all tingly. I said, "'Ass it. 'ike ellssd."

"Yeah. Exactly like LSD," Eli agreed.

I swallowed and said, "What did the lab get on the remains of the *arcenciel* glop it left on the gym floor after we stabbed it?"

"We don't— Wait a minute," Alex called from the other room. He brought over a tablet, made an agreeable sound, and pushed it to me. "This just in." He pointed to the line he thought most appropriate. It was a line of chemical formula followed by words, which he read aloud. "'Preliminary reports indicate that this compound is a biologic agent with hallucinogenic properties—a deliriant, mildly psychedelic, and strongly dissociative, likely to cause confusion, emotional euphoria, and forgetfulness, as well as headaches and possible flashbacks.' None of our witnesses had any physical complaints, maybe because they all drink vamp blood and that keeps their brains healthy enough to withstand the compound's natural effects."

None of us mentioned that Eli now fell into that vamp-blood-drinking category, his life having been preserved until he could get to a hospital, after he'd been nearly drained by enemy vamps. I couldn't resist the glance to his neck where he sported new scars—pale and irregular, above the older scars from his time in active military duty. He narrowed his eyes at me in warning and I went back to the steak, the tablet, and the info contained in the e-mail.

Alex pointed to another line and said, "'In case of inges-tion, normal, healthy humans should break down the sub-stance within hours.' But it doesn't say what effect it might have on vamps."

I scanned the rest of the report as the possibilities of the reactions of humans and vamps went on, but it was all guess-work on the part of the researchers. I had seen the results in person. Eli had read the reports. "Oh goody," I said. "The *ar-cenciel* is a living, breathing, dream-inducing, drug-pushing, see-through dragon. Like one of those frogs people lick in the Amazon, but bigger. And can fly." I half chewed and swallowed the last of the steak, got up, and went to the bedroom where my thigh rig hung on the back of the bedroom door. I removed the scale and brought it back to the kitchen, feeling the tingles on my fingertips and residual tingles on my chest. I got a roll of paper towels and tore off a stack, setting the scale on top. I sniffed my fingers and felt a change inside my nose and head, like a sudden change of air pressure. "It's a drug, or maybe a drug and magic, working together." I washed my hands, scrub-bing the fingertips that had touched the scale. "While we're sharing information," Alex said, "we got something from George." He set another tablet in front of me, and stretched his fingers apart while touching the screen, making the text larger. In his formal way of writing e-mails, Bruiser said:

Jane and Youngers,
　　From the book I am reading and interpreting I have deduced several things that might be of interest. The writer claims to be using oral tradition and ancient writ-ings from before the time of the Sumerians, none of which survive today, so far as I am able to deduce.
　　After the flood, the remaining humans were in great disarray, having lost everything of a cultural nature, and being thrust into stone-age starvation and subsistence level standard of living. In the people of the west (this could be interpreted as the Americas), this destruction and re-creation of the entire landscape created a power vacuum which was filled by the tribal magic-users (witches) who had gifts that gave them greater chances of survival. They bounced back in the form of warriors, shapeshifters (skinwalkers?), wise men, war women, shamans, and healers, most with no mention of the im-

mune problems suffered by preadolescent and adolescent witches of today, though that may mean nothing except that it was lost to time.

They survived in this manner until the Europeans came and many of them changed, growing sick and mentally unstable. My presumption is that of the majority of scholars: The white man's bacteria and viruses killed them off, their scriptures and priests demonized them, and the white man systematically destroyed the tribal Americans in genocide.

In a place that I am deducing is the African states, the witches were feared and were often sold into slavery by their own tribal chiefs as a way of preserving their own power bases. Both Christian and Muslim proselytizers and missionaries later demonized them.

In Europe, which has a better-preserved oral history and tradition, the witches went underground, hiding what they were, except for the tribal Celts, who accepted the magic-users as the ancient gift of the gods and of God. Among the Celts, magic-users remained well respected, though carefully hidden from the Church, which proved a successful methodology from the other tribal peoples of time.

When vampires were created through dark magic and black arts (the original three were witches, if you recall) they increased their numbers by turning witches into vampires. Prior to the vampire wars and prior to the creation of the Vampira Carta, the Mithrans began to destroy the witches instead of turning them.

I have been searching the archives for information relating to the causative factor for their enmity. I suggest that you ask Leo or Grégoire for more information. I will send more as I am able.

Best,
George Dumas

Some of this info was new, and some was old stuff, and some was a new way of looking at it all. I remembered that Gee DiMercy had once told me about the Cursed of Artemis, the original name of the were-creatures. He had even proposed that my kind were part of the old story, goddess-born, whatever that meant. He wasn't willing to share more, but he had suggested that I ask some of the older vamps. I had asked the priestess Sabina, who had told me about Lolandes, whose legend became confused with, and merged into, the earth goddess, who was common to all ancient tribal peoples. Lolandes had been a witch of sorts.

The first three vampires—the Sons of Darkness and their father, Judas Iscariot—had been witches too, made from the crosses of Calvary, also known as Golgotha, the place of the skull. The spikes of Golgotha were part of that event. Sooo . . . did the instigating event of today's dangers go back that far? To the creation event of the vamps themselves? Was the spike of Golgotha *that* important?

Or did all of our current problems—the dragon, Satan's Three, the attacks on my house—go back to Lolandes? There was something here, something lost among all the info we had already gathered, something important, but just out of reach, taunting me. Dang it.

I pulled up the old memory of the witch and told the guys, "Long before the Greeks named her Artemis, there was this powerful, long-lived mortal, a witch, though different from today's witches in ways that I haven't been able to determine. Anyway, Lolandes was the most powerful witch of her time, in a time when women were revered, when political and religious power was passed through the matriarchal line. She helped humans in childbirth and cared for wild animals."

"So maybe preflood," Alex said.

I gave an eyebrow shrug that said, *Who knows?* "Lolandes could have been a witch among The People of the Straight Ways. She could have come before, or after, the flood. Myth and oral tradition is sketchy at best. Anyway, Lolandes had a hunting bird, like a falcon, that loved her and came back to her after each hunt, bringing her the kills. She loved the bird.

"One night on the full moon, a wolf killed the bird, fighting over a doe they both had targeted. Lolandes cursed the wolf with disease, something similar to rabies, that affected mind and brain. It was the were-taint. The wolf ran into the woods and started biting anything it came across. The humans and the creatures it bit became were-creatures, but all were insane. Lolandes regretted the disease and found a partial cure, which she gave to all of them except the werewolves. They stayed insane as punishment for the death of her bird."

Eli said, "No falcon would have been hunting a doe."

It was the same dispute I'd had about the creation myth of the moon-touched, the weres. "I think the bird was maybe an Anzû." Eli looked confused. I just sighed. "A storm god." Which didn't help my partner at all. "It's my night off, but I have to get dressed and weaponed up. I have to talk to Big Bird."

"Big Bir—?"

A knock sounded at the side door and Eli was instantly out of his chair, weapons drawn, his body bladed and protected behind the kitchen wall. I was on the floor, yanking the Kid out of his chair by his shoulder, and rolling our bodies across the floor until we were safe. He cussed softly the whole time, his pores reeking of fear and shock. I wasn't weaponed up, which was stupid. I'd left the thigh rig on the table to roll Alex. *Stupid, stupid, stupid.*

Eli bent and slid a nine-mil to me across the floor, the scraping sound loud in the suddenly quiet house. I grabbed it as I rolled off of Alex, taking a prone position, my lower body flat on the floor, upper chest raised, balanced on my elbows, gun in a two-hand grip. I checked it fast and triangulated our shooting positions. If Eli moved toward the door, I might shoot his legs. Using my toes, I repositioned, sliding myself over, which left more of me exposed, but decreased the chance that I'd hurt my partner.

I nodded and Eli leaned in, twisting the knob and throwing the door open all at once. Soul stood on the other side, a bag at her feet. She was holding a .45 aimed at Eli's middle. A .45 slug would have blown a hole through my partner and blasted the wall opposite. Soul looked from Eli to me and smiled. "Am I in time for dinner?"

Soul had taken one end of the couch, her legs curled and feet tucked beneath her, pretty plum-colored shoes on the floor below. Sitting there, she looked a tiny thing, all voluptuous curves and gauzy purple fabrics. Her silver-platinum hair was up in a loose bun with tendrils that looked as if they had worked their way free hanging down around her face and to her shoulders. She appeared delicate and well-bred and weary and sensual all at once, as she held a salad bowl in one hand and ate with the other. "Peanuts and cola on the flight down, and a two-hour layover at Atlanta. I detest airport food. This is delicious," she said, and placed a neat bite into her mouth.

I envied her ability to eat salad with such tidy little bites. I usually just shoveled lettuce in and wiped the dressing off my mouth later. I also envied the way Soul looked, so feminine and refined. I might be a girl now, with the dressy wardrobe to prove it, but I'd never be effortlessly sexy. Of course, Soul had looked anything but frail with the huge gun in her hands. Looks could be deceiving.

For now the gun and her luggage were all upstairs in the guest bedroom. We had another freeloader. I was getting them more and more often and didn't know how I felt about my space being invaded so regularly.

When Soul was done with the meal, she leaned over and placed the bowl on the floor, picked up her tea mug, and sipped. "Thank you, Jane. This is heavenly." It was the tea Bruiser had brought, the Something Far Too Good for Ordinary People tea. Soul was not ordinary people, and I nodded. She said, "Do you want to debrief me on everything that's taking place here?"

Soul was PsyLED, so not everything could be told, but there were a lot of things that affected the human populace, or might affect the populace. As succinctly as I could, I told her about the attack on me by the light-dragon, the appearance and fight of the light-dragon at vamp central, the bomb and the shooting. And the torture of Reach. It was disjointed because I had learned info about Reach—which had likely precipitated a lot of the things happening in New Orleans—later than the trouble started. Soul listened, and I finished with, "So what can you tell me about the *arcenciel* and why it's attacking me?"

Soul leaned back over and gathered up her salad bowl and utensils, and carried them to the kitchen. Water ran and I smelled the soap we washed dishes with. I met Eli's gaze and he gave me a microscopic shrug. "How much can she tell us?" he asked.

"I don't know."

Minutes later Soul came back through the room carrying her mug. She bent and picked up her shoes, walking barefoot through the house. At the entrance to the foyer she said, "Consider that it isn't attacking you at all. Then ask questions of me. Thank you for your hospitality. I'm tired and will turn in now." Silent as a climbing cat, Soul disappeared up the stairs.

"Well, that was no help at all," I said to Eli. "I'm going to vamp HQ and ask a few people questions. Maybe they'll be more forthcoming than Soul was. I'll be back as soon as I can."

"I'll catch some zees." As it had been a while since he'd slept, I nodded and weaponed up, leaving the house by the side door.

I let myself into vamp central and logged my weapons in with security as per Protocol Aardvark. When I satisfied security, a headset hanging around my neck but not activated, I found out where Gee DiMercy was, and took the stairs up one level, to one of the libraries. I had been to the elegant room once, while carrying a vamp head in a carton. It wasn't my best moment. This time I brought a bag of something else, a joke I hoped would go over with the Mercy Blade, the Anzû I was hoping to charm or fight, whichever got me the info I needed.

He looked up as I entered the library. No reaction showed on his face as he closed the book he was reading and pushed it across the desk. As if he'd been expecting me. Go figure. I strode across the short space, seeing from the corners of my eyes the deep piles of Oriental carpets, the leather sofas with silk velvet throws, the unlit fireplace, and the dark wood shelves filled with books. By the scent, and as far as I could see, Gee was alone. I reached the table and tossed the plastic bag across the uncluttered top where it landed and slid toward Gee. He caught the bag in one hand and laughed, a quick croak better suited to a crow than a man.

Eyes sparkling that odd, iridescent blue, he held up the bag and said, "I never ate birdseed. I eat meat on the hoof or wing."

"Not denying it? *Anzû?*" I accused.

"I have been called many things, *skinwalker*. Including Storm God. Do you not kneel in my presence?"

The small man sat deeper in his chair, tossing the bag back and forth from hand to hand. I sat across from him, as if I deserved to sit in his presence. "Nope."

Gee DiMercy laughed, this time a more human-sounding chortle. "Modern man is so vastly entertaining. But they still come to the gods to ask questions, to petition for miracles. What do you wish, little goddess." It was more a demand than a question, and I propped my elbows on the tabletop, chin in hand. Looking defenseless, which I was, if he planned to hurt me. I was betting on the immortal's desire for entertainment to keep me safe.

"I know the Sumerians and the Babylonians and the Chaldeans worshiped versions of the Anzû storm gods, which makes you, maybe, the oldest thing alive on this planet. I want to know about The People of the Straight Ways. I want to know about the flood. I want to know about the *arcenciel*. And I want to know about the thing in the basement." Up until the last statement, Gee had looked blandly polite, the way people look when you act according to expectations, which meant that Gee had been waiting for me to put things together and come to him for info. When I mentioned the basement, however, he blinked. Either Gee was the best actor in the universe—not an impossibility—or he had no idea about the basement. "Start talking," I said.

"And would I share my knowledge and wisdom for nothing, little goddess? Share with a brazen and insolent woman with nothing to offer me? In times past, those who petitioned us did so with gifts of gold and silver, offering their bodies for the delight of the heavenly beings, and the blood of their first born."

"I gave you birdseed. Eat up."

"I propose a hunt. The two of us, on the wing. Perhaps we shall hunt elk in the cold north."

My mouth fell open.

Gee laughed again at what he saw on my face. "You did not think to get away for nothing?" It was half question, half amused statement. His eyebrows went up when I didn't reply and surprise flashed across his face. "You *did* think I would share my knowledge exempt of sacrifice. You are much the child. Or the fool."

"I pick fool," I said. "I can't hunt elk. The biggest bird I can shift into—" I stopped. I had been about to say was the Bubo bubo, the Asian eagle owl. But I remembered the feathers I had taken from the death site of an Anzû. I still had one somewhere. It likely had Anzû DNA on it. Could I shift into an Anzû? And what would I be if I did? Something like excitement but darker, colder, shivered through me.

"Okay," I said before I could think it through or change my mind. "One hunt in return for answers to every question I can think of."

Gee looked to the ceiling as if he searched for heavenly protection from my foolishness. "One hunt for four questions." He grinned evilly. "Questions already asked."

"Five questions. The four questions I already asked, answered fully, in English, now, and one question of my choosing, answered fully, in English, at any time I ask it. In return I'll give you one hunt, to last no longer than twenty-four hours, to take place at a mutually agreed-upon time, no sooner than tomorrow, and no later than two weeks before the Europeans arrive."

Gee chortled, delighted. "I am not Loki to demand such strictures upon an agreement. Done," he finished, before I could comment. "Your questions were: knowledge about The People of the Straight Ways, knowledge about the great flood, knowledge about the *arcenciel*, and knowledge of what hides in the deepest scion room. Yes?"

"Yes." And maybe knowledge about Peregrinus, though I didn't say it aloud for fear it would become my unasked question by accident. We'd see.

"My answer to the last question, first. I am uninterested in the scion rooms. They all stink and are filled with ravening beasts in human form. You will have to ask the Master of the City, as the residents there are his, as are we all."

Speak for yourself, I thought. But instead of saying it, I inclined my head in a "go on" gesture.

"The People of the Straight Ways were also called the Builders. They built with stone and unfired mud bricks, which were effective at the time due to the lack of rainfall in a glacial period. Their civilization flourished over twenty thousand years ago, at the *start* of the last glacial period, and they were destroyed at the *end* of that period, some seven to ten thousand years ago, when the earth warmed almost overnight and the glaciers melted."

"Overnight," I stated, careful to make the word a not-question.

He waved a hand at me as if waving away the word. "It took over a century or so for the glacial sheet to melt, and the resultant movement of the earth, as the weight of the glaciers vanished and the northern hemispheres rose, and the floods created as ice dams burst and millions of gallons of water rushed toward the nearest seas, and the permafrost melted from stone-like ground. A hundred and twenty years of flooded hell. The floods were everywhere as cold, dry weather became hot, wet weather in only two generations. There were many series of floods. The final one, the largest and most destructive, wiped the last of the Builders' civilization off the face of the earth. Earthquakes rocked the entire world. Whole mud brick cities sank beneath the waves, cities buried in the alluvial mud and many feet of ocean, all evidence wiped away forever. It is the survivors' memories of that last flood that are memorialized in carvings and friezes and paint—the rolling waveforms, the stylized-squared forms, the doubled-over waveforms—on the archaeological sites, the world over."

My childhood in the Christian children's home flashed before my eyes. "Noah and the flood?" I asked.

Gee made a little fluffing motion with his hand. "I was not alive at the time, but I have been told by the oldest among us that Noah was obedient, but a boring and untalented preacher, a drunkard, and an egotist. His redemption came in the fact that he listened when the Anzû messengers spoke of the final destruction and built his ark. He was among the best of the Builders. He survived. Many more perished."

"The Anzû," I said, again carefully making it a statement and not a question, though the question was inherent. "Not God."

Gee pondered the dilemma of the question/statement for a moment but decided to let it go. With a bored shrug, he said, "According to the ancients, the creator spoke through the living long before there was writing to record the prehistoric stories."

I wasn't sure that he had answered my statement and also didn't know what his nonanswer said about my beliefs, so I didn't push it. "That's answers to questions one and two. I'm ready for number three."

"The *arcenciel* is a more difficult question. They do not come from this time or this world."

I remembered that Rick's cousin Sarge Walker, a pilot who lived outside of Chauvin, Louisiana, south of Houma, had once talked about liminal lines and liminal thresholds. "This isn't a question," I said. "I've heard of sites and places on Earth where the fabric of reality is thin, where one reality can bleed into another. Places where the coin stack of universes meet and mesh and sometimes things can cross over from one reality to another."

Gee DiMercy zoomed a razor-sharp look at me, one worthy of a raptor with a bunny in its sights. I put two and two together and added, slowly, "Like maybe . . . the Anzû. And the *arcenciel*. It bit you like it did Leo, but didn't hurt you near as much. And then it . . . licked you." I narrowed my eyes at him.

"Tasted your blood with its tongue. Like a dessert, a petit four," I accused.

Gee did a little *pifft* of sound. "I am delectable, yes; this is true. Liminal thresholds are theoretical, the type of conjecture toyed with when physicists have drinking parties and alcohol loosens their tongues."

I sat up and dropped my hands into my lap, palming a steel blade, a small three-inch throwing knife, though I held the blade back, against my inner arm, for close-in work, not throwing work. Just in case I really did understand the truth and he decided to kill me for it. "I was told that the Earth has three liminal lines. They supposedly curve across the Earth. One starts in southwest Mexico, curves across the Gulf of Mexico to Chauvin, Louisiana, then follows the Appalachians east and north in a curve like the trade winds sometimes make, but more stable, static, bigger, and smoother. Then it curves across the ocean."

Gee stared at me with an expression I had no way of deciphering, except that he didn't look like he wanted to rip my insides out and eat the chunks anymore. Or not as much. Still Gee didn't respond, but I could see things happening behind his eyes.

"The *arcenciel* and the Anzû both came through the liminal thresholds, didn't they?" I said. "That's why there's no real paleontological or archaeological evidence of either. That's why there are so few of you. That's why—"

"Stop. I may not bandy such information about."

"We have a deal."

"And I will contemplate how I might fulfill that *deal* without being forsworn to others no longer here."

I stood. "Okay. Meanwhile, I have a . . . a friend, of sorts. She works for PsyLED, and her name is Soul. When there's danger, she moves with a long, sinuous shape of light." I leaned in. "Would she think you tasty too?"

Gee's eyes went wide and he said, "I would speak to her."

"Yeah? Well, I'll pass along the request. Right now, she's sleeping in my guest bedroom." Gee's eyes went wider and something like avarice crossed his face, too fast for me to interpret. "I'll be doing some research on liminal lines and thresholds." I stood, walking out of the library, leaving the birdseed on the table, and keeping my body bladed and my eyes on Gee DiMercy's until the door closed between us. I broke out in a sweat, knowing he could have run me through with sword, beak, or talons before I had a chance to block. I was lucky he'd not made up his mind to kill me for my rudeness. I was betting that old beings who had been worshiped as "gods" were not totally hip to modern-day snark. I put the small blade away when I reached a place where other people were, feeling safe only when there were lots of witnesses around.

I paused in a hallway and thought about the "dark things" that Gee had said were hidden here at HQ, and the things that no one was saying. I pulled my clunky cell and dialed the Kid. "Yellowrock Secur—"

"You know that glitch we were talking about recently?" I interrupted. "The one that sent us all up and down?"

"Someone's listening?" Alex caught on fast. "The, uh"—he paused, searching for a word that would communicate without giving anything away to any sharp-eared vamps nearby—"winches, gotcha. What can I do for you?"

"Send me there. Stop at the room with all the paintings and stuff, and then send me as far as you can."

"Oh." I could tell Alex was thinking that wasn't such a good idea but he finally said, "Yeah. If you're sure."

"I'm in the mood to travel."

"I can't get past the security programs to override the system, without an insider's handprint. At least not yet. I'm working on it, though."

"I'll find someone willing."

"It's your neck. You want me to stay on?"

He meant stay in contact, the HQ internal communication lines open. "Yeah." I fumbled in the cover of the cell, pulled out the earpiece he had put there one rainy afternoon when he was playing Q to Eli's and my James and Jane Bond. I synced the cell to the radio, putting the cell back into a pocket. I had never used the upmarket syncing service but it was handy. "You there?"

"Loud and clear," Alex answered. And no one at HQ could overhear. Alex was big on back doors. He was a lot like Reach that way.

I walked into the public parts of fanghead HQ, snagging a vamp on my way. It was Mario Esposito, a dark-skinned Italian guy who thought he was way prettier and way more suave than he really was. In his low-heeled loafers, Mario was three inches shorter than me in my boots, and while that wasn't uncommon, his interest in my chest was unusual. The twenty pounds I'd put on not so long ago had given me some kind of cleavage, and Mario looked like he wanted to get up close and personal with mine. I hooked my arm through his and led the way to the elevator, as Mario shot me his best lines.

"I knew we would one day be together, *mio amore.* I knew it the first time I gazed at your body, strong and sensual and . . ."

I pushed into the elevator and nuzzled Mario's ear. "Mario, honey pie, would you swipe your palm and take me to heaven?"

Alex made a quiet gagging noise, one that faded into the background noises, even to a vamp's sharp hearing. Mario laid his hand over the reader, and hit the button for the third floor.

"Now, please," I said. "Make it so, Number Two."

The elevator doors closed. Mario's mouth descended to my neck. The vamp didn't notice my disinterest while he pressed his fangs against my skin in invitation, but he did get the downward motion of the elevator. Down and down and down. He pulled his cold lips from my throat and looked up to my face. "We are going down."

"Yes."

"Into the dark."

"Looks like it," I said, maybe a bit too nonchalantly.

A blade appeared in Mario's hands, one in each. Fast. Almost as fast as he vamped out into fighting mode. I was impressed. I pulled my nine-millimeter semiautomatic, checked the silver-round load, injected a round into the chamber, and off-safetied. With my left hand, I pulled a small LED flashlight and flipped it to turbo mode. I stuck it into the little strap on my left wrist and shook my arm, satisfied it was secure. I pulled the fourteen-inch vamp-killer and set my feet, carefully balancing my weight.

Around his fangs, Mario asked, "Why do I feel that you were, perhaps, expecting this descent into hell?"

"Because you're almost as pretty as you are smart?"

"Jesu Christo," he swore, the word choice odd for a vamp. "I am trapped with a madwoman."

The doors opened onto a lighted room, the storeroom with the paper records and the paintings. I concentrated on the painting of the four vamps, taking it in fast, Grégoire and his sick little family, memorizing the faces of his sire, his brother and sister, their clothes, and the bird jewelry. The older male was olive skinned and dark haired, with a patrician nose and a dissolute, supercilious sneer that would do Caligula proud. This would be François Le Bâtard, an illegitimate son of French royalty, pederast, abuser of children. Someone of power among the EuroVamps. The younger male, Peregrinus, looked Grégoire's age, black haired, black eyed, a beautiful fallen angel, his eyes and expression empty. The girl looked even younger, maybe twelve, dressed in a low-cut gown that revealed far too much of a body halted before puberty. Unlike Peregrinus, her face wasn't blank. She wore a look of terror that seemed to have a scent even after all these years. Grégoire stood to her side, a hand on her shoulder as if to hold her down or give her reassurance, his golden hair pulled back into a braid, his blue eyes staring right at the painter. He was wearing a tight blue outfit with a white shirt and tall boots. And he looked angry. Beyond angry. He wore a fury that appeared unfettered, uncontrolled, as wild as a mustang cornered by a cowboy with intents to capture, tame, and ride him. But the painter who had captured them all. They looked real, as if they could step off the canvas.

Beside the painting was a safe, an old black one with a big handle and a dial. Another painting stood beside it, of two females, both vamps, according to the paleness of their perfect skin. One was Adrianna, a vamp I knew and had killed, twice now. For reasons never clear to me, Leo had brought her back. Other paintings were stacked nearby, including a painting partially hidden behind a trunk. It depicted Grégoire, his siblings, and a small girl child with golden skin and black hair. I had to wonder whether the thing or things that Satan's Three were searching for might be here, in this huge room. Sadly, nothing jumped up and down waving its arms shouting, *Me, me, me!* and all I got from the experience was a chance to memorize the faces of my enemies. I needed to have the contents cataloged and photographed. Soon. When I had a free day. I laughed at the thought, feeling Mario jerk in shock at the sound.

Beside me, the terrified vamp cursed in a breath that stank of fear pheromones. He swiped his hand and pressed the main floor button. "A madwoman," he repeated. The door whooshed closed on the paintings, and Mario started to put away his weapons when he noted I was balanced and ready for . . . attack? Combat? "What have you done?" he hissed.

The elevator dropped again, this time with a little jerk, as if it didn't really want to go down. "Just checking to see if Peregrinus might be looking for something hidden down here." Mario started swearing under his breath, the words in Italian and full of religious references.

On second thought, he might have been praying.

CHAPTER 15

If Vamps Could Wet Their Pants

I grunted once just as the doors opened into utter blackness. The stench of death and rotten things whooshed into the elevator. I breathed in through my mouth. The back of my tongue was instantly coated with the reek of the grave, the stench of unwashed bodies, long-dead herbs. Cloying and vile. I steadied myself.

In turbo mode, the flash provided two hundred fifteen lumens and threw a narrow, concentrated beam three hundred seventy-one feet into the darkness. It wasn't enough. The darkness swallowed the beam of light like outer space. The silence was so profound that it filled the elevator, a hollow, echoing absence of light and sound and life, a long moment of nothingness as I swept the flash from side to side and up and down.

All I saw beyond the elevator lights was darkness with unfinished ceilings and rough-hewn beams far overhead, clay floor just beyond the elevator doors, damp and slick-looking. Old bricks appeared out of the gloom to one side, barely visible, wet and oozing and smelling of magic that held back the ground water. But there was no sound. Only an emptiness so acute it might have echoed into the next universe. I took a breath and it reverberated like a hissing, asthmatic snake. I pulled on Beast's hearing and vision. And still heard nothing.

Then there it was. A single, soft drip, bright and clear, the resonance sibilant, as the sound ricocheted around the room. I tried to determine where it originated, but chasing the bouncing sound was like chasing a bunch of rabbits—everywhere at once. The drip sounded again and I followed Mario's eyes to the left and ahead. I lifted the light there, moving it slowly left to right.

From the dark, a glimmer of something red, flashing to silver. Again. And a breath, like a winter breeze. Beside me, Mario repeatedly pressed his palm on the scanner until the doors whooshed closed. The vamp was swearing like a sailor as his hand jammed onto buttons. The elevator rose. He swallowed, his vamp tissues dry as bike tires, and he started cursing in English to make sure I knew what he was saying. Finally he wound down as the elevator opened to light and the smell of vamps and blood and humans and sex. Normal vamp smells. "You are *psicotico*," he spat. "Insane."

I grabbed his arm before he could disappear. "It was a vamp, wasn't it? Down there?"

"It might have been Lucifer himself," he said, jerking free as he strode from the elevator. "Stay away from me." Mario's clothes were dark, so I wasn't sure, but if vamps could wet their pants, he just had. And I wasn't sure why he was so negatively affected. Vamps always kept their scions chained to walls when in the devoveo, the ten years or more of madness after a human was turned. The sub-five basement had a vamp prisoner. Only one, by the smell. But I could drop that from my inquiries. A scion, no matter how important he or she might have been when human—even a king or queen—wasn't anything that Satan's Three would want. If the three were coming after something here at HQ, then it was likely that they were interested in something stored on sub-four. Could Leo have put magical items and artifacts in storage? In the safe hidden in the piles of stuff?

I left vamp central and headed across the river to Aggie One Feather's place. I needed knowledge and wisdom and oral tradition. I needed someone who knew stuff and would share it with me openly and honestly. And for free. It was hard making do with bits and pieces of history offered by people who might have reasons to hide that same info. Now that I knew enough to know what questions to ask, Aggie would dish, and the only thing she would make me pay was more honesty and self-assessment. Aggie was all about shining light on one's deep inner truths and banishing the shadows.

Because of Aggie, I wasn't the same Jane who had first come

to New Orleans. I had learned too much about myself and about my Beast. Too much about what it meant to be a victim and to make others victims. Too much about the dark night of the soul—a poetic way of describing the internal loss of meaning of oneself, and depression. I had looked it up. Because of Aggie, I had survived all that learning and maybe grown up a bit. A very little bit, according to Aggie.

Because of Aggie, because she (and sometimes her aged mother) took me to sweat and took me to water—Cherokee rites and rituals—and because she forced me to remember who and what I was, I had discovered that my inner soul home was my place of greatest strength. I had discovered the first cracks and fissures into the emptiness that was my own past, the first passageways into my own Cherokee memory.

I hadn't told Aggie much about Beast yet, and I might never. But because of her I had discovered that Beast lived in that same soul home, that same deep cavern of inner sanctum. There, nothing and no one could bind us. There we were invincible, the two of us. I had discovered that our souls, Beast's and mine, were not only in the same place; they were, to some extent, intertwined, which, so far as I knew, had never happened to a skinwalker. I had no idea what it might mean to me as I aged, as time took us to new and different places, but it had to mean something.

I turned into the road and cut the engine, coasting the SUV until it stopped, well back from the shell-based drive. I pulled the key and sat in the dark, studying the house and grounds. The security light on the pole at the end of the drive was off, the house and lawn cloaked in the night and illuminated by the moon. The light's globe was broken. Shattered. The house was dark, though Aggie's car was in the drive. No TV flickered through the windows. No lights anywhere.

I stared at the house for the space of time between heartbeats. Quietly, I opened the vehicle door, sniffed, and caught the residue of gunfire on the air. Someone had shot out the light. What else had they shot? If someone wanted to hurt me, by hurting my friends, would they know about the One Feathers? Not likely. But anything was possible. Would the two women be able to protect themselves? No. Not against a sniper or a bomb maker.

I let my Beast senses free, questing. The night crashed in,

full of the buzz of mosquitoes and the croak of frogs, but empty of any human sounds. No TV laugh tracks. No radio. No conversation. Worse, there was no smell of food on the air. No smell of wood smoke from the sweat house. I raced into the shadows to the house.

I hadn't noticed when I drew my weapon, but I was holding it in a two-handed grip beside my right leg as I crept around Aggie's house. As I stepped toward the back porch a soft creak met my ear, slow and repetitive. I halted and timed the sound to about once every two and a half seconds. Someone was on the porch, in the rocker, rocking. Shades of the Bates Motel slashed through my memory.

"Nice night."

I jerked, just ever so slightly.

"I forgot what it was like to sit out here without the light."

It was Aggie One Feather speaking, and I was pretty sure she wasn't talking to me. I achieved a breath that didn't whistle in fear. Inside me Beast chuffed with laughter and thumped the wall of my soul home with her tail.

"Yup. It nice. How much time till the power company get here?" *uni lisi,* the grandmother of many children, a Cherokee honorific for an old woman, asked, her tone garrulous.

"In time for your show, Mama."

"Them kids, they gonna fix our light?"

"Their parents said they'd pay for it, Mama. And Deputy Antonelli said he'd make sure or he'd help us press charges."

"That good. Good enough." The rocker rocked on, a peaceful sound in the night. "If I get to watch my *Jeopardy!*"

I holstered my weapon and called out, "Aggie? It's Jane Yellowrock. Ummm . . ." I thought about the fact that I always just dropped by. Maybe that wasn't the nicest thing I could do. "Ummm, are you taking callers?"

"Come around to the porch, Jane," Aggie called back. "Some kids looking for a place to neck shot out our security light and hit the electric lines."

Neck? Instantly I thought about vamps and fangs and bloodmeals. Then I realized she was talking about hooking up in the backseat of a car. Old-people slang. "Oh. I'm sorry to hear that." I made my way to the porch and up the stairs. Aggie was right; the porch and the night were nice. The house's foundation was several feet high, to protect it against hurricane storm surge, and it looked out over a backyard I had never paid much attention to. There were fruit trees and a garden behind a chicken-wired fence, smelling of freshly turned earth and frustrated rabbits. A row of bee boxes stood at the back of the property, the bees silent, the smell of honey soft on the air. I closed the door behind me, making out the location of the two women and the mama cat sitting on *uni lisi*'s lap. I took a chair. Aggie moved in the dark and I heard a gurgling sound, and smelled cold tea and fresh mint. She pushed a glass across the table to me. I took it and sipped. "Thank you." A silence filled the space between us, uncomfortable on my part. "Ummm," I said again.

Aggie made an amused humming sound. My lack of social skills was not a secret to her. Not that she would help me through it.

I puffed out a breath. "That bomb maker I called you about? If she's who I think she is, then she's also a sniper and she smells like The People."

I smelled Aggie's shock, so strong it might have actually burned through my skin, like an electric spark. Maybe I should have tried some small talk before I jumped into the mess of my life. The weather. Their health. Too late now. "She is War Woman," Aggie asked, "like you?"

"No." I hesitated. "I don't think so. She's female, and a human blood-servant. I don't think a War Woman would allow herself to be fed upon by vamps. And she's not someone I've ever smelled before."

"You being a skinwalker," *uni lisi* said, unperturbed. "That true?"

I sipped again, my mouth suddenly dry. "Yes, ma'am."

"That how you can smell what this woman is?"

"Yes, ma'am."

"And this woman who smell like The People. She chasing you?"

I started to answer and stopped. Not just targeting me at my house to kill me, but chasing me? If so, was she trying to get me to lead her somewhere? Tracking me everywhere I went? Like to here? "Maybe," I said, as the possibilities bounced around in my head. What the heck did Satan's Three *want*? The things in my possession that were magical. That was all that was left for them to be after.

"I see on the TV, 'bout them little things people stick to cars," *uni lisi* said. "So they can follow peoples. You got one on you car?"

My hands went cold on the iced tea glass. I hadn't checked. I wasn't used to being a target myself. If I had been a client, I'd have been over the car with a microscope. I set down the tea glass and hit the button for Eli. "Yeah?" he answered.

"You didn't think to check my vehicle for tracking devices, did you?"

"You were clean this morning. The only way we can be totally sure is to put a camera on it, check it every day, and park it in a vault."

"Excuse me," I said to the One Feathers, and left the porch at a run. I still had my flashlight and clicked the light on as I neared my SUV. "Anything new I should be looking for?" It might sound like a dumb question, but the market for monitoring and tracing equipment was changing and evolving so fast that keeping up required constant attention to company updates. I'd left that to Eli.

"Second- and third-gen magnetic trackers are smaller and adhere better than the first generation. They still can be fired from a cannon or tossed over a fence to land anywhere on the exterior, but even the old trackers cost five hundred bucks apiece and none of them always stick. The math sucks unless you have bottomless pockets. It's easier to walk by, open the door, and toss one under the seat, except you keep your vehicle locked. A public street is not the place to disable the alarm and attach one inside the engine compartment or the trunk. So that leaves walking by, pausing, and sticking a GPS tracking device under the wheel well or bumper. Old-style craft. They can be small enough to hide between two fingers, but those cost. Most people still use the ones the size of a pack of cigarettes. You checking now?" I grunted the affirmative and he said, "I'll hold."

I walked around the vehicle and saw nothing on the exterior. I bent and checked each wheel well. Empty except for mud from where I'd gotten stuck earlier, and the rain splashing up from the roads hadn't completely washed it clean. Anything pushed through the mud to adhere to the metal would have left an impression different from ones nature left, and the mud coating all looked uniform. I lay down and rolled under the front, then the back. Nothing was stuck to the bumpers. "I'm clean. But I want a more thorough inspection when I get home."

"Okay." He disconnected.

Back on the porch I asked, "You have a gun?"

"Course we have a gun," Aggie said, as if I'd asked a stupid question. Maybe I had. These were country women facing rabid animals, carrot-stealing rabbits, and kids with nefarious and salacious intentions. And maybe evil people looking to rob, rape, and steal.

I sat and drank half of my tea, my mouth as dry as a bone from dread. "My vehicle looks clean, but there's no way to be sure. And since I'm here now, it's too late. I'm sorry."

"We be okay," *uni lisi* said. "What you come here for tonight?"

Not to get you killed, I thought. I said, "Are there any Cherokee stories about dragons?"

"Some," Aggie said.

"There Uktena," *uni lisi* said. "He a dragon-like serpent with horns."

I repeated the name. "Ook-tay-nah?"

Aggie said, "Close enough. The first Uktena was said to be transformed from a human man in a failed assassination attempt on the sun. Most other Uktena tales have to do with Cherokee heroes slaying the Uktena monster. The dragons are malevolent and deadly."

"The assassination attempt on the sun sounds a little like Apollo. So maybe the dragons are made of light?"

"Or they aliens like that professor with the hair say."

I wasn't sure who *uni lisi* was talking about, but the idea that the *arcenciel* was an alien was a possibility—though not an alien who came to Earth in a spaceship. Rather, one who got here from another universe at a liminal threshold, a place where one universe touched another.

"Then there's the Tlanuwa." I cocked my head in question and Aggie produced it again. "Tlah-noo-wah." I nodded and she went on. "Tlanuwa are giant birds of prey with impenetrable metal feathers. They're common to the oral tradition of many southeastern tribes and may be the same things as the Thunderbird in southwestern tribal mythology."

"Now, that sounds like a spaceship," I said, but thought that it could also be a storm god. An Anzû. I had never actually seen one without its glamour blocking the way and I had never seen one fly.

Aggie shrugged, her shoulders rising and falling in the dark. "It has a strong resemblance to a jet fighter. Noisy, sleek, powerful, dangerous, and darting through the sky with a roar. You want to tell us what you're looking for?"

I described the *arcenciel*. And the Anzû. Aggie watched me as I talked, her eyes holding me in place like spears. "I'm wondering if they are real creatures that came to Earth through a liminal threshold. A weak place in reality where creatures can get to Earth."

"That old man," *uni lisi* said derisively, "that Choctaw old man. Him talk about seeing strange things down in the bayou."

"The Choctaw are south of Houma?" I asked. That was one place I'd seen the *arcenciel*, playing in the waters of a bayou.

"No. The Choctaw tribal regions went from the Gulf of Mexico to the Canadian border," Aggie said. My eyes went wide in surprise.

"But in the last war, our people beat them good." *Uni lisi* sounded satisfied, the way a soccer mom might when recounting an old high school rivalry.

Aggie ignored it and said, "Locally the tribal members are represented by the Biloxi-Chitimacha Confederation of Muskogees, but they're composed of an amalgamation of several tribes which include Biloxi, Chitimacha, Choctaw, Acolapissa, and Atakapa."

I nodded, but current tribal politics didn't help me.

"Each community is governed by its own tribal council and advised by their respective Council of Elders," *uni lisi* said. "That old man, he talk about thing he see in the bayou and the swamps. Him a member of the Grand Caillou/Dulac Band, but there the Isle de Jean Charles Band, and the Bayou Lafourche Band too."

"All three bands are ancestrally related. Mama was being courted by a leader of the Grand Caillou/Dulac Band, but he was killed trying to save a family during Hurricane Rita. That's the old man she's talking about."

"Him too old for me anyway. I need me a young man." *Uni lisi* cackled with glee.

"Was there any specific place where he saw the creatures?" I asked.

"Nah." *Uni lisi* waved her hand in the air as if it was all unimportant. "He seen them when he smoking wacky weed. He a crazy old man."

Aggie added, "He did say once that the Uktena tried to talk to him. That his ancestor killed one with a steel knife and drank its blood, and that it made him strong. But he didn't say where any of this happened."

"How about a Cherokee flood story?" I asked.

"There a silly story about a dog who tell a man to build a raft, and then that dog, he tell the man to throw him into the water to kill him. Stupid dog, he was. Then the flood came and the man on the raft lived but all the other peoples were just a pile of bones."

"Their spirits danced," Aggie said, looking troubled. "It sounded like the pile of their bones dancing. Mama's beau said he heard it once." She nodded and sipped her tea, her eyes far away, in the past of the old stories. When she spoke again, she sounded uneasy. "Like a pile of bones . . . *dancing*. I always hated that image."

Uni lisi waved her hand again. "Some stories silly. This one silly. You don' be unhappy about this silly story or about that old man. That a long time ago." But her voice no longer sounded like the story was silly, or that she had stopped grieving for her old man.

Out front I heard a truck turn into the cul-de-sac. Truck lights swept the property as it went around my SUV and circled the small turn-around of the cul-de-sac. I slipped out and determined it was indeed a power company truck, and its diesel engine was idling as a man with a powerful flashlight stood beneath the pole, looking up at the damage, muttering imprecations about kids these days. I returned to the One Feathers' back porch, offered my thanks, and said my good-byes. I slipped out and to my SUV. Checked my GPS.

I called Derek and asked, "If I give you a GPS, can you send a guy to sit in a tree and keep an eye on two old ladies? Like you're doing with Leo's clan home property? I can pay."

"Sure, Legs. I'll send Blue Voodoo. He hunts. Sitting in a tree will be like a day off with pay for him."

I gave Derek the GPS and the address, described the layout, and left it to Derek and Blue Voodoo. I didn't know the guy well, but he was one of Derek's longtime men. The One Feathers would be safe from anyone targeting my friends to get at me.

Without turning on my lights, I started the engine and backed out of the street. Where would a tribal elder have heard a sound in the bayou, a sound like bones dancing?

I was no closer to discovering anything, spinning my wheels. But something about dancing bones sounded important. And sad.

With the night off, I could have changed and let Beast hunt, but it felt too dangerous to shape-shift and play. Too much was going wrong and I had too little information. And yet, the *arcenciel* had gray energies like the ones where I changed form. So . . . maybe it wasn't play. Maybe it would be research. I didn't know but I decided to stay human, for now.

I was still on the west side of the river when I saw an SUV like the ones I'd seen before, maybe tailing me, though this one was grayish in the night, not black. I asked my cell to dial the Kid, and when he answered, I said, "You remember the license plates Eli and I got you for the black SUVs that were tailing us?" I knew the Kid would remember, so I didn't wait for an answer. The question was rhetorical. "What did they come back as?"

"Local leases. Both came back to a Paul Reaver, not Revere, but Reaver."

"Fake name?" I asked, as I slowed, letting the vehicle close the gap on me.

"Probably, but the credit card is good, so whoever created the ID did a good job. The cars have GPS, which I got, and I've been following them. Both are currently near the corner of Beryl Street and Jewel Street, hear Harlequin Park. Eli rode by, talked to a neighbor who says they are nice people. Nice house. Rental. You need me to send you a photo?"

The tail vehicle pulled up fast and its lights hit my mirrors, blinding me. My heart rate sped and I reached to the passenger seat and pulled a nine-mil from the thigh holster. "Is there another car rented under the same name?"

"No. I checked. Why?"

The SUV took that moment to pull around me and roar off. It was full of people and was blasting some heavy bass beat into the night and trailing odors of weed and booze. Teenaged rockers, full of hormones. I let the tension drain away, even as I memorized the license plate. "No," I said, hearing the relief in my voice. "But just for grins, run this plate." I gave him the number. "And is Soul there?"

"She went out about half an hour ago."

"I'll get back to you." I ended the call and wondered how much of what I was seeing and worrying about was nothing and how much was various supernatural beings hiding things from me. Maybe it was time to beard the lion in her den.

Pulling over, I parked in the shadow of an abandoned warehouse, the front of the vehicle snugged up against the building.

There were lots of warehouses up and down the Mississippi, some old and fancy with intricate brickwork and some thrown together out of metal and steel. This was a newer, and therefore uglier one, with tall grasses growing up in cracked concrete and birds flying through broken glass in the ventilation windows high off the ground. There were no security cameras that I could I see, and I was far enough off the road so that traffic cams would have a hard time picking anything up, if there even was a traffic cam on the isolated road.

I rolled down the window and sniffed the night air, smelling rats and feral cats and exhaust. A far-off skunk. Dead fish. Water. No people had been here recently. I made sure that the thigh holster Bruiser had provided was secure on the passenger seat beside me. Loosened both nine-mils and chambered a round in each. Standard ammo, not silver. It would likely be rednecks or gangbangers, not supernats, who would bother me out here.

I slouched down in the vehicle seat and took a chance; I dialed Soul. She picked up instantly. "What have you learned?" she asked.

"Too much and too little. I need you to confirm that you are the same species of creature as the *arcenciel* that attacked Leo and Gee DiMercy. Gee hints that it might be so. And I need to know what the gray place of the change is—that's what I call the shape-changing energies that seem to operate outside ordinary Earth physics and time. And I need to know now."

Soul didn't answer at first, and I rolled the window down an inch so I could hear anyone or anything approaching. The window was still cracked from when the light-dragon hit my vehicle. I really needed to get that fixed before a cop pulled me over and ticketed me. By the unchanging scents, there was still nothing anywhere around, only the smells of small animals, the heady heaviness of freshwater, the soft susurration of the wind, and the deeper, more powerful vibration of the river on the other side of the levee.

"I will call you back," she said, and the call ended.

I waited for perhaps two minutes, before I began to wonder whether she had blown me off, or if maybe she had meant she would call me back later. Then my cell rang, an unknown number on it. *Burner phone?*

"Yellowrock," I said.

Soul said, "Some have hinted that you are dangerous, with

your questions and your species-gifts untaught and unproven. Those same have proposed that you be removed to lessen the danger to the rest of us."

Removed? Meaning killed? But before I could ask, Beast pressed down on my mind with her paw. In the darkness of my mind, I saw a mental image of a puma high on a ledge over a trickle of water. Waiting, still and silent, for prey.

Soul went on. "I have offered my recommendation that you be allowed to hunt for truth where you might find it and use such truth as you might wish. An experiment that might lead the imprisoned into the light."

"Thanks," I said, my tone offended. "It's nice to have someone in my corner when I'm being judged without the chance to speak for myself. *Some who?*"

"Some of my ilk. My species, as you said."

"Okay. So there are a lot more of you than I was thinking."

"The lines are open again. For now, yes."

Which meant nothing to me. "I'm not in the mood to play games," I said, feeling tired. I closed my eyes and rubbed them with my fingertips. They felt hot and dry. "Please just answer my questions. Just this once will someone please just answer my questions without making me bleed for the answers. *Please?*"

Soul laughed, not unkindly. "I am of the Light, what some have called *arcenciel* or *essendo luci*. Light-beings. Rainbow dragons. Humans have worshiped us and witches have imprisoned us and used us for their magics for eons of time. We have come and gone upon your Earth and others like it for millennia. We like it here. Were we not hunted, more of us would choose to stay here. To raise our hatchlings here. There is water aplenty and we like the water planets best."

Finally. Finally someone who could talk to me. *Would* talk to me. With my eyes closed I felt some odd sort of darkness float out of me, a shadow heavy as a stone lifting away. "And the gray place of the change?" *Please answer me that.*

"It is here and not here. It is a place that exists within and without. It is life and death, healing and illness, light and darkness, good and evil, time and not-time. It is neither this nor that, and yet is everything. It is energy and matter as they play together like streams colliding and re-forming and flowing around boulders and islands and obstacles, ever moving forward, yet able to pool and stand still. It is the Gray Between."

I laughed, the sound broken. "That doesn't help me much, though I have figured out that it comes from inside me as much as from outside me."

"Call your energies. I will come to you."

I sat up slowly in the car seat. "You can find me when I go into the gray place of the change?"

"Of course. If I am physically close enough, I can see you through the Gray Between even when you do not enter there. Can you not see us when you are there?"

I remembered back to the sparring room when the light-dragon had come through. Had it been zeroing in on *me*? But then the sequence of events settled into me and I recalled that Bruiser had asked me to go into the gray place after the *arcenciel* had appeared and started biting. But . . . I had been pulling on Beast's strength, her speed. Were they the same thing? Did Beast's strength and her ability to slow time come from the same place, from the gray place of the change? And at my house, when I shifted into the dog . . . I had felt magic. Had the *arcenciel* tried to find me? Had it been trying to find me for a long time? Was it zeroing in on my location every time I shifted?

What about the first time I was attacked by one of the things, on Bitsa, in the city streets? I hadn't been drawing on Beast then. But maybe it had been close and had seen me in the gray place anyway? *Dang it.* I didn't know enough to make a guess, which meant experimentation was on the schedule for the night's activities.

"I don't know," I whispered. "Let's see." I set the clunky cell to the side and slouched down deeper in the SUV. I didn't try to meditate or to call upon Beast. I didn't try to find my own genetic makeup in the coiled snake of my own DNA structure. I just looked inside for the energies. And there was nothing there.

Beast rolled over in my mind, a cat on her back, looking at me upside down, her belly exposed. She chuffed at me. I was pretty sure she was laughing. Cat laughter. Which was always snark at another's expense. *Fine. You try,* I thought at her.

Instantly the gray energies rose, lifting through me, sliding around me. *Great. My cat has the power, not me.* Again Beast chuffed with laughter. And then I smelled exhaust. I opened my eyes to see lights in the rearview, lights on bright, blinding me. Doors opened. The deep basso beat of music followed multiple shapes as they left the vehicle, the SUV that blocked me in. "Soul," I whispered. "I might be in trouble."

"I see you," her voice said, over the open cell line. "Stay there."

"I'm not going anywhere," I whispered again, knowing she would hear me. I reached over and took one nine-millimeter, tucking it into my waistband at my back, the other into my fist. I rolled down, lower in the seat, into the floorboard, sitting on the accelerator. I moved the seat as far back as it would go to give me room to work. I watched the windows, and cursed the broken window that left me partially blind. I let the weapon move with my eyes, holding it in a two-hand grip.

Shadows floated beside the vehicle as the human shapes moved along the SUV. Satan's Three? Or gangbangers? I took a breath and smelled vamp, unfamiliar, powerful. Floral, like Grégoire but with hazelnut undertones. And several humans smelling of booze and weed. One of them smelled like the sniper. I was so freaking stupid.

Deep inside me, Beast growled, and I realized that she had kept the gray place of the change open. It was muted but shining, a silvered shadow of energies misting across my skin. I could change. But it would do me no good. I had blocked myself in like a mountain lion in a den. I knew better. I couldn't run. Not in time.

I heard the soft *shush* of leather on concrete and placed one of the three at the back of the SUV. Another was at the cracked window and it was a vamp. I didn't know for certain that they intended me harm, but I didn't care. I lifted the weapon to the crack at the top of the window and fired. The report was insanely loud, my hearing stopped dead, my nose clogged with the stink of a fired weapon. The shadows shifted and I heard a sound like a mouse, but recognized that it was a vamp, screaming in agony, a high-pitched ululation, the sound they make when they think they're dying, a death wail. And I could barely hear it.

I was now head-blind, except for sight. Not my best sense. I shimmied back into the knee space, my neck crooked by the steering wheel, the floorboard warm beneath me. The passenger window shattered, bowing in as if under terrific pressure, but holding together; then it was rammed a second time, spraying me with pebbled, rounded bits of glass. Instinctively, I ducked. The locks on both front doors popped. And swung open. I fired, over and over again, until the magazine was empty.

The gun was jerked from my hand and I saw it whirling into the dark, arching up high, as I was yanked out of the SUV. I landed hard on the broken concrete, banging my head. My breath whooshed from my lungs. A foot kicked down on me, hitting my chest. And my breath just stopped. Tears gathered in my eyes, reflexive to the glare of a flashlight aimed into my face.

The gray energies rose around me, burning. *Change,* Beast thought at me. *Change now!*

I reached for my skinwalker magic as a man leaned over me, pale vamp face and the long fangs of the older ones. He rested something on my chest, and I felt the freezing energies through my clothes. "You have proved useful after all," he said, his words muffled behind the gunfire-deafness, his accent Italian, or Sicilian. He leaned in and smelled me, holding me still. "I would ride you and drink you down, slowly, were there time."

Change! Beast screamed inside me.

I . . . I can't. The cold thing on my chest, I thought. *It's doing something to me.*

A pale hand holding a crystal—like a quartz crystal, about four inches long and as thick as a big man's thumb—descended and rested the quartz on my chest. Gray energies gathered around it, sucked from me, and I grunted with pain, as breath pulled back into me, like into a vacuum bottle. But the energies gathered at the crystal tip swirled around and up into the quartz . . . or diamond. Was it a diamond? And dark shadows flooded downward and inside the crystal. "You are more than you first appear, my Amazon *Chelokay.* Perhaps I shall take you with me after all." Light flickered at the edges of the night. Barely, I heard screams, smelled something fishy, and the under-tang of burning, green vegetation. The smell of bayou, maybe. It smelled familiar. This was the thing that had attacked me on Bitsa. And had attacked us in the gym at HQ. This thing had been, what? Following *me?*

In the dark there were shapes like a head and jaw, glowing eyes, an iridescent silver. Wings. Scales. Dark and light, moving away. A light-dragon. Fleeing the vamps.

A fist swung down through the glare and connected with my jaw. My head rocked back. The gray energies swirled high as my vision telescoped down. As my field of vision grew smaller and smaller, I saw two vampires chasing a rainbow, humans running, right at the edge of my failing eyesight. And then the last of my vision failed me and all I heard was shouting and an engine revving. I slumped down into the blackness of an internal night.

I woke when a palm slapped me so hard it rocked my head as badly as the fist had. Soul was standing over me, the open door of my SUV visible behind her. She hit me again, the pain and the sound ringing along with my groaning. "Stop. I'm awake." Soul seemed satisfied with her untender ministrations. She bent over the armored window, the one that was still cracked from where the *arcenciel* had rammed it, studying the cracks in detail, including the nick at the top, where my round had damaged it more.

I moaned as I rolled over, and pressed against the pain in my chest. Sitting up, I held my jaw. Soul whirled, set her eyes on me, and growled. *Okay, that's weird.*

Soul was pretty, tiny, and delicate. But as I watched, she proved that she was definitely not human. Her jaw opened way wider than a human's can. She was showing me her teeth the way Beast would show another predator her teeth in threat. I had a feeling that I was missing something crucial to this situation. "Soul. It's me. Jane." I rolled away from her, one hand behind my back gripping the nine-millimeter that was still in my waistband. The teeth looked like a warning, a predator response, not just to see me squirm, but to make sure I knew I was about to be eaten. My hand sweaty on the gun grip, I froze into stillness. "Soul? What is this?"

Magic tingled and sizzled along my skin. A wind sprang up, cold and hot at once, burning with both ice and steam. Soul's mouth elongated again. And again. Alligator long. Crocodile long. Full of teeth like needles and knives. And wrong, wrong, *wrong.* Soul was not the same person in this form, as if . . . she lost her humanity when she shed her skin. "Soul, you just saved my butt. What did I do wrong that—"

Soul hissed and spat, narrowly missing me as I flinched away. The spittle hit the metal building behind me with a whistling *splat.* I heard sizzling and smelled hot metal and acid.

"Holy crap!" I pulled the gun in my waistband and fired.

Three fast shots. And nothing happened, not to Soul. The rounds seemed to leave no mark at all. Or in my panic, I missed.

Beast shoved-rammed-punched her way into the forefront of my brain. *Change,* she screamed, clawing at my mind. Pain ricocheted through me. I inhaled and thought of Beast. Rolled over into the shadows. Until the cool metal of the warehouse at my back stopped me. Acid ran down from where she had spat at me, burning a patch of bare skin in my shoulder.

Soul lunged.

Light and shadow wrenched and twisted. The earth rearranged itself beneath me. I aimed, blew out my breath, and fired. Once, twice, three more times. Nothing hit her. The rounds passed clean through her. Through the light that was Soul. Her teeth came at me, big as a T. rex. They caught my arm and snapped down, just as she solidified and dropped onto my belly. My breath, my one precious breath, was shoved out in a strangled half scream. The smell of my blood was hot on the air. There was no pain yet. Just the sound and vibration of teeth on my bones. My stomach turned over and tried to defeat gravity. She shook me like a dog with a rabbit in its jaws. Slung me up and to the side. She let go and I landed in a spinning roll. Realized I was still in the gray place of the change. With Soul. In her natural form. Or one of them.

She leaped at me, her mouth open again. I focused on it. More cat than gator now. Striped black and yellow. *Tiger,* Beast thought. I/we snarled. Soul snarled back. With much bigger teeth.

Pelt sprouted along my arms, healing flesh and tendons on the one she had mauled. But I was twisted in my clothes. I wrenched my hips and legs, trying to get them free of the jeans and boots.

Soul pounced again and bit down onto my healing arm and shook me—clearly her method of choice for killing small prey. Like me. This time I heard the *snap-snap* of breaking bones. The pain that had been hiding exploded inside me. I heard a roaring in my ears. Which felt like a really bad thing. *Beast? I'm in trouble here.* More pain raced along my jaws and through my gut. The roaring grew louder. My body went limp.

Face wrenched in agony. Changing. Shifting. Beast screamed. Buried fangs in tiger's throat, latching down. Fur and blood and meat and . . . rich, tasty blood. Beast shook tiger. Swallowed good blood. Tiger growled and gurgled. Tiger could not breathe.

Beast played dead. Then attacked. Beast is best hunter.

Tiger whined. Blew bubbles of blood. Tiger lay still. Beast let her go and leaped to three legs, whirled and reached for tiger. Tiger was gone. Sniffed, searching for tiger. Saw light and movement among trees beside cracked, broken concrete. Light like gray place, but brighter. With wings and scales. Growling and snarling. Roaring and chuffing. Singing like birds. Soul cried, "Where is the hatchling?"

And she was gone.

Pain raced up broken leg. Beating like blood and heart. I/we gathered up Jane boots and clothes. Carried them to ess-u-vee. Leaped to front, to top of chest, above beating heart, warm from life of ess-u-vee, alive but not alive. Curled into ball on top of Jane clothes. Put jaw on boots. Closed eyes and thought of Jane.

I woke up on the warm hood of the SUV, disoriented and nauseated. Hair unbraided and draped all over me. And naked. I groaned and rolled over. Sat up. Making sure that Soul and Satan's Three were gone. No growling, no light show. No vehicle behind mine. Nothing but the smell of crushed plants, Soul blood, gunfire, and vamp on the air, mixed with something vaguely familiar that skittered around in my brain like a rat in a box before disappearing like a magic trick before I could identify it.

I rolled off the hood and dressed quickly in my blood-damp, shredded clothes, except for the panties and bra that were a total ruin. This was why I didn't invest in expensive undies.

No one drove by as I dressed; no sirens sounded in the distance. I was glad I was in the boonies with no nearby, nosy neighbors. Going commando—which was not at all comfortable, the zipper cold and pinching my skin—I shoved my feet into my boots and hunted for my guns and my cell. Seconds after becoming human again, I slid into the car, the tires ground into the concrete and spit shale, as I gunned the motor and got the heck outta Dodge, thinking, *What the heck just happened?*

I was halfway across the river before my heart rate slowed and I figured out three things. One: Driving with no windows was a lot like riding Bitsa. Two: I wasn't hungry. I had been beaten and cold-cocked by a vamp, shifted, fought a tiger, been wounded, shifted back, all in a matter of minutes, and I wasn't hungry. Shifting always used energy, energy that I took from food calories. But I wasn't hungry. In fact, I felt *amazing*, like I'd had a good meal and a beer. And like the beer worked on me like it did on humans. I wasn't buzzed, but I was *amazingly* relaxed. Which I clearly shouldn't have been. And using the term *amazing* a lot. And I had no idea why. Three: Soul was a shapeshifter. Which meant that the *arcenciels* were shapeshifters. A light-dragon and a freaking tiger and maybe other forms as well. And not a shifter who required that mass and energy remain unchanged. In her human form she weighed maybe a hundred twenty-five pounds. In her tiger form she weighed more than three hundred, if her weight on my belly had been an indication. Unless she could convert energy to mass all by her lonesome. Like maybe she had a pocket of energy she could draw on as needed to change shape and mass. *That would be handy*. The *arcenciels* had—or were—magic like I had never imagined before.

I thought through the last few minutes in the warehouse parking area as I drove, analyzing it from every memory— smell, sight, pain, taste, roaring sound, and time. Something about it was familiar in a mathematical kinda way. Like A equals B, and B equals C, so A equals C. Like that. I was doing math. My high school teachers would be so proud. I pulled up my sleeve to see an undamaged arm, healed by the shift. My life was good. Weird but good. "And I can do alphabet math. Cool."

And the best thing about the whole thing? The taste of Soul's blood. Which was why I wasn't hungry, I thought. Whatever kinda dragon-cat-shifter/*l'arenciel* Soul was, her blood was full of power. "I gotta figure out what she is. Someday," I said to the road in front of me. "For now, it's all good because I know for sure who's trying to bomb me and sniper me and tailing me. Well, it's all good, except that Soul tried to kill me." I frowned at the street because it wanted to waver to the left. "And Satan's Three are after me and it has something to do with my energies in the gray place of the change. Which is bad. Very bad. So it's not *all* good.

"Oh crap. I'm talking to myself. And I'm feeling really good. Okay. Soul's blood is full of power *and* happy juice. Like the *arcenciel* goop from the sparring room floor and from the drugged scale."

Car lights flashed into the SUV through the broken windows. My T-shirt was clawed and ripped and stiff with blood. Cool night wind touched my skin through the rents. Since I was over the river and off the bridge, I slowed, parked, and yanked the shirt off, tossing it into the passenger floor, without looking. I twisted my hair up in a bun and stuck some stakes through it to keep it in place, then pushed the stakes down because they hit the roof and hurt my scalp. Dang stakes. A toiletries bag was in back and I crawled through the SUV to get it.

From the zippered bag, I pulled a thin, short-sleeved tee and slid it over my head, which would have been easier had I done it before I staked my hair. I wasn't thinking straight yet. But my head felt light and airy and I thought that was new and different, so maybe I was metabolizing the drug like the lab's research had suggested.

I looked down at my chest. I needed to shop. I was running out of bras and work clothes, getting sword-cut and claw-slashed. This brown, yellow, and pink tee had a cute pig on it with the words *Bacon Is Meat Candy*. Ugly, though it was a perfect tee for Beast. And at least all my girlie parts were covered.

In a rush, all the manic energy drained out of me, like water flowing from my fingertips and puddling on the floor of the vehicle. My limbs went weak, my eyes were too heavy, and my head lolled back against the backseat. I was pretty sure I was passing out. I said something bad just as unconsciousness took me. My last sight was the sun trying to rise, a gray haze on the eastern sky, reflected in broken window glass everywhere.

The sun was high in the sky when I heard a hollow knocking and my cell buzzed at the same time, waking me. I picked up my cell and looked around at traffic. It took a moment to remember why I was sleeping in the back of the SUV on a crowded city street. There was a parking ticket on the windshield wiper. *Great.* And Eli stood at the broken passenger window with a peculiar look on his face. I waved Eli in, opened the cell to answer the call, moistened my cracked, dry lips, and said, "Speak to me, oh genius, geek, and computer prodigy."

"Those are pretty much all the same thing, you know. Ummm. Are you okay?" the Kid asked. "You sound kinda . . . I don't know. Happy."

"I'm always happy. Tell me something I don't know. And say hi to your brother."

I held the phone out so Eli, who was easing into the SUV, could hear.

"Yeah. Sure. Hey, Eli. Whatever. Is she okay?"

Eli closed the door on the traffic, looked me over, and shook his head, bemused. "She looks like a homeless person who spent the night in the back of an unsecured SUV, wearing a bacon shirt."

"Yeah? Get a pic. Jane, the car tailing you was a lease that came back to Florence Falcon. Florence is a false ID, with a social that originated at the same birth month and state as Paul Reaver. Florence works for Paul Reaver. Whoever created the fantastic IDs did a pis—uh, a poor job of separating the locales and the timelines. You want me to send this to Jodi?"

"Yeah. Tell her I was being tailed. And that they boxed me in and tried to kill me."

"What? Are you okay?" Alex sounded weirded out, which didn't make much sense because people were always trying to kill me. "Eli?"

"Yeah, yeah, yeah. I'm ducky," I said. Eli grunted agreement. "Jodi might want to—wait," I said. "Send the info to Jodi *and* to the ATF officer in charge of the bomb delivery. What's his name?"

"Special Agent Stanley. Got it." I could hear bewilderment in Alex's voice. "Eli, is she really okay?"

"She looks fine but the SUV is damaged."

"Later, Kid." I hung up and looked at Eli. "What's up?"

"We lost track of you on the far side of the river," he said, mildly. "It took us four hours to find you, and when I did, you were asleep."

"Oh. That was . . ." I realized he had been worried. Both of the Youngers had been terribly worried. Thinking I was hurt. Or dead. Which was really sweet, and would probably insult them if I said so. I settled on, "That was horrible of me." I crawled back into the driver's seat, explaining. "I was talking to Soul and she said she could find me in the gray place of the change, so I went into it. And I was attacked by vamps. And they beat me up and were planning to kill me or kidnap me. Then I think . . ." I pulled the tangled memories back into place, and examined the different scent patterns from the attack. "I think, maybe, an *arcenciel* came—not Soul—and the

vamps did something to it or tried to, but it got away. And they
knocked me out."

Eli was staring at me with an indecipherable expression.
"Unconscious."

"Yeah. Mostly. I think the vamps were chasing the *arcenciel*
and that's why they left me. And then Soul came and woke me
up. And attacked me, maybe because she thought I should
have saved the other *arcenciel*? Or maybe because she thought
I had attacked the *arcenciel*? Anyway, then I shifted into Beast.
And that's when it got strange."

"*That's* when it got strange."

I had a feeling that Eli was making fun of me and I squinted
at him in threat. "We fought and she turned into a three- or
four-hundred-pound tiger and I bit her throat and swallowed
her blood. And then she took off. And then I shifted back to
me. Only her blood left me drunk as a skunk, 'cause she's an
arcenciel too and their blood's really tasty." I chuffed a laugh.
"So, anyway, I got dressed and back in the SUV." I looked
around me again at the traffic. "I think I drove here and fell
asleep. Because of the druggy blood. But I'm sober now.
Mostly."

Eli shook his head slowly, still looking me over. "I thought
I'd be bored in civilian life, out of the service. I had no idea."
Eli got out of the SUV and bent back in, his head low enough
to see me. "Check your messages." He closed the door, took
the traffic ticket in his fist, and walked down the street. He got
into his own SUV, a battered, unarmored, older model, and
drove into traffic. He didn't look my way as he passed.

I checked my messages, sixteen from Alex, each increas-
ingly more panicked as he called and pinged my location. And
one from Bruiser. I returned his call and left a message, ending
with, "I'm bringing lunch. I'll be there in an hour if the traffic
is willing." I tossed the cell into the seat, wondering whether
he would be there at all. I was taking all sorts of chances. How
weird was that? I wondered whether it was the drugged blood,
and decided that it wasn't, as I was now starving, moderately
anxious about visiting Bruiser, and not feeling the least intox-
icated.

I pulled into the stream of cars and turned on the radio to
catch the Doobie Brothers singing "Black Water," which was
appropriate in so many ways. I was solving problems, identify-
ing bad guys, discovering that things were much weirder than

they seemed, and protecting the sorta innocent. Things were starting to happen here on the Mississippi. Oh yes, they were.

Only, not all of my conclusions were correct.

It was out of the way, but after a quick side trip to Cochon Butcher, I made my way to the French Quarter, turning onto St. Philip Street. Luck was with me and I slipped into a rare open parking spot on the street and locked the doors, which was stupid because I had no windows. Pocketing the keys, carrying the food bags, I walked in through the arched door to find the entrance empty. The old, Mediterranean-style building was tall-ceilinged and cool, a typical, comfortable French Quarter building. There was something homey and maybe a little well-loved-shabby about the place that was unexpectedly soothing. The entrance was quaint, the lighting modest, and the central courtyard was old-fashioned and relaxed with a burbling fountain, tropical plants and vines, table and chairs, two rockers. Old brick was exposed by broken stucco. Lots of tile. Nice. Quiet.

Standing in the arched entrance to the enclosed central courtyard, I thought about the step I was taking. I was sober, single, mostly sane, so if I was making a mistake, it wouldn't be for the wrong reason.

I stuck my free hand into a back pocket, catching my reflection in a small hanging mirror in the archway. I was too tall, still too skinny, even with the added twenty pounds. Bronzed skin. Bacon T-shirt. No makeup. Hair up in a messy mass, stakes twisted to hold it in place. I considered my ghostly reflection. Not a pretty woman. At the moment not even striking. Lanky and plain. Except for my amber eyes. They were almost exotic. Almost. But not quite.

Inside, Beast was strangely silent. As if she had withdrawn completely. Or was watching me like prey, hidden in the deeps of me.

I turned my back to the courtyard and looked at the empty entrance; pulled on Beast's hearing and listened to the voices muffled by the thick walls. Smelled fresh paint and mold and age. And I was surprised that I felt no desire at all to run.

"Miss Yellowrock?"

A large woman came toward me from the shadows, dressed in black from sneakers Velcro-ed on her wide feet to her bottle-black hair. "Yes. I'm Jane Yellowrock."

"Mr. Dumas left you a key."

"Unit eleven, right?" I took the key—a brass key, not one of the new electronic card keys.

"Up the stairs to the third floor. There is no elevator."

I nodded and followed her finger to the stairs. They were long, curving at the landings, with a wrought-iron railing and bare wood treads. I carried the key in one hand, the heavy paper bag from Cochon Butcher in the other, and recalled what I knew of the old building. Useless knowledge filling an empty mind. The St. Philip was constructed in 1839 as two separate but identical residences, built by a wealthy Sicilian immigrant for his family and his daughter's family. At that time, this section of the French Quarter was called the Sicilian Quarter, home to Italian families and businesses.

Over the years since, the building had fallen into bad disrepair, and was used as rental units through the Depression. In the 1940s the building was operated as a gentlemen's hotel by one of the most notorious madams of New Orleans—Katie of Katie's Ladies—originally my landlady, and Leo's heir, though she had owned the joint under another name. All of it unimportant. My mind was swimming through murky, narrow passageways of insignificant memory, trivial inconsequence. As my feet climbed the stairs.

The building was cool, but not cold, and I could hear window units purring and gurgling through doors on the landings, trying to take away some of the early-season humidity. On the third floor I found unit eleven. The door was marked as the Owner's Suite and, like the others, was rented out. I knocked and then looked down at my hand. Watched as it inserted the key. The lock turned, clean and well lubricated with graphite, but ancient.

I pushed open the door, closed my eyes, and inhaled, smelling more fresh paint, adhesive, stone, carpet, and his citrusy cologne. Beast moved finally. Tilting her head. *Mine . . .*

He called out, "Come in. I was just preparing a salad."

I stepped inside and closed the door. Watched as my hand locked the door latch and turned the dead bolts. When I faced the room, my boots scuffed on the carpet, the kind of carpet that you glue down in squares. The kitchen had dark wood cabinets, stainless steel appliances, and what looked like white quartz tops, similar to what Leo had going into his new clan home. An island and tall, white, upholstered bar chairs separated the cooking area from the rest of the apartment. The couches in the main room were contrasting burnt peach and brown. A wine cabinet was off the sitting area. A bedroom to the left, shrouded in shadows. The unit sported a double balcony looking over Philip Street—a pricey view, but the rooms were less ornate than I had thought he would require.

Feeling light, as if I weighed nothing at all, and at the same time as if every move I made was weighted with importance, I walked in and pivoted carefully, entering the kitchen. Bruiser stood in the small kitchen area, concentrating on the salad, letting me acclimate to being there. His attention was deeply focused on the clear glass bowl filled with greens, white cheese, cranberries, walnuts, sliced grapes, and cherry tomatoes. I set the bag on the bar, watching as he poured balsamic vinegar and olive oil over the salad concoction and tossed it with two silver spoons. Bruiser handling silver was odd. Maybe the oddest thing about the moment. Until I noticed his clothes.

I had seen him in jeans and leather and dress slacks and tuxedoes. Never in thin cotton pants, wrinkled and hanging low on his hips. He sported a thin white cotton T-shirt, his body outlined clearly. His feet were bare. I always had a thing about men's bare feet, and Bruiser's were beautiful, his toes long and dusted with dark hairs that lay flat against his skin.

His face was unshaven, the whiskers a paler brown than the roots of his hair, closer to the sun-kissed golden brown of his hair in late summer. *Mine . . .* Beast said again.

Still without looking up, he reached for the bag and removed the contents, the chilled bottle of wine first. "A good choice. Buttery with a hint of lemon."

I lifted a shoulder diffidently. He knew I hadn't picked it out myself. It was one he had ordered at Arnaud's. I didn't know whether he even remembered that. But he had liked it then, so . . .

Deftly, he opened the bottle. Poured two glasses and tasted one. I lifted the other and held it. My fingers trembled, a faint and delicate vibration. The glass was cool against my palms.

He began to remove the take-out packages. "Cochon's duck confit and . . . Andouille sausage," he said, approval in his voice. He opened another and said, "Their roast oysters on the half shell and . . . goat-stuffed biscuits. A little piece of heaven,"

and this time there was reverence in his voice. "Steamed vegetables and a side of pickled baby squash. Roast asparagus." A
smile in his voice, he said, "You brought *green* things."

I shrugged, pleased. "I was feeding you."

His teeth showed, white and even when he laughed. "And
for that I thank you. But this is a feast, Jane. There's enough
food here for days."

I lifted my eyes from the food to Bruiser's face and said, "So
we don't have to leave anytime soon." He stilled. His pupils
widened slowly as he stared at the food in his hands. Even
more slowly he lifted his gaze from the packages on the island
to take me in. His mouth opened slightly and his scent changed,
heated and . . . *heated*. It was hard to breathe. Impossible to
stand there, waiting. Uncertain what he would do.

He met my eyes, an electric spark at the connection that
shivered through me from the arches of my feet to the short
hairs on the back of my neck. He gazed at me—hair, stakes,
mouth—as if the sight of me was the air he breathed. The sun
that lit his world. The moon in the dark of a perilous night. As
if he'd been denied breath and sunlight and moon-glow for too
long.

Something turned over in me, something liquid and heavy,
like some unfinished thing in a womb, waiting to be born. It
settled low in my belly and heat spread through me, thick and
viscous and sweet, like warm honey. *Mine* . . . Beast murmured.
Mine . . .

Ours, I thought.

Ours, Beast purred back. *Ours . . . ours . . . ours.*

Carefully, but without looking at what he was doing, Bruiser
set the packages on the bar. They landed with a papery sliding
and the sharper snap of plastic. His lips parted and I thought
he might speak, but instead he came around the island, stepping as if in a martial movement, carefully balanced, ready for
a strike. When I didn't back away, he lifted a hand and slid it
around my neck. His palm was warm, feverish in a human. But
we weren't human. With the other, he reached up and removed
the stakes, one at a time, setting them on the counter. My hair
slid and tumbled, a languid glide. His hand followed, smooth-
ing my hair. Like soothing a beast.

I licked my lips. Went stiff all over. Bruiser's hands went
motionless.

I whispered, "When I was five years old, I was on the Trail

of Tears. My grandmother forced me to change into a bobcat. *Wesa*. Then she shoved me away, into the snow. Alone. I was starving. Freezing. A long time later, I don't know how long, I found a buried carcass of a deer in the ice, a rare find then, after the white man had paid our young men to kill off so many. I was eating. Not paying attention."

Bruiser's hand slid down my hair again, once, as if he stroked the pelt of a cat. His eyes held mine, giving me time.

"It was the kill of a mountain lion. She came back and caught me. Attacked. Was trying to kill me. I didn't know what I was doing. I was terrified, fighting for my life, but that was no excuse. I dropped into the gray place of the change and I stole her body. It was black magic. Her soul is inside with me still. She's a killer. Predator. So am I. If we—"

Bruiser's mouth landed on mine. He crushed me to him. If I had been human, I would have broken. I hadn't even seen him move.

His mouth slashed across mine, our teeth clacking. Bruiser's tongue scoured my lips. They felt burned, almost painful. I opened my mouth and sucked him inside. Pain ripped at my fingertips as Beast's nails pierced my flesh, and dug gently into Bruiser's sides. He didn't pull away. He laughed, into my mouth, the sound desperate and joyous. His leg separated mine, a tango step, had there been music, had we been dancing. Holding me against his body, he bent over me as we kissed, our feet moving in synchrony. He whirled us slowly, my hair slinging out.

I slid my hands up his back, beneath his shirt, claws scraping. Beast's claws, extruded from my fingertips, scraping hard enough to hurt, not deep enough to break skin.

No gray place of the change, just us, just Beast and me, in one body, at one place and time.

Bruiser slipped one hand under my shirt, his palm fevered on the skin of my belly. His scent was heated metal, citrus, and need. His hand found my bare breast and he hissed as he inhaled. Gently, he cupped me, gathering up the firm flesh. His warm fingers tightened on my nipple. His mouth disappeared and so did my T-shirt as we danced through the room. Cool air brushed across me. His lips landed on my breast and he sucked the nipple into his hot mouth so hard I gasped. Grabbed his head, pulling him even closer.

He growled. Bit my breast. A nip. "Harder," I growled back.

Instead there was a mass against the backs of my knees and the world tilted. I was falling. I wrapped one arm around him. Landed on the bed, his weight trapping me.

Trapping me.

His kissed my throat. Teeth grazing.

Trapping me! Like the night when Leo—

I tensed, my body suddenly cold. I shoved, fought. "No! Nononono!"

Bruiser pulled away, horror and understanding in his eyes. His voice fierce, he said, "This is not then. This is not *him*. This is you and me." He gripped my head in both hands so hard it hurt and he held me with his body and his eyes, the golden lights of my Beast dancing, reflected in his depths. Beast pressed a paw on the panic I hadn't even known was there. Isolating it, pulling it away from me. Her claws held me safe.

I felt the fear float away as if it fell over high falls and down-downdown, to disappear into the froth of nothingness. "Yessss," I hissed, my voice too low, too deep.

Mine . . . mine . . . mine . . .

Ours . . . ours . . . ours . . .

"Yessss."

"Mine," Bruiser said, unknowingly echoing Beast.

The parallel shocked me. I searched his face to see him staring at me. Into me. I saw the golden reflection of both parts of me in his eyes. "Yesss," I said again.

My jeans disappeared, the zipper drawing blood along my shin. The scent mixed with Bruiser's, where I'd accidently pierced his skin in my terror, both blood-scents full of need. The cool air went colder along my body. I ripped at him with my claws, and his clothes were gone. His body naked and hot. A fire of need and want. I lifted my legs and wrapped them around him. "Now," I demanded. He shoved into me. No gentleness, no tenderness. Ramming in so hard he hit the back of me. My body arched. With a scream I claimed him.

There was no more talking.

It was dusk when he managed the next coherent words. "Holy hell," he muttered. His voice was ragged and rough, his breathing not yet smooth. We lay on our backs, side by side, staring at the rough-hewn ceiling beams. Our fingers were intertwined, our hands between us. My legs rested over one of his. My hair was tied in a knot and pulled to the side out of the way. He had tied it there, his hands stroking, after we had nearly scalped me when we rolled over and fell off the bed.

My skin was abraded from his beard, all around my mouth and jaw. My breasts. Lower. He had seen the raw places, when we still had sunlight, and tried to get up and shave. I had refused. Told him about big-cats and how they marked their mates. After that, Bruiser, my Bruiser, had marked me. Everywhere. Everywhere. *Every*where.

I had bitten him, drawing blood once. Beast had kept claws out and hooked into his flesh. It had to have hurt; it had to have been excruciating. But he hadn't stopped. Bruiser was healed now. Onorios are hard to damage. Good thing.

Out front, a car horn honked. A woman laughed. I sighed, low and long.

"You're awake," he murmured.

I smiled slightly, my mouth still bruised and tender. "Mmm-hmm."

He rolled over in the shadows, propping his head onto an elbow so he could see me. "No woman, in all my long life, has ever come to me"—he tipped his head forward and quickly licked my breast, his tongue leaving the nipple to grow cool and tight. Laughter and satisfaction filled his voice—"wearing jeans and a bacon T-shirt, and nothing else." I tilted my head to see him better. The widow's peak on his forehead was a pointed darkness on his pale skin, picked out by the streetlights coming through the open balcony doors, and into the bedroom.

"Everything's better with bacon," I whispered. He rolled over and collapsed against me, his laughter so exhausted it was little more than a rough breath.

CHAPTER 16

The Plink of Blood Slowed and Stopped

We returned to the cold feast near nine. At some point in the long afternoon and evening, Bruiser had put the oysters and meat in the refrigerator. Nothing smelled spoiled and we were ravenous, and so we sat on a blanket and pillows he tossed on the couch, which he pulled away from the wall to face the balcony. In the flickering shadows of a single candle, we ate wilted salad and drank room-temperature wine and fed each other oysters and Andouille sausage with our fingers. Nothing in my entire life had ever tasted so good.

While we ate, I told him about Satan's Three and the *arcenciel* attacking me. Unlike a human man, he didn't get all protective or worried after the fact. He just listened while I talked, stroked my hair when I described the attack and the distinct scent patterns of the *arcenciels*. He agreed with me that there must have been two *arcenciels* at the warehouse, one that was there when the vamps were, and then, later, Soul. He was a man who let me be me. It was different. And nice. And sooo . . . Bruiser.

We made love again, slowly, our bodies crushed together on the couch. This time, his hands were gentle, scarcely touching, his fingertips suspended at the instant where flesh met flesh. Soft caresses, leisurely and deliberate, our pleasure withheld, rising and ebbing. When we were done, I lay beside him, limp and fulfilled, every inch of me. And every inch of him.

Out front I heard a car pull up and a door open and close. I flew from the couch so fast I was a smudged replication in the mirror near one of the balcony doors. Almost as fast, Bruiser rose up on the couch. "What?"

"Leo," I whispered. "Leo is here." Bruiser's scent changed, a smell like burned stone. "Bruiser?" Faster than a human could ever hope to move, yet seeming to glide, Bruiser rolled to his feet and disappeared into his bedroom.

He answered, his voice little more than a murmur. "The last words between my former master and I were not totally clear regarding you." From the doorway, my jeans came flying; I yanked them out of the air and onto me, careful of the killer zipper this time. A moment later Bruiser emerged wearing the thin pants and T-shirt from the afternoon.

"Not totally clear," I replied softly. "He told you to stay away from me."

"Yes. But he did not tell you to stay away from me." Bruiser sounded smug, vigilant, and meticulous. Cautious. He slid one of his dress shirts off of a hanger and over my head. As if I were a child, he rolled up the cuffs. "What? No bacon shirt for Leo?"

"No." Bruiser placed the back of his hand against my cheek for a moment, watching my face to read my reaction. "I'm having it framed to hang on the wall over my bed."

I spluttered with laughter. "Very artsy. Are we in trouble? You know he'll know what we've been up to."

"Perhaps *I* am in trouble. He already knows, I'm sure," Bruiser said, turning away. "The apartment reeks of sex. With the balcony doors open, he knew everything the moment he opened his car door. He's being excessively polite, allowing us time to get presentable." Bruiser's eyes pierced up at me. "I will attempt to control the situation."

I chuffed out a breath and picked up my silver stakes, twining my hair into a messy bun and securing it with them, easy to hand. "This should be fun," I muttered. "Not." But he had a point. Neither of us had showered since sometime in midafternoon and we'd been busy since then. Several times.

Bruiser shoved the couch back in place and tossed the blanket into the bedroom. He took a bottle of red wine from the wine cabinet and opened it. He poured it into a carafe, holding the bottle high over his head and allowing the wine to gurgle and splash down and into the crystal. "Letting it breathe, the fast way," he explained. "A sacrilege, but the best I can do under the time constraints." He removed three deep-bowled crystal glasses from a cabinet and set everything on a wood tray on the island. He put a sharp knife on the tray.

I took a seat at the bar, turning one of the white leather bar chairs at an angle so I could see the door and the balcony too. And the bed. It was neatly made. Dang. Bruiser was fast when he needed to be. And agonizingly slow when he needed to be too, for which reason I was very sore, even with Beast's fast healing. I fidgeted in the uncomfortable chair, noting only now that there were *three* white leather chairs. How handy.

A knock came at the door and Bruiser opened it. Leo stood on the other side, motionless, not breathing, not moving, his pale skin seeming to glisten in the light of the single candle still burning. Leo was wearing a black tuxedo, the tie loose at his throat. His hair, black and lustrous, lay on his shoulders. It had grown several inches in the time I'd lived in New Orleans.

"I am honored that the Master of this City would visit me," Bruiser said with polite precision. "Please come in."

Without a word, Leo entered, Derek on his heels. Derek was dressed in Enforcer leathers, weaponed up like a modern-day samurai. I tensed all over, but his eyes passed over Bruiser and me, sweeping the apartment and checking the balcony, bedroom, bathroom, closet, moving the way a human did when he's been well fed on vamp blood—fast and smooth and powerful. When Derek was satisfied, he took a place at the door, his hands hanging close to his weapons.

Bruiser ignored him and followed his former master to the island. He shot me a look that lasted half a heartbeat, intense and cutting. His eyes then shot to Derek. Pointing me to look at the Enforcer, a direction, an order, a suggestion of some kind. I hadn't fought beside Bruiser like I had with Eli. The battlefield communication wasn't yet in place; I had no idea what the look meant, except to be alert and wary and ready for anything. I could sense Bruiser's worry even over the smell of sex that permeated the place. "Would you care for a glass of wine?" Bruiser asked. "I think you will find the vintage agreeable."

Leo lifted the bottle, read the label, and raised a single eyebrow, but over the reek of sex I could detect a rising change in his scent pattern, from banked discontent to something more peppery and hot. The beginnings of anger. "Outside of Pellissier Estates in France, there are fifteen bottles of Pellissier Cabernet, 1945. My cellars contain ten of them, or they did."

"They still do," Bruiser said, ignoring the less-than-subtle accusation that he might have pilfered from the MOC's wine cellar. He poured the dark red wine into each glass. "I bought this and one other at auction last year for a dreadful sum. Though the fast aeration is a desecration, this bottle seemed an appropriate sacrifice for the moment."

I managed not to react to the word *sacrifice*, until Bruiser picked up the knife and sliced his fingertip. He held it over one of the glasses and let the blood drop into the wine. Suddenly I could hear everything: cars outside on the street below, the sound of my heartbeat, the plink of blood meeting wine, the slight shift of Derek's leathers at the door. In my peripheral vision, I made sure his hands were still empty, and I could feel his eyes on me, gauging me. I forced myself to remain sitting, compelled my body to relax against the low back of the chair, a false ease that might fool Derek, but would never fool Leo. Slowly Leo's mouth opened, and his fangs dropped down. They were ivory-toned in the dim light, tinted darker by the flickering candle, as if they were lightly coated with old blood.

Sacrifice, Bruiser had said. For taking me to bed. Which meant that, even with the fancy dismissal as blood-servant, Leo's claim on me still stood, and Bruiser's careful interpretation of the edict wasn't going to protect us. In Leo's eyes, Bruiser had stolen from the Master of the City. Leo thought it okay to sleep with anyone and everyone in singles and batches, but he wasn't much on sharing what he had claimed.

To make his anger worse, according to Del, Leo was missing Bruiser. Whom *I* had just stolen.

But despite Leo's claim, he had *never* owned me. I would not be owned.

Beast is not prey, she thought at me.

The plink of blood slowed and stopped. And I knew what Bruiser wanted even before he looked at me. Questioning. Was I willing to offer blood for the supposed wrong I'd done to the MOC?

"No," I said, heat blossoming in my gut. "I never belonged to you." I pointed at Leo. At the words, his pupils widened and his sclera began to tint scarlet. The scent of scorching pepper and the smoke of burning papyrus grew stronger. "I was never yours to give away or keep. I was never yours at all except for the job." I pointed at the bloody wine. "And I don't offer sacrifice of my blood. Not to anyone." I pointed to Bruiser. "You should have remembered that."

Bruiser blinked, something dawning in his eyes. "Too late," I said fiercely, surging from the chair and to the door. Derek shifted, the movement not subtle, intending to be seen, a warning that he would defend his boss.

To Leo I said, "You can take this job and shove it into the sun." Barefoot, anger like a flame tossed carelessly into a pile of deadwood, I picked up my keys and walked out of the apartment. And slammed the door. Inside I heard the sound of furniture breaking and a roar of rage. *Stupid men.*

My cell rang moments later. I ignored it. It rang again. I turned it off as I drove away.

Stupid men.

Stupid, *stupid* men. I tried to put the memory of Bruiser—all the memories of Bruiser I had formed in the last day—out of mind, but it wasn't working. I got angrier as I drove, as the images of Bruiser flashed before me. Bruiser stretched out on his bed. Bruiser stretched out on me. Bruiser's face when I slammed my way out of his apartment. *Worry. He'd been afraid.* "Well, I can take care of myself," I said. But . . . Leo had lost his temper when I'd left. There had been the sounds of fighting. Anger and apprehension were boiling in me by the time I neared my home, and my increased body temp released all the scents accumulated over the last hours. Passion and tenderness and sex. Such fantastic sex.

I wanted it. I wanted time to roll back and stop there, Bruiser atop my body, heaving breaths, voice ragged, calling my name. And I wanted it gone, wiped away forever as if it had never been. I cursed when a traffic light stopped me, backlighting me in a bar's bright, neon beer signs, through the broken windows. In frustration, I beat the steering wheel with my fists. The wheel bent. The driver behind me backed away and took a side street. I laughed, the sound broken and hurting.

Beast said nothing. Nothing about the hours in bed, nothing about the smells, nothing about Leo or Bruiser. Despicable Bruiser, who gave in to the old ways of his old life. No. Beast said nothing at all. She was totally silent, motionless inside me. Which just made me angrier.

I didn't want to be with people, but I had no place else to go, except to check into a hotel, and that seemed no safer than anywhere else, and might endanger humans. While I was trying to decide, my muscle memory took me the short blocks back to my house. I was forced to park a block down due to traffic, which happened only during tourist event weekends, and I had no idea which tourist event was taking place now. I stomped from the SUV—when was my bike gonna be fixed?—and down the street and through the side gate. I keyed open the door, slammed it too, said a brusque hello to the Youngers as I stormed past, then slammed the door to my bedroom.

Stripping off Bruiser's shirt, I pitched it into the garbage. The jeans followed. They smelled like Bruiser. And me. And hours in his bed. Maybe I should burn them. I turned the shower to hot. Then to hotter. I tossed the silver stakes into the corner of the small space, stepped under the scalding spray, and slammed the shower door. And proceeded to scrub myself with a loofah that one of Katie's working girls had given me for Christmas. It was saturated in perfumed soap and I hadn't been able to force myself to use it, until now, when I needed the stench to hide the other stench.

I soaped my hair and scoured the bottoms of my feet. I scrubbed everything in between as well, every part of me that Bruiser had touched, had marked with his hands and his mouth and his rough, unshaven face. I was abrading the top layer of skin and I didn't care. If that was what it took to get the reek of Bruiser off of me—

The shower door rammed open, bouncing off the wall. Leo stood there, vamped out, steam rushing to swirl around him. He lunged into the blistering stream. Screaming, "You are—"

Time stood still. Droplets of water stopped, suspended. Steam—minuscule droplets, heated nearly to the point of boiling—vibrated in place. Leo hung in the air, midleap, his face frozen in a rictus of fury. Still dressed in his tux.

There were two-inch talons on each fingertip. His lips were pulled back in a snarl. Three-inch fangs were snapped down in eating/fighting position. Eyes like pits into hell, opening inside volcanos, viewed from above as one fell into the darkness. Vamped out. Vamped out and beyond ticked off. Leo didn't like to be dissed.

Time . . . time was stopped. Or nearly so. Or I was suddenly outside of it.

Silver lights stood among the shower droplets, black motes here and there. In human form, I was in the gray place of the change. And nothing was happening. I wasn't shifting. I was just . . . here. The gray place of the change was present and real, yet not overtaking me, not running the show. In the moments

since Bruiser suggested that I offer a blood sacrifice, I had
wanted time to stop. Now it had. And I had no idea how it had
happened except that I had done this. Somehow.

*The I/we of Beast is stronger than Jane or big-cat alone.
Hayyel made us so. But there will be a price.*

Isn't there always? I thought back.

In the shower stall, the water droplets seemed a fraction of
an inch lower. Leo, a fraction of an inch closer. But I had plenty
of time. If there was such a thing.

Hayyel was an angel. The Everharts and Truebloods had
summoned him to Earth to deal with the demon that Evange-
lina Everhart Stone had summoned with the blood diamond.
The blood-magic, black arts, blood-diamond artifact that currently resided in one of my bank safe-deposit boxes, along with
the iron discs made from the spike of Golgotha and a few
pocket watches from Natchez, Mississippi—which also had
some of the iron in them, powering them. The pocket watches
did something about time, but I wasn't sure what. I had a feeling that I wasn't smart enough to figure it out, and that I'd
eventually have to find a physicist to explain it to me.

When Hayyel was fighting the demon, time did something.
It stood still and it rushed ahead all at once, all the pathways
and possibilities of the future open at one time. I hadn't seen
much of it. What I *had* seen was distorted and blended, like a
single frame from a thousand movies, overlaid and viewed at
once. Madness. Madness I had instantly forgotten, too much
for my human brain to see/internalize/analyze/understand.

Those memories now seemed to merge with the steam
droplets. Trying to rise. A distinct image in each micro globule
of water, vibrating with heat and possibility. And still too much
to take in or understand.

*Hayyel did something to you, to us, in the moments he ap-
peared,* I thought.

Yesss.

What? What did he do?

Hard to think. Hard to think like Jane. Beast shook her head
and pawed my mind, frustrated. *He showed Jane a way to . . .
true life. He showed Beast how to forgive the life that Jane had
stolen.*

*I understand that part. But that doesn't explain the images in
all the droplets. Or the fact that time has stopped* now *while Leo
is trying to kill us. It also doesn't tell us what to do about it all.*

Time slid forward again, a fraction of a second. The droplets skittered. Leo's mouth opened wider. He was really not happy. When time let up again, the poop was gonna hit the prop and it was gonna get messy.

I/we were not . . . do not understand words. This. This is what he did to us. Beast showed me a memory, one I had seen before. Two streams, roiling with white water, tumbling, plummeting down a mountain, taking different paths. Rushing over and around rocks and deadwood debris. Water dropping and falling. Coiling like living things, angry and lusting and thrusting down the peaks, an image I had seen before, and thought I understood, but . . . perhaps not.

In a tight, narrow spot, full of broken stone and flood-blasted trees, the rivers met. Became one. The eddies and currents exploded into one another. Fought one another for supremacy. Spray, icy with winter, spewed into the air. Wave trains rose and fell, cresting at the tops. Eddy lines lifted a foot above the waterline, like a fence, as the two rivers struggled for power, fought for control. And merged.

This, Beast thought, indicating the eddy line. *And this,* she thought, showing me the swirling water in a pool below, as the two rivers became one and stopped fighting for supremacy. And found a calm pool of peace. *We were broken. Alone. Fighting for dominance. First as two. Then as two merged, but not at peace. Hayyel healed us. Healed our broken soul. Gave us strength and power. But we have not accepted it. Have not taken his gift and made it ours. Have not eaten it and made it part of who we are.*

I turned my attention from Beast's memory of rivers joining to the memory of my soul home, the place/memory where my skinwalker nature was first revealed. The cavern was composed of limestone, the scent sharp and tart. In this memory it was also dark and dank, cold, without the light of the fire that was usually lit. But I knew this place that existed within me, even in the dark. I moved through the large cavern and into a small passageway, to the nook where Beast slept.

She lay on the ledge in the space she claimed as her den, belly to the cool rock. Her chin and jaw were on her paws. Her amber eyes studied me as I studied her. *If two broken souls join, are we still a broken soul? But just a bigger broken soul?*

Beast chuffed with amusement. *If we join, we are stronger. Faster. This place becomes ours, our hunting territory.*

And what does that mean?

Stronger, faster. This is always better than weaker, slower. Weaker, slower is prey.

You have a point. Especially with Leo trying to kill us. Again. But . . . you couldn't tell me this before?

Jane did not need to know before. And price of more power might be much, like Beast trying to eat whole bison. Sickness.

I remembered my last partial shift in the HQ gym. Time had slowed and I had moved even faster than normal then too. And I'd had cramps after. Incapacitating stomach cramps. That would be bad in the middle of a fight.

Beast waited, staring at me through the dark. I had scratched her behind the ears once before. Now I bent into the ledge. And Beast rose to her paws, claws out, digging into the stone beneath her. Oddly, I could feel her claws in the back of my brain, piercing. She stepped toward me. Our faces met, hers prickly and rough with stiff hairs. She tilted her face, lifting her jaw. I rubbed my face over her jaw, accepting her scent, allowing her to mark me. She dropped her head and rubbed the top of it under my jaw, taking my scent.

It was odd and disorienting. To feel both sides of a motion. Beast's and mine.

Okay. Let's do it, I thought at her.

Beast opened her mouth and showed her fangs. Her breath was hot and rich with scent patterns. Meat and milk and kits and blood. Gently she placed her fangs against my throat. I knew what needed to happen if we were to live the next second. I reached to my waist, finding the hilt of a knife. The hilt was large and coarse, crosshatched for a better grip in a sweaty hand, but too big for my small fist. It was familiar to my childhood. My father had used this knife to clean fish. He had put it into my hand, teaching me how to behead a fish, how to skin a catfish. How to scale a black bass. Fillet it for cooking or drying. It felt real, that hilt of carved bone, though the knife had been lost long ago. It felt as real as my own heartbeat, as my own lungs pulling in breath. I drew the knife and placed it at Beast's throat.

So. We both have to die, together, here, in the gray place of the change, in our soul home, to get this stronger, faster thingamajig?

Yesss.

And then we have to pay the price.

Yesss.
Fine. Now!

Beast bit down. I thrust into her throat. Pain shivered through us both. Our blood gushed out, hot, spurting. Death blood, from death strikes. Like the two rivers, our blood mingled. And became one. Fire and ice rushed through me with the pain, molten lava and glaciers calving, all of nature held in a single moment of time that wasn't. A bubble of not-here, not-now, a time of its own, potent with life and possibility, outside of other reality. That moment had a sound, like a huge bronze bell, a note that reverberated through my bones. It had a color, the dark blue of deep ocean water, full of life rolling with power. The color of a sunset, burning through the sky. And the scent of blood.

A snippet of scripture came to me. "For the life of the flesh is in the blood . . . for it is the blood that maketh an atonement for the soul." I lifted my hand, which was coated in hot blood, and licked my fingers, smelling/tasting the life force of Beast. I swallowed, her fangs caught in my throat an electrified torment at the motion. Her own throat moved against the blade buried there, as Beast swallowed my blood.

The gray energies and black motes of power vanished.

The scalding shower spilled down. Leo roared, diving toward me. Shouting, "—not released from me!"

I dropped to the wet tile floor, grabbing up the dropped stakes. My hands were tawny-pelted. My fingers knobby and strong. My claws were extended. My clawed feet scratched into the wet and slippery tile as I rose, fastfastfast, thrusting up with the silver stakes. Hard. Directly into Leo's heart.

CHAPTER 17

Deadish Leo on My Floor

He fell at my feet, into the shower, his head bouncing on the tile. His blood was a pinkish wash into the drain. I jumped back, slapping my body against the cool shower wall. Stared at Leo's back, his black tux soaked. *Holy crap. What just happened?*

Over the roaring of the water I heard the *schnick* of a round entering the chamber of a semiautomatic handgun. I looked up into Derek's face over the barrel of the weapon aimed at me. He was breathing hard, face slick with sweat, his nose bleeding. His finger tightened on the trigger. Another *schnick* sounded, and the barrel of a weapon was placed tight against Derek's head. It gave his head a little push and Derek's mouth turned down in a snarl worthy of Beast. All I could see of the second gunman was his hand and wrist, but it was Eli.

"Hey, my brother," Eli said, sounding friendly and casual. "Let's chat about this first, before I hafta kill you and then figure out where to bury the body. Though I'm thinking out in a bayou, somewhere close to gators, you dig?"

"I didn't kill Leo," I said, over the sound of the shower. "Or not yet. We have options if we act fast. Unless you kill me. Think about it."

"I smell silver and vamp blood," Derek said, breath still heaving. He must have run all the way from the St. Philip Apartments. "Silver will kill a vamp. Even a vamp like Leo. If you weren't trying to kill him, why use silver?"

"It was all I had at hand. And not if he gets fed by his maker. Or a priestess. Like I said. We have options if we act fast.

"I'm reaching behind me to shut off the shower. Then I'm going to grab a towel and we'll haul Leo out and figure out what happened and how to handle it. I was *not* trying to kill him. *He* chased *me* down, not the other way around."

I turned off the water. The bathroom was loud with the sound of Derek's breathing and water dripping. I was acutely uncomfortable with the two men in my bathroom and the nearly true-dead vamp at my pelted but mostly human-shaped feet in my shower, but I was more worried about getting shot than my embarrassment. Healing took time that this situation might not give me.

From the top of the shower stall door I pulled a towel and wrapped it around me. My hair was sticking to my skin, I had soap on me, which itched, and I smelled like a bordello from the soap, but at least I was covered.

"Eli, Derek, enough with the Mexican standoff. I'll heal from most anything Derek can do to me, but Derek won't heal. He'll be dead. And I'll have to clean up the brains, which is messy and sticky and pretty ick. Now, help me get Leo out of here." I bent and slid my hands under Leo's shoulders. I heard the appropriate—though far too slow—sounds of rounds being removed from chambers and guns being holstered.

My gut began to cramp. Nausea rose up in me. *Not now,* I told myself. *Not yet.* I breathed deeply, forcing down the pain and sickness. It didn't seem inclined to go away, but it stopped increasing, more a low ache than a twisting of my entire abdominal cavity's contents.

Derek helped me roll Leo and together we lifted him and carried him, dripping, from the bathroom, placed him on the kitchen floor, faceup. Leo usually looked dead. He didn't breathe except to talk, and his heart beat only from time to time. But lying on my floor, wet and bloody, his eyes open and human-looking now that he was sorta dead and not vamped out, he looked really dead. I bent and closed his eyes. "I'm going to get dressed. Don't touch the stakes. Derek, call Del and tell her to get a healer over here. Eli, call Bruiser and get him over here."

"Can't do that, Jane," Derek said, his voice cold as stone dust. "I left him in bad shape."

Fear shocked through me. "Do I need to call an ambulance? The cops?"

"He'll heal," Derek said shortly.

I kept the relief off my face. Any anger left in my system at Bruiser was gone. It might make me a wishy-washy woman, but I wanted Bruiser alive. If only so I could torture him for being an ass. I said, "Fine. Get me a healer—Gee, or a priestess, or someone." I left the deadish Leo on my floor and went to rinse and dry off and dress in something more formal than a damp, bloody towel. I also weaponed up in case anyone else had issues with Leo's current condition.

I was standing in the foyer, braiding my wet hair with pelted, knobby hands, trying to keep the sickness at bay, when the first *visitors* arrived. Katie entered through the side door like she had been fired through a cannon, which meant she had leaped over the brick fence in the evening gown and heels she was wearing. I wished I'd seen that. But the clothes and her presence meant that she hadn't been kept safely in HQ. Nor had Leo.

It also meant I needed a new side door. She stalked over the splinters of the old one in her stilettos. Gee DiMercy walked in behind her. I figured he had flown. Neither looked happy. I dropped the braid and stood my ground with a silver stake in one hand and a steel blade in the other. Before I could explain or defend myself, the most nutso vamp I'd ever met showed up at the front door with Bruiser over her shoulder. She didn't need an invitation to enter. The door blew off its hinges. Again. This time, crime scene tape blew in with it.

The priestess Bethany Salazar y Medina was in my house. Her gaze was empty and fathomless, but her body oozed the scents of rage and vengeance. Bruiser rested across her shoulder as if he weighed no more than the shawl on her other side. He was breathing. He was also out cold, dangling like that shawl, with artful repose. And he was bleeding, his blood soaked through Bethany's clothing.

The pain in my gut twisted and went hot. I pressed my middle with one hand, the blade pointed away from me. *Not now. Not now!*

Beast cannot stop it, she thought at me. *Price must be paid.*

"Who injured my George?" Bethany hissed. She cocked her head in that snake-way vamps have and settled all her magics on me. They prickled over my skin like lightning, ready to strike. She was nothing like the other priestess, Sabina. The power that surrounded Bethany was sharp and pitted, piercing and ephemeral. Her magics carried a scent similar to witch power, but with the bitter sting of shamanism and the yellow-ish tint and tang of cardamom. She was old, among the oldest vamps I had ever seen.

I took a breath of icy air to speak but she beat me to it. "I smell you on him," she said. "I will rip you to small shreds of flesh and cook you over my fire. I will eat you and your power—"

"Not me." I backed away fast, toward the kitchen door that hung open. Unfortunately, that put me near Katie, who was on the floor beside Leo. A quick glance told me she was the lesser danger at the moment, along with Derek, who stood in the kitchen area, weapons drawn and uncertainty on his face, as if he wasn't sure what to do in this FUBARed mess. "Is Br—George going to be okay?" I asked as I scuttled like a crab, my toes spreading and aching, growing and changing shape, start-ing to look like puma paws.

"He is *my* George. I made certain that he is always well when I remade him." Bethany looked at Leo on the floor. "You staked my Leo. I smell the stink of silver. You would kill him true-dead?"

"No," I said quickly. "Not my intent. He attacked and, umm, I happened to be holding silver stakes." *Stupid answer.*

Her eyes bored into me as she advanced, her cerulean skirts swirling, her dark-skinned flesh looking smooth and oiled in the lamplight, the toes of her bare feet spread wide on the floor. And Bruiser's blood dripping steadily behind her. "I made certain that my Leo would forever be well when I gave to him my finest and most deadly gift."

"Uh-huh. Okay. Whatever. Leo hurt George," I half lied, to keep Derek alive. His eyes went wide as he understood what I'd done. "How 'bout you put George down and help Leo?"

Bethany dropped George on the floor. His head hit first and bounced hard, his body hitting just after, the double blows mak-ing hollow, dull echoes through the flooring. *Awrighty, then,* I thought, my breath coming faster to deal with the increasing pain. She went to Leo and settled on the floor beside him. Katie and Bethany stared at each other across Leo's body, and it didn't take a mad scientist to tell that they were not the best of pals. Keeping their eyes on the floor grouping, Eli and the Kid lifted George and laid him on the couch in a boneless heap.

"What does the priestess mean, her finest and most deadly gift?" Gee DiMercy asked me. He was standing behind Katie, watching the scene with intense but inscrutable interest.

"Heck if I know. I'm just the hired help. Or I *was* the hired help. I quit." I shook my head. "But I think Leo refused my resignation and decided to kill me instead."

For some reason, that made Gee laugh, but my eyes were drawn away from him. Shadows and sparkles flowed across the wall of the foyer, reflected onto the living room walls, and into the kitchen. Prickles of magic burned on my skin. "Oh crap," I whispered.

The light-dragon flowed through the front door, into the house, and across the ceiling. It moved like the shadow of a serpent, one with wings of dappled sunlight on springwater, and opened its mouth. It had teeth like needles and knives and the distorted fun-house-mirror face of a human female. Its—her—wings were fully extended and their span was wider than the house, seeming to rise and fall through walls and out into the street.

The last time I had seen it, the *arcenciel* had been fighting the vampires who attacked me. My eyes on it, I took a breath. "Eli," I said, my voice soft. "I smell vamp."

My hands ached as claws pierced my fingertips. Pelt rippled down my body. And everything seemed to slow again, just a bit. Even the pain began to ease, which should have been a good thing, but instead made me wonder whether delaying paying the price made it go up.

In the light of the overhead fixture the *arcenciel* went visible, still glowing, but with a darker line along one side where I had stabbed her. She had already healed, but not without cost. *Can light scar?* Her wings cast streamers of light, like the afterimage glare of a camera flash combined with the arctic lights in a night sky, an effervescent opalescence, green and gold and pale shades of the rainbow, a feathery luminosity sparkling with brighter motes. Her hair was white, striped with red and black and brown. Bethany screamed and raced at the *arcenciel*, reaching, trying to grab the light. To the side, I saw Eli drawing a vamp-killer and a small subgun, seemingly out of the air. Derek flashed hand signals to him, the two fighters moving as one.

A stranger I knew only from the shadows of a fight stepped through the front door. She was copper-skinned, like me. And like me—or like me when I was prepared—she carried more weapons than a small army. She was dressed in the leathers of an Enforcer, but with an old-fashioned design and enough slices and cuts in the tanned hide to be risqué. The stink of old blood was on the leathers, hers and her opponents', ripe and dense with the reek of old pain and death. She smelled like the sniper, and the bomb maker. And she was carrying two long swords. With a single, smooth, backhand cut, she struck Bethany in the neck. The priestess dropped, falling with the blade. She hit the floor, her dark blood spattering the wall.

Before I could blink, Gee had drawn two swords and raced at the swordswoman. He was moving nearly vamp fast, but time had slowed. I could see each movement, see his body flex and contract. "My challenge to blood duel was never satisfied," he shouted, his voice low and his words slurred. "En garde!"

The woman tipped her body forward and raced at Gee, but slow, sluggish. The two met at the juncture of the foyer and the living room. In an honest-to-God sword fight. Steel clashed. A cut appeared in the wall as if by magic. A small table split in two with a crash. I had really liked that table. Not so long ago, it had been blown over when an angry air witch came visiting. Now it was nothing but splinters, like the side door. And the front door.

The Kid, who had been hiding behind the couch, grabbed me by the arm and dove to the floor with me. We landed in a painful heap; I yelped and so did he. The smell of mixed blood rose on the air and I found my feet. I was still holding the stake and the way-too-small blade. The smell of blood was grounding me fast. Adding Beast's blood to the gray place of the change had reinforced my reactions.

"Jane," Alex said, his words a laborious jumble in the slo-mo of time. "The people in the rental house and with the rented SUVs, who were following you, they moved. Eli went to check them out and they were gone and the vehicles were turned back in, but there were at least twelve people living there and they had taken photos. That's one of them." He pointed to the sword fight.

My house was full of nutso vamps, two nearly dead vamps, an injured Onorio, various sentient beings, and a stranger with swords fighting a storm god. The two with swords were moving almost too fast for sight, even my enhanced time-sight, a flashing, ringing, crashing of steel, dual circles of reflected light and the spatter of scarlet and sapphire blood on the pale walls.

Into the doorway stepped a man, dark haired, black eyed, beautiful as a dying angel. He wore jeans and a white shirt that hung open to reveal a necklace of a raptor in flight, boots and wristbands tattooed with blue birds. He shouted something but the words were lost beneath the ring and clash of steel. He was the frightened boy from the painting and the unchanged man with the crystal from the warehouse. Peregrinus. Grégoire's brother.

He carried a sword, a double-edged blade with a hand-and-a-half hilt. He raced in and stabbed up at the *arcenciel*, then tossed what looked like a length of rope over it, a rope tied with something shiny on the end. The quartz crystal. In this light I could tell it was quartz, not diamond. The light of the dragon rippled through it. Eli and Derek fired at the vamp in three-shot bursts. I smelled vamp blood, but Peregrinus didn't falter. He backed out of the house, pulling the *arcenciel* with him. As he moved, the light of the dragon flickered, dimmed, shrank to half its size, and went out. The *arcenciel* writhed once, a snapping, supple movement, and dropped to the floor. It threw out sparks of brown and black, like a dirty fire, the flames dying.

It shifted shape. In its place was a child, a skinny girl of nine or ten with cotton-candy hair and predator teeth. The shooters repositioned their weapons away and down at the sight of the child. Peregrinus tossed the small body over his shoulder, pressed the crystal to her, shouted something, and vanished through the doorway. In a single instant, the invading kidnapper and his swordswoman were gone. The house fell silent around me. I was heaving breaths as I tried to put it all together, my thoughts fragmented and confused.

The light-snake-dragon. The *arcenciel* that wasn't Soul. It had just been captured, somehow. By two members of Satan's Three. Who had totally ignored *me* the whole time. So that meant that all along . . . while they were snipering my house and putting bombs here . . . they had also been waiting for a chance to grab an *arcenciel*? How could they have known I was being attacked by one? Had Reach known there was an *arcenciel* around New Orleans? Had he gotten access to the attack on Bitsa and then given the secret up to Satan's Three? And, worse, did Satan's Three have such access to HQ's security system that they had seen the attack in the gym? I didn't know. And I didn't know how to find out or what to do about it all.

"The Devil," Katie whispered, her fangs distorting her words. I looked at her. There was blood on her chin and dribbling onto her evening gown. The dress was pale aqua silk that shimmered into ocean blue in the shadows. Her eyes, vamped out and black in the bloody sclera, stared in horror at the open front doorway. "The Devil and her master were here and we still live." She crossed herself, which looked utterly wrong on the bloody-mouthed vampire.

At the sign of religious sentiment, Bethany hissed, reached out with one hand, and pulled Leo closer to her side. She was moving weirdly, as if only part of her was working. But her neck was healing, the bleeding already stopped. She extended her own fangs with a firm snap. In a movement too fast to focus on, she buried them in Leo's throat. Gee knelt at Leo's feet and slid his palms up the MOC's pants legs so his palms met the vamp's skin. Blue light flowed down Gee's arms and beneath the cloth, into Leo, and through the MOC into the priestess and Katie. Katie shook herself and looked from the front door to the back, her eyes sweeping the room the way an old soldier might. There was something different about her suddenly, focused and determined. With no hesitation, she bit her own wrist and leaned in to dribble her powerful blood into Leo's mouth.

To my side I smelled Eli. "You okay?" I asked without turning.

"Yeah. You?"

"Ducky. Just ducky," I lied. "The Kid? Bruiser?"

"I'm good. Bruiser's breathing," Alex said.

"I'm okay too," Derek said. "No thanks for not asking."

"You got any more plywood you can cover the broken doors with?" I asked Eli as I watched the four in a group healing, the MOC between them. The MOC, whom I had staked. *Oh. My.* I had staked Leo. A titter of laughter struggled in my throat and I swallowed it down. It hurt, as if I'd stuffed something large and squirming into a too-small bag. My stomach cramped as if I'd been kicked by an elephant, and I doubled over, breathing shallowly until the pain eased.

"Yeah," Eli said, watching me, sounding too casual. "I laid in a good plywood supply, but repair work isn't in my contract. I need a raise."

I finally got a breath as the pain eased and snorted at the

comment. I said, "Partners don't get raises. They get part of the profit at year end." From the corner of my eye, I spotted a twitch of smile in reply.

"What's wrong with you?" Derek asked. No one replied and I shuffled upright, pretending nothing was wrong.

"While the doors are both sealed with plywood, we can go out through the windows." Eli pointed to the three that lined the porch beneath jalousies. His weapons were nowhere to be seen, secreted in his clothes, out of sight but easy to hand. "They used to be doors, by the way," he added, still watching me, his interest seeming casual, while it was actually far more intense than normal. He was offering unimportant information, as if fantasy-film special effects hadn't just broken out in my house. "But the doors were removed and the windows retrofitted sometime in the early nineteen hundreds. I could make them back into doors if you want," he offered. He was standing with his fists balled at his hips, assessing the house in light of our sudden lack of security, but also keeping his eyes on Derek and me. It was a nice trick. "That way we'd have more ways to get in and out next time the regular doors get broken."

"Ha-ha." I lifted my head and sniffed, alarm again racing through me. I turned, following the scent to the front of the house.

"What?" Eli barked.

That odd magical prickling sensation again raced over me. Had the light-dragon gotten free? I was still holding the weapons, which I gripped more firmly, staring at the front door. "We got more company coming."

"Details," Eli said, redrawing blades and positioning throwing knives.

"*L'arcenciel*. Coming from that way." I pointed down the front street.

"Babe, you gotta start telling us before sending out invitations," Eli drawled. "Stay down, Alex," he said to his brother as he flipped the overturned couch over him and Bruiser.

"Yeah. I'm a bad host. All these uninvited guests, and us with no hors d'oeuvres," I said back as Eli and I moved toward the front of the house and Derek retreated to cover Leo.

"Some guests don't need 'em. They bring their own." He indicated the grouping on the floor just as Bethany tugged a stake out of Leo's chest. It made a gross, sucking, grinding sound and black blood bubbled out after it, smelling of silver and death. The nutso priestess held her wrist over the open wound and blood dripped in, hers looking congealed, it was so thick. Leo still looked dead, but Bethany was moving better.

Light, brilliant as the dawning sun, glared in through the broken front door and speckled the foyer with stained-glass tints. It was like fireworks going off in the street, but silent, no pops or sizzling. The light brightened, and I narrowed my eyes against it.

Through the opening, a long snout entered, moving slowly, full of teeth. The alligator snout widened into a frilled head that was easily the size of a water buffalo. The whole buffalo. This *arcenciel* was massive.

A black tongue flicked out and back in, again, touching/ tasting the walls and the floor. It turned its head to me, eyes huge, like iridescent glass, orangey and bright. Her teeth were as long as my vamp-killer and just as sharp, meeting in the massive crocodile mouth, but her teeth were more pearly than the previous *arcenciel*, her frill containing more white and red. I sniffed. I knew this one, this creature made of light and pearls with slowly spiraling, multicolored hair. Soul.

"Holy moly," I breathed.

I felt movement beside me and Gee DiMercy walked sluggishly past, like a sleepwalker whose feet were being pulled, toward the dragon head with the alligator jaw. Gee was close enough to be the *arcenciel*'s dinner when he stopped and sank to his knees, as if he was being weighted down to the ground. He was mumbling in a language that was all consonants and hoarse coughing sounds in the back of his throat. He raised his hands and begged forgiveness. It didn't have to be in English for the sense of the words to be made. The black dragon tongue flicked forward and touched Gee's forehead, once. Again. The dragon head tilted, as if considering the taste or remembering something important. Or as if listening to the rumbling litany, which switched to English. "I failed. I failed." Gee said. "I did not know there was a hatchling, a wild one flying free. I did not know what to do. I failed, Mistress. The young one was stolen . . ."

I stayed well back, Eli at my left shoulder.

When Gee DiMercy fell silent, I moistened my lips and murmured, "Soul?" My tone was one I might use to a skittish horse, if most horses didn't bolt at first scent of me. "You want to tell us what's happening?"

The alligator lips opened, but the sound that came wasn't from the mouth. It seemed to come from all around me, like the way bells sounded in an empty cathedral. "Your magics call to us. We see you in the Grayness Between Worlds. Your magics called the hatchling. She followed you, yet you did not protect her. You allowed her to be taken."

"I did what?" *Hatchling?* Maybe I hadn't understood. The cadence of Soul's words was different in this form, as if English was a second language. As if her brain was formulated differently.

"I smelled/tasted one of my kind on your vehicle window," she said. "I had thought she was fully grown, was of the old ones, like me. The blood of the hatchling was on your hands then, but she still lived. She came to you when Satan's Three attacked you at the warehouse. Yes? She came to save you, to fight alongside you?"

"Possibly," I said, choosing my words carefully, because Soul sounded pretty confused, and a confused predator was a dangerous predator. "I took a pretty big hit that night. I saw an *arcenciel* before I passed out. I'd seen her several times. She's smaller than you." I remembered the body of the child that Peregrinus had carried out the door. *Hatchling* . . .

"You did not intend her harm?"

I shook my head.

"The old ones did not know there was a hatchling," Soul said. "There have been no young ones in over seven thousand years. Now her magic has vanished." The luminous eyes latched onto me like a snare. "You have brought us into danger. You are the witch of death; you are *liver-eater. U'tlun'ta.*" The Cherokee term for evil was husky on the dragon's breath—"hut-luna"—the syllables reverberating through me until my bones ached with the accusation. Her mouth opened to display the razor-edged teeth.

I backed up fast as more of Soul came in through the doorway and passed through the walls, a shimmering glow. Her power and light filled the house, sparkling and frozen. I was an idiot. There would have been scent on the SUV, *l'arcenciel* blood-scent on my blade. I had cleaned it, but blood, crystalline blood, might never clean completely. And in her light-form, Soul's sense of smell was probably much better than when in her human form. *I am an idiot! Idiot, idiot, idiot!*

Derek maneuvered closer, between Leo and Soul, but my attention stayed on the *arcenciel* as I continued to put it all together. Soul had smelled one of her species on the SUV and had seen the vamps attack out at the warehouse. She had known something was wrong but not how bad it really was. What had taken her so long to show up here, I didn't know, but maybe tracking a being made of light was harder than it looked. And then she finds the hatchling, just in time to see the young one killed or kidnapped by Peregrinus, her magics contained, or stolen. That was the only thing that made sense. But why didn't she go after the hatchling, if she could see it in the Gray Between? Unless . . .

"Is the smaller dragon dead?" I asked Soul. "Or was she taken prisoner, her magics hidden?" I felt a hollow dread in my gut. If she was dead, was that because I had stabbed her and wounded her in the gym? Would she have been able to fight off the vampire if she had been at full power? "I am not *u'tlun'ta*. I didn't kill the hatchling." Which totally left out the part about me stabbing her. Liar by omission, that was me.

"She saw your magic and came to you. Yet you say that you did not steal the hatchling's magic?" Soul hissed, aloud this time, her voice still ringing like bells, but deeper and more powerful than her human voice. "You do not ride her magics? Then where is she!"

"Peregrinus stole the hatchling," Gee said.

"Peregrinus." The word was filled with derision and not a little horror.

"I will help you to find her," Gee said, "and return her to the waters of life."

"What he said," I managed.

Soul rippled; a blast of light shot out, blinding us all. Eli and I stepped back, throwing our arms over our eyes. When I blinked into the blurred image of the retinal burn, I saw Soul standing in the doorway, all size-sexy of her, her silver hair and a filmy lavender dress floating in a slow breeze only she felt. "Until you texted me, I had thought the Peregrine was still in Italy," she said. "I had a lot of catching up to do, research-wise."

Soul was staring at Gee as she held out her hand in invitation. "Come to me, little bird. I smell her scent on you. She bit you, yes?" Soul laughed, not unkindly. "Let's fly together. And you can tell me all you know of the hatchling."

They vanished in a flash of gray energies, shot through with black and sapphire motes. And my house was suddenly mostly empty.

With the situation at least moderately secure, my body decided it was safe now to give in and let the stomach cramps take me over. I bent double as my insides tried to twist me apart. I had been right. Pain delayed was pain intensified. *I'm gonna die after all* was my last coherent thought.

CHAPTER 18

Werewolf Laughter

The cleanup took two hours and left the house with the cozy, lightless feel of a cave. I liked it, once I was able to breathe enough to appreciate it. Eli was less positive, but he'd find security issues in a castle, one with a mote, a drawbridge lined with C4, and rocket launchers and antiaircraft weapons mounted on the turrets. I smiled to myself at the image, limping, still holding my middle with an arm.

I put the mop away, still smelling vamp blood, even over the smells of bleach and suds, even with Leo gone to Katie's place where he could feed on the working girls, and be ministered to by the priestess until he was fully healed. He hadn't come to, while he was lying on my floor, but he had looked a bit less lifeless before his heir had hauled him over the fence, handling his body one-handed, Derek behind her, his dark skin gray with fatigue. Katie was scary strong.

The priestess had left, without a word, just walked out the front door opening and disappeared into the night. Their departures had left the house feeling too large and far more windy.

Once I was able to formulate a rational thought again, we had debated moving. It was an option. But the debate hadn't lasted long. Only that castle with the mote and the rocket launchers could protect us now.

So Eli and Alex had made the place as secure as possible, with plywood, quick-mounted motion detectors, cameras focused on the street, the side and backyards, and the wall around back. Which was ironic, as I had broken the ones Katie had put there to keep tabs on me when I first came to New Orleans. We weren't safe in this house. But after staking Leo, I wasn't safe anywhere, especially not at HQ, and the Youngers still refused to go camp out at vamp central without me. And Soul, whose luggage was still upstairs, could find me in the gray place of the change, and move through brick and plaster better than the light she seemed to be made of. Here we stayed.

We were sitting down to a quick dinner—salads, steak, microwaved potatoes, Coke for Alex, and beer for Eli and me— when the rain started again, a loud and demanding storm with wind and lightning and thunder. The meal was without music, without TV volume, with only the storm to hide the approach of strangers and enemies, and the outside cameras hooked up to the Kid's monitors. Rain beat down on the roof, the front of the house, and added a loud staccato rumble to the dinner.

I hoped the rain might be loud enough to wake Bruiser, who still slept on the couch. He lay on his side, curled in a half-fetal position. The man didn't snore, which pleased me for reasons I hadn't looked into yet.

My cell buzzed midstorm with a text from Soul that said, *We are here. See lights in house. No answer at door. NO DOOR. Please advise. Are wet.*

I chuckled and texted back, *Side gate. Enter through window.* To the guys, I said, "Soul's back and she must be human because she can text. And she's not alone, and she's wet. Oh. And she noted that we have no front door."

"She's clearly got mad powers of observation even when she's a dragon," Alex said. "Got her on the monitor. Well, well, well. This should be fun."

Eli pushed his half-eaten meal away, and went to the windows of the main room. I heard the window opening, the sash sticking and scraping. And it occurred to me that Soul might not have written that text herself. Anyone with her cell could have sent it and be holding her—

I heard Eli jump back fast. I came up with a gun in one hand and a vamp-killer in the other, and reached the living room in a single leap that made the Kid yelp in surprise before he laughed, the sound wicked and mocking.

Eli was crouched, a nine-mil in each hand, aimed at a huge, soaking wet, white, growling dog, with crystalline blue eyes. It showed Eli its teeth. Big honking teeth that I recognized. This was no dog. It was a white wolf, a werewolf. I fought the desire to shoot him. Though Beast hated his guts on principle—he *was* a canine—he had once saved my life in the middle of a werewolf attack.

He crouched and raised his shoulders, his growl a rumble that I felt through the floor. Soul was just stepping through the window, and she shouted, "Brute! Stop that!" Like Brute, Soul was soaked through to the skin—not even her magic was keeping her dry through the downpour. She shoved a dripping plastic grocery bag across the floor and hit the wolf in the side with her knee.

Brute stopped growling and closed his lips over his teeth. He looked up at Eli and chuffed. And shook. Water and the stench of wet dog flew everywhere.

I couldn't help it. I laughed. Brute snarled at me. So did Eli, who had been caught in the flying droplets. I holstered my weapons and went to the kitchen, returning with two hands full of dish towels, which I tossed to Eli and to the floor at Brute's feet. "Roll around in the towels, *dog*. Get yourself dry, or I promise I'll toss you outside to sleep on the back porch like the mongrel you are."

The wolf dropped on the pile of towels and rolled, scattering them everywhere and leaving a large wet spot on the newly cleaned floor. He huffed the whole time, werewolf laughter.

Midroll, Brute wrenched himself back to his feet, nose to the floor, snuffling and growling again. "Not to worry," I said to Brute. "It's just Leo's blood." The wolf tilted his head in a totally human gesture of astonishment and I said, "I staked him earlier for interrupting my shower and trying to kill me."

The wolf's look went blanker. His mouth opened. Closed. Opened again. This time his tongue lolled comically.

Soul asked, "Forgive me if I don't quite remember everything from before, but is he . . . ah . . . true-dead?" The look in her eyes said she was calculating how Leo's death would affect the vamp legal-system negotiations. And how long I'd be alive to tell the tale.

"I wish. But nah. Katie took him home to feed him." I handed Soul a larger towel and helped to pat her down while she started giving us the third degree, law enforcement officer–style.

"Where are the Mithrans staying? Why are they here? How many are there? Did they really hurt Reach?"

The answers were minimal and unsatisfactory, but they were all I had. "We lost them. They're supposedly after magical things to take home to the EuroVamps. Satan's Three and any humans they might have. What little intel we have suggests around ten. And I don't know. He sounded"—I frowned at the memory—"hurt."

Soul shook her head and then shook out her platinum-silver hair, running her fingers through to finger-comb the long strands. Even soaking wet she was gorgeous. Curvy, womanly, rounded. With cleavage that drew the eyes, even the eyes of straight women like me. Just elegant cleavage. "You do lead an interesting life, Jane Yellowrock," she said.

"Me? You!"

Soul laughed softly; Brute snorted, and shook again. Eli grumbled and picked up the towels, wiping the dog water and scent off the floor and furniture, keeping an eye on Brute. The wolf trotted around the couch and stopped, sniffing Bruiser from the top of his head to the tips of his socked feet. Then he made the rounds of the living room and kitchen, sniffing and studying everything. I waited, wondering what he'd pick up from the scents in the foyer.

It was pretty spectacular. Brute's ruff went up, he growled and snarled, his chest enlarged as he chuffed and snuffled, and his tail dropped to half-mast. He pressed his nose to the wood and moved back and forth across the floor, sniffing and snorting and quivering with turmoil.

"Brute?" Soul asked. He didn't look up.

"Nose suck," I said.

Soul's forehead wrinkled slightly as if trying to remember the term or what it meant. "I beg your pardon?"

"Canine noses—even wolf noses—are tied directly into the brain in ways humans can't understand. The scents link, merge, and find pathways and patterns that paint a picture. He's smelling Peregrinus and the Devil, and probably Gee and Katie and you and us. Oh. And blood. There was a sword fight in the foyer and the entry to the main room."

The PsyLED special agent looked at the busted furniture piled in the corner and the sword cut in the wall, and shook her head slightly as if trying to draw conclusions from the chaos that was my life. "This, I don't remember at all."

"It happened before you made your dramatic entrance," I said.

"Oh." She shook her head, wet hair flying, "I suppose that should make me feel better." Soul knelt by Brute and ran her fingers deep into his ruff, scratching his skin. "Brute," she said. "Attention." The snuffling stopped and the wolf rolled his blue eyes up to her, but his nose didn't leave the wood floor. "I want you to remember the scents. Tell him who they are, Jane."

"The female human is the Devil. The Mithran is called Peregrinus, and he's our enemy. He came to about here"—I pointed to the floor—"and left. The not-human that might have a slight wet-feather undertone is Gee DiMercy. Then over here we had Leo and his heir, Katie, and the vampire priestess Bethany. She smells old and crazy." I looked at Soul, who stood up, leaving her hand in the wolf's ruff. "The other scents you might make out are Derek, who you've sniffed, I think, and two *les arceniels*. Their scents are fishy and plant-like." Soul lifted her eyebrows in amusement at my description of her scent, or maybe at my attempt at speaking French.

Brute snuffled and snorted, this tone different from the earlier ones, now of affirmation. He raised his head and stood on his back feet to stick his nose into Soul's neck near her ear. He blew, fluffing her wet hair. Claws clicking, he dropped, turned around, and headed up the stairs. I said, "Do not do anything bad to any room or any piece of . . . anything. Or the threat about the back porch will be true." Brute sniffed at me and trotted on up, taking the stairs two at a time.

"Why is George Dumas asleep on your couch?" Soul asked, still in the foyer, looking over her shoulder.

"It's a long story," Eli said, making his weapons disappear. "We have steak. I can cook one under the broiler for you and feed one raw to the dog."

We could hear the growl from up the stairs at the *dog* insult.

"If you don't want him to pee in your boots, you'd better be careful," I said.

"It seems I always show at dinnertime." Soul gave us an embarrassed smile, eyeing the table. "If you have an extra potato baked, I'd rather have that, though I need to change first."

"You can't just make your clothes," I make a *poof* gesture, "*presto chango?*"

"No," Soul said primly. "I cannot."

I grunted. "So why is a werewolf here without his executioner?" Werewolves, even one touched by an angel, as this one had been, were always accompanied by a grindylow, who would kill them if they tried to pass along the were-taint.

Her voice soft, Soul said, "Pea is in-country. And there was no one else to take Brute."

I blinked. "Oh. Of course." I turned away. *In-country* was the word Rick had used when I sent him into hiding. Pea was with my ex and his were-panther girlfriend. Ask a dumb question . . .

"Yes," Soul said. "Also, Brute's nose may be useful when we go after the hatchling. If you'll excuse me . . ."

Alex stood at the bottom of the stairs blushing, his eyes carefully—very carefully—not staring at Soul's cleavage or the way her body looked, with the wet clothes plastered to her as she made her way up to her room. All the time spent with Katie's working girls was paying off in the Kid's manners.

Eli and I went back to the kitchen where I nuked my untouched cold potato and lined up condiments in front of Soul's plate. Eli used tongs to serve her salad, and set a raw steak on a plate on the floor. Faster than I could change—and I changed quick—Soul was back, wearing jeans and a lightweight sweater, her hair braided in a silver plait down her back to dry.

"When *we* go after the hatchling?" I asked, picking up the conversation where we had dropped it.

"She is a powerful weapon when being ridden. As a PsyLED special agent, I *cannot* leave her in Peregrinus' hands. And she is one of my kind, a rare and precious hatchling. I *will* not leave her in his hands."

As if we'd worked and lived together for years, we went back to eating, filling Soul in on the most recent events. It took some time, and Soul asked more questions about the missing hatchling and the vamps who took her. Some of the questions we could answer, and some were so off the wall I had no idea. Like, "How old is she? How did she first find you? Has she ever talked to you?" And my personal favorite, "What do the Mithrans who took her want?"

So far as I could tell, they wanted everything, but I said, "They came prepared with a crystal and some kind of lasso to capture an *arenciel*. Why would someone want a hatchling?"

"They are easier to ride," Soul said, again employing a prim tone.

Alex laughed, which morphed into a cough when Eli kicked him under the table. Soul looked amused at the byplay, and added, "Hatchlings are easier to control than the adults of my species. And we have magic that can be used by properly trained humans."

I told them my suspicions about Reach possibly having a file about an *arceniel* in the vicinity of New Orleans.

There was no reason now to keep secrets. We knew too much about one another to play games, so the Youngers and I shared freely. Brute finished his tour of the house while we chatted, and settled at his plate, his ears flicking as he listened to us talk. The storm began to ease as we did the debrief, a gentle drumming as the thunder faded into the distance.

We were eating dessert, which was plain vanilla ice cream with dark chocolate melted over it, when my cell rang. The rain had slowed to a mellifluous patter, and the ringer was an annoying song by Madonna. While I answered I shot the Kid a warning look for messing with my ringtone. He tried for innocent. It didn't work.

"Hey, Troll."

"Where's Katie?"

I went still. All the others turned to me and I put the call on speaker. "What do you mean, 'Where's Katie?' She jumped the fence carrying Leo over an hour ago."

"She never got here."

"On it," I said, ending the call. Moving with Beast-speed, I pulled on a headset and grabbed a flashlight out of my gobag, holding it in the hand with the vamp-killer, my right holding the nine-mil, one in the chamber. After a fractured moment of indecision, I raced to my room, and reached up into the top of my closet, for the box of charms Molly had prepared for me so long ago. I hadn't used any of them recently.

I opened the box and took out one small charm, a fishhook carved of ash, painted with a streak of sterling silver. It was packed with witch power, a charm to freeze a vamp. It was crafted to work for fifteen minutes, give or take. Plenty of time to behead a vamp, even one as strong and as old as Peregrinus. I just hoped it had been created to hold power for a long time. I hadn't asked Molly to recharge the spells on the charms. I hooked it into my T-shirt neck, securing it close at hand and easy to pull. I also took all of my silver stakes and tied the fuzzy purple T-shirt around my waist, the shirt crafted with healing in the knitted threads of the tee. Lastly, I slapped on the thigh rig.

Eli was upstairs, scouting the back of the house and yard with low-light goggles.

"Ears on," I said into the mouthpiece.

"Running a sweep now," he said.

"Okay. What do you see?"

"Back is clear on low level and infrared," Eli said over the headset. He appeared at my side, silent as a hunting lion. "Clear to go." Soul stood by the back window, her badge on her hip, a psymeter in one hand and her service weapon in the other. I wasn't sure about letting the PsyLED agent take part but I also knew she wasn't leaving. "No indication of magical power in the backyard," she said, pocketing the device.

Side by side, Eli and I left through the window, Soul behind us. Though it was clear that she wanted to take point, we knew the terrain; she didn't. In the dark, flashlights sweeping, we began quartering the backyard. Brute leaped through the window and followed, his nose to the wet, draining earth. The backyard was unchanged, as I expected it to be. I had seen Katie, with Leo, go over the back fence in a smooth leap that practically defied gravity, Derek right behind.

I nodded to Eli and he climbed the rocks—the ones still whole and not reduced to rubble—taking the highest point. Using his equipment, he scanned the yard on the other side and nodded to me. I shut off the flash and pulled on Beast's strength, leaping high, grabbing the brick top, and swinging over the fence, to land in a crouch. Mud flew up from my feet and I realized I was still barefoot. The breeze was silent but steady from upriver. All I smelled on it was food and rain and exhaust. All I heard was rain pattering down and cars and music from several directions.

One hand on the brick, I scanned Katie's back garden with Beast's night vision, a sheen of greens and grays and silvers everywhere. I sucked in scent through my lips, over my tongue, and across the roof of my mouth, trying to scent silently. I smelled rain, rain, and more rain, the ozone of lightning, and, faintly, just at the edge of my ability in this form, blood. Vamp blood, mixed varieties. Leo's blood . . . He had stopped bleeding before Katie him took away. But—

"Holy crap," I whispered to myself. If Katie killed Leo, or let someone else kill Leo, she would move to Master of the City by right of succession, according to Mithran law. Leo had been unconscious and gravely injured from the silver of my stakes, and I had let the one person guaranteed to benefit from his death at my hands take him off.

"Holy crap," I said again. To Eli, I said, "Clear." No louder, but not for the headset, I said, "Brute. Get over here."

Two seconds later the wolf landed beside me and mud flew all over me. Brute, when he had been able to achieve human form, had weighed in at more than three hundred pounds. He was still that in wolf form. "Cute," I said, wiping spatter off my face. "Sniff out everything from here to the house, please. Then I'll ask a few questions. Okay?"

Brute made a low *Rrrr* sound in the back of his throat, which I took as affirmation, and started quartering the yard like a police detective might at a crime scene. I had a sudden vision of Rick and Brute working together, taking the same steps, following the same procedures, but working as a team. Minutes passed as I stood in the mud, rain falling on my shoulders. Troll, Soul, and Eli appeared at a back window of Katie's, silhouetted by dim light from the hallway beyond. Someone had been smart, not adding new scents to the scene.

Brute covered the yard and reached the back door to Katie's before he raised his head to look over his shoulder at me. His white coat was drenched with the slow rain, as was I, and his paws were muddy to the knees. He barked, the tone telling me he was done. I slogged to him through the wet grass, my jeans dragging, and the back door opened to let us both in. There was a length of plastic on the floor in the back entrance and a stack of towels. And four working girls in various stages of undress. I accepted a large towel from Troll and dried off while Soul, kneeling on the plastic, applied another towel to the wolf.

As we both worked at drying off the rainwater, I said, "Brute." The wolf lifted his crystalline eyes to me, sat down, stared, and waited. Soul stopped drying him and put her hand into his ruff again, her eyes on me too. I said, "I need answers. Let's start with: Did Katie and Leo and Derek land on this side of the fence?"

Brute nodded once up and down. It was a strange sight, seeing a wolf mimic human behavior. I wondered whether I looked that odd when I responded to questions like a human when in animal form.

"Okay. Did they make it to the door?" Brute shook his head side to side, no. "Was there a fight?" Brute nodded. "Close to the fence?" He nodded.

"Did the fight continue for a while?" He nodded. I took a slow breath. "Did anyone die in the fight?" Brute shook his head and I let the breath out. "Do you recognize the attacker or attackers' scent?" He nodded again. "Was it Peregrinus?" Brute's big head dropped and rose slowly.

"Was anyone injured?" The skin and hair over Brute's eyes wrinkled, and I recognized his inability to answer the question. "Did you smell fresh blood?" Brute stared hard at me and dipped his head. I said the names, pausing between each for an answer. "Leo's? Katie's? Derek's? Peregrinus'? The Devil's?" I got a solemn nod with each name.

Soul said, "Peregrinus has the hatchling, Leo, and Katie. There is nothing he cannot do once he controls them."

"Okay," I said, thinking that over. "We have a limited time period to fix it all. First question is, how did they get out of the yard?"

Eli knelt and rolled towels to form a square on the plastic. "Here's the fence at our back courtyard. Here's Katie's back door. There's a long alley from Katie's backyard to the street down this side, but it's locked and a camera records everything there. There's no side yard here." He pointed to the other side, where Katie's and the house being remodeled next door were so close that you'd have a difficult time getting an old-fashioned phone book between the walls. "So we have a fight that took place in a rain- and thunderstorm, in a locked garden area. Brute? How did they get out?"

Brute whined softly, looking at the towels and up to Soul.

"Brute is having some difficulty thinking in human terms," Soul said, her tone gentle. "We think his brain has been too long in wolf form. It's okay, Brute. Can you show us if we go outside, in the yard?" Brute whined and thumped his tail before nodding. He turned and put a paw on the door, which left a muddy smear before Troll opened it. I followed the werewolf stuck in wolf form into the dark.

Outside, the rain had stopped and there was only the gurgle of water running off the roofs and through gutters, and the heavy fall of collected rainwater dripping from plant leaves and house eaves. Distantly, I heard cars splashing through the rain and jazz from uptown, R & B from downtown. The wind was still moving downstream, carrying the ever-changing scent pattern.

Nose to the ground, Brute trotted around the yard, circumscribing an area about twenty feet round. Most of the yard. Several times he put his paw down as if indicating something important on the grass or on a plant. "Soul, what's that mean, when he puts his paw down?"

"He smells blood."

"A lot of blood, then," I said, counting back to eight different places just in the circumference.

Brute trotted to the side yard and put his paws up on the building next door to Katie's, the building where I had heard hammers and skill saws earlier in the week, where the construction was taking place. I looked up and saw that a window on the attic floor was broken. "Crap," I said to Eli. The breeze had carried all scent from the window away from us, so I hadn't noticed it. I was too wedded to the nose and not enough to the eyes. "We suck as investigators," I continued. "You found the sniper out front. But I'm betting we had someone watching the back from the attic of that house."

"I'll take the front, through Katie's and out to the street," he said into my ears. He looked at Troll, taking in the broad shoulders and huge chest. "Think you can boost Janie up to the window when I give the word?"

"Piece of cake." To me, Troll said, "You find who took my Katie and you put a hole in him for me."

I nodded and sheathed my weapons. I'd need hands free to climb through a high window. I just hoped they weren't still there waiting in ambush. At that thought, I said, "Eli, take Brute with you. See if he smells them leaving through another door."

Brute woofed and raced to the house, Eli hot on his tail. Literally. Which made me smile as much as I could, knowing that the Master of the City and his heir had disappeared on my watch and under my nose.

Troll stood bent-kneed, about five feet away from the wall of the neighboring house, and linked his meaty fingers together to made a basket of his hands. I gauged the distance from his hands to the window and backed up fifteen feet. Drawing on Beast's strength, I raced toward Troll and leaped, landing with my right foot in his hands. I pushed off and up as Troll straightened his knees and simultaneously raised his arms, pushing, shoving, lifting, throwing me high, like a gymnast. I shot up and over at the window, meeting the window sash at waist level, my hands thrusting down, using the momentum to lift my legs up. I caught my balance and paused on the sash, hands and feet all together, the way a cat might stand on a narrow ledge or tree limb.

"Janie," I heard softly below me.

Before answering, I inspected the room inside, dark and shadowed. There was no one there, but the smell of fresh vamp and human blood hung thick on the air, mixing with the scents of glue, putty, wallboard, wood, and human sweat. If there was an intruder inside, one who had a better-than-human sense of smell, he or she would know I was coming.

"Janie," Troll called again.

"What," I hissed over a shoulder.

"Your feet are muddy. And bare. And the window's broken."

"I noticed," I said dryly.

"Be careful," he said. "And bring my Katie back." Vamps and their humans were big on terms of possession, but there was something tender and yearning and frightened in his voice. I so totally did not want to know about his relationship with Katie, but there was no doubt that he loved her.

On a silent breath I said, softly, "Working on it, Troll. Working on it." Then I let myself drop to the floor of the dark room, drawing my weapons, my feet on carpet and shards of glass. My weight drove the glass into my soles and I hissed at the pain of sliced flesh. I took a second step inside, trying to avoid the glass, but a needle of antique window pierced my instep. Beast, responding to the danger to my feet, dropped us into the gray place of the change and my legs morphed from the knees down. I held in a scream of pain as my bones cracked and shrank and then expanded into the half-human, half-puma, big-cat form of paw. When she was finished, I had bitten through my tongue, adding the smell of my blood to the stench of the house. I gasped when the bone pain eased and shook the glass off my hard paw pads.

The gasp drew air into my mouth, and the scent and stink of humans and freshly spilled blood filled my head. Blood-servants, several of them, had entered here earlier today. Peregrinus' men and women. The construction guys had disturbed them in the attic and died for their trouble.

Silently, I crossed the room, into the dark.

CHAPTER 19

Someone Fired. They Fought Back.

The house beside Katie's was empty except for two dead workers in the attic hallway and a dead contractor on the first floor. They had died fast and recently, their blood still liquid and running into the corners of the uneven floors, soaking into the plaster and through the cracks, pulled by gravity into the nether regions of the house. The construction van they had driven in was gone, a quick and easy way to move two injured vamps through New Orleans' unique, aging, repair-requiring architecture. No one would notice a panel van sporting a construction company logo.

The only positive thing we found in the house next to Katie's was Derek, bleeding and beaten, slumped under the eaves where he had hidden himself after getting away from Peregrinus. The marine groaned a bit and moved a lot more slowly, but he was with us mentally, once Soul rested her hands on his shoulders. I wasn't sure what she did, but it looked a lot like healing. At the very least, she made him feel better.

The crime scene went to Soul. She would rather have been looking for the hatchling, but with the deaths, she had no choice. The special agent with PsyLED took the scene over with controlled and ruthless efficiency, calling her up-line boss, calling local contacts, starting with Jodi, and then working her way down the list to all the other agencies and people she needed to contact for a vamp-on-human murder investigation. She didn't have to tell me this had FUBAR written all over it, and that I was the one who would get stuck in the middle of the mess if I was here.

I didn't stick around to see who all showed up. Eli, Derek, Brute, and I left on foot, Brute in the lead, off leash, and we ran hard to keep up as he followed the scent of Katie and Leo, Peregrinus and the Devil, following the scents of danger, discord, and blood through the night. He kept his nose in the air, tracking the van's trail through French Quarter streets. We ran across the Quarter and right back to vamp HQ. As we rounded the corner, the lights in that part of the Quarter went out, for at least four blocks, leaving a black hole in the night.

I dialed Bruiser as we ran, just in case he was conscious again, but the call went to voice mail. I left a message. "Up and at 'em, Onorio. HQ has been hit."

The two-thousand-pound gate—the one that was designed to stop a dump truck filled with explosives—was bowed in and had bounced off its roller track, damaged beyond repair. We stood in front of it, huffing and panting, taking it all in. Eli swung a low-light ocular over one eye and scanned the grounds. "Nothing. No one. Up the front or split up and take the back too?"

"I'm heading to the side entrance," Derek said, "to get my men organized." The side entrance was hidden in the brick wall and opened into Leo's office.

I nodded to him. "Be careful." To Eli, I said, "We stick together." We raced in a zigzag pattern across the unlit, unmanned, circular drive and headed for the stairs to the entrance. Three steps up, the night exploded in a blinding light. Several things happened all at once. Brute yelped. We ducked to either side of the stairs, arms up to guard our faces. Eli cursed and yanked the ocular from his eye, temporarily blinded. But there was no explosion, no shrapnel, nothing to explain the agonizing light, until it dimmed from excruciating, to merely painful, to a coruscating, scintillating brilliance. And then to darkness.

On the step stood Soul. But she wasn't even vaguely human. Her face was humanoid, but the rest of her was winged, snaky, scaled, and solid now, tiger striped, like her tiger form. A striped and stunning dragon, like the tales of old. I looked back across the streets to the sight of blue and red emergency lights flashing at the crime scene. "Soul?"

"I can stay only a moment before I'm missed at the crime scene," she said, her body flashing light again. A moment later she stood before us, in her human guise, wearing a filmy dress that moved in its own breeze. "The hatchling is alive, in the Mithran Council chambers. Reality has been folded." Her voice was deeper, growly, as if when she shifted to human, she forgot to change her vocal cords. It made the hairs on the back of my neck stand up.

"Her light patterns tell me that she unfolded time and reality, reentering this world, here, on these steps, and then folded it away again, inside," Soul said, pointing into the darkened interior. "She vanished from my sight in the Gray Between. I can't follow her trail while she is being ridden." Which meant little to me, but I had a feeling that it would, and quickly.

Soul's teeth positively gnashed together in frustration at what she saw on my face. "As you fold time, so do we," she said, as if explaining something to a particularly annoying four-year-old.

"Oh," I said. Suddenly it all made sense. *Now* I knew why they kidnapped an *arenciel*. And why they had tried to steal my energies. "*Oh!*"

"If I go after her, I'll be taken as well. I can't help her, not against a witch with a crystal and the knowledge of its use. All of my kind are vulnerable. But you're a skinwalker; you can't be taken. Please, Jane. Find her and break the crystal that imprisons her."

I stalked up the steps to Soul until our faces were on a level.

"Jane," Eli warned, his voice toneless and cautious.

"If I can find her and bring her back, I will. If I can't bring her back, I'll call for you and you'll have to chance being taken too."

Soul closed her eyes as if to hide her reaction. "Thank you." In a flash of light, she was gone. I raced into the darkness inside the front entrance. Or what was left of it.

More slowly, Eli and Brute entered. Together, we moved into the room and to the side where guests usually presented weapons and acquiesced to a pat-down, our backs to the wall. Glass in plasticized hunks and rounded beads littered the floor. The air lock, the two sets of doors, and all the bullet-resistant glass was gone, blasted in and shattered as if a rocket had taken it out, though there was no scent of anything I might associate with a rocket or a grenade or other explosive device.

There was, however, an overload of other scents. The stench of
blood and lots of it. Human, vamp, and something else that
reeked of dead fish and rotting vegetation, the way an *arcenciel*
might smell if it was dying. The stink of recently fired weapons,
hot and thick on the air.

The place was black and more silent than the beginning of
a nightmare. No lights, no soft whisper of the air-conditioning
units whirring, no sound of voices; more important, no sound
of the fancy generators I had installed. No backup lighting.

Reach. Reach had gotten his fingers into the security system
long ago. The Kid and I had tried to remove any access, and
had found several back doors into the system. But obviously
we had missed one. Or more. And Peregrinus had gotten
Reach's files. He knew everything I did. He had found a way
inside in every way that could possibly count. What I didn't
know was far more important. How did Peregrinus kidnap an
arcenciel, and how was he going to use it? What was he doing
here? Did it have something to do with the safe on sub-four?
Why did he have Leo and Katie? Where had he kept his soldiers? Because, while magic might have gotten him inside, only
trained soldiers did *this*.

Beside me, I felt Eli lift his arm as he changed out devices
on his headset and studied the foyer. Beast's eyes adjusted to
the greater dark and stared through my own, brightening the
world in greens. At my side, Brute stared/smelled into the dark
of the entry of vamp HQ and whined softly. The foyer was
empty of people, but there was blood, so much blood, pooled,
puddled, splashed, and streaked across the floor, showing me
where the injured had been pulled away from the fighting and
down hallways. Almost buried beneath it all I smelled Peregrinus, relating his stench to the washed-out scents in Katie's
yard. Fainter, I smelled the fishy smell of the *arcenciel* and her
magic, like the Gray Between, but sharper, more bitter,
scorched. Her magic, her ability to fold time, had gotten them
in, I realized. And that had to mean that capturing the *arcenciel* wasn't an end in itself, but a means to an end—Leo's *les
objets de la puissance*, *les objets de magie*.

Brute pressed close against my thigh, his body quivering, his
nose on overload. I needed a tracker. I needed the wolf in this
hunt. I needed Brute, working under orders, but Soul wasn't
here to do it.

And Brute and I had issues, despite his saving my life once.

Nerves pulsing in fear at the thought of putting away a weapon, I sheathed the vamp-killer and slid my hand into the wolf's ruff as I had seen Soul do. I pushed through the thick undercoat and touched his skin beneath the long, dense hair at his neck. He was vibrating with the excess of scent patterns.

My wide toes spread and clenched; my claws scraped at the marble floor, finding nothing to sink into. I felt Beast push me into the Gray Between again, prickles on my skin and down my throat. Brute leaped away, a four-paw, rotating leap, that put him three feet away and facing me, snarling. My nose changed shape, pelt shivered up my arms and legs and across my face. But this time it was mostly soft-tissue changes, much less painful than the foot bones changing and shifting—like sticking a finger into a light socket instead of being hit by lightning. In the midst of the change, I lifted my eyes and sought out the *arcenciel*. I saw nothing before me. Or below me. And nothing back the way we had come. I didn't know what I was doing.

I let go of the energies, and the gray place of the change eased away. Brute was staring up at me, his wolf eyes wide, his nose flaring and contracting as the smells of the place, my Beast, and my magic drove him to some edge I couldn't even imagine. He growled, his body tightening as if to attack.

I stepped to him, my fist extended for him to smell. I nudged his muzzle and ran a hand through his ruff again. "It's okay," I muttered to him. To Beast I thought, *You gotta stop doing stuff like this in the middle of an emergency.*

Jane will not stay in Beast form, she thought back, sounding worried.

"What's okay?" Eli said into the headset.

Inside me/us, Beast whistled with disquiet, a sound I recognized/remembered, one that puma kits make when they want their mother. It was weird coming from her now and I shook my head to clear her emotions away. "Nothing," I whispered to Eli. There wasn't time to explain a mostly nonverbal conversation to the one human in the group.

Brute chuffed at the spoken word and leaned against my thigh, but his quivering eased. "Brute?" I asked, my words mostly breath. "Is Peregrinus still here? Can you find him?"

Brute dropped his head to the floor and took a step into the bloody room. Eli handed me a flashlight, and I turned it on, a tiny, narrow beam of light. The wolf and my partner avoided all the blood somehow, never smearing the spatter, never leaving a print. I tried to be that careful, but I wasn't as comfortable with my paws as Brute was with his, especially in half-Beast form. And Eli was just Eli.

The wolf led us through the signs of fighting, his nose to the floor, his breath a snuffling, whuffling sound, toward the stairs where he paused as if confused, and finally led us around the corner. We found the first body there, a human, a mangled mess of gore that gave no indication of gender or immediate cause of death. There were too many lethal possibilities in the glare of my flashlight, too many scents on the air to let me know by smell alone. But the human hadn't died by sword or vamp fangs. It was something else, something I had never seen before but could instantly recognize. *L'arcenciel* teeth and fangs had done this. That or an alligator, grabbing and shaking its victim, whirling around and around underwater, tearing its dinner apart. But this person hadn't been eaten, just mangled and left behind.

From somewhere deep in the building I heard the chugging cough of a generator starting, and the tiny security lights I'd installed along both sides of the hallways began to glow. At my side, Eli swung the ocular away from his face to dangle around his neck and indicated the body. *"L'arcenciel?"* I nodded and he asked, "The hatchling Soul was talking about? Under coercion?"

"Maybe. Probably. But the *arcenciel* smells sick. Maybe dying."

Eli didn't comment on that. "He okay?" he asked, meaning Brute.

"Yeah," I lied. "He's just ducky." I nudged the wolf with a knee and we moved on, the werewolf in the lead by a head, his shoulder in constant contact with my leg.

The muted lights showed me too much. Another body, mauled like the first one, farther down the corridor. A body part half in a doorway. Things I didn't want to see, smells of people I knew mixed with the stench of bowels released in death. There was no one left alive in the foyer or the hallways that veered off. No one to rescue or save.

This had been only recently done. Peregrinus had folded time and killed the people in the house next to Katie's, folded time again and gotten here, and then folded time again and started killing people. So much damage, so fast.

Gray place of change, Beast thought at me. *Jane needs to be in gray place, place Soul calls Gray Between.*

I remembered the pain from last time. *Not if I can help it,* I thought.

Gray place, Beast demanded. *Time is changed* now.

Which meant that Peregrinus was doing things outside of time, right now, things no one could defend against. "Holy crap," I whispered. "Eli. We may have a problem."

"Ya think?"

Laughter cracked through me like dry sticks breaking, sharp and shattering and painful. I pulled Eli and the wolf back through the foyer and into the weapons room. I used Beast's strength to rip the metal door off the small locked closet there and started inspecting the weapons that had been kept there, waiting for their owners to leave. Owners that may be dead. Without speaking, Eli joined me, standing so he could see out, into the foyer.

"The *arcenciel* can affect time," I said, strapping a short-sword sheath to my left thigh for an ambidextrous draw. "Like what happens in a fight when time slows down and you can move fast, while everything else is slow."

"Yeah," he said shortly. Clearly remembering combat. His scent changed, pungent and astringent.

"The *arcenciels*—all of the species and not just this one—can do that to some extent. Like they can exist outside of time, or maybe create a bubble of time and place." I laid weapons on the nearby desk.

"So they can come here and take out a well-defended, well-armed location as fast as a platoon of Rangers."

"Faster. Like magic, but not. Probably some arcane way of shifting through the physical laws, like what happens when I shape-change. And because they can bend time or bubble it or fold it like dough, no one saw them coming."

"Someone saw them. Someone fired. They fought back."

I considered that as I added three nine-millimeter semis to my gear and enough spare mags to weigh down a donkey. I was careful, taking only weapons that used interchangeable magazines, though I lusted at the sight of a lovely .45 and Wrassler's Taurus Judge .45/.410. I picked it up and checked the load. 410 rounds. What the heck. It was five rounds of power I wouldn't have otherwise, and my part-cat hands could manage a lot more weight right now. I holstered the nine-mil I had been carrying and readied the Judge. The rounds contained steel and *arcenciels* were steel-phobic. If worse came to worst, maybe Soul could heal an injured hatchling.

Yet, even with the steel allergy, the young *arcenciel* had managed to dent the iron gate. Which had to have hurt her. "The *arcenciel* is under compulsion," I said, still putting it all together, "what Soul calls being ridden. Peregrinus can force her to do things, even painful things, things she might never do on her own."

"So Bethany, the crazy priestess, knew that an *arcenciel* could be ridden but had no idea how or what that might mean," Eli said.

I remembered Bethany trying to physically climb on the light-dragon. "Yeah. And because of all that, I might have no choice but to kill the *arcenciel* hatchling."

"You. Not us. Because you can fold time too," Eli said, his tone calm.

I nodded, knowing his eyes had adjusted to the dark. "They fought," I agreed. "Fat lotta good it did them."

"What are Satan's Three after?" he asked.

"I don't know, but I'm betting Leo has some magical items on the premises. If so, then maybe what and where were in Reach's data bank." Eli cursed and I didn't respond. I felt the same way.

From the foyer, I heard something slide. We went silent. Eli pointed to the doorway and I handed off two weapons and four mags as I dashed to the far side of the door, taking in the foyer as I moved. A hulking form was pulling itself along the hallway and into the entrance. The smell of his blood told me who it was. I gave Eli the thumbs-up sign, and pointed to me, then to the foyer. "Wrassler," I said, the word almost silent.

He pocketed the new guns and ammo, nodded, and leaned against the wall, part of his body exposed to anyone in the foyer, his weapon giving me cover. I set down the Judge and dashed out, shoving my hands under Wrassler's armpits and pulling him, sliding him across the glass-strewn floor. At my side, Brute grabbed Wrassler's shirt and pulled, his teeth buried in the cloth. He was pulling Wrassler's left arm, which was practically disconnected from the rest of him.

Back in the cubicle-sized room, I covered the doorway as Eli went into medic mode, cutting off clothing and inspecting Wrassler's makeshift tourniquets, pulling his own battlefield

tourniquets and stretchy bandages from pockets of his gobag.
I kept an eye and the Judge aimed on the foyer as I listened to
Wrassler's briefing, his voice a ragged breath of agony.

"They came in fast . . . Fastest . . . thing I ever saw. Dragon,
Peregrinus . . . his Devil. Batildis carrying both Leo and Katie.
Strong. They took out the gate. Then the air lock." He stopped
and Eli pulled a bottle of water out of a pocket, opened it, and
held it up for Wrassler to see.

"Gut wounds?" Eli asked.

"No. I'm good."

Eli held it to Wrassler's mouth and the blood-servant drank.
I glanced over my shoulder, taking him in fast. He was *good*?
He was missing a right lower leg and his left arm had effectively been amputated, though it was still attached by strings
of flesh below the tourniquet. Yeah. He was good. He was
damn good. I batted away tears and untied the T-shirt and
tossed it to Eli in the dark. "Here. Tie it on him. It's my dragon
tee, the one with a healing spell in the fibers." *Dragon tee.*
Ironic that a shirt with a dragon on it might save Wrassler from
a dragon bite.

I went back to covering the foyer, Wrassler's Judge steady
in my hands, ready to fire.

Eli tied the T-shirt around Wrassler's thigh, capped the water bottle, and went back to work.

"I was standing in security. Saw it all on-screen. Ordered
lockdown. Ordered security to fire at the dragon only. With steel.
Ordered our people to hold fire at the Mithrans and the human.
And then the shooters rushed in through the gate. Ten shooters." He swore a long line of fine and detailed curses as Eli tightened the tourniquet below his knee. Sweat was dripping off his
jaw and he started shivering. Shock. Not a good sign.

Eli laid Wrassler's body flat and lifted both thighs onto a
chair, then pulled a military-style metallic blanket from his
gobag, shook it out, and tucked it around the blood-servant.
He pulled his cell phone, looked at the screen, and said, "We're
jammed."

Wrassler nodded, his breath coming too fast, teeth chatter-
ing. "The power grid went down first. Then the generators died,
just as something jammed all coms. About two seconds later
we were hit . . ." He stopped to breathe.

Eli tucked his cell away. "Why order your guys not to target
vamps and humans?"

"They had Leo." He looked up at me, his pupils wide in a too-pale face. "I gave orders to use only steel on the dragon," he repeated, his thoughts starting to wander. "That was before the shooters came in."

I ground my teeth, knowing my friend was dying. Smelling it, tasting it on the air. *Not Wrassler. Not Wrassler,* I prayed. *Not him.*

"They went down the hallways first. Taking out everyone they found. It took maybe four seconds. We had dead and dying everywhere. When this floor was clear, they went up the stairs to Leo's office. I directed everyone there." Wrassler fell silent but I could hear him breathing, fastfastfast, shallow and desperate for air.

"Four of Derek's guys were on duty. In seconds, two were dead. Derek showed up then. I don't know where he came from, but I was never so happy . . ." Wrassler blinked and fell silent.

I looked at Eli, who was frowning at the discrepancy of timelines. No way Derek could have gotten there so quickly. Not without folding time. Or getting caught up in the *arcenciel*'s magics. Eli frowned harder, putting that ability into any strategy we might develop. He tightened Wrassler's thigh tourniquet.

Wrassler started in the middle of a different thought. "Derek ordered the rest of his guys to pull back, to take them as they left the office. But Peregrinus knew about the hidden passages and the elevator in the room next to Leo's office." The service elevator went down and opened into a room on sub-four, not far from the storage room, just like I thought. Everyone knew about the previously hidden passageways, stairs, and the service elevator, thanks to the local cops who were called in about a death not so long ago, a death on my watch. Reach had access to police reports from when a were–black panther had been murdered in Leo's office. He knew about the elevator. Therefore Peregrinus knew. My fault. So much was my fault. "Grégoire followed them into the hidden room and took on the Devil. I saw the first moves and Grégoire was bleeding pretty bad." Wrassler stopped to breathe. "No one ever beat the Devil. Not even Grégoire. And he wasn't beating her then. He ordered everyone to retreat and regroup.

"I was on the move through the back stairways. I met them

on sub-four. Derek was with me. And five more of his guys.
Firefight from hell, dude," he said to Eli. "The dragon went
solid and black as night. But it was covered in what looked like
metal scales with metallic spikes and spines along the sides and
at the tail. The rounds hit it. Crazy loud. Pretty sure it was hurt.
It was thrashing. Tail hit me in the arm. Then it picked me up
by the leg and shook me. Threw me. *So fast.* I went down.
Derek pulled me back and stuffed me into the small elevator
to take me back up. I don't know what happened then. But . . .
guessing they headed down. I made it up to Leo's office on the
last generator power before it died too."

"So you crawled down here," Eli said, "hoping to get coms
and call for backup. Cells are damaged. House lines are down.
I'm thinking EM interference."

I nodded to show I'd heard. "Who's manning security?" I
asked. The hallway floor lights were on now so the security
system was working, even if coms were down or jammed.

"Angel Tit's on." Wrassler coughed, the sound hoarse. "He's
trying to call out. Get help. Friends at the Marine Corps Support Facility on Opelousas Avenue. Water," he said to Eli.

Eli gave him the rest of the water and set a new bottle down
by his good right hand. With Beast's hearing I could tell that
Wrassler's heart was beating far too fast. If we didn't get him
help, he'd die, and soon. But if we took him for help, others
would likely die.

"Where are Sabina and Bethany?" I asked.

"Sabina's off-site, at her lair in the graveyard," Wrassler
whispered, mumbling. Dying. He was dying. "Bethany . . . She
was here," he said, sounding dazed. "She's hurt. She was . . . she
was shouting about riding the dragon. The *arcenciel*. She was
crying bloody tears." Wrassler stopped to breathe again. Eli
gave him more water. He drank it fast, some dribbling out of
his mouth. "She was talking about them taking her magic. I
saw her fall."

"Taking her magic . . ." I didn't know what that meant, not
exactly, but I remembered the pain when Peregrinus had put
the crystal on my chest. The feeling like I was dying before the
hatchling had appeared and he'd turned his attention from me.
Somewhere deep inside, it all came together. This was about
the Gray Between, and the ability to fold time. This was about
stealing and storing power for later use. Any vamp who had

control over time and could steal the magical ability from other supernats, and who had access to stored witch power, on top of the power of magical icons, would be unstoppable.

Access to the White House. The Kremlin. Fort Knox. Whoever had all that power could do anything, anytime, anywhere. And no one could stop them.

"What do you want to do, Jane?" Eli asked.

I didn't *know* what to do. This was more than "pull a stake and charge in fighting." This was military tactics and strategies—hard to think through when you don't know what the enemy wants. The enemy was still here, so he wanted something stored here. Sub-four. That was where it attacked Wrassler. My head felt like it was stuffed with wool. We had no coms, no security, no electricity. My breath sped up and the palms of my hands started to tingle with hyperventilation.

I said, "Peregrinus has all our security info, building plans, Reach's thoughts and guesses about what's on every level." I banged my head on the wall once, the sound soft and hollow. "He's had a week to play with it all. A week when the elevator's been doing strange things and the electricity's been wonky. Peregrinus probably even has the stuff I changed after I heard about Reach."

"The brownouts and the electrical troubles," Eli said. "Peregrinus caused them, searching for something?"

"I don't think so. I honestly think that's just the old electrical system showing its age. But the elevator, maybe. Peregrinus wants something stored on sub-four, which he can't get to without help, unless he can override the system with Reach's IT data. I think he's been testing to see if he can get in remotely. And he can.

"There's a safe on sub-four, probably filled with magical items. I should have gone snooping, no matter what Leo said." Sweat trickled down my torso. Beast pressed a paw onto my mind, the same way that she might calm or reprimand a kit, her claws pricking. The discomfort cleared my head and the moment of panic passed. I pulled the magical fishhook out and thought about our attacker. "It makes sense that Peregrinus caused everything—the troubles started after he got Reach—but I can't prove it." I looked down at the wolf, who was watching me with the kind of patience canines show for the human in charge. I patted his head and rubbed his ears while talking to Eli. "I want you to take Wrassler and retreat. Get us some coms. Get us help. We need fighters. Shooters. We need Sabina and her weapons."

"No, skinwalker, Enforcer, *pest*." The words were whispered with the hissing *ssss* of a snake, and an electric shock zinged through me. I shifted the Judge, cradling the huge weapon in two hands again, scanning back and forth, trying to find the source—because it hadn't come from one of us. "You need only me," the voice said. "And that *obscene* charm you hold upon your person. Together we can ride the *arcenciel*."

From her words I guessed the speaker. The more-than-half-crazy priestess. "Bethany?"

She appeared at my side with a tiny *pop* of air, moving vamp-fast. Her black skin blended into the dim light, her skirts swirling, stinking of her own blood, the cut on her neck from my house mostly healed. Her eyes glistened with an internal light that was way worse than spine-chilling. It looked like a tiny candle flame was lit inside her skull. There was blood around her mouth and I smelled both vamps and humans on her breath. Bethany had been drinking people down to heal herself. I stepped between Bethany and the guys.

"Leo is in great danger," she said, her mouth too close to my ear. "The gift is in great danger. Grégoire is in danger. Katie is near unto true-dead. There is no one else to save them but you and me."

She pointed to the charm I had hooked into my T-shirt. "With your charm you can immobilize Batildis. *I* can fight the Devil with my magic until you are free to do so. Then *I* can charm the dragon. That will allow the human fighters who await you to save the Master of the City. And together we can protect the reward I bestowed upon my Leo."

"Yeah? Peregrinus is gonna give us the *arcenciel*?"

"No. She is solid. I will ride her. She will be mine."

No way am I letting you be in charge of time, I thought. But, under the circumstances, that was a battle to fight another time. I pulled out the small charmed fishhook and stared at it. Then at Eli. "Get Wrassler to safety. Get us some help. I'm going with the crazy vamp lady, and hope she really knows that some of our humans are down there, near enough to help."

Beast, I thought. *I need more of us to . . . I don't know. Just more of us.*

Instantly the bones of my arms and legs twisted and broke. I landed on my knees in the Gray Between, my back bowing so tight that my forehead met my knees with a bang. I saw stars, glittering white motes on a black background. Then my body snapped into an arch that threw back my head. I body-slammed the floor. All breath was squeezed out of my chest.

My eyes were open, however, and I could see Eli, watching, possibly with a look of concern on his face. Yeah. His mouth was turned down on one corner. Maybe. Just a little. If I'd had air in my lungs, I might have laughed.

CHAPTER 20

Dance with the Devil

Instead of laughing, remembering what Beast had said about the Gray Between, I reached out and tried to slow down time. I had no idea what I was doing, and it felt like I was mentally swatting flies, like seeing something flying past, and trying to bring it down or slow it down with my mind only. I tried to envision my hands grabbing it. Nothing changed. Then I tried to envision a net I might toss over it. Again, nothing. In reality, outside the swirling gray energies, Eli bent over me, worry clear on his face this time. Distantly, I heard him say my name. He tried to reach into the gray place and he jumped back as if I'd Tased him. The look on his face made me chuff with laughter.

Beast pushed at the sparkling energies around us and they parted, leaving me/us lying on the cold floor of the weapons room at vamp central. The night air blowing in through the broken front entry was warm and humid, smelling of the river nearby mixed with blood and death.

I pushed to my hands and knees and caught one horrible, painful breath. It sounded like I was breathing glue, thick and sick-sounding. And I was afraid, for a too-long moment, that I was going to both throw up and lose my bowels at the same time, which would have been horribly humiliating. But then they settled and I was able to breathe.

I chuffed and looked at myself. My hands had the long-fingered, big-knuckled, bony look of my half-Beast form; my knees were stretching the denim of my jeans; my hips were narrow, jeans hanging low; my shoulders were broad and stretching the tee. My lower face was all bone and teeth. I clacked my jaws together, feeling the strength in my bite.

I looked at Eli, who had his emotionless fighting face back on. I chuffed. Power ran through me like a live wire, the sensation heady and potent. "Take 'Rrrrasssler. Go." To Wrassler, I said, "Live. Or I beat your butt." It came out "heat your hut," but he seemed to understand because the ghost of a smile crossed his face.

"You can try, Li'l Janie." He used his good hand to pull at a pocket. "More rounds for the Judge. Put a hurtin' on 'em for me."

I chuffed in agreement, bent, and took the rounds from his pocket, five more, and tucked them into my own pocket. Hoisted Wrassler up and over Eli's shoulder. How the big man managed not to scream was beyond me. I picked up the Judge. And covered the two as Eli trotted from HQ and into the night, the wolf at his side.

Clacking my oversized teeth together, I said to Bethany, "Go. I follow."

Bethany moved like the wind in the night, swirling around corners, gusting down steps, the air popping as she moved. Vamp speed. I kept up with her. Somehow. And suddenly we were in unknown and unexplored parts of the interior of the old building—unknown and unexplored by me, though Bethany had no problem making her way through them. Narrow, dank, damp corridors raced by, walls constructed of old brick on one side, newer concrete block on the other, the rare, rotting stud and bracing beam between the walls, clay and pooled water beneath our feet. Black mold on the walls. Bethany, like me, ran barefoot, splashing through puddles. There was only the sound of my breathing, the splash of water, our feet drumming on clay. Dark, darker than the underside of midnight. Even Beast's eyes failed me, and I followed by sound and feel.

We raced down a flight of old concrete stairs, slippery with mildew and water. Made a left through a brick passageway. I stumbled over something in the dark and felt dry, rotting wood beneath my paws and my thick fingertips when I righted myself.

Ahead I saw a faint light, an outline of a doorway. I stopped when Bethany did, in front of the door. I was breathing hard, my heart pounding. She wasn't even breathing. No heartbeat. So weird. I chuffed at the differences between us.

"We are on the records floor. There is a way down into the

darkness," she said. "Down into the prison, the dungeon, the place where, long ago, Amaury kept his scions safe and his enemies chained. Where Leo imprisoned my gift to him." She was talking about Amaury Pellissier, Leo's uncle and the previous MOC. And she was talking about the dark scion lair, not sub-four, where I thought we were going, but sub-five. Her lips stretched into a smile, which looked so wrong with her eyes vamping out, shining with madness.

"We must move as silent and fast as moonlight. And must leave Grégoire where he lies. No pity for the fallen. No surcease for their pain. Do you understand?"

"We sssurprizzz," I said through the teeth and fangs that mangled my jaw.

"Yes. First we must stop Batildis. Then you will engage the Devil. She will not tire. She will not be slowed. I will ride the *arcenciel*."

My mouth wouldn't say what I needed it to. It came out, "D'rrreeenhious?"

"Peregrinus will be otherwise engaged."

Which meant nothing to me, except that we were two against the Devil, two vamps, a dragon who could skate through time, and no help from the hostages. No help from anywhere.

Just me and a dance with the Devil. We were supposed to have help.

"Where humanzzz?"

"They are close, but slow and broken. We may not tarry."

It felt like part of a lie, that last part where help was nearby but not in time. But really, what choice did I have?

I looked at the door, ancient wood with dozens of raised panels and carved swirls and dimples. It had a vaguely Persian style, metal button-like things, like nipples on each raised panel. Iron strap hinges. Three iron bars holding it all together. And no doorknob.

Bethany was already vamped out. With the talons of her right fingers, she stabbed into the wood and ripped a section of door out. Again and again, until she had torn a hole near one of the hinges in the door, a hole large enough for a small child to crawl through. Then she rammed it. I could feel the force of her strike, vibrations passing through the wood beneath my paws. Which meant that anyone close enough, anyone with ears, would hear it and feel it too. The door broke, a long crack through the splintered hole. Two rams later, it fell with a massive crash. Katie leaped through. A spot of brightness leaped to the broken door.

I pivoted on my oversized paw to see Brute, a pale shadow in the black of the subbasement. He snuffled at me over his shoulder and raced after Katie. It was stupid, but seeing the werewolf thrust relief through me like a spear of happiness. And now we were three.

From somewhere far off I heard words, chanting, sounding like some foreign language. Perfect scary-movie sounds, the kinds with Satanists, big twirly mustaches, and stupid teenaged blondes in tiny bikinis going downstairs into the basement. Soulless big-bad-uglies. Human sacrifice couldn't be far behind. Too bad I didn't have a bikini. I leaped through the door after the wolf and the mad vampire priestess. Mad. We were all mad.

Laughter started in the back of my throat. We raced past the records room I had seen from the elevator, a room I recognized by the smell in the dark—old paintings, papyrus, vellum, heavy cloth paper. Inks. Wood. Bethany was right. The bad guys hadn't spent any time on sub-four. We tore down stairs I couldn't see. I saved myself a nasty fall hearing the echoes of bare feet slapping and the click of Brute's claws leaping down several feet. Holding the Judge in my right hand, the wall against my left palm, I followed, falling behind. Ahead, my enhanced nose caught the stench that had nearly buckled my knees the first time I smelled it, a combination of decaying blood, rotten herbs, vinegar, sour urine, and sick sweat. We were near the boo room.

Bethany rounded a corner. There was a huge crash. Another. Light stabbed into the dark. Light and dust and the sound of voices chanting and sobbing and the stench of blood. And silver. I rounded the corner only half a second behind Bethany. Air popped around me. The wolf was racing through the door, his body a gray-and-white smear on my retinas, fast as a vamp. Faster than me.

I had seen this sight before, the wolf racing-leaping into battle. Stupid dog. Yeah. I had thought that before. *Stupid dog*. And stupid me to race in after him. But I did. Screams sounded as I leaped through the opening. Screams and laughter. And the pong of something rotten and burning. The stink of ozone.

The light of dozens of candles stabbed my eyes. I squinted to protect them, seeing the room in front of me through Beast-lashes. Time slowed, stuttered, stopped. I was in midair, mid-leap, hanging as if gravity no longer existed. From this vantage, I took in the room as if I had all the time in the world. And maybe I did.

Chained to the wall to my right was a skeleton, a blackened thing, like twigs held together with twine. It had skin like rotten cowhide, hair in tufts, limbs splayed out like a bug. It was wrapped in heavy, tarnished, silver chains. Pocket watches dangled from smaller chains interwoven through the larger ones. Which seemed important, but something for later. The creature was fastened to the wall with spikes. It had been crucified. Silver spikes at its widespread wrists, a spike through its crossed feet. It was naked.

It was alive.

Its mouth was open with laughter, or a scream. It was bleeding from a hole in its right side, nearly black blood, thick as tar. Its eyes glittered with horror and insanity.

Beneath the thing on the wall lay Grégoire. I was pretty sure he was dead or would be in seconds. Across the way, entering from another door, was a bloody apparition, teeth bared, body in midleap. Derek. Forms were behind him. I counted three. The cavalry was here. Between us, as if in a pincer move, lay the rest of the players. Everyone, including me, was halted in midaction.

Three yards or so from the feet of the chained being lay Leo and Katie, naked and bound, bodies posed toward the ceiling but their faces turned to the thing crucified on the wall. All of the downed vamps were bleeding at necks and wrists, and their torsos had been split from neck to groin—wide, gaping wounds, slick with congealed blood. Skin pale in the candlelight, bodies unmoving, unbreathing. Undead, close to true-dead. So close. From my vantage point near the rough ceiling beams, I could see their eyes were open but glazed, their veins flat and dark like blue tracks drawn on parchment-thin, too-white skin. Weak, watery blood had dried on their white, white flesh.

Above them stood the vampire known as Peregrinus. He was dark haired, dark eyed, with a bloody mouth and three-inch-long fangs, hugely big around, some of the largest-in-diameter fangs I had ever seen. Power emanated from him like from a live wire, a glowing, humming power that lit him up from within, like a lantern in a window on a moonless night. His very skin glowed. Peregrines were tattooed on his wrists, wings out and up, legs and claws spread and reaching, beaks wide and screaming.

Peregrinus was wearing a plain loincloth, the front and back draping, much like the men of the plains tribes of North America wore theirs, but without decorative porcupine quilling or beads. And I knew the moment I saw it that it wasn't animal hide, not deer hide. It was made of skin, though. He was wearing human skin. Or vamp skin. Yeah. Vamp skin. He had tanned the skin of an enemy and was wearing it around his privates. Something told me the skin had once belonged to a female vamp who had insulted him in some way, but maybe I was projecting. Behind him lay a pile of bodies. The human soldiers he had brought with him. Looking dead.

In front of me, fixed in the moment of attack, was the white wolf, Brute, jaws wide, all three hundred plus pounds of werewolf in midleap, going for the human woman who was fighting Bethany. The Devil was dressed in black, so dark and matte that no light reflected anywhere except from her spinning blades. Though time seemed frozen, I could make out motion on the part of the human's weapons, this time the long and short swords of the *Duel Sang*. They were moving faster than I was, the swords coming together in one of the scissor motions Grégoire had tried to teach me. The movement was a stepping-forward, crosscutting, kill-move that was intended to behead or cut an opponent in half. Neck or waist, either body site was a way to die.

The swords and the fighting method had one purpose, according to Grégoire. They were made for killing Mithrans. And Bethany was about to be beheaded. Faster than I could shove either of the opponents out of the way. Faster than the wolf could stop it. At least in regular time.

Batildis stood to the side. Close to the action. Watching. Expressionless. Her fists on her hips, arms akimbo. She wasn't dressed for fighting. She was dressed for something else entirely in a long dress with full skirts, pale petticoats beneath and showing at the hem, full sleeves on a peasant blouse that left her breasts partially visible in the candlelight. Just three of them against the entire vamp HQ. Their magic and the *arcenciel*'s were that strong.

The Devil's swords moved again. This time nearly six inches. Then another half foot. Time was speeding up. I wondered if—

There wasn't time to figure it out or to determine the

chances of it working. And I had no way to calculate the physics of the possibility, even if I had taken higher maths in school. *Beast, on three,* I thought.

Beast can count to three, she chuffed.

One. Two. Three.

Still in midair, I pushed through time, reached up, and removed the fishhook-shaped amulet. Hooked Batildis with the small charm, passing it through the flesh of her neck above her gorget. Time sped up for a moment, with a crash of sound, movement, and a blur of candlelight. Still in midair, I whirled and kicked the vamp. Hard. Paralyzed by the charm in the fishhook, Batildis fell toward the Devil's blades. And all hell broke loose on earth.

Batildis fell into two pieces with a fountain of blood that shot toward the unfinished beams overhead. Horror crossed the Devil's face. The swordswoman hesitated for a fraction of a second. Just long enough for Bethany to fall on her, fangs buried in her throat. The blood-servant and fighter of legend fell back, dropping her arms, her swords pointing to the clay floor. Her mouth opened to scream. Brute leaped over them, raced to the thing on the wall, and bit its foot.

Derek, coming through the doorway, raised a weapon and shot Peregrinus. Like a hundred times. With an automatic gun that crushed the silence, that echoed against the walls. Rounds missed and ricocheted. I landed, my back paws firm and stable on the clay floor. But Derek hadn't seen me enter, leaping through a bubble of space and time given to Beast by an angel.

I took a round midcenter, just right of my navel. Another penetrated my left shoulder. Beast screamed. I fell at Derek's feet and he leaped over me, still attacking Peregrinus, firing the weapon that shattered the stillness of the room and boomed against my eardrums. Bethany rose from the Devil, the priestess' face and clothes covered with blood. The Devil stared sightlessly at the beams overhead, her swords out to the sides, her legs bent and limp, like a fallen angel of death on the clay of the earth. She no longer had a throat, just the bones of a spine. She was no longer a threat.

Bethany stood beside me, her arms out to the sides, screaming. Or, I was pretty sure she was screaming. Her head was back, her mouth was open, and her eyes glittered with fury. But the gun ripped into the air, stealing the sound, and then there was a flash of light, the scintillation of smoky wings, a flash of blacked snake tail. Peregrinus pulled reality around him in a wash of flashing energies. He was gone, the bodies of the Devil and Batildis with him, shadows on the move. Derek raced after, his men chasing behind.

I lay on the floor, cradling the Judge, the weapon that I hadn't even fired yet, as Derek's men raced after their boss. I was feeling too weak for the wounds—unless a round had hit something important, had bisected or ruptured something. Like the descending aorta or the big artery that feeds the liver. Funny. I couldn't remember the name of the artery. The cramps that resulted from playing with time hit me and I curled tight in the fetal position, gasping.

Beast? I said.

She didn't answer, which could mean something good or could mean something bad. I was facing the front of the room, and I saw Bethany stop screaming. She ripped the silver chain from Leo's wrists and ankles and picked him up, placing him below the thing on the wall, holding the MOC's head like a baby's or a lover's. As she raised back up, she paused and tore the thing's leg open. With her teeth. A trickle of black blood fell from the fresh wound into Leo's mouth. He shook as if an electric pulse had hit him. He vamped out and swallowed.

Bethany wiped her thumb through the black trickle and placed it into Grégoire's mouth. He didn't respond and she slapped him hard, rocking his head, before adding another trickle. And another. He took a breath, a wet, grinding sound like rubber over sand. She repeated the action with Katie. All three vamps were stirring. Bethany then ripped her own wrist and offered it to Leo, who latched on and drank. Grégoire, looking like an ill, bloodless child, took her other wrist. Katie crawled up Bethany and bit into her throat. Three mostly naked and blood-smeared vamps, all with their torsos cut open and gaping, feeding on the priestess. *Ick.* If I'd had breath, I might have said so, or laughed. Instead, the candlelight fluttered and telescoped down into a pinhole of vision, centered on the thing on the wall. It was staring at me. And I had a bad feeling that it knew what I was and that it wanted me. For dinner.

My last sight was of gray and black motes rising to obscure my vision. *Took you long enough,* I thought to Beast.

Beast was busy, she thought back.

And then I remembered the *arcenciel*. It had been here.

Bethany hadn't taken her or ridden her or whatever. But the pocket watches that were hanging on the crucified thing . . . Yeah, pocket watches. I'd last seen them in use in Natchez. And all the ones I'd managed to get hold of were in my safe-deposit boxes.

Now some were hung on the wall in the dungeon of the Master of the City of New Orleans and most of the Southeast. I had to wonder, as the last of the light shriveled down to a bright pinprick, where Leo had gotten his pocket watches. From Natchez? Or from my bank? Which would imply that the MOC had way more power in the human and financial world than I had known. I needed time to check all that out. Because if Leo had gotten into my boxes . . . that would totally suck.

The last of the light disappeared.

CHAPTER 21

A Bucket Full of Snakes

I came to in a room I didn't recognize. A chandelier hung over me, one of the expensive ones, lead crystal and real gold gilt, polished and so brilliant that the light reflecting back from each facet hurt my eyes. The ceiling overhead was painted like the Sistine Chapel, or another fancy cathedral in Italy, with angels and humans sitting on clouds, faces etched with ecstasy. Vampires with wings flew among the happy group, fangs out. Weird. Vamps were weird. Their art was weirder.

I took a breath. It hurt so bad that I groaned, then coughed, which hurt even worse. I wrapped my arms around my middle, feeling cold blood on my flesh. Oh yeah. Right. I probably died. Again. This was getting old. Cats had nine lives, but I had already pushed that score into unknown territory and I had to wonder how many times I could die until the one time I didn't get shifted in time.

Time.

I blinked, remembering. Beast had done something with time. Not just speeding me up, but taking me *outside* of time. A time bubble that let me do stuff inside it while the world didn't go on without me. Folded time. My guts twisted into a knot and then yanked tight. I pressed into my middle, kneading, but the charley horse only seemed to get bigger.

I tried to stretch out and thought my insides would rip in two. *Beast?*

Jane must lie still. And wait.

Wait? I can't breathe. I'm dying here.

Breast chuffed at me. *Jane is not dying. Jane has air. Jane should think of* time.

In the deeps of my soul home, Beast looked away, bored. She was lying in front of the fire pit, flames casting light and leaping shadows across her.

Time. Great. I fought to relax, to not panic, and closed my eyes.

I had actually seen a time bubble once, or maybe a time loop. I had been working with Molly way back when, and we had found a time loop in an old house that had been diagnosed as having a poltergeist. Wrong. It had a vampire stuck in a time loop, in a time bubble, with a witch. I had always been aware that time slowed down in battle. Soldiers had reported that phenomenon from time immemorial. But this was different. More distinct. More intense. Longer lasting. Now Beast and I had more control over the experience. Now Beast could do something like slow down time, fold time, at will. Or place us in a bubble at will. Freaky stuff.

Unfortunately, it looked like I would be the one to pay the price for the time shifts, not Beast.

I managed to get an elbow out and rolled over slightly, so I could see. I was on a bed, in a room with some light. Fighting panic, I pulled a pillow to my middle and shoved it hard against me. I was able to inhale. A long moment later I exhaled, slowly, slowly. My guts roiled like a bucket full of snakes. I pushed down on the nausea, hard. It would be really bad if I threw up right now. I took another breath and this time, I smelled Del everywhere, in the coverlet, on the pillows, permeating the air. This was her bedroom.

I coughed again. Stuff came up. Too tired to lift my head, I spat it onto the covers beside me. Old blood, black and phlegmy. Totally gross. Old blood meant that I hadn't shifted totally. If I'd shifted, any blood in my system would have been absorbed by the shift and rearranged inside me. In a total shift, nothing got wasted. But in a partial shift, I was starting to realize, things could be way different. Things like my level of pain, and the degree of my body's change, and the functions of my brain.

"How are you?"

I tilted my head to see Adelaide staring at me, but her head was at an angle that made my stomach roil. I closed my eyes. From behind the darkness of my lids I said, "I'm sick as a dog. How are you?"

"Alive. Thanks to your help. And thanks to the priestess."

"And Derek. Last time I saw him he was chasing Peregrinus."

"Peregrinus got away," she said shortly.

I swallowed and the nausea faded just a hint. I could hear Del moving around the room. Cleaning up my mess. "The others?" I managed to ask.

"Leo and his heir are well. Grégoire is recuperating. Derek is injured, but will survive, as will most of his men. Your wolf raced away, last seen leaping through the front entry. And . . . and Wrassler. He said to give you his thanks." I felt the mattress beneath me shift, which made sickness rise again. I swallowed it back down, desperate not to be sick, desperate to hear Del's report. I pressed the pillow harder into me. "Leo has promised him the best of prosthetics for his leg. His arm may heal."

I opened my eyes to see Del sitting on the edge of the bed. "How many dead and injured?" I asked.

Del sighed. "Of Peregrinus' fighters, ten dead and left to rot. Of ours, seven dead, two of them Derek's men. Nine injured, one critically. Four humans missing."

"Missing?" I focused on her face. Missing didn't sound right. Why would anyone be missing?

I realized I had spoken the question aloud when she said, "We don't know. But it has something to do with Bethany. After she got all the Mithrans fed, she disappeared. And she took some of our people with her."

I thought about that while I gathered my strength and pushed up with my arms, swiveling to sit upright, my knees held close, pressing the pillow into me as hard as I could. Del placed pillows behind me and I rested back on them. I was in a bedroom, a lacy, silken chamber done in shades of gold and cream and touches of sapphire. A nine-millimeter handgun— not one of mine—lay on the bedside table. The room looked like Del, all soft and reserved but with hidden surprises that could hurt you. "Sorry about the spread," I said, my breath coming easier. "What time is it?"

She shrugged and crossed her arms over her middle. "It's washable. And it's nearly three in the morning."

I could hear the vibration of generators. "I'll have to deal with the power situation."

Del nodded. I realized that we both were trying to avoid

dealing with the reality. So I took a slow, deep breath and asked, "I'm guessing that everyone knows about the thing on the wall of Leo's dungeon." Del looked away. "What was it? *Who* was it?"

She cursed softly, smelling of worry and fear. While she debated on telling me the truth or an artful lie, I managed to get my knees to uncurl an inch, and touched my belly. It was still hard, and now ached. I should never do that again. *Never.* And certainly never in the middle of a battle.

The gesture elegant and lissome, Del dropped her arms and lifted her head, her shoulders relaxing, as if freeing herself from a prison. "They called him Yo-sace, Bar-Ioudas. Joses, son of Judas, in English. He is a Son of Darkness. A child of Ioudas Issachar." She stood and walked to the door, looking elegant and delicate and all the things I would never be, blond and beautiful and graceful. She stopped at the door and looked back at me. "This changes so many things. The presence of Joses Bar-Judas, as a prisoner here, makes it quite likely that, rather than parley with them, we will go to war with the Europeans."

Shock made my chest ache again. *Leo.* Leo had known. The Son was Leo's prisoner. Leo had been . . . drinking from him. That was why the MOC was so strong. Why his primo could be saved—or brought back to life—and turned into an Onorio— because Leo had been made uberstrong by the blood of the Son. And why Grégoire's twin primos, Brandon and Brian, had been turned into Onorios.

Reach had known or guessed Leo's secrets and had given them up to Peregrinus. And this one secret had gotten humans killed.

Leo had done this. Gotten an old lady across the street from me killed. Gotten three construction workers killed. *A cop killed.* So many dead because of this secret. "Did you know he was down there?"

"No," she said, her voice expressionless. "As far as I know, no one knew but Leo, his pet priestess, and his Mithran lovers." She left the room and closed the door behind her.

The pet priestess and Leo's Mithran lovers: Bethany, Katie, and Grégoire. "Well," I said to the empty room. "That sucks. Too bad Leo didn't stay dead one of the times I killed him recently." Now I might have to kill him true-dead myself, and not stop at a simple staking.

This was Leo's fault. *All* of it was *Leo's* fault. Leo's and Reach's.

I stretched out my other leg and curled the pillow back around my middle as I thought about the thing on the wall in the basement, trying to remember what I had seen in the timeless moments while I was in the bubble, hanging in midair, and afterward when I was busy getting killed by Derek.

The thing had been male. Crucified to an old brick wall with silver stakes. The wall had been slashed repeatedly by his talons, which were more like the Wolverine's blades than most vamp claws. The damaged wall had shown some kind of metal, tarnished in the candlelight—metal studs, maybe. Black-magic items—pocket watches—had been hanging on the Son's body. Scraps of clothes. Body was mostly dried flesh, looking mummified. Eyes glittering and focused on me.

The black-magic watches contained pieces of the iron spike of Calvary, of Golgotha. The crosses of Golgotha had been used to make the thing that hung on the wall, in a black-magic ceremony.

Now Leo wanted the spike. So did the EuroVamps, who were really the earliest vamps created by the Sons of Darkness. Sooo . . . what did the iron from the spike do to the Sons? To the Son in the dungeon?

There were a lot of negatives and dangers to being turned by a vamp. Sunlight could burn them. Lack of blood could starve them. The devoveo—the years of insanity humans went through after being turned—had to be lived through, and if they didn't come out of the devoveo sane, then they were put down like rabid dogs. Then there was the delore—the insane grief they went through when one of their loved ones died. The lack of stability that only emotionally stable blood-servants brought to a vamp. Blood-thirst. Lots more.

Though the Mithrans hadn't yet found a cure for the long-chained—the scions stuck in the devoveo—the Sons of Darkness had parleyed with the Anzû to keep their progeny sane from the delore, by feeding them sips of Anzû blood. It had worked. What did Gee DiMercy—the only Anzû in Leo's territory—know about the dungeon's only prisoner? He clearly hadn't known about the *arcenciels* being around.

Not so long ago, Leo had said that the Sons of Darkness had ordered the Mithrans of the Americas to make peace with the Cursed of Artemis—the werewolves and other were-creatures. That order would have been impossible to give with a Son of Darkness chained in the basement. So where did the order to parley with the were-community come from? Leo? The other Son? The European Council like the news media said? I hated vamp politics.

Even a future parley with the witches was now suspect. Was the order to reach rapprochement with the New Orleans witch coven because Leo needed the blackened prisoner and some witch magic to accomplish . . . what? *Crap.* I had no idea.

Anger raced under my skin, burning, hot, like acid eating away at me. So many dead. Hurt. *Damn* vampire secrets. *Damn Leo Pellissier.* But I could kill him later. For now, I had a deadly puzzle to figure out.

In the basement, we had a kidnapped Son of Darkness. Leo was playing political games with the lives of humans and of his people. Black-magic pocket watches containing parts of a magical item that Leo was looking for were resting on the Son's body. And a werewolf who had been touched by an angel, had bitten the thing chained to the wall, and was running through the city with a mouthful of the Son of Darkness' blood in him. I had to wonder what the bite would mean to the werewolf.

Oh—and the Devil was dead, along with Batildis, which could only tick off Peregrinus. Though he had taken their bodies with him. Could he bring them back to life, a human with no throat and a vamp cut in two?

And the *arcenciel* hatchling was still in Peregrinus' possession. Soul was going to be really ticked off with me. After Bethany had said the *arcenciel* would be solid, I had expected to see the baby dragon, maybe held prisoner by Peregrinus via some arcane means. Or maybe with jesses and a hood, the way people trained raptors to hunt. I wasn't sure what I had seen in the basement, about the *arcenciel*. It was all confused.

I also wasn't sure what I was going to tell Soul, and she didn't seem the patient, understanding type, not when she was in light-dragon form.

The weirdness was in overlays and none of it was going to be good. Nothing was ever good in the land of the bloodsuckers. It was always FUBAR from beginning to end.

I laid my head back and studied the painting on the ceiling of Del's bedroom. All that was missing was satyrs and images of torture to make it *perfectly* weird. I let my eyes trace the feathered wings of an angel as I tried to remember what else I knew about the Sons of Darkness. Something the other priestess, Sabina, had said months ago. Sabina was way more sane than Bethany, but she had lost her humanity centuries ago too. She had told me that the eldest Son of Darkness had visited, a century ago, and had failed to rise one night. Yeah. That was it. Leo and Sabina entered his lair together, and the place had stank of violence and blood—of the Son's *holy* life blood, or so she had said, and the blood of someone or something else. That blood had been splattered on the walls. Had that blood been Bethany's? Had she brought Joses to Amaury Pellissier, the previous MOC? Or to Leo? The century timeline could work either way, but there had to be way more to the story, in order for the missing Son of Darkness to end up a prisoner in Leo's basement.

Sabina and Leo had hidden the evidence. Reach had guessed or figured it out. Now everyone knew that Joses was here. Del was right. It would mean war with the EuroVamps, unless I could figure out a way to stop it.

Overhead, the lights flickered and the room went black. Which was the first time I noticed that I was in an internal room, one with no windows, one a vamp could stay in twenty-four/seven. And Leo and Del and been getting frisky, if my memory served. I sniffed the pillow again to be sure, but I didn't smell Leo. They hadn't spent frisky time here, which relieved me in ways I hadn't expected. The lights came back on and the distant sound of generators went off. Power had been restored.

I rotated to my feet and groaned my way out of the room. I found the stairs and limped down to the locker room to clean up and change clothes, coming to a few conclusions. We needed several things: a full debrief, to find Brute, and to figure out where the *arcenciel* was in all the hullabaloo—still with Peregrinus, or escaped? We needed to know where Bethany had gone with the missing people. It was gonna be a long night.

I was on the stairs when I realized that Bruiser hadn't shown up. I pulled my cell. Communications were up and I had three text messages. Eli's said, *Heading back to vamp HQ. W alive in hospital. Edmund feeding healing him.* Alex's said, *Gimme call. Got info.* Bruiser's said, *On the way. Be safe.*

That text was more than an hour old, but so far as I knew, he hadn't shown. I texted him back. *Call me.* And then texted the Kid to track his cell. Bruiser's text was the one that mattered most.

I was in the shower when I felt cool air whoosh into the room. I shut off the water with one hand and simultaneously picked up the nine-mil. There was one in the chamber, ready to fire. The Judge was on the tiled ledge beside me, next to the shampoo.

"It's me, Legs. We need to chat." It was Derek. Who had disappeared, chasing after Peregrinus. Or helping him escape? I had to wonder whether he was in his right mind or whether he'd been rolled by a vamp who had managed to seize Grégoire, Leo, Katie, and all of vamp HQ in one night.

"Yeah?" I asked, not willing to throw back the shower curtain to see him. Knowing that if he wanted me dead, he could have already fired. I had no place to run anyway. But mostly not wanting to be naked in front of Derek. I took the weapon in a two-hand grip and spread my feet, balanced and ready. "Tell me something only we know. So that I'll know it's you talking through your mouth and not some foreign vamp who's made you his."

"You wore a party dress the first time I saw you take down a fanghead. You told me you had a magic charm to track down suckheads, but we both know you was lying."

I chuckled.

"Also," Eli said, "he's got me, with a gun about three inches from his spine."

Not again, I thought, but feeling relieved. "You boys have got to learn to play together."

"Too close, Ranger boy. I'd take you—"

"And you'd sit in a chair the rest of your life. So go ahead. Make my—"

"Go away!" I yelled. I turned the water back on and set the gun aside. They could play Ranger versus SEAL on their own time. I still had things to think through. And one of those was, why was I always the only female in the ladies' room? Was I so terrifying and creepy that all the other female security personnel who used this locker room made themselves scarce when I was here? It was kinda weird.

Once I was dressed, I read my new texts and sent several, one to tell the Kid I was headed into the security conference room.

He'd know what to do. The guys were waiting outside the locker room door when I emerged, holding up opposite walls. Eli had an abrasion on his cheek that hadn't been there the last time I saw him, and Derek was nursing a bloody lip. "Idiots." I shook my head and asked Eli to run an errand for me, fast. He nodded and took off. I asked, "Your men?"

Derek's face turned down, the lines beside his mouth making him look far older. "Red Dragon and Antifreeze are down for rehab. Trash Can and Acapulco are both dead."

He didn't want sympathy. I didn't know what he wanted, but sympathy wasn't it. I kept my eyes emotionless, but let my mouth turn down in acknowledgment of his loss. "I'd like to go to the services," I said. "Anything I can do for the families, please let me know."

He nodded once, a severe, clipped gesture, and I lifted a finger pointing to the conference room. Derek followed me down the hall into security, and I felt him behind me, more so than heard him. He moved as silently as a hunting big-cat.

If he had been rolled, then I could be a target, though I could tell by his body scent that he wasn't fighting anything; nor was he overly, abnormally calm. He smelled like himself after exercise, and he also smelled angry, but it was normal, human "It isn't fair" kind of angry, combined with a little "I need to hit something" angry. He stepped up beside me, our shoulders brushing. But his scent changed as we walked, a hint of adrenaline, an increase of testosterone. It smelled like a dominance thing, the scent telling me that the person he wanted to hit was me.

I could take him if he attacked. Most likely, I could. Probably. Maybe. Most days. Maybe not right now with my belly feeling like . . . "You shot me," I said, casually.

From the corner of my eye, I saw the satisfaction flit onto his face, as he said, "Yeah. Sorry about that." But he didn't sound sorry. His voice went harder, colder. "Leo instructed me not to call in the cops for our DBs. He says it's *too dangerous* for us to let any more *humans* in here."

I suddenly understood all the mixed signals he was giving off. I moved to the side of the hallway and stopped again, turning to him. I put a hand on his arm, feeling the rigid, corded muscles there. His black eyes glittered in his dark-skinned face, but he stared into the distance. "I'm sorry about your men," I said. "I'm *so* very sorry."

"Vodka Sunrise was injured, but had enough life to be turned. He'll be an insane suckhead for ten years, but he'll be alive, if you call that living." Sunrise had lost a tooth in Leo's service not so long ago. He was good people. All Derek's men were good people. I could smell Derek's conflict, his anger, his grief, and I tightened my fingers on his arm, letting a bit of Beast into my grip. It had to hurt, but he didn't meet my eyes. I understood that too. I wasn't human. I was one of the monsters. And I hadn't reacted with anger when one of the monsters had said no human law enforcement involvement. I was getting in deep. *Too deep? How deep did I have to get to be happy that Sunrise had been turned instead of dying?* "We'll honor their sacrifice. Your men and me. And right now, *I* honor their sacrifice."

I closed my mouth with a soft snap. I didn't have time for this, but I also didn't *not* have time for it. I shoved my conflict down deep inside and shook his arm until he looked at me. "In the ways of The People, the War Woman was responsible for restitution and revenge after battle. I am War Woman." His eyes widened slightly and his scent changed, though I couldn't tell what the pheromones meant, except more confusion. "I promise you the right to choose how our enemy will die. If you choose, then for each man true-dead, I will cause our enemy to scream until he can't scream anymore. I will let him heal. And I'll make him scream again for the next man. For the men turned, I'll bring them a cup of his still-warm blood to drink. If you choose this, the death of the one we hunt will not be clean or easy."

Derek's head went up, his mouth hard. "You're asking me to let you torture a man."

"No. I'm asking what you want done."

"Clean death," he spat. "I'm not a monster."

I smiled, and knew it was bitter. "No. You aren't. And for that I'm thankful."

He blinked several times, then said, "You don't want to . . . do what you said."

"I really, *really* don't. But for you, to honor your men, to remember your men, I would have." I let a small smile soften my face. "The last time I counted coup—to use a word *not* of The People—I was five years old and my grandmother put the knife into my hand." Derek's scent changed again, this time taking on a clearly identified horror in the chemical mixture.

"Humans, ordinary humans, can be far worse than the monsters. To torture a man when you're a child, when your mother and grandmother stand beside you and guide in the methodology and the mechanics, it changes you. It changed me, changed who I became; who I am now. But I'm willing to go back to that time if you need me to."

Derek took my hand from his arm, but instead of dropping it, he curled his fingers around my wrist and pulled my hand into a soldier's handclasp. I gripped his wrist back. "They were soldiers for the United States. We'll honor them with a soldier's burial."

We stood nearly eye to eye in the hallway, arms clasped. "Okay. Good. You want me there, I'll be there. If not, I'll understand. I'll contribute to the families' funds. And I'll get Amy Lynn to feed your man. With a little luck and her super-duper special vamp blood, he might be back in as little as two years, rather than the standard ten."

He released my arm and I let him. He said, "Savin' my mama is worth part of my soul. And bein' Leo's Enforcer sounded—"

He stopped, and I could guess what it had sounded like. Easy job, lotsa money. But it had been a devil's bargain. It always was, with fangheads.

Derek went on. "I don't understand how fangheads think. Why not call in the law for the dead humans?"

"Leo had a hard time getting the human LEOs to leave, the last time one of his people died in this building. Leo has control issues *and* danger on his turf." Derek didn't reply so I said, "Honestly, I don't really care what Leo does about the law." Oddly, it was true. Once upon a time I called in the law every time a human incident took place. But it never did any good. Leo was his own law. Always had been. Probably always would be. And I was the Enforcer who carried out his law. I had quit, but not really. I was still doing the job and wouldn't stop even when Peregrinus was dead. I still had a contract with Leo as his Enforcer for a cool half mil. And with the EuroVamps coming, this job might be the only way to keep my friends alive.

My forehead wrinkled as a thought occurred to me. "The last time someone died here, it was one of the new guys. Wayne something? He had what I thought was a hawk tattooed on his scalp. But maybe it was a peregrine?"

"I'll check back. Make sure." He pulled his cell and started thumbing around for photos of the crime scene.

"I know vamps work ahead, plan things for decades," I said thoughtfully, uncomfortable with the direction of my thoughts.

"Centuries."

"Yeah. For real. But it would be hard to put that incident together with the EuroVamps and Satan's Three, and Reach."

"No, it wouldn't. Not for a fanghead." He stopped thumbing on the screen. "Not a falcon. No. It *was* a hawk. And it was done in reds and browns, not the blue tattoos on the wrists of the fanghead and his human." He turned the cell to me and I studied the photo of the top of Hawk Head's scalp. The hawk tattoo looked nothing like the peregrine falcons sported by Peregrinus' followers, and his wrists were bare. "Hawk," Derek insisted.

"Okay. But . . . let's keep that in back of our minds, okay? I don't like coincidences."

"Jane?" Derek didn't often call me by my given name. It was Legs or Injun Princess. Not Jane. I looked my question at him. "You're a Christian. How could you do that? When you were five? How could you do it now?"

"I don't know." I laughed shortly. "I probably need therapy."

"Yeah. We all probably do."

The team was assembled in the security conference room, including a few new faces.

I remembered Wrassler telling me he was trying to get help. Carefully, I said to Derek, "Your people?"

"Grégoire's people from Atlanta," he said. "They've been in training in the swamps for the last six weeks," he reminded me. "Basic training. Leo fed on all of them. They're loyal and integrated into the communications channels. Training isn't up to my standards yet, but they'll do in a pinch."

I looked them over and shook my head. They were covered in mosquito bites, were sunburned, skinny, rangy, scruffy, and hard-eyed. They looked like they'd been rode hard and put up wet, as a horse-loving roommate in the children's home used to say, and they had the body odors that claimed they had been in-country without access to bathhouses for a *looong* time. But they also looked ready to go to war, with that hair-trigger awareness the battlefield soldier always wore. I nodded at them by way of welcome.

"They've been read in on the deets," Derek added. "We can talk freely."

Which hadn't even occurred to me. My mind had been too busy on other stuff to sweat things like humans without enough info to understand what was going on. "Too much went wrong tonight, guys," I said. "Angel, I need to see everything you have on camera. And you'll note that the stuff on the secondary control panel you installed has been integrated into this one, and a bill for the design has been submitted to Raisin. To Ernestine," I amended. One of the texts had been from the Kid telling me he had found and assimilated the secondary set.

Angel Tit's eyebrows bunched and he glanced at Derek. "Told you she'd figure it out. Told Leo and Del she'd figure it out. Told all'a y'all she'd figure it out." Derek grunted and Angel punched some spots on his integrated control screen. Security footage appeared on the overhead video screen. I watched the new men studying the videos as if their lives depended on it. And maybe they did.

The action lasted half an hour, with time not matching up anywhere as we followed from camera to camera, watching as men and women died, as Wrassler was mangled, as trained soldiers tried to ignore the changing of time and fought back. As the digital feed sputtered and went all blocky at times just as it had before from the presence of the *arcenciel*. But this time, the *arcenciel* was on-screen for only some of the occurrences of the pixelating blocks. "What's causing the interference?" I asked.

Angel swiveled in his chair and grinned at me. "This time it wasn't caused only by the light-dragon. This time the interference followed the vamp Peregrinus. I did manage to get some clear shots of him. These might explain it."

I stared at the still shots plucked from the video. The fang-head was moving at vamp speed, and on regular digital camera footage, he would have been a pixel-blur, but on the new cameras, he was fairly clear—dark hair, dark pants, white shirt, leather belt, and boots. Necklace. But the jewelry looked different from the painting in the records room, and also different from the spare, stripped-raw moments when I had seen the vamp in person. Now the necklace looked larger, darker. Different.

"On the clearest one." I pointed at the shot of my choice. "Can you zoom in and let me see the necklace?" I asked.

"This isn't TV or the movies, but yeah, I can get in a bit," Angel said. By his self-satisfied tone I knew he had already done it for himself.

The screen changed and the necklace moved front and center, bigger, but more blurred. On the chain hung the raptor in flight, the same focal he had worn for the painting centuries ago. But now it was joined by a larger, black focal, wired onto the necklace. The focal was vaguely spear-shaped, wider at the top, pointed and clear at the bottom like a jeweled crystal pulled from the earth. Something was inside it. The thing inside trailed down to a point, the same way water runs down glass, all squiggly. I didn't have to see it again. I knew what I was seeing. I knew why Soul had lost contact with the hatchling, and what the moments meant when he and the light-dragon had been in my presence. Peregrinus had captured the young *arenciel* and made it tiny. He was wearing the hatchling in a jeweled crystal, wired onto his necklace with steel wire. And *arenciels* were allergic to steel. I narrowed my eyes, letting that thought percolate until I realized that this could be what Bethany had been talking about, but hadn't understood how to accomplish the act. Peregrinus was *riding the dragon* . . .

"Depending on the learning curve, I'm guessing the necklace means Peregrinus now has access to some of the *arenciel's* power, and some of her weaknesses too, whatever they are," I said. And since I had caused the death of Peregrinus' pals, and then chased him away from killing (or eating or draining or whatever) the chained Joses Bar-Judas, I could guess that he would keep coming after me, as part of finishing whatever he originally came to accomplish. And yeah. He'd be angry.

I checked the current time on the video screen. It was an hour before dawn. I doubted that Peregrinus would be back tonight. To Derek, I said, "Get what you can from the vids. See about making this place secure. Get battery lighting on every hallway and stairwell. Get Leo, Grégoire, and Katie fed on ample human blood and somewhere safe." I felt the expression that curled my mouth down. "Get them fed on the *thing* in the basement. Its blood is strong. Peregrinus will be back, probably tonight, which gives us maybe twelve hours. I have to talk to some people. Oh. And please see that the security at the graveyard is turned off. No need to alert or disturb the local LEOs."

"Yeah," Derek said, with false complacency. "No need for the local cops to get off their fat butts just to arrest you."

"They can try." That got some laughter, which felt like a good note to leave on. I swung out of the room, to find Eli waiting in the hallway, his earbuds in. He'd been listening to the meeting.

"I made the call to Del. Where are we going?" he asked, managing to sound only mildly curious, as if the information wasn't vital, like how I took my tea, instead of how I was gonna keep us alive. I barked out a laugh and headed for the stairwell and up. "If I don't tell you, will it kill you?"

"No, but we'll waste time if I have to beat it out of you. And I might hurt my knuckles," he added thoughtfully, our feet echoing on the stairs. I shook my head, smelling blood and bowel contents, the stench of fired weapons, and the stronger reek of cleansers in the contained stairwell air. Someone had died here recently. Odds were it was one of Derek's men.

We left the stairwell and reentered the foyer. I hadn't seen it since the lights came back on. There were uniformed men and women everywhere, mopping up blood. Men and women with hammers, plywood, and power tools working on making the entry secure. Not that the plywood was going to keep Peregrinus out. No chance.

I stepped into the empty weapons room and checked Wrassler's Judge back in. No amount of firepower was going to help me where I was going. I picked up a set of keys and gestured to the back of the building.

"We jogging to the next gig too? Or are we stealing one of Leo's armored SUVs to get wherever we're going?"

"Borrowing. Not stealing."

"Pa-tay-toh, pa-tah-toh."

"Have you seen Brute or Bruiser?" I asked.

"Nope. Kinda worried about both."

We pulled out of the back security gate, the vehicle smelling like cigarettes and weed. Fast-food wrappers were in the back floorboard, along with empty Red Bull cans and what might have been empty condom packages. I'd be talking to a driver or two: some guards needed to be taught to clean up after themselves; weed might slow reaction time; having sex on the job was stupid in a dozen ways; and smoke was a dead giveaway to any enemy vamp with half a nose. A visual which made me chuff with laughter.

As I pulled up to a light, I said, "We're heading to the vamp graveyard across the river."

"I got that part."

"Yeah, well, the fun part will be me telling Sabina about the

Son of Darkness chained in the basement, always assuming she doesn't already know. And telling her about Peregrinus. And telling her we killed the Devil and Batildis." Eli grunted ruminatively, so I finished with, "And then comes the not-fun part. Asking Sabina for the sliver of the Blood Cross, to kill Grégoire's brother."

"I read your report about the shard. It was taken from the wood of Calvary that the sons of Judas Iscariot used to bring their father back to life. And thereby accidently made the first vamp." I nodded at his words. "Talking to Sabina sounds like fun," he said, overly nonchalant.

"Yeah? Last time I did this, she nearly killed Rick and me. You know all the old wives' tales about vamps being able to do stuff with their minds, like telekinesis and teleportation?" Eli grunted, still sounding bored. "Sabina can slam you against a wall with her mind alone, and hold you there, steady, while she tears out someone else's throat and drinks them down at her leisure." This time, Eli's grunt was a little less sanguine. That was a good word, *sanguine*, its roots in the color red, like blood. And by the faint scent change in Eli's sweat, he wasn't sanguine anymore.

We pulled into the graveyard to find the hinged metal arms of the gate standing open in invitation. It was the darkest part of the night, the moon below the horizon, the sun not yet risen. The white stone mausoleums stood among the white shell paths, the statues on each roof looking like something out of Europe, white marble angels holding metal swords. There were no lights. Vamps didn't need lights to see by, and any human who wandered in after dark to vandalize or find a place to neck, to use Aggie's term, was likely to end up as dinner for the priestess and then wake up with no memory of the night before. The SUV's headlights picked out the individual aboveground graves, the tree line in the distance, and the chapel. I rolled to a stop about fifteen feet away and cut the engine.

The chapel was small, though larger than the multi-casket tombs with their gated and locked doors. The chapel's windows glowed softly with candlelight, bloodred, ruby red, wine, burgundy, the pink of watered blood. That candle flicker spoke to the old ones, a sign of all things good and safe. Inside, something moved past a window, a shadow only. "You need to stay here," I said.

"I'm backup." There was disagreement in his tone.

I shifted in my seat to Eli in the dark of the car, still brightened by the glowing dash lights. "She'll assume I brought her a human to munch on."

Eli grumped, giving in, by the scent. "Really like teleportation?"

"And really like mind-warping. You need to stay in the car."

"So why am I here?"

"To tell the others and prepare for Peregrinus to attack tonight if she kills me."

"You take all the fun out of a nice drive in the country."

"I do, don't I? I'll be back in a bit."

Eli stayed in the vehicle, watching as I took the steps to the front door, knocked, and entered.

CHAPTER 22

I Am a Far Worse Devil

The priestess was sitting in a rocking chair at the front of the chapel, wearing her nunlike white robes, her pale, once-olive-skinned face glowing in the light of the candles. She pushed with a toe, the chair rocking back and then forward, back and then forward, but no way did I think she was relaxed. If I said the wrong thing or did the wrong thing, she would be on me like white on rice and faster than the speed of light. To her side was a stone bier, like a sarcophagus, the lid too heavy for me to lift alone, even with Beast helping, though I could push it aside if the need arose. Inside were the treasures she guarded. No way did I think I knew everything she hid there. No way was I eager to go exploring. Again. I'd learned my lesson the first time.

I walked between the rows of wood pews, my feet loud in the quiet place, and paused about twelve feet away. I gave a nod of respect, the closest thing to a curtsy that I could do. In the silence, marred only by the sound of the rockers on the old floor, I waited.

Her black eyes glittered as she surveyed me, her hands clasped at her waist. Rocking. Rocking. And I waited.

"What do you want, skinwalker?"

I nearly jumped but managed to hold the startled reaction in. As if she saw it anyway, a faint smile crossed the priestess' face.

I licked my lips, wondering when my mouth had gone so dry. "Joses Bar-Judas is chained in the lowest subbasement in

the Mithran Council Chambers in the French Quarter. Tonight, a group of Mithrans kidnapped Katie and a wounded
Leo, captured a juvenile *arenciel* in a necklace that one wears
around his neck, busted into HQ, and tried to set the Son of
Darkness free, or kill him to get his power, or something. We
got in the way."

Sabina said nothing, did nothing except to rock, and I
cleared my throat, feeling way worse than I did when I'd been
called to the principal's office as a kid.

"One Mithran and her blood-servant are dead. The dead
are Batildis and the Devil."

I could have sworn that Sabina tried to smile, though her
lips didn't move. "This is good. They have long been a pox on
this Earth."

"Okay. Ummm. Not so good. The lead Mithran, named Peregrinus, got away. With the *arenciel*. And he'll be back. Revenge and all. And unfinished business with Joses Bar-Judas.

"A onetime friend told me also that Peregrinus was coming
for me, for the icons I have in safety. For the things Leo has, or
might have in the safe on sub-four."

Sabina gave a slow sigh that stank of old blood. Her breath,
so seldom used, always had the scent of old death. I tried to
ignore it. "*L'arenciel. Essendo luci.* Titles I had thought never
to hear again. Rainbow. Being of light or light-being in an archaic dialect of Latin," she said. "With the *arenciel*, Joses, and
enough blood, Peregrinus will be strong enough to defeat all.
This I understand." Her brow wrinkled. "Knowledge and secrets are much harder to maintain, hidden, in this day and this
age. Once, all one had to do to hide great secrets was to kill the
humans who knew of it. No longer."

All you had to do was kill the humans. Right. But I didn't say it.

Sabina met my gaze. "What do you wish of me, she who
walks in the skins of the beasts?"

"I'd kinda like to use the sliver of the Blood Cross."

She rocked. And rocked. Beyond the windows, I could feel
the sun starting to rise. The color of the windows was clearer,
redder. The candles, oddly, seemed to cast less light, the shadows shrinking and becoming denser. It was nearly dawn. I
knew Sabina was old, but I figured that she still needed to be
out of the sunlight, probably sleeping in the huge stone sarcophagus in front of the chapel. The one with her likeness
carved in the stone.

"Do you believe?" she asked. Reading my confused expression and maybe my scent patterns, she went on. "Do you believe in the cross? In the crucifixion? In the resurrection? That the Christ was transcended, ascended to heaven? Do you believe?"

I swallowed, buying the time to think, knowing that she would smell any dissembling, any lie. Knowing that my answer was important to her. History, if not religion, had always been important to this priestess. And, the more I learned about the origins of the vamps, maybe religion too. I took a shallow breath and held out my arms as if to display myself. I said, "I am human flesh, bone, and tendon. Yet I can change shape and form, like magic, and become an animal. I know that there is another place, maybe another universe of energy and matter, but in a different form. It may power my own . . . what we call *magic*.

"I have a soul, that lives inside this body, but isn't caged by it. Even in another form, I can still maintain my identity, the sanctity of my spirit, of my soul.

"I live in a world with vampires and werewolves and Mercy Blades and *les arcenciels*," I said, stumbling over the French, "who use a magic I can't even begin to comprehend." I frowned and dropped my arms. Her expression hadn't changed, but she shook her head slowly, which didn't seem like a good sign.

"My best friend is a witch. I've seen her do what looks like magic with her gift. I've been healed with the magic of Bethany, the priestess, once, by Leo once, and by Edmund Hartley more than once. I've seen Leo raise his magic in such power that it burned on the skin of my arms. If I believe in magic, in power that I can't understand, how can I not believe in more, in stuff that's supernatural and holy and even bigger than the power I've seen myself?

"I don't think that we know everything that happened back then." I pointed to the bier that held the Blood Cross. "I don't think we *understand* everything that we *think* did happen or that we were told did happen. But there was power left in the cross and in the nails, the power of his blood. The Sons of Darkness just stole it and made it evil, as humans always make things evil. So . . . yes, ma'am. I believe."

"Even though you are *Chelokay*?"

Chelokay was one of the ways that *Cherokee* had once been pronounced. "Even though," I said. "The belief systems are not in opposition."

"The white man's Christ and his priests declared the skinwalkers to be the evil ones, the devils. Before Batildis' Chelokay blood-servant was called the Devil, the skinwalker was the devil." She cocked her head, sniffing, reading my face, my body language, my scent patterns. "And yet, you believe. Why?"

I shrugged. "I don't know. The hope of things unseen," I paraphrased, "faith, that is. That kind of hope. I want there to be something bigger, something better than the rest of us."

"And if there are *many* things bigger and better than humans?"

"Not my problem," I said, suddenly tired. "I don't care. There are bad guys, and demons, and horrible things that go bump in the night. Other things that are good, the kindness of strangers, angels on wings, messengers from above. Even a priestess in a vampire graveyard."

"I am not good. I am not kind. I am a far worse devil than the human so named and now dead."

"Maybe so. I still need the sliver of the Blood Cross. I still have to kill Peregrinus."

"To save Leo Pellissier and his wanton lovers Katherine and Grégoire?"

"I'm between the devil and the deep blue sea. So to speak."

Sabina's chair stopped rocking. And it was empty. I didn't even hear the *pop* of displaced air as she moved. She was standing by the stone sarcophagus. The lid weighed, like, four hundred pounds and she lifted it, opened it with one hand, casually, the way I might lift the lid of a jewelry box. A moment later she closed the lid, softly, gently, as if it were made of cardboard. Her back to me, she said, "You would use the cross made evil by Ioudas Issachar?"

"With your permission."

When she turned to me, she was holding a small drawstring bag. "You know its worth. That this artifact is invaluable, irreplaceable. It has left my hands only twice before, in all the long years it has been in my safekeeping, the second time to you. Now you will take it from me yet again.

"Remember my warning. To prick the skin of a vampire with even a sliver of the Blood Cross will cause him to burn, ashes to ashes, dust to dust, unto true-death. This shard of the Blood Cross will destroy the descendants of the Sons of Darkness. All others of the dark will sicken and likely die, possibly including one who walks in the skins of beasts."

I nodded. I had heard her warning before. And who knew what effect a black-arts, blood-magic device, one created to bring a dead human man back to life, would have on anyone, human or supernatural.

"You will return this to me when the Mithran Peregrinus is true-dead." Sabina held out the small drawstring bag, silk velvet outside, padded within.

I took it and felt something inside it, long and slender, like a small stake. The sliver of the Blood Cross. Yeah. Priceless. I tucked it into my shirtfront, careful to place it so it wouldn't pierce the bag and my skin and maybe kill me, and also so that I wouldn't bend wrong and break it. That seemed like a bad idea.

"Thank you, Sabina. Oh. One more thing. Tonight, a white werewolf stuck in wolf form, one who met the angel Hayyel, ran up and bit the foot of Joses Bar-Judas. Should I be worried?"

Sabina burst out laughing. It sounded like a dying seal honking combined with a set of ancient gears scraping, unused and dried out and so very not human. Vamps weren't supposed to be able to stay vamped out and laugh at the same time, but I had to wonder about Sabina, because the sound was nothing a human throat could make. It gave me the willies.

I realized she wasn't going to answer me, so I nodded and backed to the door and out onto the porch. Her cackle followed me all the way.

Eli was waiting on the porch, a weapon in each hand. "What's that noise?"

"The priestess, finding joy in my tale about Brute biting the Son of Darkness."

"Yeah?" He leaped off the short rise to the path below and led the way back to the SUV. He took the driver's side this time and I let him. As he cranked the vehicle, we could still hear her laughter. Eli said, "I can't say why, but that laughter doesn't inspire confidence."

"Our situation could be pretty grim. Either Brute will turn into a vamp-werewolf or Sabina likes the idea of the Son being bitten. Or something much, *much* worse. I'm betting it's the one behind door number three."

"Not taking that bet," he said as he drove out of the vamp graveyard. The gate closed behind us. It didn't creak or groan. Sometimes vamps lose the perfect opportunity for scary ambience.

"One question," I said as we drove into the sunrise. "The other priestess, Bethany, told me that, 'Together we can ride the *arerenciel*.' What do you think that means?"

"Rodeo?"

I laughed, the sound normal and human but tired. I was so tired. I yawned. And slumped in the seat. And fell asleep. Eli let me rest until we got back to New Orleans, waking me when we stopped at my house. I couldn't remember when I'd last really slept, and I stumbled through the side window and to my bed, where I collapsed again into dreams.

I woke sometime later, still fully clothed, to see the weapons and the sliver of the Blood Cross on the bedside table—thank goodness not on me where I might have rolled over and shot myself in the butt. I had been dreaming of Bruiser. His image hung in my mind, an image remembered from his bedroom—shirtless, pantless, everything-less except the important bits. Beast purred in the back of my mind. "Stop that," I said to her.

Bruiser and I still hadn't talked about that day. I pulled out my handy-dandy bulletproof cell phone. I had messages, but nothing from Bruiser. Even knowing that Peregrinus or a human techie could trace any call I might make, I sent Bruiser a message that said, succinctly, *Call me, dang it*, and rolled back over into sleep and into dreams that left me both agitated with longing and satisfied. Some dreams are better than others, and as dreams went, these were excellent.

It was midafternoon when I woke again and this time I stripped and showered, hoping the cool water might stand a chance of waking me up. It did clear my head, and it also allowed me time enough for my subconscious and dream-state mind to present me with a plan. It wasn't a good plan, but any plan is better than no plan. It also gave me time to figure a few things out.

Hair braided up on my head with sterling hair-stick stakes to hold the large bun in place, wearing jeans and socks and a sports bra and tee, the small bag containing the sliver of the Blood Cross hanging from my gold chain, I left my room. Eli, looking wide-awake, was cleaning his weapons at the kitchen table. Sitting cater-corner from him, Alex was working on his tablets. The Kid leaned back and switched on a fan that emitted a low-level hum of electronics. It wasn't hot in the room, though the air conditioner was humming outside, which meant he was using the fan as a low-tech voice dampener.

I poured tea that someone had obviously set to steep when they heard me get up, and I stood at the table near them. Added creamer and sugar. Cognizant of the fan's noise level, I said softly, "When was someone going to tell me that Bruiser was one of the people that Bethany took with her when she went gadabout last night?"

Alex's head jerked and his heart rate sped, though his eyes never left his screens. Eli's heart remained steady and his hands stable on the weapon he was laying out. "When we knew for sure," Eli said. A hollow place opened up inside me. I had been guessing, but—"And then when you woke. No point in waking you to tell you something you can't do anything about, now, is there?"

"You do know that talking so reasonably is one surefire way to tick a woman off?"

"The woman of my dreams has so informed me." He said it with a grin, an odd one for him, showing teeth, and he added, "And Syl accompanied the information with a head slap, which led to the most amazing—"

"Stop. Not interested," I said.

"I am," the Kid said.

"No," Eli and I both said together. Family was so wonderful. But Eli still had that odd note about him. I watched him work as I sipped, worry for Bruiser worming through me, growing. He should have called by now. "So do we have video of Bruiser and the nutso priestess leaving vamp HQ together?"

Eli tilted his head at his brother, who fiddled with a tablet before swiveling it toward me. I sat, straddling a chair, holding the warm tea mug/soup bowl in both hands propped on the chair back, to watch. Bethany was shown on three screens, dashing through darkened vamp hallways, some floors and walls streaked with blood. Brute was on her trail, racing close at her feet, his muzzle black from biting the thing on the wall, the thing called Joses Bar-Judas, and his crystalline eyes seemed to glow with light. Not good. Bethany had to know he was there.

She passed one of Derek's men. Hi-Fi, short for Vodka Hi-Fi, a mixed drink and his team name, spun from an all-out run as she touched him, to follow her. Hi-Fi and the werewolf raced after her to the front entrance, where the way was blocked by a group of men, scruffy guys in night camo—the cloth blacks and grays—and carrying guns. In front of the group was Bruiser and the two other Onorios. I hadn't seen Brandon and Brian since the *arcenciel* attack. It looked like they had gone somewhere and returned with backup.

Bethany paused long enough to reach out and touch Bruiser, standing in the busted-out entry. He was dressed in Enforcer regalia, leather and weapons enough to finish his own little war, but when she touched him, he went still; then he whipped in behind her and raced away with the others. Brandon and Brian followed. Brute was still with her too, like a good dog following its master. Hi-Fi moved after them, stumbling at first, then moving with purpose and picking up speed.

"She rolled Bruiser, Brandon, and Brian," I said. "I thought Onorios couldn't be rolled."

"Maybe not by an ordinary suckhead," Alex said, "but it looks like a priestess might be different." Slower, he said, "A priestess who was mostly responsible for George rising as an Onorio and not being turned into a scion chained to a wall. Or dead. Maybe she left a, you know, like a back door, into a fire-walled system. She has the password."

I grimaced and tried to ignore the spike of reaction. I was not jealous. I was *not*. "And the twins?"

"I got nothing there," Alex said. "I don't know when or how they were changed from blood-servants to Onorios. But if Bruiser's method—essentially dead, then brought back by the priestess—is the only way, and it may be, for all we know, then maybe she brought back Brandon and Brian too."

"Bethany, Brandon, Brian, Bruiser, and Brute," Eli murmured. "You got some good alliteration going on there, Janie."

"Ha-ha," I said to Eli. "Fine," I said to Alex, and pushed the tablet to him. I glowered at nothing and sipped my tea. "Any way to track where they went?"

"No. Sorry. Power went out in the Quarter, remember? The only reason we have this much is the one generator that came back online."

"Is there any way to track them later?"

"His cell is off. I can try to ping it. Or try to turn it back on. But if Peregrinus is in our systems, he'll get the data and location, and know that we're interested in it. In George."

I glanced at the fan, sipped my tea, and thought. Eli wasn't talking much. He was too quiet. "I called his cell earlier," I confessed. Neither guy said anything, but I knew they were thinking that it was a stupid move. "Do we know where Peregrinus is?"

"No," Alex said. "But we're all in agreement that he'll be back tonight."

"Without his backup, since they're all dead."

"Except for the *arenciel*," Eli said, his tone mild.

No one answered. I sipped some more tea. Worried about Bruiser. Then I sighed. "I need to try something. Practice something." I shrugged. "I need to enter the gray place of the change and see if I can see Soul or the hatchling. And maybe get a fix on Bruiser."

"You can do that?" Eli asked, his voice calm, sedate, nearly toneless, the tenor that told me he was preparing for battle. I should have picked up on it already.

"I have no idea. But I think I need to try."

"You could just text her," he suggested, sounding quietly rational.

"This is about more than just information. If we have to fight the hatchling, and Soul shows up and takes the hatchling's side, we might be toast. You know, since we have no idea what her powers are."

"And if she tries to eat you while you're in the gray place?"

"Hope she gets heartburn?"

"Not overly funny," Eli said. "Don't quit your day job for the comedic stage."

"I'd need better writers. Better sidekicks too. Guys with wicked T-shirts, tights, capes, and way-cool masks." They ignored me. I set the mug/bowl on the table and stood. "I'll be outside for a bit."

"I'll keep watch," Eli said, still not looking up from the weapons. Hands moving as fast as Beast might, he began reassembling the nine-mil. I watched as it practically flew back together with fine, delicate little clicks. He slammed the magazine home and racked the slide to load a round, removed the mag, added a final round, and slammed it home again. He stood and gestured to the windows at the side of the house.

I went through one, Eli behind me. I climbed up on the rocks at the back of the house in the rock garden that had been part of the requirements for me to come to New Orleans in the first place. I still didn't know where Katie had gotten boulders or how much it had cost her to have them shipped in, but they were much the worse for wear, several chipped and ground down to a medium rock sand from the times I had needed mass to shift into an animal bigger than I was. Beast had stopped asking to be big so much recently, since I gained a few pounds.

I settled on the largest boulder and crossed my knees, leaning back against a smaller rock. I no longer needed to get into a lotus to enter the gray place of the change, but sitting on the rocks in that position was habit. I just closed my eyes and thought about the place I needed to be. It was inside me. I sighed and smiled. All along it had been inside me. And outside me. And probably everywhere.

I felt the energies rise and spread through and around me like a faintly tingling mist. It was cooler than the air, the darker motes of energies sharp and pinging where they touched my skin. I didn't know if I'd need to say her name aloud or just think it. I was flying by the seat of my pants, after all, just like usual. Be sad if I really did get eaten this time.

I opened my eyes to see Eli on the side porch, his handgun in one hand and a vamp-killer-sized short sword in the other, except that the blade was all steel, no silver plating. Not for vamps. Steel for Soul. Like steel for Gee DiMercy. Who, last time I saw him, was being mesmerized by the bigger *arcenciel*. Interesting. Both species with an aversion to steel, both tied to the creation myth of the Cursed of Artemis. Had Artemis been an *arcenciel*? They had left my house together as if they'd recognized each other's species, if not each other personally.

"Soul," I called. "Girrard DiMercy." I waited for several minutes, then called again, this time thinking about the snake dragon and the Anzû, picturing them in my mind. Again I waited. And waited. And called again. And nothing. Either what I was doing couldn't be done by a skinwalker, or I was doing it wrong.

I tried picturing the gray energies as not a cloud around me, but more a thing that existed everywhere, something that I was part of. Light and matter, two parts of a whole. With dark matter and dark energy in there somewhere. Physics I didn't understand but was a part of. I dropped deeper into the gray place—the Gray Between—and let myself look out and around, seeing not the world I knew, but a gray net of light and dark, some places dense with dots of energy, some not so dense, tiny dots pulsating. Everything quivered. Everything had movement. Some slower than others, some much faster, the minute vibrations in all things. The thought came to me. This was the unlimited possibilities of the all-space. Which made no sense at all. And yet did.

I felt lighter somehow, effervescent, as if I could fly or float away. As if I could do anything. I laughed, and the vibration of my laughter seemed to affect the area around me and out like rings in a pond when you toss in a stone. This was the way I felt when I had consumed enough alcohol to feel a hint of a buzz, the way I felt when I bit Soul. Suddenly Soul was there, in front of me. She was in her winged, sparkling snake form, and standing on her head was a blue and scarlet-winged bird. Her snake-like tail rattled and shook, sounding like dry bones. "Speak, Jane. *U'tlun'ta*."

"I'm not a liver-eater," I groused.

"You neither *are* a liver-eater nor are you *not* a liver-eater."

"Schrödinger's cat."

"Schrödinger was a foolish human, but wiser than most. What do you want?"

"Peregrinus has the hatchling. He captured her in a . . . something. She's hanging on his necklace."

Soul showed me her teeth. All of them. And there were a lot of teeth, some as long as my arm. "She was vulnerable to his call because you wounded her with steel," she said.

She had figured that out. Or Gee had told her. "I know. And I'm sorry. But I need your help to find Peregrinus, kill him, and free the hatchling."

She pulled back a short distance, like a snake coiling back on itself. "You would help the young one? Even after she killed humans in the vampire council chambers? Why?"

"Why not? Peregrinus forced her. I want Peregrinus dead. You want the baby *arcenciel* back safe and sound. We're stronger together than alone."

"I will assist as I can," Soul said, "but the hatchling can bind time and space. She can alter energies at will. She is young enough to go where she wishes, or where her captor wishes, once he learns how to ride her. Peregrinus is intelligent. He will have learned from taking the young one and by now will certainly be capable of capturing me as well. I was a prisoner of time once and will not be so again." She gnashed her teeth and they clacked like pearls against bamboo, a poetic thought totally unlike me. Rather, they sounded like bones rattling. Yeah. Better.

"My kind make a dangerous weapon in the hands of others," Soul said, "as would my little bird."

"I'll keep that in mind. Speaking of little birds, can Gee DiMercy find Bethany, the vampire priestess, and the Onorios, and tell them to contact me?"

"This he can do. Go, little bird. Make alliance with the vampire priestess."

Gee chirped and spread his wings, blinking out of sight. I had no idea where he'd gone, or whether he could manipulate the gray place of the change on his own, or whether Soul just did it for him. So many questions and so few answers. "Thank you," I said, as formally as I knew how.

Soul winked out of sight. The last thing I heard as she disappeared was the sounds of her tail and her teeth, like bones rattling, like dry bones dancing. Yeah. It was all coming together: the myths, the oral tradition, the scriptures, the lost People of the Straight Ways, and the Builders. All tying in with the weak places between universes and the loss of all civilization through flood, the mythos that tied almost all ancient peoples together.

I opened my eyes to my vacant backyard.

Eli was standing on the porch, his eyes sweeping across the yard, back and forth. "Eli, we need to weapon up and get to vamp HQ."

He didn't answer, just swiveled on a heel and headed back in through the open window. We really needed to get the doors fixed. Yeah. Some easy, lazy, sunny, summer day.

We made a run to Walmart for camping supplies and to a storage unit that my partner had rented and not told me about, and we still got to vamp HQ in plenty of time to prepare. I turned Eli and Alex loose with the new supplies. My lousy plan was coming together, but there was plenty of room for things to go horribly wrong.

CHAPTER 23

The Keeper of the Iron Spike

The staff had been decreased to shooters, swordsmen, and techies. No one who could be killed easily was still in vamp HQ. Housekeeping and the culinary staff were at Grégoire's under heavy guard, maintenance crews at skeleton levels. It was like a stripped-down Aardvark Protocol. All the blood-servants and vamps on hand were old ones—looking well fed and grim, geared up for battle. I had never seen a vamp war, but it must have been a bloody business by the number of blades the vamps carried.

They were, to a fanghead, wearing chain-mail armor, with titanium gorgets and steel gauntlets with fingers that looked like metal roly-polies. They still moved with the graceful speed of the vamp, but now they clanked, just a bit.

On my part, I was decked out in my best fighting gear—the fancy leathers with plastic joint protectors and lots of silver-plated titanium chain mail. My hair braided into a fighting queue, close to my skull. Tall combat boots and more blades than I usually carried. No long, flat sword. Not yet. Hopefully not ever. But the new thigh holster, yeah. And every other weapon I could think of, with the exception of my shotgun. It wasn't helpful in close-quarters shooting when I might take out friendly forces along with the big-bad-uglies.

The Kid and Angel Tit were rigging backup coms, the stuff we had picked up from the storage unit, all over the place, putting portable CNBs—communications nexus boxes—on every stairwell and floor. The CNB tactical radio system was designed to work in places where physical or electromagnetic interference was high. Or underground. And on battery power. We had used them before and they had worked great, but the specs were limited. They had to be aligned, pointing in proper places and directions. It took time to set up and the system was clunky. It was also easy to ruin. A swift kick to any box would stop all comms from that location. So the Kid instructed that they were all to be duct-taped to the ceilings, which was pretty smart. Eli put the humans to work with the tape and positioning new battery-powered backup lights on the floors. It was low-tech, but was also better than nothing, and not something Peregrinus was likely to be expecting, since most of it had been purchased with cash and not recorded on credit cards.

Go, Eli and his paranoid survivalist instincts and hoarding nature. Not that I would tell him that. He'd either be insulted or arrogantly proud. Or both.

Eli and Derek agreed on locations for shooters. It would be a pain to create such a lousy plan and then get taken out by friendly fire, when it *should* be much more likely to be eaten by a vamp or a rainbow dragon or drained by the Son of Darkness.

When everything was in place, I sent Alex and the last of the maintenance staff down to double-check the generators. Eli had covered them with metal heating blankets, the kind that he had used to preserve Wrassler's body heat. It was a long shot, but maybe the little amount of reflective material would bounce any magic EM attacks off. Since we were all trying new paraphernalia and untested theories, I taped a single obfuscation charm on top of the first generator. It might work to keep any spell from finding and stopping the generators. Who knew? But it was the only obfuscation charm I had.

When he was finished with the generators, Alex settled in to the security console with Angel Tit. If this worked, we'd want footage of it. If it didn't, well, maybe our survivors could learn from our stupidity. Derek and his team and four vamp fighters were stationed at the front entrance. Eli and I chose to man the back entrance under the porte cochere, and took all the new men from the swamps with us. They'd had showers, been fed, and gotten some rest. They looked a lot less scruffy, a lot more operational, and smelled a lot better. I figured Peregrinus wouldn't use the same entrance twice and we had to make sure that he went in the right direction when he came in. So at both

entrances we had positioned fighters to herd him where we
wanted him.

On the ground floor at the back, Eli put his hands and arms
to work, torqueing his body to open the elevator doors. The
elevator wasn't there, just the dark shaft, which was empty all
the way to the basement, filled only with a stink on the air that
spoke of mold and rot. At the bottom were the doors that
would open to Joses Bar-Judas' prison. And our pitiful plan.

Eli and his guys settled in to wait, their purpose to lead the
attackers to the open shaft and down, and I got ready to carry
out my part of the plan. Which was when I was summoned by
His Regal Grumpiness via a text message from Del that asked
me to come to Leo's office.

I put the cell in a pocket and looked up to see Eli watching
me. "Leo."

"You haven't seen him since he was bound on the floor of
the catacombs."

"Worse. I haven't talked to the MOC since he tried to kill
me in my bathroom. And it's a dungeon. Catacombs are long
tunnels."

Eli smiled. It wasn't his battle smile, which was all adrenaline and cold intent. It wasn't the smile he used for his lady
love. It was the smile he'd have worn every day had he not
chosen the military for his job. Had he not seen and done
things that hardened him. It was friendship.

I shrugged. "Leo wants me in his office."

He looked at his watch. "It's early yet. I don't think they'll
attack this soon after sunset. You got a cross with you?"

"Thirteen. Even better. I have a piece of the Blood Cross."

"Thirteen." His smile widened. "Lucky number. Be careful.
And pick up Wrassler's Judge on the way. He texted that he
wanted you to use it today."

"Yeah. Okay. That's . . ." I shook my head at the ludicrous-
ness of what I was about to say. "That is so nice."

I took the stairs because the elevator shaft was open with the
elevator locked on the top floor as part of my lousy plan. "Yellowrock in stairway *B*," I said into my headset. "Heading up."

"Copy, stairway *B*," Angel Tit said back.

I increased my speed, picked up Wrassler's weapon, and
reached Leo's office fast. I wanted to get this over with and
didn't want to be on this floor when the trouble hit. I knocked
on the door, which was cracked open, and stepped inside. On

the air currents I smelled Leo and Grégoire and Katie. And Del. Oh, goody. The vamp council's top members all in one place just for me.

Stopping at the opening to the office, I waited. The silence was disturbing on an organic, biological level. No breathing except Del's and mine, only two hearts beating. Del sat at the desk, a legal pad before her, a pen in her hand, and was dressed in a black sword-fighting suit, her hair up in a severe bun. She didn't look at me, which told me something, but not what. Nothing on the vamps moved except their eyes. The three studied me in my Enforcer gear as I studied them.

Leo and Katie were sitting on wooden stools at his desk, which made sense, as they were weaponed up like the love children of samurai warriors and the Terminator, and sitting in a chair would have been impossible. Grégoire was leaning against the wall, looking lazy, or as lazy as the unbreathing undead can.

Their battle gear was downright pretty. Grégoire's was a dark gold leather with an overlay of bright brass-over-steel chain mail that caught the light. Leo's was black leather overlaid with blackened titanium chain mail and the entire outfit seemed to absorb the light. They made quite a pair. Katie's battle gear was white with steel and looked all wrong with her white skin and ash blond hair, until I saw the white hood and face plate, like a beekeeper's hood or a fancy version of the sword-fighting gear worn in Blood Challenges. Del had guns on her. At least three that I could see from my angle. I hadn't remembered that Del was a gun-gal.

Since no one said anything, I decided to make offense my best . . . offense. "You didn't call me up here to kill me, did you? Or to pay me back for staking you? Because last time I saw you upright, you were . . . rude."

A fleeting smile crossed Leo's face. "You are safe. The error of my ways has been pointed out to me by my primo and lawyer, Adelaide." A faint smile lit Del's eyes when she glanced up at me. Her eyebrows lifted in some kind of warning before her attention dropped back to the paper. "My Enforcer," Leo said. "I ask that you allow me to bind you, that we might communicate in the coming battle."

It sounded like a formality but I wanted to make sure he knew I was serious. I pulled a silver cross out of my neckband to dangle over my gorget. It was already glowing, with such powerful vamps present, and it brightened my dark clothing. My voice had no inflection at all when I spoke. "No."

"Why do you stay with our master, Leo?" Grégoire asked.

"Money. And because I'm learning stuff I need to know." I hooked my thumbs in my utility belt and kept my knees loose, my body balanced. I looked as relaxed as he did, but I was ready to move. My hands were positioned directly over my red-handled .380s, which I'd made ready to fire as I climbed the stairs.

"Such as?" Grégoire asked.

When I answered, I looked at Leo, not his heir and his spare heir. "I've learned the reason why all the vamps have such an interest in Leo's prime real estate. Swamps and a river and ports and jazz aren't reason enough. The real reason isn't even because of the world political situation. Most of the reason is because of the magical things that are missing from vamp history. For a while, the EuroVamps thought you had them and that kept you safe, as they were afraid to attack you." I let some of my anger at him creep into my voice. "But because of what's hanging in the basement, all that's changed. Joses Bar-Judas. The Son of Darkness. Is. *Hanging.* In. Your. *Basement.*"

Leo was staring at his hands, loosely clasped on the table. Katie was resting across the tabletop, her head in the crook of her arm, staring at him, her face unguarded, and at ease, almost human. Her eyes . . . soft.

Holy crap. Katie is in love with Leo.

Mate, Beast thought at me.

"Yeah," I said to all of them.

Leo nodded once, the light catching the curve of his jaw.

My voice hard, I went on. "When Peregrinus got Reach's files, he got more than hints about artifacts. He found out about the SOD." Leo nodded again. "Now? *Knowing* it's down there—that *he's* down there—means that they'll start coming. It's out—*all your secrets are known now,* even if only to a limited number of people. The secret is out. Soon they'll *all* know."

"Yes," Leo said.

"And what will you do with Joses?"

"Do?"

"Yeah. Leave him on the wall, chained and starving?"

Leo laughed, but the sound wasn't human. It was the royal laughter of a king who was ticked off. "Shall I set him free?

Joses was riding his own *arcenciel*, which was set free by accident in the fight to take him prisoner. The bite it gave him tore him near unto true-death and stole what remained of his humanity. He has been raving for decades."

"But one bit you. And Gee." I stopped. *"Oh!"* The understanding hung in my mind like a single candle flame in a dark cavern. "Once you had him, you were stumped. You couldn't set him free. You couldn't bring him back to sanity or control him. So you hung him up to cure, like a scion. You three had been drinking from Joses—who had survived an *arcenciel* bite—for years, and Gee from you. You were immune."

"It seems so," Leo agreed.

"Holy crap." I stared at him, trying to make sense of all the possibilities that had just occurred to me. "You drank from him, like, regularly because his blood is so powerful. But you couldn't control him until you got hold of the pocket watches I found in Natchez. Once you had a few of them with the discs made of the iron spike inside, you had a way to manage him. At least a little bit."

"The Keeper of the Iron Spike of Golgotha can wield all power over all Mithrans, even the Sons of Darkness," Grégoire said. It sounded like a quote from a story or a history. He adjusted his posture, standing straight, his feet flat on the floor. He no longer looked like a teenager lounging. Weapons bristled on him, blades of every shape and variety and style. He looked what he was, the best fighter in the Americas. And my Beast didn't like the way he was looking at us. There was a challenge in his eyes. I shifted my own body, inching my palms down over the guns.

"Men," Katie spat. She stood too, and stared back and forth between the other vamps. "No one knew for *certain* that Joses Bar-Judas was here until *that foul creature Reach* was taken," she said. "Our enemies De Allyon, Silandre, and Lotus began this crisis, with black magic, not her." Katie pointed at me.

"What she said," I said. "Had any of your enemies *known* Joses was a prisoner, they would have brought the war here first, hoping to steal your artifacts, combine their artifacts with the Son of Darkness, and rule the world of the Mithrans. Boom. Game over, months ago."

"But you discovered only the pocket watches, and not the spike," Leo said. "Without it I am not enough to rule."

It sounded oddly like an accusation, as if I hadn't done my

job. Since Leo wanted the spike, and I hadn't found it, I actually hadn't done my job. Go figure. I grunted, a nonspecific sound.

"It is still missing or in the hands of another," Katie said. "If we had the spike now, we could control the Son and maintain peace. But we do not. There will be war on the shores of this land for possession of the artifacts of power, for control of Leo's prisoner and Joses' gift of power, and for the right to possess and to ride *les arcenciels*."

"His gift of power?" Bethany had talked about the gift she had given Leo. Had Bethany broken the crystal that set the *arcenciel* free and brought down Joses for Leo as some sort of gift? Bethany had wanted to ride the *arcenciel*, maybe because she had seen it when it got free the first time. She had tried to literally ride it in the gym. It made an awful sort of sense for a crazy priestess. I doubted the vamps would tell me if I asked, so I led the way in indirectly and asked instead, "Ride?"

Grégoire said, "To encase them in crystal from the earth and use their power. It is not a difficult process. All one needs is a length of quartz crystal, enough blood, and the proper power source, such as the Spike of the Hill of the Skull. Power is what we discuss. Who has it and how we use it."

"Sadly," Katie said, "it is easy to free them. The slightest crack and they may escape."

"A dangerous slave is then set free," Grégoire said.

"Uh- huh." Slave? Yeah. *Slave.* Vamps were used to keeping slaves. "Bethany has three Onorios, some humans, and a werewolf in her control, and a desire to ride the *arcenciel*," I said. All the vamps turned to me. Not one of them looked human when they did it. More like statues whose heads suddenly spun on their marble necks. Even Del raised her head, with something like horror on her face. Grégoire's voice was full of shock when he said, "My boys are—"

My earpiece squealed and I jerked. "Incoming! Incoming!"

Something shook the entire building, like a bomb going off. The air pressure changed as a concussive wave battered through. I heard screaming in my earbud and from the front entrance. A second explosion followed.

And all hell broke loose. Again.

I had made a huge mistake. Because all of Peregrinus' humans had been drained and left dead in the basement, I assumed that he was out of blood-servants. I had expected primarily a magical attack. I got a human one.

I was rushing from the office and down the stairs, the vamps left to get downstairs on their own. "Yellowrock on the way down," I said into my mic.

I heard automatic arms fire as I raced. Screaming and the sounds of pain and anger. Orders being given. Derek in command mode, telling men where to move and what to do. From his words it was clear that an explosive device, maybe a rocket, had taken out the front entry again, and that more than a dozen attackers were racing up the outer front stairs. Where had Peregrinus gotten more soldiers?

I reached the stairs to the foyer. Part of the wall to my right exploded outward and on through the wall to my left. I dropped and crawled to the top of the stairs. I could smell blood and feces and the stink of fired weapons. The entry was full of fighters, both vamps and humans, the unknown humans wearing jeans, hoodies, and gang tats. I stayed low, moving like Beast on all fours, analyzing the scene below. I wasn't getting down to Eli this way. Leo, Grégoire, and Katie leaped over me, over the stair railing, and landed on the marble floor of the entryway. Like a well-seasoned team, they started to clear the floor of opposition. Katie fell in a rain of automatic weapons fire, blood blooming across her chest. Leo and Grégoire pulled her to safety behind a wall.

The vamps at this assault point were all ours. I could tell by the smell of them. They smelled of the thing in the basement. They had fed on it. Not that it would help them. The attackers were using guns and explosive devices, not fancy, outdated flat swords. Being faster than a normal vamp sword fighter was useless here. This was war as *mankind* had envisioned it. Nothing elegant about it. Just efficient and deadly.

If this attack was by humans only, then the attacking vamp or vamps were elsewhere. Before I headed down the stairwell I keyed my mic and said, "Eli?"

"Go ahead."

"No enemy combatant vamps at front entrance strike. Humans only."

"Copy that. No encom action here."

I started to say that didn't make sense when he barked, "Incoming!"

There was an explosion. A big one. I felt it through my knees and palms on the floor and I jerked the earbud out of my ear to save my hearing.

"Eli," I whispered, sticking the earpiece back in.

"Position to the basement as per plan," he ordered me.

It was where I'd still be if I hadn't wanted to see what Leo had to say. Curiosity killed . . . not the cat . . . killed my friends? But Eli was alive. "Okay," I said, relief surging through me as I backtracked through HQ.

"Roger, Jane. Or copy. Not okay. Never okay."

I smiled and said, "Okay." I thought about how I could get to the basement now. It wasn't going to be easy, dang it, but at least we still had electricity and lights. I retraced my steps to Leo's office and through one of the no-longer-hidden passageways and into the room that was situated over the green room, the waiting room that guests used when they came for appointments. The room I'd last eaten oatmeal in. The room that had a hidden elevator shaft behind it. I called the elevator and the door opened immediately. The cage was just that, a brass cage, tiny and swaying, with an uneven floor. Only one or two people could ride at a time, so the invaders wouldn't split up their forces to take it. The cage wobbled as I stepped in. I pushed the cage doors shut and the outside doors closed too. There were numbers on the buttons but they didn't correspond to anything that made sense, so I took a guess and punched the lowest button to the right.

The cage shook and dropped two feet. I stumbled and grabbed the ancient handrail to steady myself. "Going down," I said. "Hopefully not at gravity speed." I thought I heard Alex chortle, but someone cut off the sound.

The elevator ground its way down with no more drops. It opened on a floor I didn't recognize, however, a musty area with no lights and a scent I remembered. I was one floor too high, on sub-four, the storage floor. And I was in a small, closed space. In the dark. I switched on my flash and saw clothes hanging in rows, circa somewhere in the early nineteen hundreds. The cloth was rotting and the clothing was falling off the padded hangers. I was in a closet. Still using the flash, I found the closet door and opened it to reveal a bedroom. No windows, lots of rotten wall hangings and wallpaper falling off the walls. It smelled of dust, dead insects, rot, black mold, and vaguely of a vamp I recognized. Adrianna. The room's door was locked from the outside. Had the flame-haired beauty been kept prisoner here? Or kept a prisoner here?

Fortunately it was an old, *old* door. I drew on a little of

Beast's power and put one hand on the jamb. With the other hand I yanked on the knob. The hinges fell off and the door broke in splinters. I leaped back as it fell inward, and then forward through the broken opening. I was in a dark hallway. The Judge in a two-hand grip, held low at my thigh, the flash Velcroed to my wristband, I opened squeaky doors to the left and right, seeing nothing new, everything old, with lots of storage rooms stacked with trunks and furniture, smelling of things that were no longer in use.

Then I opened a door that didn't squeak. Inside, the room was clean and modern. And a security console was set there. I tapped my mic and said, "Alex. I just found the physical location of the second security console you hacked and merged. I have no idea what to do with it. But mark my location and send someone down here later to officially hard-wire it into the routine one. On the orders of the Enforcer," I added, in case Leo got ticked off when he heard about it and wanted to tear someone a new one. He could try that on me.

"Roger that, Janie," Alex said. "And, hey, Jane? We might have a problem. Soul and about a dozen cop cars just pulled into the open gate and up to the front door."

"Crap," I said into the mic. "Do not try to stop them. Repeat, do not. Get Del up there to tell her what's going on. Let them know it's vamp business. Maybe that will keep them in one place until the legal beagles decide how to handle the sounds of gunfire on U.S. soil."

"Will do."

I backed out of the secondary security room and found a branching hallway with stairs up and down. I went down, my feet against the wall where the rotten treads might still be strong enough to support my weight.

It took me less than a minute to discover that the stairway went all the way to the lowest subbasement and a small pocket door. Carefully, silently, I lifted up on the small latch and slid the door open. Beyond was complete darkness. Which I totally did not expect. My body protected behind the jamb, I used my flash to inspect the room, and it was indeed the room where Joses lived—or hung undead on the wall, a rack of bones in a man-shaped bag of worn and torn leathery skin. I moved the flash across him for a moment—making sure he was still secured there—before taking in the rest of the room.

It was vacant, smelling of blood and death. The clay floor

where the dead had lain was empty, only dark stains every-where to show the recent deaths. Again, I shined the light on the wall where the prisoner hung. He was watching me, black eyes glittering in the dark, the metal of the wall picked out by the glare of the light.

I moved the flash back and forth, taking in everything. The thing's talons were embedded in the brick of the wall; rusted iron and tarnished silver bands held him in place, the bands running horizontally around the room, attached to vertical I beams retrofitted in the corners. The holes where his fingers were buried, deep in the brick, showed exposed copper wires. I smelled the stink of burned flesh and ozone on the air. That hadda hurt. Yeah. He was nutso. But that might explain why there were brownouts and electrical problems.

Gee DiMercy appeared in my flash, just inside the room, but hovering, a foot off the floor. I jumped back in shock, and he laughed, his voice bouncing off the walls. I wanted to hit him, but he wasn't really there. Just a shadow of himself, spec-tral as any ghost. "What!" I demanded, forcing my heart rate to slow, trying to catch my breath.

"The priestess speaks lies. She is full of deceit." And he van-ished.

I brought my heart rate under control and blew out my ten-sion. *Dang Mercy Blade.*

I pushed the thought of Gee DiMercy away and chose where I would wait, to the left of the elevator. I stepped through, pulling the door behind me. I shot the flash over Joses and caught him smiling. It wasn't a pretty sight. His fangs were like a sabertooth cat, upper and lower, and his tongue was a black strip jutting between his jagged incisors. Yuckers. I flipped the light away from the prisoner and stepped into the room.

"Aaaaah." The breath echoed, bouncing back from the walls.

I flinched and spun, shining the flash back on the prisoner.

"I am visited yet again by *U'tlun'ta*, warrior of The People," he said.

That didn't sound insane, or not the gibbering insanity of the usual rogue vamp. Not wanting to actually chat, I grunted at him.

"Do you not bow? Do you not genuflect in the presence of one worshipped as a god?"

"Shut up," I said as I considered the elevator door. This close, I could hear the sounds of gunfire and the shrill screams of the injured. And the *thump* as something or someone landed on the floor of the elevator shaft. But the door didn't open. The gunfire continued. I crossed the room.

"Release me and I shall give you a third of my kingdom." I heard the breath grate in his lungs and realized he was about to shout.

Midstep, I pulled a silver-plated throwing knife and focused the flash on him.

"I shall—"

I threw the blade. It spun through the dark and sank into his throat. He made a soft squeaking sound and went silent. "War Women do not miss," I whispered, only partway lying, "not with knives." Though he wasn't dead, not even now. A vamp that old could heal from a dose of silver. However, it did take care of the annoyance factor.

I took my place beside the elevator door and steadied Wrassler's Judge. The kick was gonna be bad, but if I managed to blow Peregrinus' head off before the battle started down here, it would be worth it. That was the plan. Like I'd said, it was lousy. And simple. But sometimes lousy and simple were best.

From behind me, I heard a *thump* and flipped off my flashlight. The pocket door slid open. Light speared the darkness. Air whooshed down and into the basement. I smelled Bethany, Onorios, and humans in need of deodorant. Great. Just what I needed. *Not.*

"Spread out," Bruiser murmured softly, barely at the edge of hearing. His voice was intended for his dedicated headset, one not tied into mine. I knew that because I heard his voice through the air, not through the electronics. "Get in position. Stay well away from the man on the wall."

"Ain't no man, dude. Ain't human," a human said.

"Better reason to stay from him," Brandon or Brian said, humor in his voice.

By sound, I knew that they took up positions. Their flashlights never caught me in the glare, allowing me to decide what I wanted to do. And I decided not to share my position with them. I didn't know how compromised Bruiser was. Or *if* he was. Or . . . It was too much to think about.

Readying the heavy gun in two hands, I took a stance with

one heel braced on the wall and both knees bent. I lowered the weapon and relaxed my shoulders. Keyed my mouthpiece and tapped it twice, code for *I'm in position*.

I turned off the mouthpiece, breathed in and out, and shrugged my shoulders. *Okay, Beast. I'm gonna need some of that time thing you do,* I thought at her, *for as long as you can hold it. Don't let me down, girl.*

Price will be high.

Yeah. I figured. And I had hoped to never do this again. Silly me.

In the back of my mind Beast snorted and padded forward, taking up the forefront of my mind. She stared out through my eyes, which I kept turned away from the rest of the room to hide their glow. I stood in the dark, in a room with the Son of Darkness, armed Onorios, an insane outclan priestess, and humans. Stupid. Really stupid. But smart to be quiet if they were not on my side in this little battle to come.

Together, Beast and I waited.

Around the edges of the door I saw flashes of light and heard hollow booms. The door thundered, vibrations that shuddered my eardrums. Seen through the crack in the elevator opening, there was an unfinished room on the other side of the elevator shaft, some twenty-by-twenty feet in size. With the elevator secured at the top story of vamp HQ, there was room for close-quarters fighting beyond the doors. *Very* close-quarters fighting. On the other side of the closed elevator doors I heard a bellow of anger and the clash of swords.

CHAPTER 24

I Probably Shouldn't Trust Me Either

The elevator doors blew inward, just missing me as I stepped back into the dark. It took a few long seconds to interpret what I was seeing/hearing/smelling. Leo stood in the shaft, wreathed in shadows, stinking of combat and explosive residue and his own blood. His swords were circling in La Destreza. To his right Katie fought, her swords whirling, her clothing catching the light, pulling it all to her, her grace and brilliance seeming to make the shadows darker. The two stepped toward the dungeon, toward me, feet lifting lightly, as if in a dance. But they had been injured with both swords and gunfire, numerous times, and crimson stained their clothes.

Peregrinus followed, lunging, lunging, lunging, his swords flashing. Humans took cover behind him, their guns firing at the dancing vamps. From the room where Bruiser and the others waited, shots were returned, steady, targeted shots, not random cover fire. Two of Peregrinus' humans fell. The street gang raced behind the walls, out of sight. Their guns fell silent.

The gunfire assured me that whatever Bruiser and his boys had planned, it wasn't to let Peregrinus win, which meant that Bethany was still on Leo's side. That was good to know.

Katie moved out from Leo's side as the fighting spread past my hiding place, into the room. That put her in line with Peregrinus. In my line of fire.

Peregrinus was dressed in plate metal from head to foot, looking like Iron Man, if Iron Man had worn blue armor splashed with bloody trim like macabre lace. He also wore the quartz crystal necklace, with the smoky inclusion of a dragon.

And Katie was still in my way. If I missed.

Peregrinus lunged again and again, moving farther into the room. Faster than even Beast could follow. At his back another form appeared, landing in a crouch as if dropped from the floor above.

Holy crap. The Devil.

She was still alive.

Peregrinus had fed her quickly enough to save her. *Impossible.* Unless he himself had already fed from the Son of Darkness. Yeah. Sure. He had done that the first thing when he got here. Drink. Get stronger. Drink down his humans, Naturaleza-style, the ones he'd left in a drained pile. Then start whatever ceremony he had been planning on. Which, if priestesses weren't necessary for the change, could mean that the Devil was an Onorio . . . *Holy crap.*

The Devil raced through the fighters, avoiding everything, every sword, every gun, her own swords spinning with the grace of angels' wings, steel wings of death. Her fighting method was different from other vamps'. Not just lunge-lunge-lunge, but rather step-step-lunge, step-lunge, step-step-lunge, like a dance. Add in a lunging pirouette with a lunging sword sweep, like a bird's wing with death on the flight feathers, and it was beautiful and deadly and mesmerizing. Around her, three human fighters fell, their cries and blood and the stench of bowels released in death adding to the chaos. And with the rhythm of the Devil's steps, her dance of death, I had a clear shot.

Now, I whispered to Beast. Together we stepped into the Gray Between. Time stuttered and shuddered and slowed. Stopped. Or nearly so. Though the Devil's swords still moved, ever so slowly.

I slid between her blades, easing between the cutting edges. The swords slid an inch. Two more. Three. *Careful. Careful,* I thought. If Beast lost control, I would be in several pieces before my eyes could blink. I wasn't sure I could heal if I was in pieces. I had never died that way before. A shaft of light thrust through the path of the Devil's blades, illuminating Bruiser, leaping high, toward her. His mouth was open in a scream, his face full of wrath and lethal purpose. His blades were out to the sides, like a raptor in flight. But he wasn't going to survive the leap. Faster than he was falling through the air, the Devil's blades turned toward him. Only an inch at a time, but I could see the trajectory of the swords and the bloody death to come. My heart clenched, a painful contraction. *No . . .*

I stepped close and placed the working end of the Judge against the side of the Devil's neck, into the freshly healed scars left by vamp fangs. Making sure her swords were still out of cutting range, and Bruiser out of range of any through-and-through .410 pellets, I squeezed the trigger. It took a lot more muscle than I expected. And it took a lot longer. I squeezed and squeezed, muscles trembling, the trigger moving slowly. Finally, the gun clicked. Shook.

The explosion was a visual thing as much as a tactile experience, the barrel shoving back in my hands, leaving a small space between the barrel and the Devil's neck. A puff of hot gray smoke appeared, burning her skin, a low roar that grew in volume. Pellets emerged in a tight, narrow pattern.

My hands fought the kick, which was slow and heavy, trying to shove my arms up. The pellets and something plastic-like began to depress the skin of her neck, pierce the flesh. Disappear inside her. Spread out, the pattern widening. Her cervical spine snapped. I held my position as the barrel emptied.

As soon as the barrel of the gun was empty, I ducked and backed away. And my belly began to cramp. It started faster this time, and harder. Deeper. I grunted with pain and doubled over. I stumbled and dropped to one knee, gripping my belly with one hand, while the other still held the Judge. I managed a partial breath and tilted my head to see my handiwork.

Nothing had happened. The smoke from the shot still filled the air. I breathed it in, smelling blood, barely tingeing the air. Human blood, smelling a lot like Onorio blood. The Devil's blood.

I had just killed a human with malice aforethought, with malevolence and planning. An assassination. I had killed a human while I was in no danger of my own life. I had just committed murder. I blew out a breath, forced myself up into a crouch, my guts on fire. Lurching, I reversed my path through the fighting until my back touched the wall. The brick was cold and wet and slick. The Devil's swords faltered. A faint hesitation in movement. I watched as shotgun pellets burst from her throat. Out the far side of her neck. Her head tilted. Her eyes started going wide. Her knees went weak. Time sped in juddering, shuddering motions, like stop-and-go photography.

Bruiser was landing within the path of the Devil's swords, his arms beginning to fling outward to deflect the Devil's strikes. He would have survived the landing. He might even have survived the Devil's assault. I could have disabled her. I could have done any number of nonlethal things to assure Bruiser's life. Instead I killed her.

No one would thank me. Not the cops she had killed. Not their families. Not Reach, whom she had tortured.

I am a murderer. An arm of vengeance. The words were bitter in my thoughts.

Beast huffed in grim delight. *Beast is best hunter.*

In for a dollar, in for a death. I forced myself upright and walked to the vamp, approaching Peregrinus from behind. He had dropped his short sword and was lifting a hand, his fingers nearly touching the crystal quartz prison on his chest. He was getting ready to use it, to force the hatchling to work for him, to twist time. He was going to ride the *arcenciel.* At his side, Bethany also reached, her black eyes glittering, her gold earrings and beads halted in flight, her face fully vamped out. Desire and avarice wrenched her expression into something feral and fierce. If she got the crystal, things might go from pan to fire.

I pushed my body past the pain and reached around. Slid my fingers between Peregrinus' hand and the necklace. Took the crystal quartz that hung around his neck, gripped it in one hand, and yanked. The thong holding it in place snapped and flew free, suspended in the air. Wrapping around my wrist with a quick bite of pain as the leather ends linked with my speed, my bubble in time. The crystal was cold in my hand, like holding dry ice, a burning frost. I curled my fist tighter and turned away from the fighting.

Nausea flooded up my throat and I gagged. My abdomen coiled and spiraled and knotted. I vomited and the splash that hit the wall was pure blood. *That can't be good.*

I fell and felt a sword pass slowly over me, the roar of battle like a far-off jet engine, battering my eardrums. I cradled the crystal against my body as I heaved, and heaved. More and more blood erupted from me. The world spun drunkenly. I had lost too much blood. Something inside me had ruptured and it wasn't healing over, not while I was in the bubble of time.

Price, Beast thought at me. *Price is high. Must stop now.*

I left Peregrinus fighting the two vamps, knowing that Bethany had been thwarted in whatever her goals might have been. Bruiser and the other Onorios would protect Leo, Katie, and Grégoire, no matter what Bethany might have wanted or planned. And without the crystal, without riding the *arcenciel,* and without the Devil, Peregrinus was done.

I looked at the thing hanging on the wall of Leo's dungeon, believing in my gut that it needed to be beheaded. Beast's fear response might be the only proof, but I trusted it more than I trusted logic or evidence. Of all the things in the dungeon, in the sub-five basement, *that* psycho thing needed killing. I couldn't get there, do the deed, and get the *arcenciel* up, outside, and free before I died, however, not without blood in my veins, so that was a moral decision I didn't have to make.

I took the crystal to the elevator shaft and looked up. I could see part of Eli's face, a few floors up, leaning over the edge and trying to get a view. He had probably heard the Judge fire by now.

Still in the gray place of the change, the energies moved around me like black fireflies, but slower, jerky, not fluid and smooth. I bent and set the crystal on the clay floor. I snapped open the pocket on the thigh holster Bruiser had given me and pulled out the hatchling's scale and set it beside the crystal.

I shouted, "Soul! I've got the hatchling!"

From behind, I heard a sound, a single ringing bell, as sword blade impacted sword blade. The note rang out for what felt like seconds, low and deep and sonorous. Above me, a ray of light appeared and illuminated the shaft. A flashlight had been turned on and was shining down.

From the dungeon came the low, deep clang of swords and the first boom of the Judge reverberating. Time was catching up with me.

I knelt, pulled a vamp-killer, and reversed it. I brought the hilt down on the smoky crystal. It shattered slowly with tiny cracks and splits and a near-metallic clang. A black metallic claw emerged, followed by a shoulder and wing, all metal, and covered by spines. It occurred to me that, for the moment, the dungeon might be the best place for me. I backed away, back into the scion lair, as *time* in the Gray Between, and the bubble of time around the previously imprisoned *arcenciel,* synchronized into its own version of slo-mo.

The imprisoned *arcenciel* leaped from the crystal quartz into the air. In midflight, her wings beginning to spread, she changed from metallic to a rainbow of lights. Landed on the floor of the elevator shaft several floors above, next to Eli's head, still looking down. Lights like a dozen rainbows shifted from her like pixie dust. She called, a ringing, silver tone, like the sound of a thousand bells and the warmth of sunlight. She looked back once and met my eyes. She called again, the sound like carillons ringing. With a leap, she flew out of sight, toward the outer door, which Eli had left open and unguarded for just this moment. I fell to my butt, the pain wrenching as if I were being cut in two. I had committed murder tonight, killed without combat, with sneak attack. An assassination. The death roiled in my stomach and burned there like acid. The Devil had needed to die, but her life and death sat on my soul like weights.

I understood why Joses had worn an *arcenciel*. I understood why vamps wanted them. Riding one let them do, in a limited way, what the *arcenciels* and Beast could do naturally—enter the Gray Between and move outside of time. But without the pain of the *price* placed on me/us by an angel.

For now, Joses was a prisoner, and the *arcenciel* was free. It might not be perfect, but it was good enough.

Now no one had access to folded time, to time bubbles, but me—if I was willing to nearly die—and my Beast. And the *arcenciels*.

And maybe the Anzû.

Crap. I sheathed my blade. Oh well. Nothing was perfect. Nothing.

I vomited blood one last time, falling forward onto the clay floor beside the scale left behind by the *arcenciel* and the shattered crystal prison. I bounced, my head turned to see into the battleground. My hand landed beside me, still holding the Judge. My skin was white-white-white, bluish, nearly purple, empty of blood and low on oxygen. And still my guts pulled and tore and the sick taste of blood and stomach acid coated my mouth.

Change, Beast thought at me. *Now.*

Reaching into the Gray Between, I sought her form. Time began to slide forward in blocks of action, quaking, trembling motions still too slow for reality. The explosion of the Judge still echoed. The screams of battle ripped across my eardrums, faster now. And again, faster still, as time began to unfold.

A light as bright as a phosphorescent torch lit the elevator shaft. Peregrinus danced back, and back, into the light, his feet moving around me where I lay. The fight followed him, his men firing, the sounds like a dozen bass drums beating all at once.

In the same instant, the Devil fell and Grégoire whirled and leaped to cut across Peregrinus' torso. Brother fighting brother, the oldest tale of them all. Peregrinus' knees buckled, but he wasn't finished. The vamp was too strong, too old, too powerful for most weapons. He had, after all, brought the Devil back to life. Moving as if my hand weighed fifty pounds, I released the Judge and pulled the bag holding the sliver of the Blood Cross. Ripped the bag free from my neck. Slid the pointed end from the drawstring opening.

I gripped the sliver through the bag, careful not to touch it, my hand shaking as if I were dying. I thrust the splinter of wood forward, through the seam of his fighting leathers, into Peregrinus' calf.

Still caught in the remnants of the time warp of the Gray Between, I saw a tiny explosion of fire at the point of impact. The progression of burn as the vampire began to burst into flame. A heated glow I could feel on the skin of my fingertips and my face. The power thrust through his body into his veins, into his arteries. Instantly, he blazed. His whole core lighting with power. With the heat of the sun. For a long while, I could see his bones, his ribs, the shape of his pelvis and shoulders.

Peregrinus slowly dropped to his knees. He wrenched back his head and screamed.

And he burned. And burned. Bright against my retinas. Lighting the darkness of the dungeon.

He fell. Landing beside me, too close, the heat like a phosphorous flare, scorching my skin. I closed my eyes as he burned into dust.

Ashes to ashes, dust to dust, I thought.

I lifted my head and met the eyes of the Son of Darkness. Within the energies of the Gray Between, I said, "I don't need or want anything you have to offer. Not now. Not ever." I didn't know whether he heard me, in the bubble of folded time, and I didn't care; I simply needed to say the words. I tucked the sliver of the Blood Cross into my gorget and let Beast pull me into the change. Pain like flaming silk flowed along my bones and through my veins. I shifted. I changed.

* * *

Screams and sounds of guns hit Beast ears. Fire burned tips of Beast pelt. Beast rolled. Lay twisted in Jane clothes. Gorget too tight on Beast neck. Choking. But sliver of cross weapon was in gorget. In Beast's care.

Beast clawed out of Jane clothes and leaped away from burning body. Rushing through dark room, close to thing on wall, to open doorway and up narrow stairs, racing like climbing cliff. Human met Beast in hallway and opened door. I crouched and snarled, showing killing teeth, smelling Jane-kin. Not blood kin, but kin in human ways. Ways of choice. Jane trusted human Eli like littermate. Eli stepped away from door, hands out to sides, empty of weapons—human sign of *not fighting.* Beast crawled on belly to open door. Was sleeping den of Del.

Opened mouth and pulled in air with *scree* of sound. Smelling, tasting, knowing room was empty. Beast gathered paws close and leaped inside, to land in middle of bed. Fresh cloths covered bed, smelling of sweetness instead of Jane sickness. Beast lay still, staring at door, at Eli. "You want me to loosen the gorget?" he asked. "It looks tight."

I hissed at him, showing killing teeth. *Jane's weapon. Stay away or Beast will hurt you.*

Eli touched his head in way that meant nothing to Beast. "I'll bring you a steak in just a bit," he said. He closed door.

Beast is hungry. Steak is good. Bison is better.

Beast woke, *knowing.* Smelled mate. Smelled Bruiser. Memories of Bruiser and Jane and mating scents filled mind. Had marked mate. Had been marked by mate. Ear tabs flicked. Beast stared at door. Waiting. Patient predator. Gathered paws close. Heard Bruiser voice on other side of door.

Door opened. Bruiser came in. Beast showed killing teeth. *Did not ask you into den.* Beast narrowed eyes at mate, hissing, remembering. Bruiser went away with priestess. Bethany. Vampire was good hunter. Trying to take mate? Bruiser was *Beast* mate. Snarled. *My mate!*

Bruiser scent changed. Foot kicked plate on floor, plate smelling of blood and cow. Had been good blood and cow. Heated. Eli had put salt on cow meat. Liked salt. Bruiser looked from Beast to plate and back.

Bruiser moved slow. Closed door behind him. "Jane?"

Growled, snarled. *Am Beast. Jane sleeps in den of mind. Am Beast!*

"I don't know if you can hear me but . . ." Bruiser scent changed again. Grew warm. Possessive. "You are utterly beautiful."

Beast chuffed. Lifted tail tip into air. Covered killing teeth with lips. Stared at mate. *Good mate*. Beast opened mouth and drew in scent with *scree* of sound. Bruiser flinched. Beast chuffed. Was good for mate to know Beast was powerful. Bruiser had good scent. Good mate scent. Bruiser came into den, across soft floor to den bed of Del.

"May I touch you? Without getting bloody mauled?"

Beast showed killing teeth again, thinking. Wanted Bruiser to touch. Jane wanted Bruiser for mate. For more than kits. Did not understand mate for more than kits. But Jane . . . was confusing. Lay head to paws, like sleeping. Stared at Bruiser. Bruiser walked closer, moving slow. Was smart to approach Beast slow. Beast had killing teeth and claws.

Bruiser reached den bed. Could feel his heat. Was warmer than human. Liked heat. Liked scent. Vibration of purr rumbled through Beast body, soothing. *Purrrrrr. Purrrrrr.*

Bruiser put hand out for Beast to breathe in scent. Heated scent. All Bruiser. No scent of Bethany. Was pleased Bruiser had not mated with Bethany. Priestess would be hard to kill.

Bruiser fingers touched head. Smoothed pelt. Rubbed ears and under jaw and under tight gorget. *Purred*. Tilted head so Bruiser could get to tender spots. "You are truly beautiful. In both of your forms. I wonder if you know that? If you know how you make my heart break every time I look at you."

Bruiser stroked hand along body and Beast rolled over, to lay on back, exposing tummy for rub. Bruiser laughed and leaned over to give good belly rub. Long time later he stood straight and said, "I have to go now, beautiful lady. Or ladies. I'm not sure of the proper term anymore. But I'll be back."

He patted tummy and Beast rolled over fast. Caught Bruiser hand in killing teeth. Bruiser stopped like rabbit in field. Beast let go and raised up. Put front legs on Bruiser shoulders. Put face to Bruiser's, breathing in scent. Breathing in breath. Leaned in and rubbed head and jaw over Bruiser. Scent marking mate. *Mine . . .*

Beast dropped down and curled into tight ball to sleep.

Bruiser chuffed out breath stinking of fear and desire. "Bloody hell . . ." Bruiser left Del den.

At dusk I woke to find a bowl of hot oatmeal, fixed the way I liked it, with milk and sugar, on the bedside table. A headset and clean clothes were there as well, jeans, belt, undies, and T-shirt folded neatly, a pair of sandals on the floor below them. And the gorget was still on my neck, with the sliver of the Blood Cross hooked in the rings. I touched it, feeling it blister on my skin. I touched my belly and found a knot there, hot and burning. I wasn't completely healed.

I never want to do that again, I thought to Beast. She panted back at me, her agreement flooding through me. Careful not to touch the sliver of ancient wood, I removed the gorget and dressed, packing the gorget into a pillowcase and tying it to my belt, thinking as I moved.

Peregrinus was dead. The Devil and Batildis were dead, for good this time. The *arcenciel* was free.

It was over. Or this part was. Now the battle would start, the battle to find and take possession of the iron spike. I didn't trust anyone but me to have it. And after committing murder with no remorse, I probably shouldn't trust me either.

I wasn't far from Leo's office and I made my way there, seeing the signs of repair and cleanup. In Leo's office, I closed the doors to the hidden room and the elevator, and made my way down another of Leo's hidden escape routes, through vamp HQ, and outside the stone gate, a pathway I only half remembered, from what seemed like ages ago.

I stepped into the early night and the outer brick wall closed behind me. The breeze was warm and muggy, a heat wave coming in off the Gulf, bringing more rain and lightning. I could feel the leading edge of the storm approaching, ozone in the air. I keyed my mic on and walked around the block. "This is Yellowrock. I'm outside. How are things inside?"

"Full of spirit and badges, as expected, ma'am," the Kid said, letting me know he was on-site and running security and that we had lots of company. "Vamp HQ is calm and quiet, ma'am."

"Cops are with you?"

"Yes, ma'am. That's a roger. They are here and wish to speak with Ms. Yellowrock when you see her, ma'am."

"Uh-huh. We'll talk later." I tapped the headset to open

Eli's channel. "I'm out front, staying out of sight of the cameras. Your brother has Soul and her human law enforcement officers in the security room."

"Copy that," Eli said. "Good to hear you're alive."

"It's good to be alive. I'm in the mood for Mona Lisa's. Deep-dish pizza."

"What? No talking to the feds?"

"God, no."

"Let's see if I can get out of here and head that way. The Kid can join us at his leisure or when he gets away from Soul, whichever happens first. Maybe we'll leave leftovers."

Over my earbud I heard the Kid say, "You are evil, just evil, man."

"Yes. Yes, I am," Eli said.

EPILOGUE

Bound by Oaths of Loyalty

It was one week from the day Bruiser had taken me to Arnaud's. It had been a week of battles, death, and funerals, and I was sleep deprived and sad and . . . close to depressed. I hated being depressed. I'd been depressed once and it sucked.

Yet here I was, sitting in the Clover Grill, staring at the sign reading, DANCING ONLY IN THE AISLES, NOT ON THE TABLES, courting depression.

I had gotten to the diner early to scope out the place and had taken the table farthest in. There were only four so it hadn't been a hard choice, my back to a wall, facing the door. Waiting. For an hour now. Checking my cell for messages every few minutes. Bruiser was late. Or worse. He wasn't coming. The place was filling up with lunch customers. I held up a finger to the short-order cook and he nodded, throwing my burger on the grill. Even if I had to eat alone, I was eating. But my heart hurt.

I twirled my beer on the table, making smeared rings. Trying not to think. In the days since the death of Peregrinus and his pals, Bruiser and I had talked a lot, but only on the phone, not in person. We'd both been busy, long hours and long days, me and Wise Ass getting security totally stripped and rebuilt at fanghead central and in Leo's new house. Getting the new system up and running, and tracking down leads to make sure the city's vamps were safe. Fixing the electricity problem by disconnecting the wires in sub-five from the rest of the system.

Finding Peregrinus' stuff and taking it. Trying to figure out what some of it was. Bruiser had been doing Onorio things.

Most of our convos had been about Bethany and Leo and Bruiser's life, which was way more complicated than mine was. He might not be Leo's primo anymore, but he was bound by oaths of loyalty to the vamps in New Orleans. He wasn't free to move around the country, not for years. My contracts would be up in a few months or a year—assuming I survived the EuroVamps' visit and the coming war. I didn't have plans yet, but staying around New Orleans without work wasn't in the cards. Bruiser and I had talked around the big question of *us*, but hadn't really talked yet. Had settled nothing. Talking didn't really ever settle anything. It was doing that mattered.

My food was deposited in front of me: wonderfully greasy burger and greasy fries, pickle. I tossed a scalding-hot potato into my mouth and picked up my burger. Another meal was placed in front of me, across the small table. "Starting without me, my Jane?"

Mouth open for the bite, I looked up and watched as Bruiser lifted a jeans-clad leg over the back of the chair across from me and settled into place. He dropped flowers on the table, a bouquet of nonaromatic lilies and fresh tea leaves, which were almost impossible to find. A smile crossed my face, as I remembered him telling me that men should always give me flowers.

He picked up his burger and said, "'I eat at diners and fast-food joints and drink beer. My dates and I talk about guns and the newest horror or action flick. I wear jeans and boots and no makeup.' I believe that was the exact quote. And yet, you are wearing lipstick in that amazing shade of red that makes me want to take you right here, on this beat-up old table." He bit into his burger.

Heated chills raced through me as I watched his hands cradling the burger. And . . . Bruiser in jeans and Western boots. And a button-up shirt, crisply starched. Sleeves rolled up to reveal his tanned arms. Oh . . . my . . .

Talking around the ground meat, he said, "Eat up, Jane. We have guns to talk about and then the entire *Kill Bill* series, which I watched last night in preparation for our date, just so I would be ready for today."

I bit my burger, hardly tasting it. I chewed and swallowed

and said, "You're going to spend the day with me. Talking about *Kill Bill*."

"And eating." He swallowed and reached out, tracing my jaw with one long, heated finger. "And making love. Hurry up, Jane. Today is going to be quite . . . busy."

ABOUT THE AUTHOR

Faith Hunter was born in Louisiana and raised all over the South. She writes full-time, tries to keep house, and is a workaholic with a passion for travel, jewelry making, orchids, skulls, Class II and III white-water kayaking, and writing.

Many of the orchid pics on her Facebook fan page show skulls juxtaposed with orchid blooms; the bones are from roadkill prepared by taxidermists or a pal named Mud. In her collection are a fox skull, a cat skull, a dog skull, a goat skull (that is, unfortunately, falling apart), a cow skull, the jawbone of an ass, and a wild boar skull, complete with tusks. She recently purchased a mountain lion skull, and would love to have the thigh bone and skull of an African lion (one that died of old age, of course).

She and her husband own thirteen kayaks at last count, and love to RV, as they travel with their dogs to white-water rivers all over the Southeast.

Love Jane Yellowrock? Then meet Thorn St. Croix. Read on for the opening chapter of *Bloodring*, the first novel in Faith Hunter's Rogue Mage series. Available from Roc.

I stared into the hills as my mount clomped below me, his massive hooves digging into snow and ice. Above us a fighter jet streaked across the sky, leaving a trail that glowed bright against the fiery sunset. A faint sense of alarm raced across my skin, and I gathered up the reins, tightening my knees against Homer's sides, pressing my walking stick against the huge horse.

A sonic boom exploded across the peaks, shaking through snow-laden trees. Ice and snow pitched down in heavy sheets and lumps. A dog yelped. The Friesian set his hooves, dropped his head, and kicked. "Stones and blood," I hissed as I rammed into the saddle horn. The boom echoed like rifle shot. Homer's back arched. If he bucked, I was a goner.

I concentrated on the bloodstone handle of my walking stick and pulled the horse to me, reins firm as I whispered soothing, seemingly nonsense words no one would interpret as a chant. The bloodstone pulsed as it projected a sense of calm into him, a use of stored power that didn't affect my own drained resources. The sonic boom came back from the nearby mountains, a ricochet of man-made thunder.

The mule in front of us hee-hawed and kicked out, white rimming his eyes, lips wide, and teeth showing as the boom reverberated through the farther peaks. Down the length of the mule train, other animals reacted as the fear spread, some bucking in a frenzy, throwing packs into drifts, squealing as lead ropes tangled, trumpeting fear.

Homer relaxed his back, sidestepped, and danced like a young colt before planting his hooves again. He blew out a rib-racking sigh and shook himself, ears twitching as he settled. Deftly, I repositioned the supplies and packs he'd dislodged, rubbing a bruised thigh that had taken a wallop from a twenty-pound pack of stone.

Hoop Marks and his assistant guides swung down from their own mounts and steadied the more fractious stock. All along the short train, the startled horses and mules settled as riders worked to control them. Homer looked on, ears twitching.

Behind me, a big Clydesdale relaxed, shuddering with a ripple of muscle and thick winter coat, his rider following the wave of motion with practiced ease. Audric was a salvage miner, and he knew his horses. I nodded to my old friend, and he tipped his hat to me before repositioning his stock on Clyde's back.

A final echo rumbled from the mountains. Almost as one, we turned to the peaks above us, listening fearfully for the telltale roar of an avalanche.

Sonic booms were rare in the Appalachians these days, and I wondered what had caused the military overflight. I slid the walking stick into its leather loop. It was useful for balance while taking a stroll in snow, but its real purpose was as a weapon. Its concealed blade was deadly, as was its talisman hilt, hiding in plain sight. However, the bloodstone handle-hilt was now almost drained of power, and when we stopped for the night, I'd have to find a safe, secluded place to draw power for it and for the amulets I carried, or my neomage attributes would begin to display themselves.

I'm a neomage, a witchy-woman. Though contrary rumors persist, claiming mages still roam the world free, I'm the only one of my kind not a prisoner, the only one in the entire world of humans who is unregulated, unlicensed. The only one uncontrolled.

All the others of my race are restricted to Enclaves, protected in enforced captivity. Enclaves are gilded cages, prisons of privilege and power, but cages nonetheless. Neomages are allowed out only with seraph permission, and then we have to wear a sigil of office and bracelets with satellite GPS locator chips in them. We're followed by the humans, watched, and sent back fast when our services are no longer needed or when our visas expire. As if we're contagious. Or dangerous.

Enclave was both prison and haven for mages, keeping us safe from the politically powerful, conservative, religious orthodox humans who hated us, and giving us a place to live as our natures and gifts demanded. It was a great place for a mage-child to grow up, but when my gift blossomed at age fourteen, my mind opened in a unique way. The thoughts of all twelve hundred mages captive in the New Orleans Enclave opened to me at once. I nearly went mad. If I went back, I'd go quietly—or loudly screaming—insane.

In the woods around us, shadows lengthened and darkened. Mule handlers looked around, jittery. I sent out a quick mind-skim. There were no supernats present, no demons, no mages, no seraphs, no *others*. Well, except for me. But I couldn't exactly tell them that. I chuckled under my breath as Homer snorted and slapped me with his tail. That would be dandy. Survive for a decade in the human world only to be exposed by something so simple as a sonic boom and a case of trail exhaustion. I'd be tortured, slowly, over a period of days, tarred and feathered, chopped into pieces, and dumped in the snow to rot.

If the seraphs located me first, I'd be sent back to Enclave and I'd still die. I'm allergic to others of my kind—really allergic—fatally so. The Enclave death would be a little slower, a little less bloody than the human version. Humans kill with steel, a public beheading, but only after I was disemboweled, eviscerated, and flayed alive. And all that after I *entertained* the guards for a few days. As ways to go, the execution of an unlicensed witchy-woman rates up there with the top ten gruesome methods of capital punishment. With my energies nearly gone, a conjure to calm the horses could give me away.

"Light's goin,' " Hoop called out. "We'll stop here for the night. Everyone takes care of his own mount before anything else. Then circle and gather deadwood. Last, we cook. Anyone who don't work, don't eat."

Behind me, a man grumbled beneath his breath about the unfairness of paying good money for a spot on the mule train and then having to work. I grinned at him and he shrugged when he realized he'd been heard. "Can't blame a man for griping. Besides, I haven't ridden a horse since I was a kid. I have blisters on my blisters."

I eased my right leg over Homer's back and slid the long distance to the ground. My knees protested, aching after the day in the saddle. "I have a few blisters this trip myself. Good boy," I said to the big horse, and dropped the reins, running a hand along his side. He stomped his satisfaction and I felt his deep sense of comfort at the end of the day's travel.

We could have stopped sooner, but Hoop had hoped to make the campsite where the trail rejoined the old Blue Ridge Parkway. Now we were forced to camp in a ring of trees instead of the easily fortified site ahead. If the denizens of Darkness came out to hunt, we'd be sitting ducks.

Unstrapping the heavy pack containing my most valuable finds from the Salvage and Mineral Swap Meet in Boone, I dropped it to the earth and covered it with the saddle. My luggage and pack went to the side. I removed all the tools I needed to groom the horse and clean his feet, and added the bag of oats and grain. A pale dusk closed in around us before I got the horse brushed down and draped in a blanket, a pile of food and a half bale of hay at his feet.

The professional guides were faster and had taken care of their own mounts and the pack animals and dug a firepit in the time it took the paying customers to get our mounts groomed. The equines were edgy, picking up anxiety from their humans, making the job slower for us amateurs. Hoop's dogs trotted back and forth among us, tails tight to their bodies, ruffs raised, sniffing for danger. As we worked, both clients and handlers glanced fearfully into the night. Demons and their spawn often hid in the dark, watching humans like predators watched tasty herd animals. So far as my weakened senses could detect, there was nothing out there. But there was a lot I couldn't say and still keep my head.

"Gather wood!" I didn't notice who called the command, but we all moved into the forest, me using my walking stick for balance. There was no talking. The sense of trepidation was palpable, though the night was friendly, the moon rising, no snow or ice in the forecast. Above, early stars twinkled, cold and bright at this altitude. I moved away from the others, deep into the tall trees: oak, hickory, fir, cedar. At a distance, I found a huge boulder rounded up from the snow.

Checking to see that I was alone, I lay flat on the boulder, my cheek against frozen granite, the walking stick between my torso and the rock. And I called up power. Not a raging roar of mage-might, but a slow, steady trickle. Without words, without a chant that might give me away, I channeled energy into the bloodstone handle between my breasts, into the amulets hidden beneath my clothes, and pulled a measure into my own flesh, needing the succor. It took long minutes, and I sighed with relief as my body soaked up strength.

Satisfied, as refreshed as if I had taken a nap, I stood, stretched, bent, and picked up deadwood, traipsing through the trees and boulders for firewood—wood that was a lot more abundant this far away from the trail. My night vision is better than most humans', and though I'm small for an adult and was the only female on the train, I gathered an armload in record time. Working far off the beaten path has its rewards.

I smelled it when the wind changed. Old blood. A lot of old blood. I dropped the firewood, drew the blade from the walking-stick sheath, and opened my mage-sight to survey the surrounding territory. The world of snow and ice glimmered with a sour-lemon glow, as if it were ailing, sickly.

Mage-sight is more than human sight in that it sees energy as well as matter. The retinas of human eyes pick up little energy, seeing light only after it's absorbed or reflected. But mages see the world of matter with an overlay of energy, picked up by the extra lenses that surround our retinas. We see power and life, the leftover workings of creation. When we use the sight, the energies are sometimes real, sometimes representational, experience teaching us to identify and translate the visions, sort of like picking out images from a three-dimensional pattern.

I'm a stone mage, a worker of rocks and gems, and the energy of creation; hence, only stone looks powerful and healthy to me when I'm using mage-sight. Rain, ice, sleet or snow, each of which is water that has passed through air, always looks unhealthy, as does moonlight, sunlight, the movement of the wind, or currents of surface water—anything except stone. This high in the mountains, snow lay thick and crusted everywhere, weak, pale, a part of nature that leached power from me—except for a dull gray area to the east, beyond the stone where I had recharged my energies.

Moving with the speed of my race, sword in one hand, walking-stick sheath, a weapon in itself, in the other, I rushed toward the site.

I tripped over a boot. It was sticking from the snow, bootlaces crusted with blood and ice. Human blood had been spilled here, a lot of it, and the snow was saturated. The earth reeked of fear and pain and horror, and to my mage-sight, it glowed with the blackened energy of death. I caught a whiff of Darkness.

Adrenaline coursed through my veins, and I stepped into the cat stance, blade and walking stick held low as I circled the site. Bones poked up from the ice, and I identified a femur, the fragile bones of a hand, tendons still holding fingers together. A jawbone thrust toward the sky. Placing my feet carefully, I eased in. Teeth marks, long and deep, scored an arm bone. Predator teeth, unlike any beast known to nature. Supernat teeth. The teeth of Darkness.

Devil-spawn travel in packs, drink blood and eat human flesh. While it's still alive. A really bad way to go. And spawn would know what I was in an instant if they were downwind of me. As a mage, I'd be worth more to a spawn than a fresh meal. I'd be prime breeding material for their masters.

I'd rather be eaten.

A skull stared at me from an outcropping of rock. A tree close by had been raked with talons, or with desperate human fingers trying to get away, trying to climb. As my sight adjusted to the falling light, a rock shelf protruding from the earth took on a glow displaying pick marks. A strip mine. Now that I knew what to look for, I saw a pick, the blackened metal pitted by ichor, a lantern, bags of supplies hanging from trees, other gear stacked near the rock with their ore. One tent pole still stood. On it was what I assumed to be a hat, until my eyes adjusted and it resolved into a second skull. Old death. Weeks, perhaps months, old.

A stench of sulfur reached me. Dropping the sight, I skimmed until I found the source: a tiny hole in the earth near the rock they had been working. I understood what had happened. The miners had been working a claim on the surface — because no one in his right mind went underground, not anymore — and they had accidentally broken through to a cavern or an old, abandoned underground mine. Darkness had scented them. Supper . . .

I moved to the hole in the earth. It was leaking only a hint of sulfur and brimstone, and the soil around was smooth, trackless. Spawn hadn't used this entrance in a long time. I glanced up at the sky. Still bright enough that the nocturnal devil-spawn were sleeping. If I could cover the entrance, they wouldn't smell us. Probably. Maybe.

Sheathing the blade, I went to the cases the miners had piled against the rocks, and pulled a likely one off the top. It hit the ground with a whump but was light enough for me to drag it over the snow, leaving a trail through the carnage. The bag fit over the entrance, and the reek of Darkness was instantly choked off. My life had been too peaceful. I'd gotten lazy. I should have smelled it the moment I entered the woods. Now it was gone.

Satisfied I had done all I could, I tramped to my pile of deadwood and back to camp, glad of the nearness of so many humans, horses, and dogs that trotted about. I dumped the wood beside the fire pit at the center of the small clearing. Hoop Marks and his second in command, Hoop Jr., tossed in broken limbs and lit the fire with a small can of kerosene and a pack of matches. Flames roared and danced, sending shadows capering into the surrounding forest. The presence of fire sent a welcome feeling of safety through the group, though only earthly predators would fear the flame. No supernat of Darkness would care about a little fire if it was hungry. Fire made them feel right at home.

I caught Hoop's eye and gestured to the edge of the woods. The taciturn man followed when I walked away, and listened with growing concern to my tale of the miners. I thought he might curse when I told him of the teeth marks on the bones, but he stopped himself in time. Cursing aloud near a hellhole was a sure way of inviting Darkness to you. In other locales it might attract seraphic punishment or draw the ire of the church. Thoughtless language could result in death-by-dinner, seraphic vengeance, or priestly branding. Instead, he ground out, "I'll radio it in. You don't tell nobody, you hear? I got something that'll keep us safe." And without asking me why I had wandered so far from camp, alone, he walked away.

Smoke and supper cooking wafted through camp as I rolled out my sleeping bag and pumped up the air mattress. Even with the smell of old death still in my nostrils, my mouth watered. I wanted nothing more than to curl up, eat and sleep, but I needed to move through the horses and mules first. Trying to be inconspicuous, touching each one as surreptitiously as possible, I let the walking stick's amulet-handle brush each animal with calm.

It was a risk, if anyone recognized a mage-conjure, but there was no way I was letting the stock bolt and stampede away if startled in the night. I had no desire to walk miles through several feet of hard-packed snow to reach the nearest train tracks, then wait days in the cold, without a bath or adequate supplies, for a train that might get stranded in a blizzard and not come until snowmelt in spring. No way. Living in perpetual winter was bad enough, and though the ubiquitous *they* said it was only a *mini*–ice age, it was still pretty dang cold.

So I walked along the picket line and murmured soothing words, touching the stock one by one. I loved horses. I hated that they were the only dependable method of transport through the mountains ten months out of the year, but I loved the beasts themselves. They didn't care that I was an unlicensed neomage hiding among the humans. With them I could be myself, if only for a moment or two. I lay my cheek against the shoulder of a particularly worried mare. She exhaled as serenity seeped into her and turned liquid brown eyes to me in appreciation, blowing warm horse breath in my face. "You're welcome," I whispered.

Just before I got to the end of the string, Hoop sang out, "Charmed circle. Charmed circle for the night."

I looked up in surprise, my movements as frozen as the night air. Hoop Jr. was walking bent over, a fifty-pound bag of salt in his arms, his steps moving clockwise. Though human, he was making a conjure circle. Instinctively, I cast out with a mind-skim, though I knew I was the only mage here. But now I scented a charmed *something*. From a leather case, Hoop Sr. pulled out a branch that glowed softly to my mage-sight. Hoop's "something to keep us safe." The tag on the tip of the branch proclaimed it a legally purchased charm, unlike my unlicensed amulets. It would be empowered by the salt in the ring, offering us protection. I hurried down the line of horses and mules, trusting that my movements were hidden by the night, and made it to the circle before it was closed.

Stepping through the opening in the salt, I nodded again as I passed Audric. The big black man shouldered his packs and carried them toward the fire pit. He didn't talk much, but he and Thorn's Gems had done a lot of business since he discovered and claimed a previously untouched city site for salvage. Because he had a tendresse for one of my business partners, he brought his findings to us first and stayed with us while in town. The arrangement worked out well, and when his claim petered out, we all hoped he'd put down roots and stay, maybe buy in as the fourth partner.

"All's coming in, get in," Hoop Sr. sang out. "All's staying out'll be shot if trouble hits and you try to cross the salt ring." There was a cold finality to his tone. "Devil-spawn been spotted round here. I take no chances with my life or yours 'less you choose to act stupid and get yourself shot."

"Devil-spawn? Here?" The speaker was the man who had griped about the workload.

"Yeah. Drained a woman and three kids at a cabin up near Linville." He didn't mention the carnage within shooting distance of us. Smart man.

I spared a quick glance for my horse, who was already snoozing. A faint pop sizzled along my nerve endings as the circle closed and the energy of the spell from the mage-branch snapped in place. I wasn't an earth mage, but I appreciated the conjure's simple elegance. A strong shield-protection-invisibility incantation had been stored in the cells of the branch. The stock were in danger from passing predators, but the rest of us were effectively invisible to anyone, human or supernat.

Night enveloped us in its black mantle as we gathered for a supper of venison stew. Someone passed around a flask of moonshine. No one said anything against it. Most took a swallow or two against the cold. I drank water and ate only stewed vegetables. Meat disagrees with me. Liquor on a mule train at night just seems stupid.

Tired to the bone, I rolled into my heated, down-filled sleeping bag and looked up at the cold, clear sky. The moon was nearly full, its rays shining on seven inches of fresh snow. It was a good night for a moon mage, a water mage, even a weather mage, but not a night to induce a feeling of vitality or well-being in a bone-tired stone mage. The entire world glowed with moon power, brilliant and beautiful, but draining to my own strength. I rolled in my bedding and stopped, caught by a tint of color in the velvet black sky. A thick ring of bloody red circled the pure white orb, far out in the night. *A bloodring.* I almost swore under my breath but choked it back, a painful sound, close to a sob.

The last time there was a bloodring on the moon, my twin sister died. Rose had been a licensed mage, living in Atlanta, supposedly safe, yet she had vanished, leaving a wide, freezing pool of blood and signs of a struggle, within minutes after Lolo, the priestess of Enclave, phoned us both with warnings. The prophecy hadn't helped then and it wouldn't help now. Portents never helped. They offered only a single moment to catch a breath before I was trounced by whatever they foretold.

If Lolo had called with a warning tonight, it was on my answering machine. Even for me, the distance to Enclave was too great to hear the mind-voice of the priestess.

I shivered, looking up from my sleeping bag. A feasting site, now a bloodring. It was a hazy, frothing circle, swirling like the breath of the Dragon in the Revelation, holy words taught to every mage from the womb up. "And there appeared another wonder in heaven; and behold a great red dragon. . . . And his tail drew the third part of the stars of heaven, and did cast them to the earth: and the dragon stood before the woman. . . . And there was war in heaven: Michael and his seraphim fought against the dragon; and the dragon fought, and his seraphim." The tale of the Last War.

Shivering, I gripped the amulets tied around my waist and my walking stick, the blade loosed in the sheath, the prime amulet of its hilt tight in my palm. Much later, exhausted, I slept.

Lucas checked his watch as he slipped out of the office and moved into the alley, ice crunching beneath his boots, breath a half-seen fog in the night. He was still on schedule, though pushing the boundaries. Cold froze his ears and nose, numbed his fingers and feet, congealed his blood, seeped into his bones, even through the layers of clothes, down-filled vest, and hood. He slipped, barely catching himself before hitting the icy ground. He cursed beneath his breath as he steadied himself on the alley wall. *Seraph stones, it's cold.*

But he was almost done. The last of the amethyst would soon be in Thorn's hands, just as the Mistress Amethyst had demanded. In another hour he would be free of his burden. He'd be out of danger. He felt for the ring on his finger, turning it so the sharp edge was against his flesh. He hitched the heavy backpack higher, its nylon straps cutting into his palm and across his shoulder.

The dark above was absolute, moon and stars hidden by the tall buildings at his sides. Ahead, there was only the distant security light at the intersection of the alley, where it joined the larger delivery lane and emptied into the street. Into safety.

A rustle startled him. A flash of movement. A dog burst from the burned-out hulk of an old Volkswagen and bolted back the way he had come. A second followed. Two small pups huddled in the warm nest they deserted, yellow coats barely visible. Lucas blew out a gust of irritation and worthless fear and hoped the larger mutts made it back to the makeshift den before the weather took them all down. It was so cold, the puppies wouldn't survive long. Even the smells of dog, urine, old beer, and garbage were frozen.

He moved into the deeper dark, toward the distant light, but slowed. The alley narrowed, the walls at his sides invisible in the night; his billowing breath vanished. He glanced up, his eyes drawn to the relative brightness of the sky. A chill that had nothing to do with the temperature chased down his spine. The rooftops were bare, the gutters and eaves festooned with icicles, moon and clouds beyond. One of the puppies mewled behind him.

Lucas stepped through the dark, his pace increasing as panic coiled itself around him. He was nearly running by the time he reached the pool of light marking the alleys' junction. Slowing, he passed two scooters and a tangle of bicycles leaning against a wall, all secured with steel chains, tires frozen in the ice. He stepped into the light and the safety it offered.

Above, there was a crackle, a sharp snap of metal. His head lifted, but his eyes were drawn ahead to a stack of boxes and firewood. To the man standing there. *Sweet Mother of God . . . not a man. A shadow.* "No!" Lucas tried to whirl, skidding on icy pavement before he could complete the move. Two others ran toward him, human movements, human slow.

"Get him!"

The first man collided with him, followed instantly by the other, their bodies twin blows. His boots gave on the slippery surface. He went to one knee, breath a pained grunt.

A fist pounded across the back of his neck. A leg reared back. Screaming, he covered his head with an arm. A rain of blows and kicks landed. The backpack was jerked away, opening and spilling.

As he fell, he tightened a fist around the ring, its sharp edge slicing into his flesh. He groaned out the words she had given him to use, but only in extremis. The sound of the syllables was lost beneath the rain of blows. "Zadkiel, hear me. Holy Amethyst—" A boot took him in the jaw, knocking back his head. He saw the wings unfurl on the roof above him. Darkness closed in. Teeth sank deep in his throat. Cold took him. The final words of the chant went unspoken.